MEGGIN CABOT

is

"UTTERLY REMARKABLE!"
Atlanta Journal-Constitution

"THOROUGHLY CHARMING!"
Stella Cameron

"A WRITER OF REMARKABLE SKILL!"
Publishers Weekly

"UNIQUE...A TRUE JOY!"
Romantic Times

"IRREPRESSIBLE!"
Associated Press

"SEXY, ROMANTIC...DELIGHTFUL!"
Jill Jones

"OH MY GOD, JACK!"

Her eyes, he noticed, were so large they seemed to consume the rest of her face. Her breath wasn't coming out in gasps either, he now realized. She was sobbing. Tearlessly, but still sobbing. He'd never seen anyone look so terrified.

"It's okay," he said, reaching out to wrap an arm around her neck and drag her toward him. "Hey, it's okay."

For a moment, it was like she was someone else. The cocky, contemptuous Lou Calabrese he was so used to disappeared, replaced by this stranger with dewy eyes and trembling lips. Lou reached up to cling to his jacket, burying her face in his chest. Amazingly, a twinge of desire shot through him.

It was just as he was wondering if he ought to make a move—it wouldn't really be taking advantage, he thought, of her momentary weakness to tilt her chin up and kiss those lips that for once were still, and so beckoningly red and moistly parted—that Lou suddenly tensed, stepped out of his embrace, and hauled back and slugged him . . .

"It is a true joy to listen to Cabot's unique voice."
Romantic Times

"Cabot writes romance almost without peer."
Publishers Weekly (*Starred Review*)

Also by Meggin Cabot

THE BOY NEXT DOOR

MEGGIN CABOT

She Went All the Way

AVON BOOKS
An Imprint of HarperCollinsPublishers

This novel is a work of fiction. Any references to real people, events, establishments, organizations, or locales are intended only to give the fiction a sense of reality and authenticity, and are used fictitiously. All other names, characters, and places, and all dialogue and incidents portrayed in this book are the product of the author's imagination.

AVON BOOKS
An Imprint of HarperCollins*Publishers*
10 East 53rd Street
New York, New York 10022-5299

Copyright © 2002 by Meggin Cabot
Excerpts from *The Lady is Tempted* copyright © 2002 by Cathy Maxwell; *Her Highness, My Wife* copyright © 2002 by Cheryl Griffin; *Shadow Dance* copyright © 1989, 2002 by Susan Andersen; *The Woman Most Likely To . . .* copyright © 2002 by Alison Hart; *Untie My Heart* copyright © 2002 by Judith Ivory, Inc.; *She Went All the Way* copyright © 2002 by Meggin Cabot
ISBN: 0-06-008544-4
www.avonromance.com

First Avon Books paperback printing: December 2002

Avon Trademark Reg. U.S. Pat. Off. and in Other Countries, Marca Registrada, Hecho en U.S.A.
HarperCollins® is a registered trademark of HarperCollins Publishers Inc.

Printed in the U.S.A.

10 9 8 7 6 5 4 3 2 1

For Benjamin

ACKNOWLEDGMENTS

The author wishes to thank the following people for their help and support: Beth Ader, Jennifer Brown, SWAT officer Matt Cabot, Bill Contardi, Carrie Feron, Michele Jaffe, Laura Langlie, and David Walton.

1

WEDDING SURPRISE OF THE YEAR
Hindenburg stars' red-hot romance sparks controversy: Actors Bruno di Blase and Greta Woolston wed in media firestorm . . .

It blossomed on the set of *Hindenburg*, last year's mega-movie blockbuster, which broke all previous earnings records and garnered seven Academy Awards, including Best Picture: a romance that, unlike the relationship of the heroic characters the two stars portrayed on screen, many said would never last. Now two of the hottest stars in Hollywood have delighted fans by making their big-screen romance a reality. . . .

"Yo."

Officer Nick Calabrese stared down at the front page of the New York *Post*. The *Post*, man. The freaking thing had made the *Post*. Even worse, the *front page* of the *Post*.

"Yo, a little help over here, please?"

Nick glanced at the other papers lining the front of the newsstand. The *Daily News* had it, too. *Newsday*. Even

USA Today. About the only paper it hadn't made the cover of was the *New York Times*, and Nick was certain it would be in there somewhere. The Metro section, probably.

Jesus!

"Yo, Calabrese," snarled Officer Gerard "G" West, as he struggled to place handcuffs on a local junkie who was proving reluctant to come along quietly. "You gonna stand there readin' the funnies, or are you gonna help me with this guy?"

Nick picked up a copy of the *Post* and strolled over to his partner, pointing to the picture of the attractive couple on the cover and tilting it so that the struggling captive could see the photo, too.

"Look at this," he said. "See this guy? The one in the tux? That's my sister's boyfriend. Or was."

The junkie peering at the photo didn't seem to notice when G used this momentary distraction to snap his cuffs in place.

"Get outta town," the man said.

"No," Nick said. "Really."

Even G, still holding the junkie by the arms, looked skeptical.

"Yeah," he said, sarcastically. "And my sister's dating Denzel Washington. C'mon, Nick. I wanna get a hashbrown down at the Ds. You know they stop servin'em after ten-thirty."

"I am telling you," Nick said, holding the paper out so that the owner of the newsstand, who'd been looking on with interest, could see the photo, too. "That is my sister's boyfriend. Two of 'em were livin' together up until about a few months ago, and the rat went and married somebody else behind her back. Can you believe that?"

The newsstand owner replied, his Bangladeshi accent so thick that his English was barely understandable, "No, sir, that I cannot believe."

"She wrote that movie, you know," Nick said to the newsstand owner. "My sister did. The one that made them both so famous."

"You are shitting me, sir," the newsstand owner said politely.

"No, I'm not," Nick said. "I swear it. Lou wrote it as, you know, a whadduyacallit. A vehicle. For Barry."

"Who is Barry, sir?" the newsstand owner wanted to know.

"This guy." Nick pointed at the paper. "Bruno di Blase. That's not his real name. That's his, you know, stage name. His real name is Barry. Barry Kimmel. He grew up in our neighborhood out on the island. I used to make him eat bugs." He noticed the disapproving look his partner sent him, and said, with a shrug, "Well, you know. We were kids."

G, still holding onto the junkie, grunted. "Oh, yeah. Barry. I forgot. Tough break for Lou. You don't stop squirming around, I swear to God—"

The junkie however, was having a hard time containing his excitement. "Hey, s'that really true?" he asked Nick. "Your sister really shacked up with that guy from *Hindenburg*?"

"Watch it," Nick growled. "My sister never shacked up with anybody, understand?"

"Well," G said. "Not anymore, anyway. I mean, not now that the guy's married to—"

"You watch it, too." Nick flashed his partner a look of annoyance over the top of the diminutive criminal's head while he dug into his pocket and extracted some change, which he tried to give to the owner of the newsstand in exchange for the copy of the *Post* he held beneath one arm.

"Oh, no, sir," the newsstand operator said graciously. "It is on the house. You are keeping our streets safe for law-abiding citizens."

Nick, pleased, slipped the change back into his pocket. "Hey," he said. "Thanks."

"And please to tell your sister," the newsstand owner called, "that I enjoyed her film, *Hindenburg*, very much. As did my wife. It was truly a moving triumph of the human spirit."

"Sure thing," Nick said, as they moved towards the squad car. "Jesus, I still can't believe it. Barry eloped on her! The poor kid."

STAR-STUDDED NUPTIALS

It happened in the newly created *Hindenburg* Room—featuring memorabilia from the hit movie of that name—in the Trump Casino in Las Vegas. *Hindenburg* stars Bruno di Blase and Greta Woolston tied the knot, just days after Ms. Woolston's well-publicized split from longtime boyfriend, action-adventure star Jack Townsend.

Townsend, who rose to fame during his four-year stint as the moody Dr. Paul Rourke on the hit television medical drama, "*STAT*," and later went on to star as renegade detective Pete Logan in the highly popular *Copkiller* movies, does not appear to have taken news of his ex's elopement in stride.

"Good Lord." Eleanor Townsend looked down at the paper folded so neatly on the silver tray. "What is this, Richards?"

The butler cleared his throat. "I took the liberty, madam, of picking up a copy of the *Post* this morning as I was walking Alessandro. As you can see, there is a story on the first page that I believe will interest you."

Eleanor, after flashing her butler of thirty years a look that was as affectionate as it was reproachful, reached over the Yorkie perched on her lap, lifted the paper from the tray, and, slipping on her spectacles, inspected the front page.

"Ah, yes," she said, after scanning the article beneath the full color photo. "I see. How distressful. 'According to sources at the Anchorage Four Seasons Hotel, where Townsend is staying during location filming of *Copkiller IV*, the sound of breaking glass was heard from the star's suite shortly after news of the wedding was announced on the evening news,'" she read aloud. "'By the time hotel security arrived, a French door had been shattered, several fist-sized holes were found in the hotel room walls, and a love seat had been set on fire.' Good heavens."

"There is no word," Richards said, "as to whether or not Master Jack was arrested."

"No." Eleanor perused the article. "No, it appears not. Fist-sized holes in the wall, indeed! And a love seat in flames? Jack would never have done anything so childish. Besides, he couldn't possibly have cared for the Woolston woman that much. She was so terribly . . . common. Though it's so difficult to tell when they have a British accent."

"It was, perhaps," Richards ventured, as he lifted a silver coffee urn and refilled Eleanor's china cup, "not so much that she married so soon after their breakup, but to whom."

"Yes," Eleanor said, squinting at the photo on the paper's first page. "I see. Bruno di Blase. He played the hero in that movie everyone was talking about last year? The one about the . . . what is it called again? Oh, yes. The blimp?"

"Indeed, madam," Richards said. "*Hindenburg*. A moving triumph of the human spirit, I am told."

Eleanor lifted a carefully groomed eyebrow. "Oh, dear. Di Blase. I wonder if he is one of the Tuscan di Blases. You know, that lovely family I met in Florence last spring?"

"I believe, madam," Richards said, after clearing his throat once, "that di Blase is a stage name."

Eleanor put down the paper with a shudder. "Oh, Richards," she cried. "How dreadful. That any woman should drop Jack for a man with a *stage* name—"

"I always rather suspected," Richards said, evenly, "that Miss Woolston's name might have been . . . well, improved upon, in some small fashion."

Eleanor plucked her glasses from her nose and looked horrified. "No! But you might be right. It's probably something dreadful. Doris Mudge, or Vivian Sloth, or some such."

"Allegra," Richards said, deliberately, "Mooch."

Eleanor shuddered. "Stop. Not *Allegra*. Not before *breakfast*."

"My apologies, madam. Shall we attempt to reach Master Jack, and see if we can be of aid?"

Eleanor examined her elegant gold watch. "No, there isn't any point. He's impossible to reach most of the time, but especially when he's on location. And after something like this he won't get anywhere near a phone. Oh, Richards." She heaved a sigh. "It's starting to look as if it's going to be quite a long while before I ever see any grandchildren, doesn't it?"

CELEBRITIES SCORNED

Although Jack Townsend himself has yet to comment publicly on ex-girlfriend Greta Woolston's sudden elopement with Bruno di Blase, her *Hindenburg* costar, the marriage appears to have been as big a shock to family and friends as to fans. Academy Award–winning *Hindenburg* screenwriter Lou Calabrese, longtime girlfriend of the new groom, has also yet to issue a public statement . . .

"Damned right we have no statement," Beverly Tennant snarled at the newspaper, which she then threw, with savage force, in the general direction of her office's gilt trashcan. "Chloe," she bellowed. "Chloe!"

A harried-looking young woman came catapulting into the office, clearly having only just arrived, her ear-muffs still on, her coat not yet unbuttoned, and two cups of steaming coffee in her hands.

"Oh," Beverly said, noticing the steaming cups. "For me?"

Chloe nodded, trying to catch her breath. "I . . . saw . . ." she panted, "the . . . headlines . . . on my way in. I figured you'd need . . . a double. I got nonfat foam."

"You are a lifesaver," Beverly said. She tapped on her desktop with a well-manicured nail. "Put it here. And hold all my calls. I'm going to try to get hold of her."

"Oh." Chloe hurried to place the steaming cup where her employer had indicated. "Could you tell Lou hi from me? And tell her I'm really sorry. Tell her if it's any consolation, none of us—here at the agency, I mean—think Bruno di Blase is as hot as everyone is making out. I mean . . . we don't represent him, do we?"

Beverly, her fingers poised over speed dial buttons, sent her assistant a withering look.

"We do not," she said. "But I will deliver your message. I'm sure it will be a great comfort to her."

Chloe, abashed, hurried from the office, closing the door carefully behind her.

As soon as she was gone, Beverly, who'd slipped her feet from her Manolo Blahniks, leaned back and plopped her heels on her desk, peeled the lid from her cappuccino, and dialed her client's Los Angeles number.

"Be there," she muttered, as the first ring sounded. "Be there, be there, be there . . ."

Lou's machine clicked on. "Hi. We're not here right now, but if you leave a message at the tone, we'll be sure to give you a call back real soon—"

Beverly winced at the use of the word "we." But there was nothing except sympathy in her tone as she cooed into the phone, "Lou, honey, it's Bev. If you're there, pick up. I know it's"—she looked at her diamond-chip–encrusted watch and made a swift calculation—"six in the morning there, God, how can you stand it? But listen, sweetie, I'm telling you, this is the best thing that ever happened to you. Believe me, I've been there, I know. The man is pond scum. Worse than pond scum. He's the scum that grows on . . . other scum."

Satisfied with this description, Beverly went on, "And she's just British white trash. The two of them deserve each other. Where are you, anyway? Don't tell me you've gone all West Coast, and taken up jogging, or yoga, or something horrible like that . . ."

Beverly slid her heels off the desk and sat up straight in her swivel chair, as if struck by sudden inspiration. "Oh, God, that's *right*. You were headed up to the shoot today, weren't you, to talk Tim Lord out of blowing up that mountain and getting all those environmentalists' panties in a wad. God, what a dope I am. Here I am blathering to your machine and you're off in . . . God, the wilds of Alaska. I am so sorry. *Alaska*, of all places. I shudder to—"

Beverly shook herself. "But no, wait, that's *good*. It's good you're in Alaska, Lou. Alaska will keep your mind off . . . well, I don't suppose it will, actually, since Jack Townsend will be there, won't he? I know how you feel about him. God. Well, anyway, honey, call me. And as soon as you're back, we'll do *lunch*."

Beverly hung up. She looked glumly down at her cappuccino. "Oh, God," she said to no one in particular. "Poor Lou. Right about now, I'll bet she's wishing she never wrote the thing in the first place."

2

"Oh, God." Lou Calabrese dropped her head to the sticky airport lounge table. "Why did I ever write the stupid thing?"

Vicky Lord, seated across the table, regarded her friend with an expression of concern on her carefully made-up face. "Lou, honey. You're gettin' ketchup in your hair."

"What does it matter?" Ketchup or not, the tabletop felt cool against Lou's forehead. "If I wanted to give him a vehicle, why didn't I just buy him a Porsche?"

"Honey, lift up your head. You don't know what people might've been doin' on that table."

"Sure, he'd still have driven away from me just as fast," Lou went on, miserably, keeping her head where it was. "But every single person in the western world wouldn't know about it. It wouldn't have been on CNN."

"Now, Lou," Vicky said. She opened her Prada handbag, which she'd kept carefully positioned in her lap so as to avoid condiment stains. "Not every single person in the western world knows about Barry and Greta. I'm sure there's some of those hermits in Montana—you know, the ones with the bombs—who haven't heard about it."

"Oh, God," Lou wailed. "Why couldn't I have written a romantic comedy instead? They never would have gotten together on the set of a romantic comedy. It would have been too, you know. *Predictable.* Their publicists would never have allowed it."

"Now, Lou, honey," Vicky said again, as she dug through the contents of her purse. "You can't blame it all on *Hindenburg.* You and Barry were having problems way before *Hindenburg,* if I remember correctly."

Lou, not moving her head from the table, blinked at her friend. Morning sunlight was slanting in through the airport lounge windows, and a pinkish beam had settled on Vicky, who looked angelic in its rosy light.

But then, Vicky Lord always looked angelic. She hadn't been the Noxema girl for five years running just because of her flawless skin. Oh, no. Vicky *glowed*, and from the *inside.* In a way that Lou, who spent way too much time in front of a computer screen, knew she would never glow, inside or out.

"Sure," Lou said. "Sure we were having problems. We'd been together for what, ten years? Ten years, and the guy wouldn't commit. I'd say that was a *problem.*"

Lou didn't know why she felt compelled to explain herself to the angelic vision seated across from her. Vicky would never understand. Vicky, model, actress, and current Hollywood It Girl, had always gotten everything she had ever wanted.

Well, that wasn't quite true. There'd been one thing Vicky had wanted and hadn't gotten, a guy she'd been crazy about, who'd thrown her over the minute she, like Lou, had mentioned the C word. True, that had been years ago, and Vicky was happily married now—to a man who so thoroughly adored her, their marriage was routinely held up as one of the most successful in Hollywood.

But maybe—just maybe—she could still see where Lou was coming from.

"Barry told me the reason he couldn't commit to our relationship was because he didn't want me to be saddled with an out-of-work actor for a husband," Lou said. "So I wrote something that I hoped would bring him some work."

Vicky found what she'd been looking for in her purse—her Christian Dior compact. She opened it so that she could examine her new collagen-enhanced lips.

"Honey," Vicky said, as she regarded her reflection. "You didn't just write him something that would bring him more work. You wrote him something that turned him from Mr. Nobody to Mr. Eight Figures in about five minutes flat. And how did he reward you?" Vicky looked up from her compact and directed the full force of her azure-eyed gaze at her friend. "By runnin' off with that blond ice-bitch. What I don't get is why all of this is such a shock to you. I mean, he moved out way before this, didn't he? How long ago?"

"Weeks ago." Lou's voice was mournful. "But he didn't say anything about having fallen in love with somebody else. He just said he didn't think he could commit after all."

"When what he meant—obviously—was that he couldn't commit to *you*. Honey, I've been there. Jack pulled the same old fast one on me, remember? Only in his case, he still hasn't seemed to find Ms. Right. Maybe because for him there *is* no Ms. Right." Vicky shook her head, and happened to spy the reflection of the terminal's coffee stand in her compact mirror. "Can you *believe* they don't have espresso here? I mean, I realize Anchorage is not LA, but it's still *America*, isn't it?"

"God!" Lou exclaimed. She lifted her head from the table, but kept her forehead in her hands. "When I think of everything I did for him! I tell you, writing that stupid thing was the worst mistake I ever made."

Apparently satisfied with her lipliner, Vicky closed her compact and slipped it back into her bag. "Taking up with Barry was the worst mistake you ever made," she said. "Writing *Hindenburg* was a stroke of genius. For heaven's sake, Lou, it's become an American classic."

"Classic piece of crap," Lou said, bitterly.

"It was short on depth," Vicky said, with a shrug. "I'll give you that. But the action scenes were to die for. And those love scenes between Barry and Gret . . ." Lou didn't miss Vicky shaking herself out of the thoughtful reverie into which she'd slipped. Biting her lower lip—ruining her liner as she did so—Vicky's expression was guilty as she said, "Oh, God, hon. I'm sorry."

"No." Lou slumped in her hard plastic chair. "No, it's all right. I can take it. I mean, it's not like any of this is a total surprise. I certainly had my suspicions. Unlike *some* people."

Vicky raised an eyebrow. "If you mean Jack," she said, "he knew."

Lou let out a bitter laugh. "Oh, come on, Vick. He did not. He had no clue."

"About Greta and Barry?" Vicky shook her head until her bob shimmered. "I'm telling you, he knew. He's not as dumb as you like to think, Lou."

"He dumped you, didn't he?" Lou demanded. "If that's not the dumbest thing anybody ever did, I don't know what is."

"Aren't you sweet," Vicky said, with another of her beatific smiles. "But honey, I swear to you, he didn't trash his hotel room because of Greta. I mean, for him to have been that upset, he'd have to have, you know. *Cared* about her."

"And that's a biological impossibility," Lou muttered, "for someone who doesn't even have a heart."

As Vicky, one of the many starlets Jack had left in his wake, ought to have been able to attest to. The only man in Hollywood who'd had more affairs than Jack Townsend was Tim Lord, director of both *Hindenburg* and this most recent *Copkiller* sequel . . .

But at least Jack did his conquests the favor of not marrying them and then dragging them forever through the divorce courts, something Tim Lord did on a fairly regular basis. Vicky was Tim's third wife. The man had an unfortunate tendency—not uncommon in Hollywood— to marry his leading ladies, and though Vicky's part in *Hindenburg*—as the wife of the doomed airship's captain— had been small, she'd nevertheless managed to steal the hearts of both audiences and the film's director.

Still, Vicky hadn't exactly jumped from the frying pan and into the fire going from Jack to Tim. She adored her new husband, while Tim was obviously smitten by her, whereas Jack . . .

Well, the day Jack Townsend cared for anyone whose name wasn't Jack Townsend was the day Lou would appear poolside at the Beverly Hills Hotel wearing only a thong.

"Oh, look," Vicky said, brightening. "Here comes someone who looks unwashed. Maybe he can tell us what's taking so long with our ride."

The unwashed gentleman did prove to be a member of their flight crew. He was, disconcertingly, their pilot.

"We're just waiting on Mr. Townsend," the burly, wool-capped individual informed them, politely, "and then we'll be on our way."

Lou was not certain she'd heard him correctly.

"Jack Townsend?" she echoed, hoarsely, her eyes going wide. "Did you say you're waiting for *Jack Townsend*?"

The pilot was hard-pressed to drag his gaze from the effervescent Vicky, but he managed.

"That's right, ma'am," he said to Lou, before reluctantly— as, like all men, he was drawn to Vicky Lord's ethereal beauty like a moth to a flame—shuffling off again.

"Oh, my God," Lou said, clutching the tabletop with white-knuckled fingers. She glanced at Vicky, but the latter was busy pulling out her cell phone. Hesitantly, Lou asked, "Did you . . . did you hear what he just said, Vick?"

"What he *said?*" Vicky looked disgusted. "What about what he had *on?* Have you ever in your life seen so much plaid on one human being? Who wasn't an extra in *Braveheart*, I mean?"

Lou blinked at her friend. It seemed incredible to her that Vicky could have just heard that the man who had torn her heart in two was on his way to this very airport, and yet all she seemed concerned about was outerwear of the locals.

But that was Vicky. It was one of the reasons Lou had remained friends with her for so long . . . Vicky could be utterly shallow at times, it was true, possessing a complete inability to pass by a designer shoe store without stopping in to make a purchase. But she had an equal weakness for those who were down on their luck, and was incapable of encountering homeless people without stopping to thrust hundred dollar bills into their hands.

"Jack's going to be on our plane, Vicky," Lou explained, because she wasn't certain Vicky understood this. *"Jack Townsend."*

"Well, of course," Vicky said, distractedly. "Why shouldn't my day be completely shot to hell? He must have missed the earlier flight, thanks to all that hoopla back at the hotel. *Why* isn't this phone working? What is wrong with this godforsaken place? First no espresso, now this."

"Vicky," Lou hissed. She had to hiss because it felt as if something was gripping her throat very tightly. Something . . . or someone. Lou's mind flew back to *Hollow Man*, starring Kevin Bacon, parts of which she'd watched in her hotel room the night before. Scientist becomes invisible and goes around terrorizing his colleagues . . .

Vicky, holding the cell phone to her ear, complained, "I don't understand what is going on here. Why can't I get a signal? Where the hell are we, anyway, Siberia?"

"Vicky." Lou's voice came back in full force, filled with wonder—and admiration. "How can you be so calm? The man stomped on your heartstrings, and you're about to get on a plane with him like it's . . . like it's nothing. Whereas I'm still ready to kill him for what he did to you. What's your secret? Really. I'm dying to know."

Vicky closed her cell phone with an impatient snap, then stuffed it back into her bag. "It's called *acting*," she said. "I swear, I should get an Academy Award for Outstanding Performance as Jack Townsend's ex." Then, glancing at her slim gold watch, Vicky made a face. Except that of course, even contorted, her features remained impossibly pretty. "If I'm going to schedule that lymphatic drainage massage, I have to call now." Vicky stood up. "I'm going to find a pay phone."

"Vicky." Fortunately, Lou hadn't had any breakfast. If she'd had, she was fairly certain it would be coming back up right then. "I really think I'm going to be sick."

"Oh, you are not," Vicky said. "Go find the little girls' room and wash that stuff off your head. The last thing you want if you're going to tangle with Tim over that environmentalist thing is to show up at the set with ketchup in your hair."

Spinning around on her slender stiletto heels, Vicky marched off, leaving Lou, white-faced and short of breath, still gripping the tabletop.

"All right," Lou said to herself. Fortunately, with the exception of the woman behind the counter at the coffee stand, she was the only person in the small, rundown private terminal, and so did not have to fear being overheard. "I can do this. I can get on a plane with Jack Townsend. If Vicky can do it, I can, easy. I just won't speak to him. That's all. I mean, just because his ex ran off with my ex, that's no reason for things to change between us. I never spoke to him before, if I could help it. Why start now?"

Fortified by these assurances, Lou climbed to her feet and, shouldering her purse—and the much heavier bag containing her laptop—found the door marked Women. The bathroom was not as bad as she'd thought it would be. The lighting over the sink was generous—a little too bright, actually. She could see the deep circles under her eyes only too well.

Wet paper towels applied to her unruly auburn curls solved the ketchup problem. The purple shadows under her eyes were going to be a more difficult fix. Lou fished a stick of concealer from her purse. Miraculously, it did the trick. Too bad, she thought, there was no concealer for her life. Ex-boyfriend causing you to suffer from low self-image? Just dab on a little of this, and voilà! He's gone! It's like he never existed.

Concealer for emotional scars. Lou smiled at her reflection. That was a good one. Maybe she'd put it in her novel.

Then she stopped smiling. Lipstick. Definitely needed lipstick.

She found some at the bottom of her bag, and slicked it on. Even better. She was starting to look almost human. If she walked out of this restroom and ran into Barry, she doubted he'd be able to tell the emotional wreck he'd made her. Why, all that running she'd done on her at-home treadmill, determined to sweat Barry out of her system, had actually given her some muscle tone. And the weight she'd lost after Barry had moved out—a direct result of a diet of nothing but peanut brittle, the only thing Lou had been able to keep down during that low period of her life—made her seem almost as ethereal as the third Mrs. Tim Lord.

Almost. But not quite. Because there was a hint of wariness in Lou's formerly trusting brown eyes—so like the gaze, her brothers had always asserted, of a golden retriever—that kept her appearance firmly rooted in earthly, not heavenly, stratums.

Now her eyes, Lou decided, were more like those of a golden retriever who'd survived an ingestion of antifreeze.

Barry, she thought, those wary brown eyes narrowing in the mirror before her. *It's all your fault, Barry.*

Except that it wasn't. Lou knew perfectly well that if anyone was to blame for what had happened, it was her. She never ought to have fallen for Barry Kimmel in the first place.

For one thing, of course, Barry was an actor. And if Lou had learned anything in her years in LA, it was never to trust an actor. Never trust one, and never, ever, fall in love with one.

How was she to have known that, though, back in high school on Long Island? Although they'd grown up down the street from one another, Barry had never deigned to notice lowly Lou Calabrese until their senior year, when she'd finally managed to shed the layer of puppy fat she'd worn for most of her life, and convinced everyone to stop calling her Carrots by dyeing her copper-colored curls mahogany. Just like that, Barry Kimmel had asked her out. Barry Kimmel, the hottest boy in Bay Haven Central High School's Drama Club.

Hot, yes. And for a while—a long while—that had been enough. But even Lou, smitten as she'd been, had grown uneasy early into the relationship. Barry was gorgeous. No one could deny that.

But what about funny? Had Barry had the slightest trace of a sense of humor? No, not at all. Granted, few people shared the boisterous Calabrese family's enthusiasm for ribald jokes, but Barry had seemed to find them particularly offensive. Then again, since most of her brothers' pranks had centered around Barry, could Lou blame him, really, for not finding them funny?

And moody? If he did not think he was getting the attention he felt he deserved from whomever—his drama coach, the other actors, Lou—Barry had had a pronounced tendency to sulk. A lot.

Well, Barry was an artist, after all. No one, least of all Lou—or so Barry insisted—could understand the angst an actor went through with every new role, trying to get to the core of his character, to find exactly the right intonation for each line. How Lou, a mere writer, could even dare to compare the two forms of creative expression—writing and acting—was beyond Barry. Writing, as everyone knew, was simply a craft. Acting, however, was art.

The saddest part of all was that for a long time, Lou had actually believed him.

But God, how handsome he'd been . . . a teen girl's walking fantasy of how a boyfriend should look. Barry had been Lou's Nevarre (Rutger Hauer, *Ladyhawke*), her Lloyd Dobbler (John Cusack, *Say Anything*), her Hawkeye (Daniel Day Lewis, *Last of the Mohicans*).

Her everything.

And the fact that he'd wanted *her*, chubby Carrots Calabrese . . . it had been a dream come true for a girl who'd always cared more for movies than she ever had for fashion or makeup. Barry Kimmel had wanted *her*, Lou Calabrese, not Candy Sparks, cheerleading captain and star of every musical Bay Haven Central put on, or Amber

Castiglione, homecoming queen and possessor of a professionally done portfolio of modeling headshots. It was a coup, Lou's landing Barry Kimmel, an almost unheard of victory for fat brainy girls everywhere.

Until now. Now, ten years later, it appeared that Candy and Amber had won after all. Because wasn't that who Greta Woolston was, really? Just a British version of Candy, a European Amber? Barry, saddled with a Lou all those years, had suddenly realized he didn't have to be. He could have all the Candy he wanted . . .

. . . now that he had his own money to pay for it, thanks to Lou, who'd foolishly provided him with the means to earn the kind of paycheck that attracted women like Candy . . . and Greta Woolston.

"You've gotten so cynical," Barry had said to Lou, as he'd been moving out. "So hardened about everything." This observation, Lou was fairly certain, was due to the fact that, rather than throwing herself prostrate at his feet and begging him not to go, she'd politely held the door open while Barry struggled past with a box filled with his CDs.

"I feel like the girl I moved to California with, the one filled with all those hopes and dreams," he'd told her, "is gone."

"Because she grew up, Barry," Lou had said. "Thanks to you."

Remembering the pain that had lanced through her as his words hit home—was it true? Was that why Barry had fallen for Greta? Because of her luminescent vulnerability, the appearance she gave of being completely incapable of taking care of herself, her almost palpable need for someone to watch over her, a sensation Lou was fairly certain she had never aroused in any man?—Lou wrenched her gaze from her reflection.

"Stop it," she whispered to herself. "Just stop it. Pull

yourself together. You're not Carrots Calabrese anymore. You're not. You're Lou Calabrese." She straightened her shoulders and gazed into her own wary, weary eyes. "You're an award-winning screenwriter, soon to be an award-winning novelist . . ."

If she ever finished her novel, the first chapter of which she'd only just begun a few nights ago, about a woman betrayed by her high school sweetheart, and brought to wholeness again through the love of a good man . . . an entirely fictional creation since Lou was now convinced that, with the possible exception of her father and brothers, there was no such thing as a good man.

"When Greta Woolston can't get a part because her implants are hanging down to her knees," Lou said to her reflection in the bathroom mirror, "you'll still be writing. Your best asset isn't made out of silicon. In the meantime, just remember this: *no more actors*. Now, cheer up."

The pep talk didn't work. Lou stared at the smile she'd plastered onto her newly glossed lips, then gave up. She couldn't smile. But she couldn't cry either. Maybe Barry had been right. Maybe she *was* too cynical.

Yeah, and maybe Jack Townsend hadn't meant to break her best friend's heart.

Disgusted, Lou spun around and threw open the door to the terminal . . .

And collided with Jack Townsend, who was standing by the coffee counter, looking absurdly at ease—and handsome—in jeans and a brown leather coat.

"Oh, there she is." Vicky, having returned from her phone call, wore a faintly frantic expression. On Vicky, of course, even frantic looked gorgeous. "Look what the cat drug in, Lou. Well, I can see that you've discovered that for yourself."

Jack Townsend looked up from the cup of coffee he

had barely managed to keep from dropping, thanks to Lou's graceless exit from the ladies' room.

And the minute those cool blue eyes met hers, Lou felt her face turning a deep, burning umber. She'd long ago stopped dyeing her hair a darker shade than its natural auburn, since by the time she'd entered college, everyone seemed to have forgotten about the whole Carrots Calabrese thing.

But there were still times she yearned to be anything but a redhead, and now was one of them. She blushed often and easily . . . so easily that sometimes all she had to do was think about blushing, and she found herself doing it. The *Excuse me* she'd been about to utter for having run into him died on her tongue. All ability to formulate even the simplest of sentences left her as heat consumed her face. Suddenly, Lou Calabrese was on fire.

But any woman, Lou told herself—not just a redhead whose ex-boyfriend had run off with his ex-girlfriend— would blush upon encountering Jack Townsend. That's because he was, not to put too fine a point on it, six foot two inches and two hundred pounds of hard muscle, all wrapped in an irresistibly long-limbed package. With his thick dark hair already turning noticeably gray in spots, and his nose that was no longer aquiline due, it was rumored, to a long-ago prep school fight—the guy was one of the Manhattan Townsends, of Townsend Securities, born with a silver spoon in his mouth and legacies coming out of his finely sculpted rear end—Jack fell far short of being the teen heartthrob material Barry had always been. Barry—aka Bruno di Blase—was a bit of a pretty boy, truth be told. Jack Townsend would never, ever be considered even remotely pretty . . . let alone a boy.

But he was good-looking. More than good-looking. With his piercing blue-eyed gaze and dark, invariably razor-stubbled jaw, Jack Townsend was, in the opinion of many a moviegoer, God's gift to heterosexual women everywhere. Even more astonishingly, he did not appear to know it: Not for Jack Townsend the Armani suits and leather pants Barry traditionally sported, or the Hollywood parties and clubs Barry haunted, in hopes (though Barry denied this) of paparazzi snapping his photo. Jack Townsend, when not working, kept to himself on his seventy-acre ranch in Salinas, almost never appearing in public except to promote his next film . . . a fact Lou guessed had probably contributed to the dissolution of his relationship with press-hungry Greta Woolston more than anything else.

But Greta ought to have known that in taking up with Jack Townsend she was not aligning herself with a man comfortable with the trappings of Hollywood stardom. Why, Jack Townsend, Lou knew for a fact, having witnessed the spectacle herself on more than one occasion, would not allow body doubles or even stuntmen to take his place during nude scenes or action sequences. And makeup? Not on Jack Townsend's face. No one touched that head, not even hairstylists . . . which explained the sprinkle of gray.

And the dark circles—so like her own—Jack Townsend currently sported under his eyes? Tim Lord was going to have to pay a fortune to have them removed after filming, frame by agonizing frame, since Jack would sooner eat glass than wear concealer, even for his closeups.

Yes, Jack Townsend was many things: a makeup artist's nightmare, a director's sure ticket to box office success, and just about every woman in America's dream date.

But one thing Jack Townsend was not, in spite of his incredibly good looks and laid back charm, was one of Lou's favorite people.

And it was obvious by the look on Jack's face when she

bumped into him that Lou's feelings of intense dislike were heartily returned. Jack glanced at Lou—seeming to look straight through her with those preternaturally blue eyes—then looked away again, and muttered, in that sardonic tone in which he said just about everything, "Oh. It's you."

Was it possible that this day, Lou wondered, which had not started out at all auspiciously, could get any worse?

3

Lou. It would have to have been Lou, wouldn't it?

Oh, well. He ought to have expected it, the way things had been going. From last night's debacle in the hotel suite—courtesy of Melanie Dupre—to this morning's mad dash to escape the press staked out in the lobby, not to mention the picketing environmentalists, furious over the state's decision to allow Tim Lord to go ahead and blow up part of Mount McKinley—Jack Townsend's life had turned into one long continuous nightmare.

No, nightmare wasn't right. It wasn't a nightmare. Nightmares were frightening. This was just . . .

Ridiculous.

Really. He was irritated at himself for having gotten into the situation in the first place. Now would come the endless questions, the speculation, the suspicion, the snickers.

And he couldn't tell them it was all Melanie's fault. He couldn't say, "I decided I'd had my fill of actresses, so I told Melanie she was going to have to go, and she trashed my room." No, he couldn't say that, because that wouldn't be gentlemanly.

And though Jack felt that his cold, somewhat autocratic father hadn't taught him all that much, one thing he had learned from Gilbert Townsend was never to kiss and tell. The drawback to this rule, which Jack never failed to adhere to, was that from this day forward, he would never be able to check into a hotel without arousing comments about love seats.

And now this. Lou Calabrese. Perfect. She would, of course, have picked this day, of all days, to pay a visit to the set.

Not that Jack was ever unhappy to see a pretty woman show up anywhere. It was just when that woman happened to be Lou Calabrese that he tended to mind.

Because Lou Calabrese, to put it bluntly, was a pain in the ass.

All writers were impossible. He knew that only too well, having taken up with his fair share of them in the past. But screenwriters were the worst. Temperamental, self-absorbed artistes, with delusions of grandeur and an inflated sense of their own importance.

And Lou Calabrese was the worst of them all. Change one word of her precious dialogue, and an actor—as Jack knew only too well—would never hear the end of it. Why Tim Lord had agreed to work with her again, Jack couldn't imagine.

Then again, Tim was probably unaware of just how much of a pain Lou Calabrese could be. Greta and Bruno probably hadn't made any filmworthy ad libs during the shooting of *Hindenburg*. Neither one of them was exactly rocket scientist material.

Not, of course, that Lou's dialogue wasn't usually right on. Hey, it had won her an Oscar, right? But still. *It's al-*

ways funny until someone gets hurt. Who did she think she was kidding? Arnold had *Hasta la vista, baby.* Eastwood, *Make my day.* Willis had *Yippee-ki-yay* expletive deleted.

But Jack Townsend was supposed to be happy with *It's always funny until someone gets hurt?*

"Oh." Vicky looked from Lou to Jack and then back again. "Right. You two go way back. The original *Cop-killer.* God. What was that, like, five years ago?"

"Six," Lou said.

Jack would have to have been deaf to have missed the acid in her tone. Oh, so the feeling was mutual, was it? Like that wasn't completely obvious, given the indignities he'd been forced to undergo as Detective Pete Logan in *Copkiller II* and *III.*

Hey, fine with him. She wasn't exactly his favorite person in the world, either.

"Six years. I can't believe it's been that long. . . ."

Vicky's voice trailed off. She seemed to get the message that it might be better if she just shut up. That had been, Jack remembered now, the good thing about Vicky: she wasn't dumb. A little flaky, with her t'ai chi and her deep tissue massages and her bringing home every stray animal that came her way and all of that, but smart enough when it counted. Except for that whole—what was it again? Oh, yeah—intimacy issues thing. Whatever *that* had been about.

Now Vicky was looking at her watch. "Oops, sorry, I gotta go."

Lou's eyes—already ridiculously enormous, although their size might have been partly due to their darkness in her pale face; she looked like she'd gotten about as much sleep as he had—widened. Really, what good were eyes like that, Jack couldn't help wondering, on a *screenwriter?* They were leading lady eyes . . . or ingenue eyes, at the very least. They were wasted on a woman who spent eight hours a day in front of a computer monitor.

As was, he couldn't help thinking, that body. If Lou thought she could hide those curves under that thick cable-knit sweater and brown wool slacks, she was sadly mistaken. Even a less practiced gaze than his own could detect the narrow waist, high round breasts, and slender legs those loose-fitting garments were supposed to hide. She was tall, too, at least five eight, and that was without the help of two-inch heels on her boots. Lou Calabrese had the kind of endlessly long legs a man wouldn't mind having wrapped around him on a winter's night. . . .

Now what had put *that* image into his head?

Maybe the same thing that caused him to reflect that Lou Calabrese's hair, a shoulder-length riot of russet-colored curls, seemed to cry out for fingers to be plunged into its thick waves. It even had the appearance of being natural, both in color and curl, making it, according to the dictates of the current Hollywood style for sleek blond bobs like Greta's and Vicky's, hopelessly retro. . . .

A fact about which Lou apparently either didn't know or didn't care. The bronze-colored parka she wore over the cable-knit sweater, more functional than figure-flattering, bore out the latter theory. There might, Jack reflected, be something uniquely refreshing about being with a woman who was not a slave to the whims of the world of fashion. Especially a woman who'd look good no matter what she put on.

Still, Lou Calabrese? He pitied the man Lou Calabrese sunk her sensibly short nails into next. Those kind of looks coupled with a brain capable of summoning up the myriad tortures she regularly inflicted upon her hapless character, Detective Logan? A deadly combination.

Look how she managed the defenseless female thing.

She was doing it right in front of him, right now, those lush raspberry-colored lips parted in distress, those brown eyes wide and dewy-looking as she asked Vicky, "Go where?"

If Jack hadn't decided a long time ago that Lou Calabrese was devoid of human emotion, he might have felt some manly protectiveness for her, she looked so genuinely alarmed.

As it was, however, he knew she'd welcome his help about as much as she'd welcome a swarm of killer bees. Look how grateful she'd been over the "I need a bigger gun" thing. Had *that* ever not turned out the way he'd anticipated.

"But you can't go, Vicky," Lou was saying. "I thought you were flying out with us to the set."

"I was, honey," Vicky said. Vicky, Jack remembered, had always been very loose with the endearments. No one else, he was quite sure, would ever refer to Lou Calabrese as honey. Sweet as she might look, *honey* Lou was definitely not. "But when I called in just now for my messages, there was one from Tim. He phoned down from the set. Something's wrong with Elijah. A little fever, I guess. The hotel called him up in Myra. So now I've got to go do the stepmommy thing. I'll catch up with you this afternoon, though, I swear. I mean, unless the kid's gangrenous."

This news was clearly distressing to Lou. She reached out and grabbed Vicky's arm.

"Vicky," Jack heard her growl. No, really. Growled, like a tiger. Much in the way she'd growled at him, the day he'd substituted the *It's always funny until someone gets hurt* line with the *I need a bigger gun* thing. Only this time, she used less expletives. "I swear to God, if you leave me alone with—"

Jack was distracted from this interesting conversation

by the woman behind the coffee counter, who suddenly, and quite shrilly, declared, "Why, you're Jack Townsend!"

Jack blinked at the pleasant-looking middle-aged woman who'd provided him with that much needed cup of coffee.

"Yes," he said, realizing that really, there was no way of getting out of it. "I am."

"Oh, my Lord," the woman cried, her eyes bulging. "Oh, my Lord, I wasn't sure at first, but now I heard you talk, it is, it *is* you!"

Jack, tired as he was, couldn't help grinning a little. Fans were almost as big a pain in the ass as screenwriters. Yet without them, just like screenwriters, Jack wouldn't be where he was today.

Not that, particularly on a morning like this one, he considered that such an enviable position.

"Yes," he said, because there was no use denying it. "It's me."

The woman's face broke into a beatific smile.

"I'm Marie," the woman gushed. "Mr. Townsend, I can't tell you what a hoot this is. I heard you were here, you know, in Alaska, filmin', but I never thought I'd actually lay eyes on you myself. Did you know that you are my favorite actor of all time? *All* time. '*STAT*' was my favorite show . . . well, until you left it. It went totally downhill from there, I don't care what anybody says. And *Copkiller* is my favorite movie."

The pause in her babbling stream of compliments enabled Jack to jump in with, "Thank you very much, Marie. I—"

But he didn't get a chance to finish, because as Jack started to crumple his coffee cup, its contents drained, Marie, behind the counter, screamed, "No!" When Jack glanced at her in astonishment, the woman added, with a sheepish blush, "I was gonna keep it. You know, the cup Jack Townsend drank my coffee from."

Jack looked down at the crumpled cup. This—not the long hours, the months spent away from home, the endless script changes he was forced to commit to memory at a moment's notice, the hounding of the press—was what he hated most. People—fans—saving his used drink containers, napkins, on one memorable occasion, even a Kleenex. There was no one—no one single person on this earth—whose used Kleenex Jack would want to keep, and he could not understand the compulsion to do so in anyone else . . . particularly when it was *his* used Kleenex in question.

"How about I sign something for you?" he offered gamely while shoving the cup into the trash. "That might, you know, impress people more than an old coffee cup."

"Oh!" Marie shoved a pen and notepad across the counter at him. "If you don't mind. Can you make it out to Marie?"

"Sure I can," Jack said, lifting the pen.

"And can you write *it*?" Marie grinned at him shyly. "You know. Pete Logan's famous line."

Jack, conscious that Lou was watching, couldn't help but smile. It had to gall her, he knew, how popular that line had become.

"Sure," he said, and scribbled, *I need a bigger gun* above his signature. "Here you go," he said, when he was finished, handing pen and pad back to her. "Have a good one."

Marie beamed. She also, he noticed with a grimace, fished his coffee cup from the trash, and set it carefully aside.

Why, he asked himself, not for the first time that day, or

even that hour, hadn't he become a lawyer, the way his father had wanted him to?

But Marie wasn't done.

"Hey," she said, widening her eyes at Vicky. "You—you played the captain's wife! In *Hindenburg*!"

Vicky's smile brightened her face like a new dawn.

"Yes," she said. "That was me."

"Can you sign this for me?" Marie asked, shoving a napkin and pen in Vicky's direction.

"Sure," Vicky said, with a smile, and stepped forward to seize the pen. She would, Jack knew, accompany her signature with a smiley face and heart. He had yet to meet a woman in Hollywood who could resist adding a smiley face or heart to her autograph. Greta had even occasionally doodled a star by her name . . . well before she'd ever become one, making the whole thing seem a sort of self-fulfilling prophecy.

Marie dragged her gaze towards Lou, looking hopeful. "What about you?" she asked. "Are you somebody famous, too?"

Jack, expecting to hear a long recital of projects on which Lou Calabrese had worked, prepared to restrain a yawn. No writer that he'd ever met could resist tooting her own horn, and Lou's list of accomplishments was a particularly impressive one, as everyone knew—*Variety* having endlessly reported the fact—that she'd sold her very first screenplay, the original *Copkiller*, at the tender age of twenty-two.

But he stopped mid-yawn when, to his surprise, Lou merely shrugged and said, her smile every bit as brittle as Vicky's had been beguiling, "Sorry. I'm just a writer."

Just a writer? *Just a writer*? That was like saying that . . . well, that Tim Lord was just a director. Just a writer? It had been a long, long time since Jack had heard so self-effacing a statement from a member of Hollywood's elite. He regarded Lou Calabrese curiously. What, he wondered, was going on here?

Marie, however, was visibly disappointed.

"Oh," she said. Then she seemed to rally. "Well, would you mind signing something for me anyway?" she asked, taking her pen back from Vicky. "Because you never know, honey. Maybe you'll be famous someday, too, like these two."

That was when Lou did something extraordinary. She smiled.

And when Lou Calabrese smiled, Jack was surprised to see, her face went from being merely pretty to downright beautiful, something he had never before had occasion to notice, since Lou generally wore a look of extreme dissatisfaction while watching him perform the role of Detective Logan.

"Thanks," she said, to Marie, in a voice that, like the smile, he'd never heard her use before. The reason the smile, he realized, was so striking was because its warmth was reflected in those deep brown eyes, a rarity in LA circles, where most smiles were about as genuine as the teeth they tended to reveal. She scrawled her name on the proffered napkin. No smiley face, Jack noticed. No heart. And certainly no star.

"Here you go," Lou Calabrese said.

It was right then that the large man in a plaid shirt approached them, looking unaccountably nervous.

"Mr. Townsend?" he asked.

Vicky chimed in, again before Jack could get a word in, "Yes, Mr. Townsend's here now. But there's been a change of plans. I'm going back to the hotel."

Plaid Shirt nodded. "Whatever you say, ma'am." To Jack, he said, "I'm Sam. I'll be your pilot today. Whenever you're ready, then, we can take off."

"We're ready," Lou said, quickly. So quickly, in fact, that Jack wondered if she was as anxious as he was to get out of Anchorage—or perhaps it was only that she wanted to spend as little time as possible in his presence.

The pilot looked startled.

"Uh," he stammered. "You're, uh, coming, too, miss?"

"Of course I'm coming, too," Lou said. Her voice was still growly, like she'd just woken up. Bed voice, they called it. Unlike bed head, bed voice was a good thing. For an actor, anyway. For a screenwriter, though—especially when coupled with a set of what could only be called bedroom eyes—it was merely distracting. At least, Jack found it so.

"Uh—" The pilot looked confused. "Uh, are you sure? I thought you were supposed to go with Mrs. Lord."

Lou shook her head, looking puzzled. "No. No, I'm still heading out to Myra, as scheduled."

The pilot glanced down at his flight manifest. "Uh. It says here one passenger."

"Well, it's wrong. It should be three. Now it's two."

"Um. Okay. I guess." The pilot reached beneath his knit cap to scratch his head . . . not, in Jack's book, a very encouraging sign. "If you say so, miss."

Above their heads, the airport terminal's sound system crackled to life. A local radio station DJ advised them that snow was in the forecast, then announced that, in celebration of *Hindenburg* stars' Greta Woolston and Bruno di Blase's elopement, he was playing the Academy Award–winning song from the movie's soundtrack. A second later, the first chords of "My Love Burns for You Tonight" began to rain tinnily down upon them.

Perfect. Freaking perfect.

Jack wasn't the only one, however, who seemed unhappy about this. Without another glance at either Jack or Vicky, Lou, her coat over one arm, and her purse and computer bag on the other, let out a strangled scream, then rushed after the burly bush pilot as he made his way from the terminal, her thick red curls bouncing as she ran.

Academy Award winner or no, "My Love Burns for You Tonight" was, without a doubt, one of the stupidest songs Jack had ever heard. It was also one of the catchiest.

And now it was going to be stuck in his head for the rest of the day. Lou's too, if the scream had been any indication.

Could things possibly get any worse?

Apparently so.

Because when Vicky stood on tiptoe to kiss him goodbye—women like Vicky kissed everyone goodbye. She'd have kissed Lou goodbye, only she got away before Vicky got the chance—he realized that, as a matter of fact, his day *could* get much worse. That was when Vicky chose to say, in a whisper he was certain could be heard all the way across the terminal, "If you'd just stayed with me, none of this ever would have happened."

Well, what had he expected? Vicky wasn't the type to keep her mouth shut. When Vicky had something to say, by God, she said it. Intimacy issues. That's what she'd accused him of having. That was why, she'd told him, he didn't feel the same way about her that she felt about him. Intimacy issues. Jack, she'd said, was just too damned protective of his heart ever to allow himself to open up and possibly get hurt.

Yeah. That was it. Just because he didn't give his heart away with every autograph, the way Vicky did. . . .

Still, Vicky's outspokenness had been one of the most appealing things about her, and had almost made putting up with the rest of the Vicky package—the brief flirtation with the Kabala, the macrobiotic diet, the stray llama—worth it.

Almost. But in the end, not quite. Because he was protecting his heart, of course.

It wasn't his heart he was protecting a minute later when he stepped out onto the bitterly cold tarmac and felt icy fingers of wind stab at him. Pulling his leather coat more closely around him, Jack hurried towards the aircraft waiting on the tarmac . . . then balked. This was not, as he had assumed, the turbo-prop eight-seater that ferried the director and other members of the production crew too important to bunk down in what passed for hotel accommodations in Myra. No, this was a helicopter.

And not a very big one, either.

Lou was already in the backseat, a set of headphones over her ears and an expression on her face that revealed her enthusiasm at the prospect of flying in this contraption was equal to his own. Or maybe it was just the fact that she'd be flying in it with *him* that had her nose in the air.

"What happened to the Cessna?" Jack asked the pilot, having to raise his voice to be heard above the winter wind and the slowly rotating blades overhead.

"Um, the Cessna Caravan's unavailable, sir," the pilot shouted. "This is all we've got."

Jack scowled. He had no fear of flying, but he definitely preferred to stick to aircrafts that comfortably fit more than four.

"You don't have anything bigger?" he asked.

"Um," the pilot said, looking, to Jack, disconcertingly nervous for someone with whom he was supposed to trust his life. "This R-44's brand new. Mr. Lord's been using it for his aerial shots, and that's it. It's completely safe. Really, Mr. Townsend."

Lou, in the backseat, glared at him, and said, in that growly voice of hers, "In or out, flyboy. It's freezing out there."

Jack set his jaw. What was with this woman, anyway? He could understand her still being mad about the *I need a bigger gun* thing—she had made her ire over that more than known, if the indignities she'd subjected Pete Logan to in subsequent films was any indication.

But come on! That had been years ago! Sure, redheads were supposed to have tempers, but this was getting ridiculous. Just how long could this girl hold a grudge, anyway?

Then he recalled, belatedly, that Lou was a friend of Vicky's. Had the two of them, he wondered, spent the ride from the hotel to the airport dissecting their exes? Undoubtedly. Which was just great. Now he was going to have to weather not only the rage of an offended artiste, but the wrath of a loyal friend of a woman he'd supposedly scorned.

Still, you'd think that, considering what had happened the night before, he and Lou being in the same boat now, she'd cut him a little slack. And if you thought about it, the whole thing was her fault anyway. If she hadn't written that stupid blimp movie in the first place, Greta and that idiot di Blase might never have met.

Besides, no way did she have it anywhere near as rough as he did. Oh, no. As far as he knew, he'd been the only one in that hotel room last night, trying to talk Melanie Dupre out of venting her rage at him on an innocent couch. Or love seat, as the press, with an uncharacteristic flash of irony, was calling it.

Yeah, sure, Lou'd lost her boyfriend. But she didn't have half-crazed actresses lighting her hotel room furniture on fire, now, did she?

"Fine," Jack said, tamping down, with some effort, his misgivings about the aircraft, its stammering pilot, and most of all, his fetching, if ill-tempered, fellow passenger. "Let's go."

He pretended not to hear Lou's muttered, "Alleluia."

One advantage of the R-44 over the turbo-prop, Jack

soon learned, was that polite conversation with his fellow passenger was impossible. For one thing, she sat alone in the backseat: Sam had insisted he needed Jack's weight "up front" to "balance things out." For another, the pounding of the propeller blades overhead made it impossible to hear what anyone was saying, save through the voice-activated microphones attached to the headphones Sam insisted they wear. Jack, exhausted as he was, found the fact that no one appeared to expect him to make small talk extremely satisfying. As the chopper lifted, then sailed from the airport, he gazed out through the large windscreen before him, watching the outskirts of Anchorage shrink below them, then gradually give way to a blanket of white, dotted by the occasional cluster of green pine trees.

Alaska. He'd been amused when he'd first read the script, and seen that the plot called for a considerable amount of the film's action to be conducted in a fictional mining town situated at the base of Mount McKinley. Pete Logan, for a simple New York City homicide dick, certainly seemed to get around. He had, in his past three films alone, spent time in Tibet, Uzbekistan, Bolivia, and Belize. And now Alaska, to round out his world tour.

Interestingly, Pete always seemed to be sent to some of the most dangerous places on earth, a fact that Jack attributed to the desire of the character's creator to make things as uncomfortable as possible for the man who played him. He never let on to Lou that the truth of the matter was that Jack enjoyed the location shoots immensely, and minded neither the desert heat nor the arctic cold of the various locales in which she chose to set her plots.

The fact that, in all of these exotic districts, Detective Logan was invariably forced to drop his pants, however, rancored somewhat. It was one thing to go chasing after diamond smugglers in Nepal. It was quite another to be stripped naked and strung up in a temple by those smugglers, only to be beaten on the ass with bamboo poles.

That kind of thing Jack—but apparently not the American viewing public, who had enjoyed *Copkiller II* immensely, helping it to gross over three hundred million in domestic box office alone—had a small problem with.

Fortunately, the only scene in the current *Copkiller* requiring Jack to appear less than fully clothed was the one in the hot tub right before sassy assistant district attorney Rebecca Wells gets electrocuted. Lou must have been a little off her game while writing this one. Apparently, his only punishment this time was to be a month-long sojourn in the forty-ninth state.

Which was hardly a punishment. Alaska was beautiful . . . from what Jack had seen of it, anyway. It was a little hard to judge, since the bulk of his sightseeing consisted of the Anchorage Four Seasons and the small mountain town, some two hundred miles north of Myra. Between the two, from what he'd observed, existed only forest. Well, forest mixed with mountains covered with vast expanses of white. Hardly, he thought, a thorough example of all that the great state of Alaska had to offer.

Still, if he'd had to be anywhere when news of Greta's elopement hit, better Alaska than LA. Far from the reach of "Access Hollywood" and "Entertainment Tonight," Jack felt almost . . . well, at home. And when filming was over, he hoped to take a few weeks off and do some ice-fishing. One of the guys on the crew had offered to loan him his cabin—

"Mr. Townsend."

It was only when the pilot's voice, coming over his headphones, crackled noisily in Jack's ears that he realized he'd dozed off. Well, it wasn't any wonder, really. Melanie's temper tantrum the night before, and its unfortunate consequences—in the form of hotel security, the fire department, and finally, the police, showing up in his suite—had kept him up until four in the morning. He was really going to have to learn, one of these days, to quit consorting with actresses. His mother was right: every little thing developed into a full-scale drama to them. Jack wasn't sure how much longer he could take the constant theatrics.

On the other hand, when did he ever meet an attractive woman who *wasn't* an actress? Unbidden, his gaze slid towards the redhead in the backseat. Not an actress, that was for sure. But certainly a major league—

It was only when Jack's gaze fell on Lou's face that he realized her expression was not one of boredom, as would have been expected on a not entirely comfortable helicopter ride. Nor did she appear to be nauseous, a common reaction to flying in what was, admittedly, fairly choppy air space.

No, Lou wore an expression of abject horror. And this time, it did not appear to be because he had said or done—as he'd seemed constantly to have done since the day they'd first met, six years earlier—the wrong thing. Following the direction of her gaze, Jack realized Lou was staring fixedly at the revolver the pilot was pointing at Jack's head.

"Mr. Townsend," the pilot said. "I think you need a bigger gun. Or just any gun, actually."

4

Tim Lord stared at the closed trailer door. "Rebecca" was written across the masking tape stuck to the door. But he would have known that Melanie Dupre—the actress playing Pete Logan's love interest—was inside simply by the sounds of breaking glass and prolonged, animal-like screams coming through the door.

"She's been like that all morning," Melanie Dupre's personal assistant, whose name Tim could never remember, informed him glumly.

Tim listened as what sounded like a tower of CDs toppled over. He winced. He wondered if the studio's insurance would pay for the damage, or if, to teach Miss Dupre a badly needed lesson, they might deduct the cost of replacement from her paycheck.

"Is this," he asked the PA curiously, "on account of the whole elopement thing? You know, Greta and Bruno?"

"I don't think so," the PA said. Like most personal assistants, this one was a distant relative of Melanie's, and bore a passing resemblance to the actress. The PA, however, had a pretty severe case of acne that marred her otherwise attractive features. Tim wondered why Melanie didn't fix the girl up with her dermatologist. She had one of the best in LA, after all. Tim knew, because Melanie's contract stipulated that the studio pay for her chemical peels during shooting.

"I think," the PA said softly, as if Melanie, inside the trailer, might possibly overhear her, in spite of all the noise she was making breaking things, "that Mr. Townsend, you know. Kinda broke up with her last night."

Tim nodded. Of course. He ought to have known. It was very rarely a good thing when a pair of actors chose to take their on-screen chemistry out for a spin behind the cameras, and Jack Townsend and Melanie had, recently. There was always the possibility their relationship might crumble during shooting, and make things on the set . . . well, awkward. Tim had enough personal experience with that sort of thing to have known better.

The same could not be said of Jack Townsend and Melanie Dupre, apparently.

Why him? Really. Why today? Why the hell had Greta Woolston and Bruno di Blase had to have chosen last night, of all nights, to elope, an act which had no doubted prompted Jack's sudden decision to reorganize his priorities?

And why had he chosen this movie, of all movies, to follow up *Hindenburg?* Why hadn't he signed on for some nice little indie flick? Hey, it had worked for Jack Townsend, hadn't it?

"Mel?" Tim reached up and rapped sharply on the trailer door with the back of his knuckles. "Mel, it's me, Tim. Tim Lord. Can I come in?"

Before Melanie had a chance to respond, Paul Thompkins, one of the assistant directors, came hurrying up, the tips of his ears, sticking out from beneath his *Copkiller II* baseball hat, bright red from the cold. It was a relatively balmy twenty degrees, with predictions of the temperature dropping another ten degrees in the coming hour.

But that was nothing. Yesterday, it had been five below. One cameraman had nearly lost a finger to frostbite.

Why had Lou chosen an arctic setting for this, the last of the *Copkiller* movies? Why couldn't she have set this thing in Hawaii? There were dangerous criminals hiding out in Hawaii, weren't there? Lou was taking her dislike of Jack Townsend, and her desire to see him as uncomfortable as she could possibly make him, way too far. After all, "I need a bigger gun" *was* a better line than "It's always funny until someone gets hurt." Just ask any test audience.

"Tim," Paul leaned down to whisper. Tim Lord, in spite of the cowboy boots he habitually sported, the ones with the two-inch heels, was only a little over five feet, six inches tall, a fact that rancored him even more than the *New York Times* film critic who'd called *Hindenburg* "a cloying and masturbatory work from a director who thinks a mite too highly of himself."

"Just got word from Anchorage," Paul whispered. "The chopper with Jack in it is on its way."

"Great," Tim said. "Great." He took a deep breath, drew himself up as tall as he could, then rapped harder on the trailer door. "Melanie? Honey, it's Tim. Listen, let me in, would you? We need to talk."

"And," Paul whispered, apparently so Melanie's PA wouldn't hear, "they say there's another cold front moving in. This one should be a doozy. It's supposed to dump another ten inches."

"Swell," Tim said, feeling his heart sink. Still, you wouldn't have noticed, from his voice, that anything was amiss. Anything at all. It was the director's job to maintain an aura of calm control at all times. No matter how much your world might be spinning completely out of control, never let it show. Never let them see you sweat. "That's just swell."

Turning back to the door, he called, "Mel, honey, Jack's going to be here in a little while. We're going to have to start filming. You know, the mine scene. We've got a storm coming, and I—"

Suddenly enough that even the PA jumped, the door to Melanie Dupre's trailer ripped open. Melanie, still in costume, but with badly smeared mascara, glared down at Tim. Even Melanie Dupre, delicately boned poppet that she was, was taller than Academy Award–winning director Tim Lord.

"Do you have any idea," Melanie demanded, in a voice clogged with tears, "what that jerk said to me last night? *Do you?*"

Though he wouldn't have thought such a thing possible, Tim felt his heart sink even more. Two more days. That was all that was left of the shoot. Two more days, and he could have gotten everything he needed and returned to L.A. to begin editing.

Really, he did not need this. He did not need romantic trouble between the talent, on top of protesting treehuggers, rabid animal-rights lovers, bad weather, and everything else.

No one, he'd noticed, had called Jack Townsend's indie *Hamlet* masturbatory or cloying, that he'd noticed. Sure, the thing hadn't done a fraction of the business *Hindenburg* had, but it had received glowing reviews—even one from the *New York Times*.

Somehow, Tim didn't imagine *Copkiller IV* was going to pull in glowing reviews from anybody.

"Now, Mel," Tim said, in what he hoped was a soothing voice. "You know Jack. He gets testy right before an important shot. . . ."

"It has nothing to do with the film!" Melanie all but shrieked. Her voice did not carry far, however, with all the snow. Tim doubted the crew, setting up in front of the mouth to the abandoned mine, could hear her. Thank God.

"That is what is wrong with you people," Melanie shrieked. "You think everything revolves around your stupid film! Well, this has nothing to do with *Copkiller*, Tim. It has to do with the fact that Jack Townsend is a selfish, manipulative di—"

Over by the mine shaft, a siren went off. The special effects crew had rigged the detonators, and were preparing to do a test run of the explosion. They needed everyone to move back twenty feet to avoid flying shards of wood and gravel.

"—and I am not going to be used anymore," Melanie, who'd kept talking right through the warning siren, continued when it was shut down. "This is it, Tim. I will not work with him. Not a second longer. Understand?"

A distant rumble indicated that the explosion had gone off without a hitch. Now the crew would be scrambling to rig up the explosives for the actual shoot. In a very short while, they'd be ready for the principals.

"Mel," Tim said soothingly. "I understand you're going through a hard time right now. We're all stressed. You know it always gets like this in the final days of a shoot. But I'm asking you to understand that Jack's going through an even harder time than the rest of us. I mean, Greta—"

He knew immediately he should not have brought up La Woolston. The part of Mimi, the heroine of *Hindenburg*, had been the most sought-after role in Hollywood two years ago, and Melanie—along with three dozen other starlets, not to mention several rock divas and one television talk show hostess—had been bitterly disappointed when it had gone to Greta, and not to her.

"Oh, God!" Melanie cried, her face crumpling. "How could you, Tim? How *could* you?"

The trailer door slammed shut again. Tim, the PA, and Paul all exchanged glances.

"Maybe," the PA ventured, after a moment, "I should phone her therapist."

"Maybe," Tim said, curtly, "you should have done that a half-hour ago."

While the PA went slinking shame-facedly away, the assistant director cleared his throat. Tim threw him an aggrieved look. "What now?" he wanted to know.

"Um," the assistant director said, lifting a hand to the headset attached to one of his bright red ears. "It's just that I got confirmation that Lou's with him. Townsend, I mean."

Tim stared at the other man in horror. "What . . . what are you saying?"

"Um," Paul said nervously. "She took the same chopper. Lou. And Jack. In the same small, enclosed space."

Tim reached up to clutch his head. No. No, this could not be happening.

"My God," Paul breathed. "They'll kill each other."

Vicky Lord slammed the door to her hotel suite and leaned back against it, heavily. Or as heavily as a woman who kept as eagle an eye as she did on her hundred pound, fifteen percent body fat, small-boned frame as Vicky did—could lean.

"My God," she said, to Lupe, who looked up at her employer with surprise from the magazine she'd been perusing in front of "The View." "Those reporters are relentless. I can't believe I made it through that lobby in one piece.

'Mrs. Lord! Mrs. Lord! Do you have any comment, Mrs. Lord, on the Di Blase/Woolston elopement? Do you know how Jack Townsend's doing this morning? Is he suicidal?' And those environmentalists! You'd think Tim was threatening to blow up a kitten farm, instead of an old abandoned mine shaft, the way they're carrying on." Eyeing the bottle of whiskey set out on top of the hotel suite bar, Vicky hurried over to it and poured herself a glass. "Just a quick one," she said, to Lupe, who'd hidden the magazine and switched off the TV. "I need it, after all that."

Lupe, as was her custom, said nothing, but got up and retrieved the fur coat her mistress had dropped onto the floor. Designed to look like imitation mink, the coat was in fact genuine chinchilla, but would have fooled even the most ardent paint-carrying animal activist.

"Why are you home so early, Mrs. Lord?" Lupe asked, as she went to the closet and carefully hung the coat up. "Is it the storm? I heard about it on the news."

"Storm?" With the whiskey sitting nicely at the bottom of her stomach with the egg white omelette and hot water and lemon she'd had for breakfast, Vicky went to the vast bank of windows on the far side of the suite's living room and looked out at the thick wall of clouds barreling down from the mountains. "Good Lord. Now that *is* a storm. Well, isn't that just perfect? Now I'll be stuck in here all day with little Lord Fauntleroy, and not even a chance of a reprieve for shopping. As if," she added with a sigh, "there were anything to buy in this godforsaken place anyway."

She turned away from the window and said, "All right, just give it to me straight. Has he barfed? Because you know how I am about vomit."

Lupe gazed at her employer with undisguised bewilderment. There was much Lupe did not understand about the Lord household, but the new Mrs. Lord was the most perplexing thing of all. Though Lupe had to say this one was better than the last one, who, towards the end, when it became clear she was about to be replaced with a younger, newer model, had frightened Lupe with her sudden keen interest in body-building and handguns.

"I don't know what you mean, Mrs. Lord," Lupe said. "Who is barfing?"

Vicky's pretty features creased with impatience. "Elijah," she said. "I got a message he was sick."

Lupe shook her head. "Elijah is not sick. He is down at the pool with the rest of the children and the nanny. They were playing *Jaws*, last I checked."

Vicky sank down onto the place on the couch Lupe had just vacated, and picked up the very same magazine and started to flip through it.

"That's okay, Lupe," she said. "You don't have to worry about sparing my feelings. I'm totally good. I knew what I was getting into with this stepmom thing when I took it on. Just give it to me straight. How bad is it? I mean, it's not projectile, is it?"

"Mrs. Lord." Lupe held out both hands in a gesture of helplessness. "I do not know what you are talking about. Elijah is not sick. He is downstairs, swimming in the indoor pool. I am to order lunch in one hour. That is all I know. Last time I see Elijah, he was fine." The kid had been more than fine. He'd hurled a Lego battlecruiser at her. But Lupe knew better than to waste her breath complaining about the children's behavior to their stepmother, who would—could—do nothing about it.

Vicky looked up from the magazine—the newest issue of *Vogue*—and said, "Wait a minute. If the kid's not sick, why did Tim get a message that he was?"

"I do not know, Mrs. Lord. I did not call Mr. Lord. Elijah is fine. At least, he ate all his Count Chocula this morning."

Vicky eyed her maid. "So you're saying I got called

away from the airport, all the way back to the hotel, for nothing?"

"There has been some mistake," Lupe said, with a shrug. "Maybe the hotel make a mistake? But it is not so bad. You would not want to go to the set in this." She nodded at the windows, where she could see snow starting to fall. "You could be trapped on that mountain all night."

Vicky, following the direction of Lupe's gaze, gasped. "You're right. Ugh, that looks nasty. Glad I'm here instead." Then, with a prettily constricted brow, she added, "Poor Jack and Lou, flying in all that. Hope they'll be all right."

Frank Calabrese looked down at the numbers he'd carefully copied out onto the emergency contact list he kept by the telephone in the kitchen. After forty years on the force, Frank had learned a thing or two. Never, for instance, to wear white undershirts: the pale material peeking from the V of his uniform collar made a perfect target for perps who wanted to be sure to hit him above his bulletproof vest.

Not that, in all his time on the force, he'd ever been shot at. Still, it never hurt to be prepared. And black undershirts had the added bonus of not showing the stains from the meatball sandwiches he liked to have for lunch.

But more edifying than his years in the New York Police Department had been the four decades Frank had spent parenting his five children—admittedly with the help of his now deceased wife, Helen. But for the past ten years, anyway, since Helen's death from breast cancer, he'd been handling the parenting duties alone, and, not to brag, he'd been doing a pretty good job of it, thanks.

And while the kids were mostly grown up now, and not necessarily in need of constant supervision, one thing he'd learned was that it behooved a parent to keep all of his children's phone numbers in one place—along with other important numbers, such as the nearest pizza place that delivered, and the toll-free hotline to secure Yankee tickets—in easy access to the phone.

Now he squinted down at the list he'd composed—he was far-sighted, but too stubborn to put on the glasses his optometrist had prescribed, except when he was reading the spy novels he found so engrossing since he'd retired. Finally, he found the number he was looking for, and, with one last glance at the paper spread out in front of him on the kitchen table, he dialed.

She didn't pick up, of course. She rarely did. He didn't know why she even kept a cell phone if she wasn't ever going to answer it. The voice mail came on, encouraging him to leave a message. He wasn't sure if he ought to. If Helen were alive, she'd know whether or not leaving a message for one's jilted daughter, acknowledging the jilt, was appropriate.

But after careful consideration, he decided he didn't care if it was indecorous to leave a message about what he'd seen that morning in the paper, and when the tone sounded, he said, "Lou. It's Dad. Listen. I saw it. In the papers. About Barry."

Now what to add? "I never liked the guy anyway"? No. He had tried that with Nick, when he and Angie split up, and what had happened? They'd gotten right back together, and Nick, that idiot, had told Angie what his father had said, and Frank had gotten nothing but malevolent looks from this youngest son's girlfriend for the rest of the time they'd gone out, which had mercifully only been for a few more months. Still, it had been downright uncomfortable there, for a while.

So he couldn't tell the truth: that he had always hated Barry Kimmel, had thought him a panty-waist since the first day Lou had brought him home, that day the jerk had

stood out on his porch in his white chinos and pink—
pink!—Izod shirt and spoken to Helen in that fake
Kennedy way of his, until Frank had longed to wipe the
smirk off the kid's face. Frank knew smarm when he saw
it, and Barry Kimmel was the king of smarm.

He tried instead for a toned-down version of what he
longed to tell her, but couldn't: "What can I say, kiddo?
The guy doesn't deserve a girl like you. Am I right, or
what? I mean, any guy who would rather marry some air-
brushed floozy than my little girl. . . . So, look, don't
worry about it. You know what your mother would say, if
she were here. There're a lot of fish in the sea, and, uh,
your ship will come in one of these days, and, um, he was
never good enough for you, anyway."

Somehow that didn't sound quite right. Helen had said
something like it, however, the time Adam had split up
with his first significant other, so Frank just went with it.

"Yeah," he said. "That's it. Well, I hope you're doing
okay out there in La La Land. You know if you want to
come home, your room's always ready for you. I know the
guys'd all love to see you. And you don't have to worry
about getting the celebrity treatment around here. We
won't let you forget your roots, you know, Oscar or not.
Hey, speaking of that Oscar, you know what you ought to
do with it, don't you? I mean, to Barry. Well, I probably
shouldn't say—"

He broke off and ran a hand across his face. Helen, he
reflected, had always known what to say to Lou. It didn't
matter so much with the boys. You could say anything to
them—even Adam, the sensitive one—and they'd be all
right. Lou, though. She'd always been different. "My genius daughter," Helen had called her, and she hadn't been
far wrong. Lou had never been like the boys, and not just
because she was a girl, either. She just . . . well, she analyzed things too much. A good quality for a writer, he sup-

posed, but not so hot for a cop. Cops who analyzed stuff too much, rather than going by instinct . . . well, they usually ended up dead.

Fortunately Lou's instincts had always been pretty good, too. Well, except where her choice of boyfriends was concerned.

"So, uh, listen," Frank said, into the phone. "Call me when you get this message, huh? We're worried about you. We want to make sure you're, you know, okay. Don't go, you know, running off to join one of those goofy celebrity cults out there, or something, okay? Okay. Call me."

He hung up. Had that been too much? He looked down at the photo of Barry and that Woolston woman, the one from the *Hindenburg* movie, hanging onto one another and laughing over a wedding cake shaped— whimsically, he supposed Adam would say—like a blimp.

No, he thought. That hadn't been too much at all. If he knew Lou, she'd probably gone running off to the mountains somewhere to lick her wounds and recover in private.

He just hoped she'd taken her cell phone with her. Unlike the boys, Lou, well, she had never really been that great in a crisis.

5

ou couldn't believe it. Really, this could not be happening. As if the past twenty-four hours had not been awful enough, now she was trapped in a helicopter, five hundred feet in the air, with Jack Townsend and a lunatic bush pilot.

There was no justice. There was simply no justice in the world.

Well, she supposed she'd asked for it. The studio wouldn't have been half so eager to sign on for another *Copkiller* script if it hadn't been for the meteoric success of *Hindenburg*, proving once again that if she had just written a nice little romantic comedy, instead of a damned triumph of the human spirit, her life would have been a lot simpler.

"Whoa," Jack said, when those electric-blue eyes of his finally registered that there was a .38 pointed at his face. "Hey. Wait a minute."

"I'm really sorry, Mr. Townsend," Sam, the pilot, said, again, his deep voice sounding genuinely penitent in Lou's headset. "But I gotta do what they tell me."

"Are you kidding with this?" Jack, to his credit, did not sound panicked. He wasn't even scared, as far as Lou could tell. He was even remembering to speak into the microphone hanging off the side of his headset so that Sam could hear him. "Come on. You're going to shoot me? Inside your ride?"

Sam nodded, sadly. "And push you out," he said. "That's why we couldn't take the Cessna."

"But . . ." Lou didn't know if Jack was stalling for time, or if he really wanted to know. Whichever the reason, he asked, without the least bit of his usual sarcasm, only an air of bewilderment, "Why?"

Sam shrugged his heavy shoulders. "I already told you," he said. "I got orders. I don't do it, they don't pay me. And I really need the money, Mr. Townsend. I owe some people. Now, if you could just—"

Lou, her heart thumping, and her mouth dry as bone, nevertheless unfastened her seat belt so that she could lean forward. Trying to recall the numerous stories her father had told at the dinner table of dealing with difficult, weapon-wielding perps, she said, in what she hoped was a calm, soothing voice, "This is ridiculous, Sam. You can't shoot Jack Townsend. What's everybody going to say when we show up at the set without him?"

Sam looked back at her apologetically. "We ain't going to the set, miss. See, I'm supposed to dispose of Mr. Townsend, then fly to—well, you don't need to know. But they got my pay waiting for me there. I'm retiring after this, see?"

Lou swallowed. It felt as if there was sand in her mouth. *The Mummy Returns*, 2001. A lot of sand had flown around in that one. "What about me?" she rasped.

And even though she'd expected his next words, they still chilled her, far more than the frigid air the helicopter's heater couldn't quite dispel.

"You weren't supposed to be on this flight. There ain't supposed to be any witnesses."

No. Of course not. That's why Vicky had been called away at the last minute, wasn't it? But they'd evidently forgotten about Lou—whoever had arranged for Jack Townsend's murder, that is.

Well, and why not? She was, after all, only a screenwriter, and everyone knew how disposable screenwriters were. There wasn't a Starbucks employee in America who didn't have at least one screenplay hidden away in a drawer somewhere.

"Look," Jack said, and Lou recognized his friendly, reasonable tone as the same one he employed while doing hostage negotiation scenes as Detective Pete Logan. "Um, Sam, is it? Look, Sam, I'm sure whoever is paying you to kill me has offered you quite a lot for your services. But I'm a pretty well-off guy. How about I double your paycheck, and you let me live?"

Lou nearly sprang from her seat. It was a ploy straight out of *Copkiller II*, a ploy she herself had written. But Jack had the presence of mind to remember it, and put it to good use in a bad situation, something she never seemed able to do . . . apply her character's fictional experiences to her true-life ones, that is. Other people's characters, sure, but never her own.

The pilot shook his head until his jowly double chin swayed. "You must think I'm pretty stupid," he said, again not sounding in the least resentful. He just sounded . . . well, sad. "I know you're just gonna turn me in later," he went on. "There's only one way this can end. And I think you know what I mean."

Lou stared, transfixed with fear, at the heavyset man seated in front of her, pointing a gun so nonchalantly at Jack Townsend's heart. It wasn't until something compelled her to shift her gaze slightly to the right that she noticed that Jack was staring, too . . . only not at his would-be assassin. No, Jack was staring at *her*.

And for the first time in the six years that she'd known Jack Townsend, Lou really felt that that penetrating gaze of his was actually seeing her . . . seeing her as something other than the crazy screenwriter who wouldn't let him change her lines . . . *really* seeing her, and in some way she could not discern, urging her to. . . .

Well, to do something. Only what? What was *she* supposed to do? Get the guy in a headlock? Oh, yeah, that would work.

"Oh, God," Jack cried, breaking eye contact with her, and, to her very great alarm, suddenly rolling his head against the back of his seat. "Oh, God, I can't believe this is happening!"

Lou, startled, spent only a second or two wondering what he was doing. Jack could be a jerk, certainly, but he was no coward. He hadn't even been afraid to do that stunt she'd thought up for *Copkiller II*, the one with the eels and the cement mixer. . . .

Then, suddenly, she knew. She knew exactly what Jack was doing. Act two, scene five of *Copkiller III*. Was it possible that Sam had not seen the movie? If so, he was the only man in his demographic—between forty-five and sixty, resident of the northwestern quarter of the United States—to have missed it.

But apparently he had missed it, since, taken aback, Sam stammered, "Now, Mr. Townsend. Don't be like that—"

"For the love of God, man," Jack cried, and reached out to grasp the pilot by the shoulder. "Don't do it. Don't throw your life away, living as a wanted felon, always on the run."

"Hey, wait a minute," Sam sputtered. "Wait just a second. . . ."

Lou, meanwhile, had thrown herself onto the floor, just as Pete Logan's hapless partner, Dan Gardner, was always forced to do, when Logan got up to his theatrical antics. Lou had no idea what she hoped to find on the floor of the aircraft, but the R-44 was small, and storage space seemed to her to be at a minimum. If she were going to store something—something that might, in a pinch, serve as a weapon—it would be under the seats.

Underneath her seat, Lou saw a box marked "Emergency Use Only." Well, this was certainly an emergency, if she'd ever encountered one before. Scrambling to pull the box towards her, she prayed Jack would keep the man occupied while she dug through it.

"What kind of life is that?" Jack demanded. "Always looking over one shoulder, just one step ahead of the law—"

"The law can't get me in Mexico," Sam said. "And I don't reckon, once I'm on those pearly white beaches, I'm going to be doing much lookin' over my shoulder—"

"Think about it, Sam," Jack assured him. "Don't you think they'll extradite you, if they find you? I am an international celebrity. The entire world is going to mourn my demise, and cry out for justice."

Lou, on her hands and knees, looked up to roll her eyes at this. Could he *be* more of an actor?

"But they can't get me," Sam said, truculently, "once I'm safe in Mexico."

The lid pried from the top of the box, Lou uttered a prayer of private thanks. She had found exactly what she'd been looking for. After carefully loading and hefting it—it was surprisingly heavy—she pointed it at the back of Sam's head, and cried, "Freeze, dirtbag!" just as Rebecca had, in *Copkiller III*.

Only when Sam didn't freeze, and Lou continued to

hear in her headset, "I mean, look, I'm not proud of this, but a man's gotta do what a man's gotta do," did Lou realize she hadn't spoken into the mike.

"Sam," she said, this time speaking into the mike, and holding the mouth of the flare gun level with his temple. "Put the gun down. Now."

Jack, she noticed, had taken one look at her, and gone gray beneath his razor stubble. Well, what else had he expected her to do? It wasn't like she had much of a choice. It was the flare gun or nothing, thanks. She ignored him.

"Wh-what?" Sam looked confused. Clearly, he was not used to having flare guns waved in his face. "What are you doing?"

"I am going to put a flare through your skull," Lou informed him in a voice she imagined was quite steady—like Dirty Harry's in *The Enforcer*—"if you don't put the gun down."

Sam turned to look at her, an expression of indignation on his face. "You ain't going to shoot me," he said, as if this were something Lou ought to know perfectly well.

"Yes, I will," Lou assured him. "I most certainly will. You bet I will."

Oh, damn, Lou thought to herself, wincing. Three times. Three times she'd said it. People who stated something three times were invariably lying, her father had always told her. But maybe Sam, who was clearly on the opposite side of the law than Frank Calabrese had never heard this. . . .

Or maybe he had. He was still staring at her. His eyes, she could not help noticing, were blue, just like Jack Townsend's. But Sam's were a different sort of blue—a paler, inferior blue, without that dark rim separating the iris from the white part, that dark rim that had made so many fans of "*STAT*" sit up and take notice of the tall, brooding Dr. Rourke. . . .

"You ain't going to shoot me," Sam said, again, as reasonably as if he were speaking to a child. "You ain't going to shoot nobody. You ain't got it in you."

Lou blinked at him. He was right, of course. She wasn't going to shoot him . . . or anyone else, for that matter. Her father had been a New York City cop for forty years, and he had never once shot anyone. All four of her brothers were employed by various law enforcement agencies, and none of them had ever shot anyone, either. Oh, they'd drawn their weapons, plenty of times, but when it came to pulling the trigger, not one of them had ever been in a situation where deadly force had been necessary. . . .

Except for Nick, who'd once had to shoot a rottweiler that wouldn't let emergency rescue workers near her wounded owner. But he'd used a rubber bullet, and the dog had recovered nicely, though she had not much appreciated the many visits Nick had paid to her sickbed.

Lou's grip on the flare gun wavered a little. "All right," she said, her voice now sounding, to her own ears, less like Clint's and more, unfortunately, like Sally Field's. "All right, well, maybe I won't shoot you in the head, but I could certainly shoot you in the leg, and that's bound to hurt—"

Sam shook his head.

"Sweetheart," he said, "you shoot me, and this thing'll go down, understand? Like a stone."

Lou flinched. Oh, God, she hadn't thought of that. Her grip on the heavy metal gun wavered even more. . . .

"I don't think so," Jack Townsend said, in his deep, even voice. Lou wasn't the only one who glanced at him in astonishment. Sam was open-mouthed, too. They'd both seemed to have forgotten the existence of a third party in the cabin, so intense had been their own exchange.

"I've flown R-44s before, you see," Jack went on, conversationally.

Lou, in spite of herself, was surprised. "You have?"

"Sure," Jack said, with a shrug of those broad, heavy shoulders of his. "In Berger's *Spy Time*. You might remember it. Grossed sixty-five million domestic its first week out."

Lou nearly dropped the gun. Not only would Jeffrey Berger—who'd had the unmitigated gall to reject *Hindenburg* after Lou's agent had sent him a copy of the first draft—never allow one of his actors to do his own stunts, such as operate a heavy piece of machinery like an R-44, but *Spy Time* had grossed nowhere near that much total, let alone in its first week.

But the look Jack shot her reminded her to keep her mind on the task at hand, and accordingly, she pressed the flare gun more closely to the side of the pilot's head.

"Okay," she said. "See? We'll be just fine without you. So drop the gun."

Sam, who was evidently aware of neither Jeffrey Berger's conservative direction nor *Spy Time*'s dismal box office receipts, heaved a sigh and, to Lou's very great surprise, handed the .38 to Jack.

Apparently remembering everything he had learned on the sets of the *Copkiller* movies, Jack held the revolver in both hands, his index finger to one side of the trigger to keep from accidentally pulling it before he had to.

"All right," he said, in a much different tone of voice than the one in which he'd asked Sam, for the love of God, to think about what he was doing. Now he sounded calm. Deadly calm. Lou felt a chill, Jack Townsend sounded so calm.

Or maybe the chill was because they were still hurtling

through the arctic air at an enormous speed with the safety catches of a number of dangerous weapons released.

"Now," Jack went on, coolly. "Turn this bird around."

Lou was glad she wasn't looking down the barrel of that magnum. Or into Jack Townsend's blue eyes, which had grown, as they regarded the pilot, as cold as the floor upon which she knelt. If Jack Townsend had ever looked at Greta like that, Lou could totally understand the woman leaving him for Barry, whose meanest gaze wouldn't have frightened a kindergartner.

Sam apparently agreed with her, since he said, with a slight moan, "Oh my God. What have I done? What have I done?"

"Don't worry about it," Jack said. "Just fly the plane."

"They're going to kill me," Sam was intoning in a high-pitched whine. "I show up in Myra, they're going to kill me, don't you see?"

"Just fly the plane," Jack said, again.

That was when Lou, gazing through the wide windshield, saw something that caused her to cry out. Only because she was too shocked to remember to speak into her mike, no one heard her.

"Now you just keep flying," Jack was saying, in a soothing voice, "nice and easy, and I'll put in a good word for you—"

"Geese!" Lou cried, this time into the mike, and pointing straight ahead.

But it was too late. They'd been flying so low, thanks to Sam's cockpit nervous breakdown, that they were in the thick of the flock before anyone could do anything.

And when one of the birds slammed into the windshield in an explosion of blood and feathers, the force of the impact was enough to throw Lou, still kneeling on the floor, forward, until her forehead connected solidly with the metal frame on the back of the pilot's seat. The blow, which made her see stars, also caused her to lose her hold on the flare gun.

Which fell with a clatter to the floor of the aircraft, and promptly went off, causing her to see a completely different set of stars.

In the shower of sparks and smoke that followed, Lou had time to think, *gaggle*. Not flock. A *gaggle* of geese was what they'd run into. Gaggle of geese. Flock of . . .

Seagulls.

"Look out!" she heard Jack Townsend yell. He didn't need to speak into the mike. He'd yelled with enough volume to be heard above the heavy whomp-whomp-whomp of the propeller blades overhead, and the sizzle of the flare as it bounced from wall to wall until settling, with a terrific burst of flames, into the control panel in front of them.

"Oh, Jesus," Sam, the pilot, shrieked, as he threw up his arms to protect his face from the cascade of sparks. "Oh, Jesus!"

Flock of seagulls, Lou, who was thrown back into her seat, had time to think. Barry had always loved them, had all their CDs. That's what that box had been full of, the one he'd been holding that day he'd accused her of having grown so cynical. Flock of Seagulls CDs. And pan-flute music. Barry had always had a thing for pan-flute music.

Jack Townsend's face loomed in front of her, silhouetted by the smoke and flames behind him. "Put your seat belt on," he yelled. Lou, staring at him, did as he asked, but she couldn't help thinking that really, Jack Townsend thought mighty highly of himself. Who did he think he was, anyway? Some kind of movie star?

This thought caused her no end of amusement. At least until, through the smoke that was rapidly filling the small cabin, she saw something hurtling towards the windshield that caused her throat to close up.

And that something was the ground.

6

And then she was surrounded by seagulls. White, fluffy seagulls, their feathers pressing all around her, like angels' wings.

Only not exactly like angels' wings. Because angels were supposed to be kind, heavenly creatures.

These angels, on the other hand, were sitting on her. They were suffocating her. Hurting her. *Burning* her.

Lou opened her eyes.

She was lying in the snow. Snow, not feathers, was what was burning her. Not burning her, really, but it did not feel very comfortable, lying in the snow. Her head hurt. Really hurt, in a way it hadn't hurt since the morning after Barry had left with all his CDs, and she, never a very practiced drinker, had consumed the whole of a bottle of Bailey's Irish Cream, along with a box of peanut brittle a neighbor kid, raising money for his school band, had sold her.

Wincing painfully against the harsh white glare of the snow and, above it, the vast expanse of equally white Alaskan sky, she rose to her elbows. . . .

And instantly wished she had not. Not because of the

pain that shot through her skull—although that was excruciating—but because a few dozen yards away, its nose embedded deeply into the snow, and its rotor blades askew, lay the smoking wreckage of the helicopter.

Gasping, she started to climb to her feet. What she'd intended to do, she was never afterwards certain. What little she knew of first aid she had garnered entirely from her many seasons of faithful "*STAT*" viewing. She had never even been a Girl Scout, much less a lifeguard. Still, she had seen Dr. Paul Rourke perform CPR on dozens of unconscious crash victims—most memorably the fifth-season premiere which had featured the overturned high school fan bus—and she was confident she could do as good a job, if not better.

Her rush to aid her fellow crash victims was halted, however, and not just by the sudden increase of pain in her skull, or the fact that her vision, from her sudden burst of activity, began to swim. No, the hand that clamped down over her wrist, with a grip like iron, also had something to do with it.

Dragging her gaze from the crumpled wreckage of the helicopter, Lou found herself looking into the eyes of the owner of that hand. Jack Townsend's coolly uncompromising, ice-chip blue eyes. The eyes for which directors all over Hollywood were willing to shell out fifteen million dollars a film.

So he was not lying amidst all that charred and smoking metal after all. It looked as if she was not going to have to pull him, unconscious, from the crash site. In fact, it was beginning to look a little as if the opposite had happened: that he, in fact, had saved her.

A part of her, it had to be admitted, felt faintly dismayed by this. Was it really true? Did she really have to owe her life now to the man who had not only cruelly rejected one of her best friends, but had made the asinine phrase "I need a bigger gun" into household words?

"Where do you think you're going?" he wanted to know. His voice—that deep, even voice, nearly always tinged with sarcasm and which was also part of that fifteen-million-dollar package—sounded oddly muffled to Lou. That was when she realized it was snowing. Lightly, but steadily. Flakes were settling into Jack Townsend's hair, already flecked with white, to the dismay of colorists throughout LA. Things always sounded muffled, Lou had noticed, when it was snowing. Even the voices of professional actors who'd trained at the Yale School of Drama.

Lou gestured lamely at the smoldering heap that had once been a helicopter. "Is he . . . is he . . . ?"

"Not yet," Jack said. "He's over there." He pointed at a heap of plaid lying a few feet away, beneath a tall, snow-covered pine tree. "Alive. Unfortunately." And then he let go of her wrist.

Released from his supportive grip, Lou sank like a stone back down into the snow. Whoa. She probably should not have gotten up so fast. She'd crumpled like Pinocchio without his strings, before he became a real boy. And probably, she thought to herself, about as gracefully, too.

Jack looked down at her. "Hey," he said, the usual irony in his tone replaced with something that Lou, in her dazed state, almost mistook for concern. "Are you all right?"

"Oh," Lou said, reaching up to brush away the tears that had suddenly appeared, from out of nowhere, in her eyes. "Sure. Sure. I'm just fine." She was not sure which dismayed her more, the fact that she was stranded in the wilderness with Jack Townsend, or the fact that she was crying in front of him. "I'm just peachy. I'm totally used to having guns pointed at me by hired hit men, and then crash-landing in the woods in the middle of the frozen tundra. Happens to me all the time."

Jack's tone went from concerned back to coolly ironic in a second. "This isn't tundra," he informed her. "We're in the mountains. Tundra is flat."

"Whatever," Lou said. She couldn't believe this was happening. She really couldn't. "It's just . . ." Her gaze slid over to the unconscious Sam. "Is he hurt badly?"

Jack shrugged his broad shoulders. "Bump on the head, is all I can see. Not as big as yours, but still pretty impressive looking."

Lou reached up and felt, defensively, along her forehead. Oh, yes. There it was. An egg-shaped swelling just beneath her hairline. How attractive. Not, of course, that she cared how she looked in front of Jack Townsend.

"So that's it?" she asked, tracing the outline of the bump, but studying the pilot, where he lay a few yards away. "You're not going to try to . . . I don't know. Resuscitate him?"

"Hey," Jack said, spreading his hands wide. She noticed he'd slipped on a pair of leather gloves. "I'm not a real doctor. I just played one on TV."

She grimaced at him. "You know what I mean. Shouldn't we . . . I don't know. Do something for him?"

"Why?" Jack asked, that fifteen-million-dollar voice suddenly hard. "He was going to kill us, remember?"

"Obviously you care," she said, with some asperity, "or you wouldn't have dragged him to safety, now, would you?"

"Well," Jack said, giving another shrug, this one uncomfortable. "Couldn't very well leave him to die, now, could I? I mean, he's got kids."

"Kids?" Lou was having a hard time believing any of this. Was she really sitting in the snow, having this conversation with Jack Townsend? Had the two of them really survived a helicopter crash in the Alaskan outback? Or was this Bizarro World, an alternate reality, like in *Super-*

man? It certainly *felt* like Bizarro World. "What kids? How do you know he had kids?"

Oh, yes, definitely Bizarro World. In the real world, Jack Townsend would not sit down in the snow beside her and dig, as he was doing now, a cheap black leather wallet from his coat pocket, then flip it open. A half-dozen school portraits, in a long plastic holder, tumbled out.

"Four of 'em," he informed her. "I know, I was as surprised as you are. Sam didn't strike me as the fatherly type either."

The children were all, Lou couldn't help noticing, in need of a good deal of orthodontia. No wonder the guy needed money. . . .

Then she tore her gaze from the wallet, and swung it accusingly towards Jack Townsend's face.

"You picked an unconscious man's pocket?" she asked.

Jack shrugged for a third time and began to fold the photos back into the wallet. "Hey," he said. "Somebody paid him to kill me. I thought there might be something in here that would tell me who that person was."

Lou's gaze wavered uncertainly from his face to the wallet and back again. "Was there?" she couldn't help asking, finally, when he did not elaborate.

"Nope." Jack dropped the wallet back into his pocket.

Lou studied his profile for a moment. "You didn't know he had kids," she couldn't help pointing out, drily, "until after you pulled him out."

"Well," Jack admitted, with obvious reluctance. "That's true, I guess."

Amazing. The guy had a heart after all. If she lived through this, she was going to have to apologize to Vicky for having doubted her on that score.

If she lived through this. The more Lou became aware of her surroundings, the more she began to doubt the likelihood of her lasting the afternoon. Everywhere she looked, she saw only smoke, and snow, and trees, and the rising slope of the mountain they'd crashed into.

My God, she thought. It's *And I Alone Survived*, that 1978 film about the woman whose plane crashed somewhere ... the Sierra Madres, maybe? And she had to climb down the mountain and wandered for days, looking for a telephone so she could call her loved ones and let them know she was all right. ...

Startled, Lou reached into the pocket of her parka, and drew out her cell phone.

"Don't bother," came Jack Townsend's wry voice. "I already tried. There aren't any relay towers out here."

Lou shook her head, staring angrily down at the tiny screen. "I pay seventy bucks a month for this piece of junk," she said. "Seventy bucks. And does it ever work? God, no. Drive through the canyon ... nothing. Crashland in Alaska. Nothing. I can't even access my messages," she added, after pushing send several times, and holding the phone to her slowly freezing ear.

"What do you want to bet," Jack said in that same dry tone, "one of those messages is from someone who tried to reach you before we left, with some urgent reason why you weren't supposed to fly out to Myra?"

She glanced at him. Snow was settling, in a gentle dusting, across his broad, leather-jacketed shoulders. She wondered if he was cold. She was cold, and she was in a down-filled ski parka. All he had on was a beaten brown leather jacket. Unlined, from what she could see.

Well, what had he needed a warm coat for? He just strolled from the plane to the limo to his heated trailer to the set. *She* was the one who'd been planning on standing around, freezing her toes off, trying to talk Tim Lord out of creating a real-life environmental disaster in order to realistically film the one she'd invented for the film.

Then the meaning of his words sunk in.

"You mean like Vicky," she said, "with Elijah getting sick?"

"Exactly." He regarded her steadily, still wearing that faint look of amusement on his achingly handsome face.

"So if I had just checked my messages before getting on that stupid helicopter. . . ." Her voice trailed off.

"Then you'd be safely back in Anchorage," Jack finished for her.

Lou looked at the smoking helicopter, at the scar it had made in the earth. She looked at Sam, the pilot, stretched out in the snow with a slightly bemused expression on his face, his mouth sagging open as he breathed, none too quietly. Not snoring, exactly, but not breathing easy, that was for sure. Then she looked at Jack Townsend, looking so cool and self-assured in his jeans and leather jacket. *He* didn't look as if his butt, like Lou's, was slowly freezing. *He* didn't look as if his head, like Lou's, was pounding. *He* didn't look as if the thought of being trapped in the Alaskan woods without a working cell phone, food, or even a dry place to sit, was the slightest bit disconcerting.

If she had just checked her messages, right now she could be back at the hotel with Vicky, reading magazines, ordering hamburgers and hot fudge sundaes from room service, and watching the Lifetime movie channel. Maybe even watching *And I Alone Survived* and joking about it.

"Damn," Lou burst out, angrily, her eyes stinging—maybe from the cold, but more likely from the injustice of it all.

"Of course," Jack said, without even a hint of his usual dry, ironic tone, "if you had, I'd be dead."

She blinked at him. "What?"

"I'd be dead," Jack said, again, as simply as if he were telling his PA what he wanted for lunch. "You saved my life."

Lou was so startled to hear this that she did the very

first thing that came to mind. And that was to deny it. "I did not."

"Sorry to have to be the one to break it to you," Jack said, "but yeah, you did."

She narrowed her eyes at him. She couldn't tell whether he was joking or serious. That was, of course, the problem with Jack Townsend. Well, one of the many. His sense of humor was so dry that most people couldn't tell he was joking at all.

Like now, for instance. Was he serious? Did he honestly think she'd saved his life? *Had* she saved his life? No. No, not hardly. Saved her own life, maybe. Sure. That's what she'd been doing. Because why would she bother to save the life of a commitment-phobic egoist like Jack Townsend?

"What made you think of it, anyway?" Jack asked suddenly. Well, suddenly to Lou, anyway.

"Think of what?" she asked.

"The thing," Jack explained patiently, as if to a mental patient, "with the flare gun."

"Oh." The flare gun. Of course. "*Breakfast Club*," she said.

He looked startled. "I beg your pardon?"

"*The Breakfast Club*," she said again, enunciating more carefully this time. "John Hughes, 1985. Anthony Michael Hall's character gets detention for bringing a flare gun to school. He meant to kill himself with it, but it accidentally went off in his locker. Remember?" She studied his face for signs of recognition. "By the director of *Sixteen Candles*?"

"Sorry," he said, as politely as if declining seconds at a dinner party. "I don't really watch movies all that much."

For a moment, Lou forgot she was the victim of an attempted murder and a helicopter crash, and gaped at him as if he had just done something completely out of keeping with his manly image, such as order a champagne cocktail or burst into a falsetto rendition of "I Feel Pretty."

"You're an *actor*," she cried, "and you're telling me you don't really watch movies all that much?"

"Hazard of the trade," Jack said with a shrug. "The magic of Hollywood doesn't hold much allure when you know all the secrets behind the tricks."

Lou shook her head. Oh, yes. They were definitely in Bizarro World now. No doubt about it.

"But *The Breakfast Club*," she said. "I mean, come on. That movie's an American teen classic. It defined a generation." What did he do on Sunday afternoons, if not lay around and watch movies on TV, the way Lou did?

"Maybe," Jack ventured, as if he hoped to change the subject, "we should build a fire."

"A fire?" She gaped at him. Maybe he had gotten a conk on the noggin, just like her and Sam, and was hallucinating, or something. The girl in *And I Alone Survived* had hallucinated quite a bit, from thirst and hunger, but all she had ever seen were trailer parks and the occasional Native American spirit guide. How much better the film would have been if she'd hallucinated about something entertaining, or at least lascivious, such as . . . well, Jack Townsend with his clothes off. Lou sincerely hoped that if worse came to worst and she started hallucinating, it was of something along those lines . . . but only if she could be assured Jack would never find out.

"What do you think *that* is?" Lou pointed at the burning hulk of metal a dozen yards away. "What, you're worried when they start looking for us, they won't be able to spot us? Townsend, I don't think they're going to have any problem."

"Actually," he said, in the same polite tone he'd used before, "I was thinking a fire we might actually be able to get close to, for warmth. You're shivering, you know."

She was, of course. Shivering. But she'd hoped he

wouldn't notice. It was bad enough she'd been *uncon-scious* in front of him. The last thing she wanted was to show weakness in front of Jack Townsend.

So he wasn't hallucinating after all. She heaved a sigh. No, that would have been too much to hope. That Jack Townsend might have suffered a concussion and would hopefully remember none of this, most specifically the part where he had saved her life by pulling her uncon-scious body from the burning wreckage of the helicopter.

Because now, of course, she owed him one. And how was she supposed to maintain a healthy and ongoing con-tempt for him—which she had to, out of loyalty to Vicky—if she owed him one?

On the other hand, if he really did believe this thing about her saving his life, maybe they were even. If so, and they lived through this, she could still hate him without impunity. . . .

It was as she was thinking this that Jack, who'd climbed to his feet and begun picking up branches that the heli-copter had knocked to the ground, leaned down and heft a particularly large stick. The back of his leather jacket hiked up as he bent over, and she was awarded a denim-clad view of the famous Jack Townsend ass, the one women all over America gladly shelled out ten bucks a pop to see on the big screen.

And here she was, in the middle of Alaska, with that butt all to herself.

Not that she wanted it. No, thank you. She was cer-tainly not going to make *that* mistake again. No more ac-tors for her. So what if this one seemed to be concerned about her physical comfort, and had saved her life, and oh, yes, looked better in a pair of jeans than any man Lou had ever seen in her life? *I need a bigger gun.* Right there was reason enough not to give him the time of day, let alone her sorely abused heart.

Besides, hadn't he had the very bad taste to dump her best friend and take up with Greta Woolston instead?

Jack turned around and approached the place where she sat, dropping the pieces of wood he'd collected into a pile at her feet. If he noticed that her cheeks, which had gone up in flames the minute he'd turned around, were burning, he didn't say anything about it. Maybe he thought it was due to the wind, and not the fact that she had, just seconds before, been ogling his hindquarters.

"A lot of it's wet," he said.

Hardly noticing the cold now, she was blushing so hard, Lou said, "Wet? What's wet?"

He looked down at her curiously. "The wood," he said. "Are you sure you're all right?"

"Fine," Lou said quickly. Too quickly. "Why?"

"Because you look. . . ." He paused, as if searching for the right word. "Funny."

Funny. Great. Because her face was as red as a strawberry, maybe? Yeah, real funny.

Then, to her relief, he looked away.

"We might as well give it a try," he said, glancing at the burning heap of metal before them. "I'd rather not get too close to that if I don't have to. Who knows if it's still gonna blow. You got any matches?"

She assumed a look of complete disdain, hoping he would not guess that she'd been admiring his butt.

"No, I don't have any matches," she said, huffily. "I live in LA, where smoking is outlawed. Why would I have matches?"

He seemed very surprised to hear this.

"I thought all screenwriters smoked," he said.

"I thought all actors smoked," she countered.

They fell silent. All Lou could hear was the hiss of the snow as it fell on the burning helicopter. Not even a bird. And definitely not any search planes, out looking for them yet. Lou didn't say anything, because she didn't want to alarm her fellow crash survivor. But the snow suddenly seemed to be falling a lot more thickly. And quite a bit faster.

"I'll bet our friend Sam's a smoker," Jack said suddenly, starting to his feet. "I'll go check."

This time it was she who stopped him by grabbing onto the back of his coat—being careful not to look at what lay beneath it, however.

"Aw, come on," she said. "Leave the guy alone."

Jack looked impatient. "Lou," he said. "He's not going to mind my rifling through his pockets. He's out cold."

"Still," Lou said. "It's not right. It's . . . it's creepy." She couldn't explain her repugnance over the idea of Jack touching Sam. She tried to change the subject, to distract him. Such tactics had usually worked with Barry, whose attention span had been extremely limited. "And besides, isn't there some beacon or something that goes off whenever a plane crashes that alerts everyone back in the tower that it's down? I mean, someone knows we're out here, right? Someone will be here any minute to rescue us. Any minute now. And even if there isn't a black box or whatever, they're bound to notice over in Myra if we don't show up, right? I mean, Tim's probably on the phone with the Mounties or whoever right now."

"Sure," Jack Townsend said. Was it her imagination, or did it sound as if he was just trying to appease her? "Sure he is."

"Right," she said, with false cheer. "They'll be here any minute. So have a seat."

Jack gently peeled her fingers from his coat. "I will," he said. "But first, I'm going to get some matches, and then I'm going to build a fire to keep us warm."

Dismayed that she hadn't, in fact, managed to get him

to forget about searching Sam for matches, she cried, "But—"

"Look, I'm not suggesting we eat him," Jack said before adding darkly, "yet. I'm just saying, I am not going to freeze to death if I can help it. It's called survival, honey. You better get used to it."

She narrowed her eyes after him as he strode through the swirling snow. *It's called survival, honey. You better get used to it.*

Not a bad line, really. She kind of liked it. She had to hand it to Jack. He was a fair wordsmith, for an actor. Maybe she could use that line sometime. Not in this film. It was too late. But maybe in her novel. Yes, her novel, the one that was going to catapult her out of the film business forever, and maybe land her on a nice farm somewhere far, far away from the Santa Monica Freeway. . . .

Suddenly, she sprang to her feet, then staggered as her head swam from the sudden movement.

"My laptop!" she cried. "Oh, my God! Where's my laptop?"

Jack glanced up at her from where he was bent over the pilot, going through his pockets once more.

"It's all right," he said, seeming puzzled by her outburst. Well, and why shouldn't he be? Clearly, he thought her a headcase. He couldn't understand, he didn't know what it was like. "It's right over there."

She looked in the direction he pointed to now. Her laptop, in its computer case, sat a few feet away, unscathed except for the snow that had already begun to carpet it.

She pounced upon it, cradling it to her chest as her heart began to slow its frantic pace, and her head stopped spinning.

She was being ridiculous, she knew. It was only a computer, after all. But it had that chapter on it. The first thing she'd been able to write since that rat fink Barry had left, taking with him, she'd been sure for a while, not only her heart but her creativity, as well.

But no. No, he hadn't gotten it all. That chapter was proof. And the proof was safe. Because, she thought with a sickening feeling, Jack Townsend had saved it. Saved her first chapter, and her, too.

She glanced over at him. It appeared his search for matches was not going well. He looked annoyed, and slightly disgusted, as he picked through Sam's pockets.

Good God. The reality of her situation was finally starting to sink in. This wasn't Bizarro World. This was the *real* world. And she was stranded. Stranded in a clearing amidst a thick cluster of pine trees, on a sloping hillside. In Alaska. In the middle of nowhere. Next to the smoking heap that had once been a helicopter.

And it was snowing. And it was cold. And her head hurt.

And over there was Jack Townsend, the last man in the world—with the possible exception of Barry Kimmel—that she'd ever want to be stranded with in the Alaskan wilderness. Or anywhere, for that matter. And someone wanted him dead—wanted it enough not to mind if a few other people, namely Lou Calabrese, went right along with him.

Great. Just great. Just what, precisely, had she ever done to deserve *this*?

7

"I don't *care* about your piddling problems, Marvin," Beverly Tennant snarled into the phone. "Do you hear me? Let me repeat it, in case you didn't understand. *I . . . don't . . . care.*"

The door to Beverly's office, which someone had been tapping on for some time throughout Beverly's conversation, opened a tentative few inches, and Chloe peered in, looking pale and a little sick to her stomach.

"No, Marvin," Beverly said, waving for Chloe to come all the way in. "No. How many different ways do I have to say it? *Nyet. Nein.* Not gonna happen."

Chloe, standing in front of her employer's desk, twisted her fingers together nervously. Beverly held up one manicured index finger for the girl to wait.

"I said mauve, and I meant mauve, Marvin," Beverly said. "I did not mean purple, or lavender, or goddamn vermillion. I want mauve. And if you can't get me mauve, Marvin, then as far as I am concerned, this relationship is through."

Placing her hand over the mouthpiece of the receiver,

Beverly explained to her assistant, "Marvin, my contractor. I think he might actually be brain dead. I'm not sure how he manages to walk around and form sentences and all of that. It is probably one of those medical miracles they're always talking about on the channel nine news. But clearly, the man is operating under brain stem guidance only."

"Ms. Tennant," Chloe said. The girl looked as if she might, at any moment, lose her lunch, which Beverly happened to know had been takeout kung pao chicken. "That was Tim Lord on the phone just now. I tried to break in and get you for him, but—"

"I know, sweetie," Beverly said. "I'm sorry I didn't pick up. But you don't know how hard it is for me to get this bastard on the line. Do you have any idea what kind of crap he's trying to pull now? I ordered these mauve tiles for the downstairs powder room, and you know what he delivered? He—" She broke off and, removing her hand, barked into the receiver, "Oh, you think so, do you? Well, we'll just see what my lawyer has to say about that. Oh, won't I? You just wait and see, buster—"

"Lou Calabrese," Chloe said, in a dazed voice.

Beverly raised a carefully plucked eyebrow at her assistant. "What did you say, sweetie? No, I did not mean you, Marvin. You think I would call you sweetie, you bum? I want my money back. If I can't have my mauve tiles, then I want my money back—"

"The helicopter went down," Chloe said through bloodless lips. "The helicopter carrying Lou and . . . and Jack Townsend went down."

Beverly froze with the telephone receiver glued to her ear. The voice of the far-off Marvin could be heard, offering up excuses for the missing tiles.

"They think it crashed," Chloe said. Her eyes were filled with tears. "Into McKinley Park. Only they don't know if there are any survivors, because there's a storm, and they can't send a plane out to look for . . . for . . ." The last two words were a painful whisper: "The wreckage."

Beverly dropped the phone. "Oh my God," she said. "Oh . . . my God."

Through the receiver, they could both hear Marvin, saying something about a shipload of mauve Italian tile being held up in customs. Neither of them moved to hang up the phone.

"Faster, Richards," Eleanor Townsend leaned forward to say.

"I am going as fast as the law allows, madam," the butler, who was now acting in his capacity as chauffeur, Mrs. Townsend's regular driver having the day off, replied.

"Bugger the law," Eleanor said. "Drive in the . . . the whatever it's called."

"The emergency vehicle lane, madam?"

"Yes, that."

"I think not, madam," Richards said. "You are not going to be able to help Master Jack from inside a jail cell. Or, God forbid, a hospital room."

"I cannot miss this flight, Richards," Eleanor, in the backseat with Alessandro and a small overnight bag on her lap, informed him. "It's the last direct flight of the day to Anchorage."

"We will not miss the flight, Mrs. Townsend," Richards said, in his calm voice. "I assure you, we will be there in plenty of time."

"Certainly we will," Eleanor said. "If you drive in the what's it called."

"The emergency vehicle lane. Perhaps if you were to call Mr. Lord back, he might have some good news—"

"Nice try, Richards," Eleanor said, turning up the collar of her fox fur coat. "But I have said all I have to say to Mr.

Lord. The next time he hears from me, it will be through my lawyers. Imagine, sending my son out in a helicopter, in inclement weather! You can be assured the studio won't soon hear the end of this outrage."

"I am certain Master Jack is all right," the butler said, as the Bentley inched forward another six inches, towards the rear bumper of the car in front of it. "He is, as you know, quite a resourceful young man."

"He ought to have listened to his father," Eleanor said, firmly. "If he had just become a lawyer, the way Gilbert wanted him to, instead of a film actor, of all things. . . ."

"Master Jack has done rather well for himself," the butler said. "And I quite enjoyed his last film. The independent, Shakespeare one."

"*Hamlet*," Eleanor said. "And it was lovely. But, really, Richards. I love my son—I do. But if he had to be an actor, why film? What is so wrong with the stage, I ask you? Stage actors are a good deal more respectable, I think. And they are never required to take helicopters."

"Nor," Richards pointed out, "are they generally required to disrobe quite as often as Master Jack has, in his more profitable films."

"Yes," Eleanor said. "You know, I don't believe I have a single friend left who has not witnessed my son in his altogether. It is quite embarrassing, Richards."

"Perhaps," Richards said, comfortingly, "when you see Master Jack, you can have a word with him about it."

"Surely," Eleanor went on, "it can't be necessary for him to disrobe in every film he's in. There must be some scripts that don't require nudity, don't you think? There was none in *Hamlet*."

"Yes," Richards said. "But that film only grossed about nine million, domestic, if you'll remember, madam."

Eleanor sighed, gazing sightlessly through the window as New York rain fell in a steady curtain against the car. "I just don't know. I suppose it's good that he's so successful. You know he ran off to California with only about twenty dollars in his pocket, after his father cut him off. Jack truly is a self-made man. Still, money isn't everything, is it? You cannot put a price on dignity. And Gilbert did leave him very well taken care of. I can't imagine he needs more than a hundred thousand a year to run that ranch of his." Eleanor's voice caught raggedly. "Oh, Richards. If something should have happened to him, whatever are we going to do with all those horses?"

"Shhh, madam," Richards said. And, lifting a tissue from the box on the empty passenger seat beside him, he passed it back to the rear of the car. "Chin up, Mrs. Townsend. I'm sure Master Jack is fine. Just fine."

It was right then that the sound of a police siren became audible. Eleanor looked up from the tissue and said, "Oh, Richards. Perhaps there's been an accident up ahead, and that's why the traffic is so bad."

"Indubitably, madam," the butler replied. "I do hope no one has been seriously injured."

But when the squad car streaked past, suddenly, with a great squealing of tires, Richards pulled the Bentley out into the emergency lane, following in the police car's wake.

Eleanor, thrown back rather roughly against the butter-colored leather seat, had to hold quite tightly to Alessandro to keep him from being similarly jostled.

"Richards!" she cried. "Whatever do you think you're doing?"

"Getting you to the airport," came the butler's calm reply, "in time for your flight, madam."

"Can't this thing go any faster?" Adam complained.

"Jesus," Nick said. "I'm already going ninety. What more do you want? It's a freaking Chevy."

"Hey." Luke, in the backseat, was craning his neck to see behind him. "We got some kind of a tail. A Bentley."

"Where?" Nick tried to look.

"For the love of God," Frank Calabrese cried, smacking his youngest son in the back of the head. "Keep your eyes on the road."

"Yeah," Dean said, from where he was wedged between his father and second eldest brother. "You want to get us killed, too?"

A silence fell over the inside of the squad car, broken only by the incessant whine of the siren.

"Oh, nice one, Dean," Adam said, from the front seat.

"You know what I mean," Dean said.

"Way to exercise some tact," Luke said.

"Look." Dean, who'd only made detective a few weeks before, tried to explain himself. "That's not what I meant, and you know it. I do *not* think she's dead. I'm just say-ing—"

"Your sister isn't dead," Frank Calabrese snapped. "Nick, I swear to God, if you don't put that pedal to the metal—"

"Geez, Dad," Adam said. "What have you been watch-ing lately? *Smokey and the Bandit*?"

"Could you," Luke asked, in annoyance, "possibly be more gay?"

"Could you," Adam wanted to know, "possibly be more hetero?"

"Could all of you," Nick said from between gritted teeth as he clutched the wheel of the squad car he'd taken off the island of Manhattan without exactly getting the proper clearance first, "possibly *shut up* and let me drive?"

Everyone tried to oblige him. For about sixty seconds.

"That Bentley's still behind us," Luke informed them all. "He's breathing your exhaust, little bro."

"What do you want me to do about it?" Nick snapped. "Pull over and write him a ticket?"

Adam glanced at his watch. "We still got time. I mean, long as Dad hasn't got any carry on. . . ."

"I am breaking," Nick said, tensely, "about nine hundred laws here, guys. Cut me a little slack, will you?"

"You're doing a fine job," Frank said. "A fine, fine job. The rest of you boys, leave your brother alone. Just because he's the only one of you still in uniform."

"Hey," Nick said. "I *like* being a cop."

"I liked being a cop," Dean said. "I just like having a life more."

Adam snickered. "Like narcotics detectives have lives."

"More'n homicide detectives do," Dean fired back.

"I just never looked good," Luke reflected, "in blue."

Nick, glancing into the rearview mirror, saw his father's expression, and said, "Dad. Come on. They're kidding."

"I don't," Frank Calabrese said, "see anything funny about any of this."

"Release of nervous tension, Dad," Adam said. "We all know Lou's fine."

"Yeah," Dean said. "You think a *plane crash* is gonna kill her? Not Lou."

"Not as many times as she's seen *Zero Hour*," Luke agreed. "My God, she probably could have flown that bird herself, she saw that movie so many times."

"It was a helicopter," Frank said, woodenly, "not a plane. A helicopter, they said."

The brothers exchanged glances.

"Well," Dean offered. "A helicopter is like a plane. I bet she could have, you know. Flown it even more easily." His voice trailed off.

"Look, Dad," Luke said. "She's fine, okay? I mean, she's a tough kid, way too tough to let a lousy helicopter crash kill her. Remember that time she got hit in the head with that softball?"

"Yeah," Adam said. "She still ran around the bases. Every last one of them."

"Even though she was playing outfield at the time," Dean added.

"It'd take a lot more than a downed chopper," Nick said as he took the turn off to the airport, his siren still blaring, "to kill Lou Calabrese."

"I hope to God," Frank muttered, "that you're right. Because truthfully, I don't think I could stand it if she left me to deal with you four clowns alone."

The door to the Lords' hotel suite opened, and Tim Lord, looking haggard and chilled to the bone, stepped inside.

"Oh, hi, honey," Vicky Lord said from her position on the couch, from which she had not moved all day, having an aversion to snow. "You're home early. How was your day?"

Tim stared at his wife in utter disbelief. He did not move to take off his parka or his hat. He just looked at her, stretched out on the white couch, in the rosy glow from the lamp at one end of the room, a pile of magazines stacked up on the floor in front of her, and the remains of midafternoon tea on the coffee table in front of her. On the suite's sound system, a tape of the ocean waves was playing. The sound of gulls crying was an odd contrast to the sight in the windows behind Vicky's couch, which was of an all-out blizzard.

"Haven't you heard?" Tim asked, numbly.

"Heard what?" Vicky turned a page of her magazine. She'd finished the *Vogue* hours ago, and was now on a copy of *Teen Beat*, left behind by her eldest stepdaughter. "About the storm? God, did I ever. They wouldn't shut up about it. I had to turn the TV off. It wasn't such a sacrifice, though. You should see what they've done to Todd's hair on 'General Hospital.' I mean, I am all for transplants, but come on, get a professional to insert them. The guy looks like he's got corn stalks growing out of his head."

Tim staggered forward a few feet, then sank into a nearby chair. "Where are the children?"

"Oh," Vicky said, reaching over and lifting up her teacup. "Lupe took 'em over to that video arcade across the street. Elijah's not sick, you know. I don't know what you were talking about with that message this morning. He's fit as a fiddle. He even bit Anastasia right on the—"

"Jack Townsend's dead," Tim said.

"—arm. I had to force them into separate corners, because they wouldn't stop—" She broke off suddenly and blinked her expertly lined eyes at him. "What . . . what did you say?"

"The helicopter went down," Tim said. He reached up, a dazed expression on his face, and pulled off the knit cap that had been covering his gray hair. "Somewhere along McKinley. They can't . . . because of the storm, they can't send out search planes. If he survived the crash—Jack, I mean—they don't expect he'll live through the night. The temperature's expected to drop to—"

Suddenly Vicky was up and off the couch, standing in her stockinged feet, both hands raised as if to ward something off. Her face had gone as white as the couch behind her.

"No," she said, backing away from him. "No."

Tim tiredly began pulling off his gloves. "Vick," he said. "I tried calling here all afternoon. You must have had your phone off, as usual. They're gone, Vick. Jack, and Lou Calabrese, too, apparently."

Vicky continued to back away from him until she banged into the glass dining table, with seating for twelve, a necessity for a man with as many children—and staff to care for them—as Tim Lord had.

"That's not true," Vicky said. Her makeup stood out starkly on her pale face. "Jack . . . Lou . . . I mean, I just saw them. At the airport. Just a few hours ago. And they were fine. I mean, they were fighting—you know how they hate each other—but they were fine."

Tim peeled off his coat. "Well," he said. "They're not fine anymore. Is there any whiskey, Vick? Because I could really use a whiskey."

"Jack Townsend." Vicky stood by the table, hugging herself. She was shaking. Even from where he sat, he could see that she was shaking. "Jack Townsend is *not* dead."

Tim would have gotten up and put his arms around her if he hadn't been so tired. As it was, he simply slumped back into his chair and said, "Yes, Vick. He is."

Vicky, after staring at him for ten seconds more, whirled around and ran to the master bedroom. The door slammed behind her. A minute later, Tim heard the sound of bathwater running. To hide, he knew, the sound of her sobs.

He sat where he was, watching the snow come down, hard and fast, against the windows.

"Damn," he said as he stared, like someone transfixed, at the flakes. "God damn."

8

Well, Jack thought. At least she wasn't crying.

That was one thing to be thankful for, anyway.

A lot of women, Jack knew, would have been. Crying. Clinging to him. Making a nuisance of themselves.

But she wasn't. She wasn't exactly falling over herself in an effort to thank him, either, he noticed, for dragging her out of that burning hunk of tin. But at least she wasn't crying. She was just sitting there, those darkly opaque eyes completely unreadable.

Well, except for the resentment. That he could make out, no problem.

It was pretty unfair, in his opinion, to resent someone who'd recently pulled you, unconscious, out of a charred helicopter, and remembered to save your laptop, too. But she resented him anyway.

He supposed he couldn't blame her. There was the whole *I need a bigger gun* thing. That had to hurt. And then the stuff with Vicky, which he had never even been able to explain satisfactorily to himself, let alone anyone else. And now all this, which was apparently his fault, as well. After all, it had been him, not her, Sam had been hired to kill.

And what about that, anyway? Just who in hell wanted him dead so much that they were willing to pay money to see it happen? He hadn't, so far as he knew, offended anybody lately. He hadn't even been in any bar fights. And he certainly hadn't slept with any married women. So what was up with that?

"Are you paying attention, Townsend?" Lou was asking imperiously. "I mean, if you're gonna do something, at least do it right."

He looked up from the hypnotically dancing flames in front of him.

"Oh, hey," he said, when his brain, which seemed to be growing sluggish with the cold, finally registered what he was seeing. "You got a fire started."

"It's called tinder," she explained, as if she were speaking to a four-year-old. "You don't just throw a whole bunch of sticks in a pile and light them, okay, Ranger Rick? You have to find tinder first, and light it, and then gently blow."

He liked the way her lips looked when she said the word *blow*.

"Didn't you ever see *Cast Away*?" she went on, tossing Sam's lighter back to Jack in disgust.

"Can't say that I did." How was it, he wondered, that he'd never before noticed how hot Lou Calabrese was? Oh, sure, he'd known she was attractive. She'd always looked good, you know, at the *Copkiller* premieres, and that night she'd won the Oscar for *Hindenburg*, and she'd been in that slinky black number Greta had snidely told everyone was an Armani knockoff.

But for some reason, out in the Alaskan wilderness, with a goose egg on her head and the wind making her color high, Lou Calabrese looked hotter than she had in a sleeveless evening gown. Maybe it was because, he realized, this was the first time he was seeing her without Barry Kimmel hanging all over her. That guy really annoyed him, and had done so long before he'd run off with Greta. Maybe it had been that bit part he'd done on "*STAT*," way back before either of them had gotten famous. Barry—or Bruno, as Jack supposed he was now calling himself—had kept coming around his dressing room, asking Jack if he'd known where was a good place to score some chicks. Chicks, for God's sake. Jack had done his best to blow the guy off.

And now it turns out he'd had this chick here waiting for him at home the whole time. Jack really did hate his profession sometimes. Oh, he loved to act. But he really despised his fellow actors.

"Just remember," Lou was saying. "In the future, *tinder*. That's what it's all about."

"Is there a movie," Jack wanted to know, "that you haven't seen?"

"No," came her reply, which was accompanied by a sweet smile that completely disarmed him for a moment, until other words came along with it. "Unlike some people," she said, "I wasn't born with a silver spoon in my mouth, so I had to entertain myself the way the common folk do."

"Gosh," Jack said. "Is that a jibe at my supposedly over-privileged upbringing?"

"There's nothing supposedly about it," she said. "You're a Townsend. I think we all know what that means." She glanced at the unconscious man beside whom she'd insisted upon building the fire. "Except possibly Sam here. I doubt he reads the society page all that much."

"Or maybe he does," Jack said thoughtfully. Lou's fire had begun to crackle merrily, but its battle against the wind and snow, which was growing ever thicker, looked as if it might be a losing one. "Maybe that's why . . . you know."

She raised her eyebrows.

"What, you think Paris Hilton is jealous?" she wanted to know. "You're stealing all her limelight, or something? So she hired Sam here to off the competition?"

"It's as good a theory as any, at this point," Jack said. "This might come as a shock to you, but there really aren't that many people out there who've expressed a desire to kill me."

"Really," Lou said, clearly unconvinced.

"I'm serious. There are very few people I don't get along with. I'm an immensely charming guy."

"Except to screenwriters," she pointed out.

"Except to *some* screenwriters."

"Hey," she said, brightening. "Maybe the Screenwriters' Guild got together, took up a collection, and paid Sam here to off actors like you who go around changing our lines. It'd be nice to think my dues were going towards a worthy cause."

He glared at her. "Look. *It's always funny until someone gets hurt* is not something I feel that my character—"

"*Your* character?" She hooted. "Excuse me. He's *my* character. I made him up. I think I would know what he would say and what he wouldn't say. And one thing he'd never say is *I need a bigger*—"

Jack held up a hand, but not for the reason she evidently thought, to shut her up. No, he held up a hand because . . .

"Do you hear something?" he asked.

She fell silent. It was growing darker and darker on the deep hillside. The sun, which had never really put in an appearance all day, seemed to be giving up. Still, there was enough light for him to see all the bright white flakes of snow in her thick red curls. The tip of her nose was bright pink, and there were matching splotches of pink on either cheek. Her lips, which had lost any trace of makeup long ago, were cherry red, and, he couldn't help noticing, enticingly moist.

Too bad what kept coming out between them wasn't half so appealing.

"That is so like you, Townsend," she complained. "Start an argument and then pretend like you heard something so the other person has to shut up and you automatically win—"

"Seriously," he said. "I thought I heard an engine."

Immediately, she looked up towards the sky.

"Well, it's about time," she said. "What were they waiting for, an engraved invitation?"

But as seconds passed, and the two of them strained their ears, it became apparent that whatever Jack had heard, it wasn't a plane.

"Are you sure R-44's even have a tracer beacon?" she asked, after a little while.

Still scanning the snowy sky, he shrugged. "How would I know?"

She gave a little hiccup of outrage. It was, he thought, kind of cute. Or would have been, if it hadn't been coming out of her.

"*You don't know?*" she practically screamed. "Didn't you say you flew your own R-44 in *Spy Time?*"

"That," Jack said, uncomfortably, "was a bit of an exaggeration."

"Oh, I'll say it was." She snorted. "As is the idea that *Spy Time* ever grossed sixty-five million domestic. Puh-lease."

"Maybe," Jack said, "I meant total."

"In Jeff Berger's dreams," she said. "He hasn't had a hit since *Baby Trouble*, and that was ten years ago."

If there was one thing Jack couldn't stand, it was exactly this. That was why he'd bought the ranch in Salinas.

Still within a commutable distance of LA—well, by jet—but far enough away that he almost never had to have conversations with people about points and gross net deficits (except, occasionally, with his agent) the ranch was more of a retreat than it was merely a home. The ranch, in a way, was how he stayed sane in a world of cocktail parties, four-hundred-dollar lunches, and "Entertainment Tonight."

Still, this, he thought, was better than the alternative. Which was Lou using her overactive writer's imagination to picture what was going to happen after the light faded completely and the wolves came out.

"Not too fond of Jeff, are you?" he said, because the wind was rising and her fire was going out and the man who'd tried to kill them lay half-dead in front of them and they were trapped together in the middle of nowhere for who knew how long, and he wanted to keep her mind off what he was thinking, which was that in the morning, their bodies were going to be found, frozen together like a couple of fruit pops.

"Why should I be fond of Jeff?" Lou wanted to know.

There was no reason, of course, for anyone to be fond of Jeff Berger. He was a fairly typical example of a Hollywood B movie director, without scruples or tact, whose taste in jokes ran towards the execrable. Jack had only taken the part in *Spy Time* to pay his rent, which, in the days after he'd run away from home, and before he'd joined the cast of *"STAT,"* had been a source of constant worry, since he could not—would not—ask his father, who disapproved of his only child's career choice, for a loan.

But there were better reasons to hate Jeff Berger than his raunchy taste in jokes. He had, for instance, a set of roving hands. He could not seem to direct a film without being slapped with a sexual harassment suit afterwards.

"He make a pass at you?" Jack asked, because he could

see her being Jeff's type, in that she was young and female. Oh, and attractive, of course.

"Duh," she said, scornfully. "But way worse, he rejected *Hindenburg*. I mean, I admit, he'd have been all wrong for it, but that he had the gall to reject it?" She shook her head. "He called it puerile. The man who directed *Frat Party USA* called *Hindenburg* puerile. And while I certainly don't consider *Hindenburg* a cinematic classic, it wasn't puerile."

They were not sitting closely enough together that their shoulders touched. If they had been, and she'd been crying—the way any other woman properly would have been, under the circumstances, instead of sitting there castigating him for never having seen *Cast Away* or *The Breakfast Club*—he would have put his arm around her, in the hopes of comforting her.

And, being that she was more than passably attractive—when she wasn't scowling—and that he was, well, who he was, chances were they might have found a more agreeable way to pass the hours before they were rescued than sitting there bickering like a couple of kids.

But she wasn't crying, and his arm wasn't around her. Still, though they weren't touching, he felt her tense beside him.

And then, a second later, she was on her feet and screaming like a banshee. A pretty banshee, but a banshee all the same.

"Over here," she was screaming, as she ran through the snow, waving her arms wildly. "We're over here!"

That was when he heard it. The same sound he'd heard before, only closer this time, and more distinguishable. An engine. Not a plane engine, or even a helicopter, but an engine of some kind, and heading towards them.

Then he saw it, a bright spot weaving through the trees towards them. A snowmobile.

They were rescued.

"Hey!" Jack sprang to his feet, spraying enough snow as he did so that Lou's pitiful little fire immediately went out. But that didn't matter, he told himself. Because they were rescued. At last, they were rescued, and soon he'd be back in his warm suite at the hotel. . . .

With Melanie yelling at him some more, and maybe even throwing things. And who knew? Perhaps this time she might set flame to more than just a love seat.

It didn't matter. Because if there was anything good that could come out of almost getting killed, it was that suddenly, one's priorities became very, very clear. And Jack's main priority, he realized, was to get rid of everything in his life that was remotely connected to Hollywood.

It was irksome that this, of course, was exactly what his father had warned him about, all those years ago—that Jack would eventually get tired of playing let's pretend all day, and end up wishing he had a "real" job. Jack had refused to listen at the time—had defied his father by dropping out of Yale and moving out to LA to prove him wrong—but now he was starting to wonder if his love for acting hadn't stemmed so much from true love for the craft as from a desire to escape the destiny his father had planned out for him—assistant VP, then VP, then president, and then eventually CEO of Townsend Securities. Sure, he'd been successful—meteorically successful—at his chosen profession.

But it wasn't a challenge anymore. As far as he was concerned, the studio could wave goodbye to Jack Townsend. Jack was chucking it all in. Enough was enough, already.

"Hey!" he called, running after Lou in the snow. Fortunately he had on his waterproof cowboy boots . . . not ideal for traversing wintry terrain, but hey, how was he supposed to have known he'd be slogging down a mountainside?

The snowmobiler, coming up the steep slope towards them, did not appear to be a state employee, if his bright yellow-and-red parka was any indication. Just some random Alaskan, out for a spin. Or maybe he'd seen the smoke from the smoldering helicopter and had driven up the mountain to check it out.

Whatever the case, he was fast approaching them. They were rescued. Soon Jack would be back at the hotel, where the first thing he'd do was check anonymously into a new room, as far away as possible from Melanie. The second thing he'd do was call the police. Because, after all, somebody had tried to kill him.

And then? Well, he wasn't sure. But he had a strange, nagging feeling that Lou Calabrese was going to be involved, somehow.

Which was ridiculous, because she really, really wasn't his type. For one thing, she, unlike almost every other woman he'd encountered since entering puberty, seemed completely immune to what he knew, without being conceited, were his exceptional good looks. Hey, a guy could not get voted one of *People* magazine's Fifty Most Beautiful People ten years in a row and not come away with the knowledge that women found him appealing.

All except Lou Calabrese, who apparently found him about as appealing as week-old string cheese.

And while he didn't think his work on *"STAT,"* or the dozen or so movies he had made, really qualified him as a swell person or anything, he was, not to put it too bluntly, one of the highest-paid actors in Hollywood. And there was a reason for that, and it didn't, as Lou Calabrese clearly thought, have anything to do with how he looked: he was simply a damned good actor.

But even though women all over America seemed to realize this, and hordes of them, like Marie back at the airport coffee shop, were prepared to swoon over his crumpled beverage containers, the fact that one seemed not in the least impressed by him—seemed, in fact, actively to dislike him—weighed more heavily on his mind than he knew it should. Especially considering the fact that he currently had way bigger problems, such as how he was going to finish this film with his co-star so assiduously hating his guts, and how he was going to get out of these woods before succumbing to hypothermia, and, oh, yeah, why someone was trying to kill him. All these things were much more important than the fact that Lou Calabrese didn't like him.

Although telling himself this didn't do the least bit of good. Nor did reminding himself that Lou Calabrese was a bit weird, with her obsession for movie lore and that stupid laptop, that even now was banging against her hip as she ran. Weird or not, she still had all that gorgeous red hair, and those dark eyes that were almost hypnotically beautiful—even when they were filled with derision for him. But derision was better than what he saw in the eyes of most of the people who looked at him, which was cartoon dollar signs . . .

But there really was no getting around the weird part. Especially when, as suddenly as she'd started to run, Lou jerked to a halt, freezing in her tracks like the jackrabbits back at his ranch when he happened to come across them.

Jack barreled into her, of course. She fell forward, into the snow, with an "Oof." He scrambled to help her back to her feet and took an undue amount of pleasure in the fact that her parka had hiked up above her hips, so that he had an unimpeded view of her backside. He was gratified to note that he'd been right about those wool pants: they hid an ass any body double back in LA would be glad to claim as her own.

"What's the matter?" Jack wanted to know, as Lou, trying to catch her breath, leaned forward, with her hands on her knees. "Why'd you stop?"

"Something. . . ." she panted, peering through the trees as the snowmobiler continued to speed towards them. "Not . . . right. . . ."

He looked. The snowmobiler *was* doing something strange as he came hurtling towards them . . . reaching behind his back, seeming to struggle with something fastened back there.

"It's just a walkie-talkie," Jack said, not breathing too easily himself. Even for a guy who'd been training for a couple of hours a day to stay in shape for his nude scenes, it was no joke, running at full tilt through two feet of snow, even downhill. "He's going to radio for—"

But when, a second later, an explosion ripped through the quiet woods—and it wasn't the helicopter blowing up, either—Jack realized that what the snowmobiler had been reaching for hadn't been a walkie-talkie at all. No, what it was, he saw, in growing horror, was a—

"*Run!*" Lou yelled, grabbing his arm.

He needed no further urging. Spinning around, he began careening down the mountainside, Lou slipping and sliding along beside him. Another explosion sounded, and this time, the branches on a nearby tree flew off, sending tiny shards of wood and snow raining down upon them.

They were being shot at. And from the looks of the damage to that tree, by a sawed-off shotgun.

"Here!" Suddenly, Lou was pulling him down behind something, another tree, only this one seemed to have fallen some time ago. It was covered with snow. Not, Jack thought, a very good place to hide. Couldn't a blast from a shotgun penetrate a hollow log like this one?

But hiding did not appear to be Lou's plan.

"Sam's gun," Lou yelled. There was no chance of their voices being overheard above the whine of the snowmobile . . . not to mention the crack of the shotgun. She gripped the collar of his jacket. "Do you still have it?"

Wordlessly, Jack drew out the revolver Sam had been waving in his face. He'd rescued it, and not the flare gun, from the burning helicopter, because he'd been certain they'd be found without the help of the flare gun, and Sam's revolver, he'd felt, was vital evidence in the attempt that had been made on his life. Jack didn't know all that much about guns. Except for the time he'd gone on a ride along with some LAPD beat cops, to get a feel for real-life police work for the first *Copkiller*, he had never even held a handgun loaded with anything but blanks.

But Lou apparently knew a thing or two about firearms, since a second later she'd stripped off her gloves and was clutching the revolver in both hands, resting the sides of her palms on top of the log, and lining up her target with only her left eye open. Her right was squeezed shut tight, not a particularly reassuring sight.

"A little closer," she said. He noticed, even more disconcertingly, that both her voice and her fingers were trembling uncontrollably. "A little closer. . . ."

Crack! The shotgun went off, showering them with pieces of the bark. Then, even as Jack was ducking, he heard the steady *pop . . . pop . . . pop* of Sam's revolver, a controlled staccato so close to his ears that when they stopped, he could hear nothing else at all.

But he could still see. And what he saw were a pair of long black blades, coming straight at them. He grabbed Lou by the hood of her parka and pulled her down, just as the snowmobile went sailing over them, its sleek underbelly bearing scuff marks, and the body of the driver slumped lifelessly over the controls, his features hidden behind snow goggles over a bright red face mask.

And then, a few seconds later, another explosion, this one much louder than any of the shotgun blasts. Jack instinctively flung himself across Lou, shielding her from the sudden rain of debris that fell, like tiny missiles, all around them. The pieces that landed on the ground were immediately extinguished, leaving hissing, smoking craters in the snow. Other pieces bounced harmlessly off Jack's leather coat.

It wasn't until the shower of flaming snowmobile parts was over that Jack dared raise his head. And when he did, the first thing he saw was Lou's face, pale but resolute, beneath him.

But if he'd expected any womanly display of emotion—tears, or even hysterics—he was destined to be disappointed once again. Because all she said, when she parted those deeply pink lips, was, "Jeez, you weigh a ton. Get offa me."

It was right about then that Jack decided he could sort of see why Bruno di Blase had left Lou for Greta. A guy like Bruno—or Barry, or whatever his name was—didn't have a chance in hell of ever impressing a girl like Lou. Greta, on the other hand, had been awed merely by Jack's ability to correctly read a map.

Slowly—though not really painfully, since except for some snow that had made its way down his charcoal black cashmere sweater, he appeared to have been unscathed by what had occurred—he peeled himself from her. The minute he did so, she rolled over, the gun still poised in both hands, and pointed it in the direction the explosion had come from.

"I think," Jack observed wryly, "you got him."

She had, too. Snowmobile and driver were both gone.

All that was left was a black gouge in the earth, right in front of the enormous pine tree the snowmobile had plowed into, full speed. Black, acrid smoke, like the kind pouring from the helicopter, floated up from a few of the larger chunks of charred rubble. Jack felt no desire to approach these chunks to investigate more fully just what, exactly, they might be.

Lou, on her knees in the snow, let Sam's gun drop to her lap, as if it had suddenly grown far too heavy for her to comfortably hold. But she didn't sit that way for long. That was because, off in the distance, they both heard a sound that had once been welcome, but which now had an ominous ring to it.

Snowmobiles.

More of them.

A *lot* more.

"Come on," Jack said, reaching down to take her arm. "Let's get out of here."

"Wait," she said, even as he was dragging her to her feet. "Wait a minute. You don't know who it is. Maybe this time it's the good guys."

"You want to stick around to find out?" he demanded.

With a little moan, she followed him as he began once more to streak down the mountainside. But not without a final word of complaint.

"Just who in hell," she grumbled, in a voice he was pretty sure she was trying to keep from shaking, "did you piss off so much, Townsend?"

He only wished he knew.

9

Seven thousand and twenty-six.

That's how many miles were on the speedometer of Lou's treadmill back in LA. Seven thousand and twenty-six miles she had alternately walked and run in the past six years, since moving to the West Coast with only a BA in creative writing and a newly completed script—the first *Copkiller*—to her name.

And Barry, of course. She'd had Barry, too.

Almost five hundred of those miles she'd put on her treadmill just in the months since she and Barry had split up. She had had a lot of nervous energy to get out, and what better way than to pound it off on her treadmill while watching "Judge Judy"?

But that was different. Running in her own home, on a treadmill, in her Nikes, was completely different than running through the woods in two-inch heels, through yard-deep snow and in freezing temperatures, with a laptop and purse strung over her shoulders. Her feet weren't the only things that felt as if they were going to burst. She was pretty sure her lungs were going to, too.

"Wait," she gasped, grabbing onto the closest pine tree for support, and clinging to it as she tried to catch her breath. "I . . . can't. I . . . can't . . . run . . . anymore."

Thankfully, Jack looked as winded as she was. And he, as she well knew, was in top condition. It was in his contract, of course, that he had to be. Detective Pete Logan was many things, but out of shape was not one of them.

"We . . . gotta . . . keep . . . going," he panted, leaning forward to rest his hands on his knees. "Come on, Lou. They're right behind us."

"*Were* right behind us," she corrected him. Now that her breathing was growing more even, she strained her ears, but could hear nothing save the sound of their breathing. "I think . . . I really think we might have lost them."

It would have been hard not to. With the sun all but gone from the sky, and the snow coming down more thickly than ever, it was difficult to see more than a few yards ahead of them as they'd run. Snow and trees. That was all Lou could see. Snow and trees.

And as they raced between those trees, Lou could not help thinking that they must have been as difficult to distinguish against the snow as the fallen logs and bracken they were forced to leap over in their mad dash for safety.

As if there were such a thing in this godforsaken place.

"Listen," Lou said, reaching out to lay a hand on Jack's shoulder. "Do you hear them?"

They were silent for a moment. There was no sound—no sound at all save the hiss of snow landing in their hair and on their shoulders. The snow and the wind, as it moved through the pines around them. It wasn't gale force yet, but it was a cold, strong wind. A wind that indicated, to Lou, at least, that things were going to get worse before they got better.

She could barely make out Jack's features. It wasn't yet

nightfall, but what little sun there had been was gone, leaving only a dank gray sky overhead, growing ever darker as the minutes passed. Still, she had seen his face often enough—in dailies, on the big screen, and on her own television set, back in his *"STAT"* days—to tell by his expression that he, too, was listening for the whine of a snowmobile engine.

"I don't hear anything," he said, finally.

"Me neither," Lou said. "Do you think we lost them?"

"Might have." He squinted at the snow that was rapidly filling the footprints they'd left behind . . . but not rapidly enough. "Trees are kind of thick here. Be hard for them to follow, except on foot. And that. Well, that wouldn't be difficult, given the tracks we've left."

Lou let go of both the tree and his shoulder, and started looking around for a low-lying branch.

"We can use it to wipe out our footprints," she explained to him. "Like in *A Simple Plan*."

"Oh, sure," he said. "So instead of following our tracks, they can follow the branch marks."

Lou felt something hot well up unpleasantly inside her. Much to her chagrin, it was tears, brought on by anger and fear.

"Look," she said to him in a loud whisper. "I could do without the sarcasm, okay? We wouldn't be here if it weren't for you, so just try not to be such a jerk about all of this, okay?"

"Jerk?" He straightened and eyed her. "What'd *I* do?"

"I don't know," she shot back, thankful that the cold wind provided her with plenty of excuse for why her eyes were watering. If he should happen to notice, that is. "But something to get someone mad enough to kill you. Not just kill you, Townsend, but hunt you down like a dog. Now find a branch. Preferably one with the needles still on it."

Jack, much to her relief, said nothing more and began to look around for the branch she'd requested. Lou was glad, since she could barely see, her eyes were so filled with tears. God, what had she ever done to deserve this? Stranded in the middle of nowhere with a prima donna movie star who'd apparently never seen a single survival movie in his life. She'd be lucky to get out of here with just a few toes and fingers lost to frostbite. The way things were beginning to look, they would not survive the night.

At least, not unless they built an igloo. In *Shoot to Kill*, Sydney Poitier and Tom Berenger survived a night in a blizzard by burrowing under the snow and huddling together for warmth. In the movie, it had been a comical scene. In reality, the thought of huddling under the snow with Jack Townsend even for a few minutes made Lou's skin feel strangely hot, despite the fact that she was convinced she was half frozen. There were millions of women in America to whom the thought of passing a night in an igloo with Jack Townsend might not seem like such a chore. Lou, however, was not one of them.

Dear God, she prayed. Let it not come to that.

And then, a second later, it appeared her prayer might have been answered.

"Hey," Jack said, from a dozen yards away, where he'd gone to look for branches. "C'mere. Look at this."

Lou, thinking at first that he'd spied more snowmobilers, nearly collapsed in the snow with an *I give up already*. But Jack wasn't looking in the direction from which the snowmobilers had come. Instead, he was squinting ahead of them, his eyes narrowed against the snow and wind.

"What?" Lou demanded, coming to his side and attempting to follow his gaze. But all she could see was trees. Trees, and snow, coming down harder than ever. "I don't see anything."

"There," he said, pointing straight ahead. "Do you see that?"

Lou shook her head. "All I see is snow."

"Not there," Jack Townsend said, and abruptly, he moved behind her, clapped two hands over her ears, and turned her head in the direction he'd been peering. "*There.*"

Until Jack put his hands on her ears, Lou had not realized how cold they were. Her ears, that is. They were numb with cold, since she had no hat, only her thick red hair to protect them. Jack's warmth seemed to sear her through the leather of his gloves. She could feel a similar warmth emanating from him all down her back, though only his hands were touching her. Suddenly, the idea of staying the night with him in a hole dug into the snow didn't seem all that unappealing. Not if it meant she could have more of that warmth, all to herself.

Good God! What was she thinking? This was Jack Townsend. *Jack Townsend*, movie star, heir to Townsend Securities, *actor*. Actor, Lou. *Actor*. Which meant vain, incapable of loyalty, and as Vicky could attest only too well, terminally commitment-shy.

The alarm bells clanging full pitch, Lou ignored the welcome warmth flowing from those hands, and looked in the direction Jack was pointing her face.

And then she saw it. A rectangular shape, silhouetted black against the gray sky, stuck out against the treetops. She couldn't tell what it was. Not a house, surely, because it was in the air, not on the ground. But it was rectangular. There was no doubt about that. And rectangular meant man-made.

"What is it?" Lou asked, all thoughts of snuggling under the snow with Jack Townsend mercifully wiped from her mind. "What could it be?"

"I don't know," Jack said. "I thought I was hallucinating, but if you see it, too. . . ." Abruptly, he dropped his hands from her head and wrapped those warm, strong fingers around one of her arms. "Let's go find out."

Lou noticed the hand on her arm. How could she not? Much as she might have disliked him, she could not deny that Jack Townsend had a magnetic quality that made it difficult for people to drag their gaze from him when he was on screen, and even harder for anyone—well, all right, Lou—to shrug off any hand he might happen to lay upon her.

But this time she happened to be grateful for the hand. Because in his eagerness to investigate the mysterious rectangle in the sky, he was propelling her through the snow. And it was a lot easier, she discovered, to slog along in her heels, with that laptop weighing her down, when someone was pushing her. Towrope, she thought. That's what they needed. A towrope . . .

And then they were standing at the base of the rectangular thing, craning their neck and blinking against the thickly falling snow to get a better look at it.

"It's a ranger station," Jack said finally.

It was, too. Built on long wooden supports, the dark green shack hovered like a child's tree house above them, with only a rickety-looking wooden ladder leading up to the trapdoor in its floor. It looked gloomy and uninhabitable, as if it hadn't been used in years.

It also looked like a perfect place for spiders and other creepy crawly things to hang out.

"Come on," Jack said, releasing her arm and starting to climb.

"I'm not going in there," Lou declared.

"Fine." Jack didn't even glance down at her. He'd reached the trapdoor, and was pushing on it. "Stay down there and freeze. Personally, I'm getting in out of this wind."

And then the trapdoor swung open with a groan from its rusty hinges and Jack pulled himself inside. She had a glimpse of his long, denim-clad legs, then just his cowboy boots—cowboy boots! Perfect—and then he was gone.

Standing beneath the treehouse, the snow beginning to blow sideways into her eyes because of a sudden shift in the arctic wind, Lou waited for the structure to crumble to pieces beneath Jack's weight. She could hear the floorboards creaking as he walked across the small—surely only nine feet by nine feet—space.

But nothing collapsed. Nothing—Jack, for instance— came hurtling down to the ground.

Jack's face appeared in the opening for the trapdoor.

"Hey," he said, looking genuinely celebratory. "You're never going to believe this. There's a cot up here. And blankets. Come on. We can wait out the blizzard in here. You can bet that's what our friends on the snowmobiles are doing, too. We should be safe enough for a while."

Blizzard? Lou blinked. The wind whistled around her, slicing through the wool of her slacks. She was wearing hose beneath them, but they didn't help to keep out the bitter cold. Her eyes were watering. The snow fell in a steady white curtain around her.

Oh, yes. Blizzard seemed about right.

"Lou." Jack leaned through the trapdoor, peering down at her bewilderedly. "What is wrong with you? Didn't you hear me? We can sit out the storm in here. And all this snow will cover any tracks we made. With any luck, they'll think we froze to death behind some tree. Come on."

Getting dark out. Perfect. Night was falling. Well, not really. It was probably only late afternoon. But in Alaska, in winter, it was pretty much dark all the time, just like in the summer it was almost always light out.

And she was going to spend the night in a ranger's station with Jack Townsend. Jack Townsend, one of America's hottest Hollywood idols.

Great. Just great.

"Lou?" Jack was beginning to sound pissed off. "Are you all right?"

She took a deep, shuddery breath.

"Are there spiders?" she asked, her voice sounding thin even before it was snatched away and tossed around by the wind.

"Are there *what*?" Jack's face, which she could not see all that well through the snow and the quickly descending darkness, appeared to wear an expression of incredulity. "*Spiders?*"

Lou nodded, not trusting herself to speak again. She did not want him to hear the fear in her voice. Though which she feared more, the potential for spiders or spending the night in a small shack with Jack Townsend, she could not say.

"Lou," Jack said, in his usual ironic tone. "There are no spiders, okay? Spiders can't generally exist in sub-arctic temperatures."

Lou had known that, of course. She'd just wanted to be sure. She stepped forward and put her foot on the first rung of the ladder, then reached up and grasped the one above her head. She disliked spiders more than she disliked heights, but the truth was, she wasn't wild about either.

Jack, however, was still chuckling as he grabbed her by both arms the minute she climbed within reach, and pulled her into the dark shack.

"Spiders," he said, swinging the trapdoor shut behind

her. "You're perfectly all right about shooting people, but spiders you've got a problem with."

"I shot that guy in self-defense," Lou said, as she stood in the semi-darkness. The only light came through the small observation windows set at regular intervals in each of the four walls. Fortunately they were glassed-in, though the glass was incredibly dirty. "He was going to kill us."

"I didn't say I didn't approve," Jack pointed out. "Only that your fear of arachnids isn't in keeping with your Annie Oakley aim."

Jack, after digging Sam's lighter from his coat pocket, lit it.

The orange glow the tiny blaze created was enough for Lou to get a really good look around the room in which she found herself. It was impossibly small, but mercifully did manage to shelter them from both the snow and the wind, which had risen to shrieking pitch outside. There wasn't much in the way of furnishings, just a single army-issue type cot, a bookshelf with a few copies of *National Geographic* on it, and a file cabinet.

But it was dry; it was out of the wind; it was clean enough; there certainly weren't any spiders. And for now, it was home. It was all Lou could do to keep from collapsing in a heap where she stood.

Instead, she managed to make the few feet of distance between where she stood and the cot, and then collapsed onto it. Fortunately, it managed to hold together beneath her weight, despite some ominous creaking.

"I want you to know something," Lou said as she sat there, shivering.

"Oh, yeah?" he said, distractedly, yanking open the file cabinet and drawers and peering into them one by one by the glow of Sam's lighter. "What's that?"

"If we get out of this alive," Lou said, feeling her cheeks and ears begin to tingle, sure signs she'd been suffering from the first stages of frostbite, "I am going to kill you myself."

Jack only smiled. Though not as if he found anything funny. The smile was rueful. And of course, since it was coming from Jack, it was sinfully attractive.

"Why am I not surprised?" he wondered. "Look, Lou. If you're thinking I did something to make these people come after me, I'm telling you right now, I didn't. I don't have the slightest idea what I could have done to get somebody mad enough to kill me."

"Oh," Lou said, disentangling herself from the straps to her laptop and purse, and setting them carefully aside. "You know."

"I'm telling you," Jack said, in a less than patient tone, "I don't."

"Oh, come on, Townsend," Lou said, not sounding so patient herself. "Nobody sends hired assassins after a perfectly innocent man. You had to have done *something*. Now what is it? Just tell me, so I can have some idea what we're up against. Is it drugs?"

Jack sent her the same glare he used to give Meredith, the chief administrator at County General who'd always been urging Dr. Paul Rourke not to be so hot-headed, back on "*STAT.*" "I don't do drugs, Lou," he said laconically.

Lou chewed on her lower lip. She knew that, of course. Besides the fact that Jack had never been in any trouble over that sort of thing, the studio routinely screened their actors now as part of their contractual bargaining.

But you never knew. A small-town girl and a cop's daughter, Lou had never experimented with illegal substances, and had been shocked upon moving to LA to discover how casually everyone else seemed to. Lou still hadn't gotten over how many people in the business continued to "party," in spite of the number of their colleagues and peers who'd gone to jail and rehab for doing so, proof that you could take the girl out of the small town, but not the small town out of the girl.

But there'd never been a whisper of Jack Townsend liking a toot now and then. So if it wasn't a drug debt, what was it that was making so many people want him dead?

Lou glanced at him. "Gambling?"

He grimaced. "Lou. Come on."

"Well, it has to be *something*," Lou cried. "It can't be a woman. I mean, Greta dumped you. If it were the other way around, I'd say why not? I mean, I could see Greta Woolston hiring a team of commandos to off you, but—"

Her voice trailed off as she caught a glimpse of Jack's face, right before the flame on Sam's lighter flickered, and went out.

"Oh . . . my . . . God," she said, slowly. "You mean, there's someone else?" She couldn't say how she knew it, but there it was, all over his face. "Already?"

Jack shook his head, almost as if he were shaking off an unpleasant thought. "No," he said. "I mean, yes, there's someone else. Well, sort of. But she couldn't have—"

"Aw, geez," Lou said, rolling her eyes in disgust. "What is with you guys, anyway? You can't stand to be alone in your bed, even for a week? Who is she, Townsend? And I swear to God, if you say Angelina Jolie, I will freaking kill you."

Jack glared at her. "It's not Angelina Jolie, all right? And it's not like that, it was just . . . I made a mistake. I shouldn't have let it happen, but it did, and last night, I tried to tell her, and she went a little crazy, and—"

"Last night?" Lou stared. "Last night? You mean at the hotel? But who—" Then her eyes widened. "Melanie? You and *Melanie Dupre*? Aw, Jack, you've got to be kidding me."

"Look." Jack, in the semi-darkness, looked serious. She hadn't seen him look this serious since—well, since the last time he'd had a gun pointed at his head, which had only been a few hours ago. "It was my fault. I admit it. It started a couple of weeks ago, and it just got out of control. Last night, when we heard the news about Greta and, um, Barry, she got . . . well, she started talking about how maybe we should do, you know, what they did—elope— and I told her my feelings on the subject of matrimony and she . . . well, she—"

Lou held up a single hand. "Don't tell me. I already know. She lit your love seat on fire."

"Well," Jack said, sounding relieved that he didn't have to explain. "It was a couch, really. But—"

"And you think Melanie Dupre," Lou interrupted, "star of *Manhattan Junior High*, is the one who hired the A-team out there?" Lou shook her head. "No. I think not."

Jack, who'd stripped off his gloves for a minute, reached up to rub his face, over which a coarse growth of razor stubble had already sprouted. "No," he said. "I guess not. Melanie's not really the shoot-a-guy-and-shove-him-out-of-a-helicopter type of girl. She's more call-the-*Enquirer*-and-spill-all type."

Lou was still shaking her head. "Melanie Dupre," she said, to herself. "*Melanie Dupre.*"

"Hey," Jack said, glaring at her. "You barely even know her. She's a very warm, kind-hearted individual—"

"Oh, please," Lou said. "Like you were really interested in her heart. What are you, a cardiologist now? Give me a break. The girl has the intellect of Hines cake frosting, and you know it."

"Well." Jack slipped his gloves back on. They were out of the wind, all right, but that didn't make the temperature any more bearable. "In any case, I guess that rules her out."

"I'll say." Lou had to restrain a laugh. Not that there was anything so amusing about the situation. Here she was stranded, hundreds of miles from nowhere, in the middle of a blizzard, with an actor. And not just any actor, either, but Jack Townsend, the ex of her own ex's current flame.

But still. Melanie Dupre. Melanie Dupre, who'd been stunned the day her on-set nutritionist revealed that there was actually very little fiber in fruit roll-ups. Even Greta Woolston was sharper than Melanie.

As if he'd read her thoughts, Jack said, suddenly, "Can we possibly talk about something else?"

"Oh." Lou flattened a hand to her chest and blinked rapidly. "I'm sorry. Have I offended you by suggesting that we discuss the reason someone might be trying to kill you? Gosh, I just can't apologize enough for being interested in *why I am currently on the run for my life!*"

Jack stared down at her. In the meager light, he looked handsomer than she'd ever seen him. "Well, you handle yourself pretty well for someone who isn't accustomed to being shot at. Where'd you learn to fire a gun like that, anyway?"

Lou glared broodily at the floor. "Oh, that," she said. "My dad taught me."

"Really?" Jack looked surprised. "Did he hunt?"

"No," Lou said. "He was a cop with the New York City Police Department for forty years."

Jack looked interested. Not like he was just being polite, either, but like he really cared. But of course, he was an actor, so it was entirely possible his interest was feigned. "Oh?"

Lou nodded. She didn't care if he was pretending or

not. She always enjoyed talking about her family, because, though the Calabreses irritated her to distraction sometimes, she was proud of every single last one of them.

"When we were little, and my mom got so sick of us hanging around the house she couldn't stand it anymore," she explained, "she used to send us all out with Dad to get ice cream. Only instead of ice cream, he'd take us to the shooting range and have us take turns with his service pistol."

Jack's eyebrows went up. Way up.

"How paternal of him," was all he said, however.

Lou shrugged. "It was his way, I guess, of telling us he loved us."

"Us?" Jack raised his dark eyebrows. "You have siblings?"

"Four older brothers," Lou said. She waited to see his reaction before she added, "All of them grew up to be cops."

He didn't, however, look scared. Instead, he looked impressed.

"And you grew up to be a screenwriter who writes about them. Cops, I mean. When you aren't writing about exploding blimps, anyway. Your mom and dad must be pretty proud," he said.

"Well." Lou was pleased that there wasn't so much as a hitch in her voice as she replied, "My mom died ten years ago. But yeah, she was proud. Dad, too. Although, you know, we were a handful growing up."

"I can imagine," Jack said, mildly. "So now I know where the inspiration for Pete Logan came from."

She glanced at him darkly. "Yes. He's sort of a mix of all four of my brothers—"

"Which would be why you don't appreciate it when I change his lines, huh?" Jack definitely looked amused now.

"Well," Lou said, unable to keep a hint of sourness from her tone, "that's part of it, yeah."

"Right. The rest of it is just plain artistic vanity," Jack said.

"It is not," Lou cried defensively. "I just don't think you have the kind of grasp on the character that—"

"—that you have, I know, I know." Jack grinned. It was that same sarcastic grin he wore practically every time he spoke, the same one he had on in all the *Copkiller* posters. Why was he never serious around her? She knew he was capable of seriousness, because she'd seen the art house version of *Hamlet* he'd done—though nothing short of rescue from this arctic hell would ever induce her to admit she'd bought a ticket to something Jack Townsend had directed and starred in. He'd made a moving Hamlet, a character Lou had always considered something of a sap.

And he hadn't worn that grin once during the entire film.

"Well," he said, still grinning. "Now that I know how well you handle a gun, you can be pretty much assured I won't be ad-libbing anymore—"

She felt a shudder pass through her. She wasn't cold anymore—at least, not as much as when that icy wind had been ripping through her. No, the shudder wasn't because she was cold—though of course she was. It was because he'd reminded her of something she'd been trying to put out of her mind. Something she didn't want to remember, and something she definitely didn't want to discuss.

And that was the fact that she'd taken a man's life.

Granted, he'd been trying to kill her. Still, it wasn't easy, realizing that she was the first person in her family actually to end a life. And she was the only one who wasn't a member of a law enforcement agency.

"It isn't funny," she said, with a sort of hiccupy sob.

Where the sob had come from, she didn't know. But she was glad for it, since it wiped the smirk right off Jack Townsend's face.

"Hey," he said, looking alarmed. "Look. I didn't mean—"

"Oh, didn't you?" Her voice caught. God, what was happening to her? As a matter of course, Lou tried never to get emotional around the people she worked with. It was hard enough to be a working writer in Hollywood, without throwing the fact that she was a *female* writer into the mix. The old-boy network was still alive and well in most of the studios Lou'd worked for, and she knew few female movie executives who did not complain of having hit the glass ceiling at some point during their careers. The one thing Lou most dreaded was being accused of being too emotional, too "soft," to be taken seriously.

And now here she was, practically crying, in front of the one person she most wanted to be taken seriously by. . . .

Her brief hope that he might not have noticed either the catch in her voice or the tears that had sprung suddenly to her eyes was extinguished when he said, in a startled voice, "Hey, Lou. I can understand why you might be upset, but—"

"No, you can't." Lou's voice cracked. Oh, God, why couldn't she just suck it up, and take it like a man? Why did she have to start crying now, in front of *him*?

But there was nothing she could do. There was no holding it back. It came flooding from her, like water from a dam, all her pent-up feelings over what had just occurred.

"You can't possibly know why I'm so upset," Lou said. She could hear her voice rising, but she didn't care anymore. "I killed a man today, all right? And I would just like to know why. Why he was trying to kill me. You. Us. *Is that so much to ask?*"

And suddenly, she was melting, tears streaming from her eyes, making the man before her disappear in a soggy blur.

Great. Just great. Now she was crying—*crying*—in front of Jack Townsend. So much for not showing weakness in his presence. So much for trying to maintain a dignified and professional appearance. She was bawling her head off, while he just stood there looking down at her, as open-mouthed as if she'd just revealed that in her spare time she liked to watch old reruns of *Battlestar Gallactica*.

Well, what did she expect? Here was a man who would willingly spend time with Melanie Dupre, who had to be one of the stupidest people on the planet. He couldn't possibly have the slightest idea how normal women behaved, because he had probably never in his life spent more than five minutes in the company of a normal woman . . . except maybe to sign autographs for them.

Well, screw him. She wasn't going to stop crying just to make him feel better, or because it didn't look very professional of her. Now that she'd got a good healthy head of steam on, she was beginning to feel a lot better. Even the snow coming down in a white sheet just outside the windows seemed less ominous, now that tears were dripping down her face with just as much velocity. The darkness that was fast encroaching what little sky she could see through those dirty panes wasn't bothering her half so much now that she was snuffling away. She could even hear her father's voice, in the sound of the wind as it pummeled the four walls around them. *Hey, the guy was a mutt*, Frank Calabrese was saying. *He deserved to get popped. Don't feel bad, kiddo. In the end, it was you or him, and what, would you rather it'd been you?*

Lou was just beginning to think she'd about cried herself out when something completely unexpected happened, something that almost made her choke back her tears altogether.

And that was that Jack Townsend had slipped an arm around her.

 **10**

Well, he'd been expecting them, hadn't he? Tears. Lou's tears. He'd even been a little weirded out when they hadn't come.

He ought to have known it would take more than simply crash-landing in the Alaskan wilderness to bring tears to the eyes of Lou Calabrese. No, it had taken driving a bullet into another man's skull to bring on the waterworks.

Well, Jack could respect that.

Now at least he knew what to do. It had been a little confusing before. He wasn't used to women who acted— and talked—like men. Almost all of his relationships with women were flirtatious in nature. Lou Calabrese was just about the only woman he'd ever known—with the exception of his mother, of course—who had always seemed completely oblivious to his, er, charms. Not oblivious to the fact that other women found him attractive, of course. Otherwise, why would she keep writing all those scenes in which Pete Logan was required to drop trou?

But she had never given him any reason to think that she personally found him attractive. In fact, for most of the time he'd known her, she'd been quite openly hostile towards him.

Which was why he had never known quite how to act around her. Jack wasn't used to being disliked. Oh, sure, there were people in Hollywood with whom he didn't get along. Jeff Berger, for one, whom Jack had once given a black eye over a disagreement about a scene. And he wasn't all that fond of Russell Crowe.

But Lou was the only woman in Hollywood with whom Jack had anything like an adversarial relationship.

Which just made the fact that he was currently sitting on a rickety cot in an abandoned forest ranger station with his arm around her all the more bizarre.

"Shhh," he said, patting her on the shoulder as she cried, because that, he had discovered, tended to have a soothing effect on women. "It's all right. Everything is going to be all right."

"No, it's not," Lou said, in a tear-choked voice. "Just ask S-Sam."

"I'm sure Sam's fine," Jack said, although he was not sure of any such thing.

"N-No, he's not." Lou sniffled. "He's either still lying out there, with snow piling up on him, or—"

"Or his buddies found him, and got him medical treatment."

"They didn't," Lou sobbed. "They wouldn't. I'm sure they just left him out there to die."

Jack was having some trouble summoning up sympathy for Sam Kowalski. He didn't want to admit to Lou that the only reason he'd dragged the guy from the copter in the first place was so that he could get a good look through his pockets.

Instead, he said, "I bet you're wrong. I bet Sam's doing fine. I bet he's warmer than we are, right now. I bet he's snug in some hospital bed somewhere, and that they've got him pumped full of wonderful, mind-altering painkillers."

Lou made a snorting sound. He realized that she was laughing. Just a little. Still, it was a good sign.

He noticed something else, too. He couldn't help it. And that was the fact that the shoulder he was patting was, beneath the down of the parka Lou wore, a particularly finely sculpted one. He told himself it was just the fact that they were a million miles from nowhere that her hair, softly brushing his face now and then, smelled so good. And it was just the tears that were making her dark eyes seem so large and brilliant, just as they made her lips seem so hypnotically moist and kissable. . . .

At least until Lou, who'd abruptly stopped sobbing the minute his arm had gone around her, looked up at him with those wet, bewitching eyes, and asked, "What do you think you're doing?"

Jack wasn't used to women questioning him when he made friendly overtures towards them. Keeping his arm where it was, he said, not very lucidly—it was hard to be lucid with her hair giving off such a pleasant odor of orange blossoms—"Me? I'm comforting you."

"Yeah?" She ducked out from beneath his arm and stood up. "Well, do me a favor," she said, her voice husky with tears, though she was no longer crying. "Comfort me from a distance."

"Lou," he said, reasonably. Or at least he hoped he sounded reasonable. He didn't actually feel very reasonable. Something about her body, as it had felt pressed up against his side, had unsettled him—more even than the fact that they were stranded in the middle of nowhere with armed snowmobilers chasing them had unsettled him. "Look. It's okay to be scared. Hell, *I'm*—"

"I'm fine," Lou said, in something more like her normal voice. "Okay? It's all good over here. You just stay over there. Understand?"

He raised an eyebrow, but didn't say anything. Clearly, Lou's dislike for him far outweighed her fear over their current situation. This was a sobering—and infuriating—thought.

"I'm starving," Lou announced.

Jack glanced at her. Now that she mentioned it, he realized he was kind of hungry too. Kind of hungry? He was ravenous. He'd had nothing to eat since dinner the night before. And that had only been half a steak and a few fries, since the news of Greta and Barry's elopement had reached him midmeal, and Melanie had started right in on the theatrics. . . .

"Maybe somebody left something," he said, getting up and looking around the room. "You know. K rations, or something. Whatever it is forest rangers eat."

Lou had lifted her purse and was rifling through it, her long red curls hiding her face. "There was nothing in the file cabinet?" she asked, into her bag.

"I didn't get all the way through it." Jack went back over to the file cabinet and yanked open the first drawer once again. He stared blearily into it, not really seeing all the files and papers jammed into it. What was with Lou Calabrese, anyway? It was true the two of them had never had the best working relationship, due primarily to her own sensitivity about her work and Jack's insistence on authenticity. And it was true about him and Vicky not parting on the best of terms. But that had been ages ago. So what was up with Lou Calabrese?

Women usually liked Jack. He could say that without being conceited, because it was a fact. He didn't know why this was so—whether it was because he'd always gotten along with his mother, or if it was simply because he genuinely liked women. He'd even been able to maintain cordial relationships with his exes—well, except for Melanie. But look at Vicky. She understood that he could not give her what she wanted—a wedding ring—but did she hate him? Far from it, so far as he knew. Lou seemed to have a bigger problem with their breakup than Vicky did.

So what was wrong with Lou Calabrese? When she'd looked at him just then, after he'd put his arm around her, he could have sworn he'd seen fear in those gentle brown eyes. Fear? Fear of what? Him? What for? Jack had never done anything to Lou Calabrese.

Well, okay, there was the *I need a bigger gun* thing. But come on. She couldn't possibly feel threatened because he'd changed one measly line of her precious script . . . even if it had been her first script, the one she'd sold just out of college, the one that had made her a name in Hollywood. Writers, he knew, were funny about their work, thought about scripts the way some people thought about their children, and couldn't bear to hear them criticized. . . .

Still, hadn't she walked away from *Hindenburg* with an Academy Award? Wasn't that proof enough for her that she could write? What did it matter that he'd changed a single line? Okay, maybe an important line. And maybe the line he'd substituted for it had turned into a catch phrase that thirteen-year-old boys all over the country were wearing on T-shirts and writing on their skateboards.

But come on. That meant he couldn't even put an arm around her, when she was crying, without getting his head bit off?

"Aha!"

He looked over his shoulder and spied Lou pulling something from her bag. Something wrapped in tinfoil.

"I knew I had some in here somewhere," she said, holding the object high. She'd unzipped her parka, he noticed, and though the cable-knit sweater she wore beneath it was on the bulky side, he didn't have any problem at all making out what lay beneath it, which were two extremely fine—and that was without, he was reasonably certain, the aid of silicon—breasts.

"What's that?" Jack asked, though he didn't care, really. His appetite had fled, to be replaced by a hunger of another kind . . . a hunger he was pretty much assured he was not going to get to appease any time soon.

"Peanut brittle," Lou said. Then she turned back to her bag. "And I'm pretty sure I've got some wintergreen Lifesavers in here somewhere, too. What about you?"

Jack dragged his gaze reluctantly away from the front of her sweater, and turned his attention back to the file cabinet. What was he thinking, anyway? He wasn't even sure he *liked* Lou Calabrese. Why should he? She certainly didn't like him.

And what had all that hooting about Melanie Dupre been about? Sure, Melanie was no rocket scientist, but it wasn't like she was some innocent babe in the woods, either. Melanie knew which way was up.

"Townsend?" Lou's voice was still husky from her tears. "Any luck?"

"No," he said, slamming the first drawer closed, and opening the second. "Not unless you count what looks like a lot of data about the migratory habits of the arctic tern. Apparently, somebody's doing their dissertation on . . . hey. Wait a minute."

He struck paydirt in the third drawer. A box of saltines, a half dozen little Denny's jelly packets, and. . . .

"Eureka," he said, and pulled out the half-full bottle of Cutty Sark that had been hidden, deep in the back of the bottom drawer, beneath a paperback Audubon guide to birds of North America. "God, I love ornithologists."

Lou, clearly unimpressed by the whiskey, looked hopefully at the jelly packets. "Are any of those orange marmalade?"

"Excuse me." Jack presented the bottle with a flourish, the way Vanna White turned over the letters on "Wheel of Fortune." "Perhaps you failed to notice what I am brandishing here. Blended, I realize. But it's still a perfectly palatable whiskey. I know, because I used to partake of the Cutty regularly back before I could afford single malt."

Lou, sinking back onto the cot, was peeling back the tinfoil from the brick of peanut brittle.

"I wouldn't know," she said, biting into the candy. "I don't drink. Throw those crackers over here. And the jelly. Is there a knife, or anything?"

"You do too drink," Jack said, closing the file cabinet drawer with his foot, since his arms were full of whiskey and crackers. "I saw you drinking champagne at the *Copkiller III* premiere."

"I don't drink hard liquor," she said, chewing. She held the brick of peanut brittle towards him. "Want some?"

"No, I don't," Jack said, settling down on the cot beside her—and ignoring her wary look as he did so. "How can you eat that stuff? Doesn't it stick to your teeth?"

Lou seemed to reflect on this. "Yeah," she said after a minute. "But it comes loose eventually. And then you have a tasty snack for later."

"That," Jack said, dumping the saltines and the jelly onto the cot between them, but keeping hold of the whiskey bottle, "is disgusting."

"Oh, and what you're doing isn't?" she asked, as he pulled the stopper from the bottle's mouth and lifted it to his lips. "You don't have the slightest idea who was drinking from that bottle last."

Jack, feeling the fiery liquid course down his gut, said, "No, I don't. And I don't care, either. Besides, the alcohol'll have killed whatever germs the guy might have been carrying, if the cold didn't get'em first." He held the bottle out towards her. "Come on. Have a toke."

"Uh, no," Lou said. She'd opened the box of saltines, and was dipping them, one after another, into one of the packets of jelly. "I told you, I don't do hard liquor. The last time I did it, I woke up the next morning feeling like my head was going to explode."

"Yeah? Well, what were you drinking?"

It was hard to tell in the dark, but he thought her cheeks turned a little redder. She muttered something indistinct.

"I beg your pardon?" he asked.

"Bailey's Irish Cream," she said more clearly.

"Oh, you poor innocent," Jack said. "No wonder. But you see, that's not real liquor. Real liquor is your friend."

"Liquor," Lou assured him, "has never been my friend."

"Yeah," Jack said, reaching for a saltine of his own. "Under normal circumstances. But this is hardly what I'd call normal circumstances. I mean, come on. You're stranded with a man you despise in the arctic wilderness in the middle of a blizzard."

"I don't despise you," Lou said, using a cracker to scrape up what was left in the jelly packet she'd peeled open.

"Yeah," Jack said. He was not successful in squelching a feeling of triumph that she had admitted she didn't despise him. It was ridiculous, he knew. To be happy that she didn't hate him. What was he, in the seventh grade again? "But you don't like me."

"Well, that's true," she said matter-of-factly.

Great. He'd had to push it, hadn't he? Why couldn't he ever leave well enough alone?

Fine. Two could play that game.

"And you survived a helicopter crash," he pointed out. "And not one, but two murder attempts."

"Don't remind me," she said, going for the peanut brittle again.

"And you shot a guy," he couldn't help adding.

She glared at him. "Do you have a death wish?" she wanted to know.

"And right about now—" He looked at the glow-in-the-dark face of his watch. "Yeah, I'd say right about now, your ex and my ex are probably slipping into a heart-shaped Jacuzzi, sipping some Dom, and nibbling on oysters in the half-shell . . . and each other, of course—"

"Gimme that." Lou leaned over and snatched the bottle of Cutty from him, then brought it to her lips. After she'd choked down a swallow and handed the bottle back to him with stinging eyes and an aggrieved expression, she said, "Just remember, you asked for this."

"I know," Jack said. "I'm a big, bad man, debauching nubile young screenwriters—"

She snorted. "Oh, yeah? If this is an example of your debauching technique, I swear I don't see how you get laid so often."

Now he was the one who was choking. "Wh-what?"

"Oh, please," she said, rolling her eyes. "You heard me. Is there any woman in the business you haven't slept with?" She took the bottle from him and took another pull on it. "With the exception of me, of course?" she asked, after she'd stopped coughing.

"As a matter of fact," he said with wounded dignity, "there is."

"Oh, yeah? Who?"

"I haven't slept with Meryl Streep," he said. "Yet. But hope springs eternal."

She laughed. When Lou Calabrese laughed, it was impossible to remember that the temperature was well below freezing, and that an arctic blast was buffeting the four meager walls around them. Lou Calabrese's laughter was like the sun coming out after a month of rain. Like a cold beer after a long hot hike. Like a hot shower after freezing all day. It was amazing to him that he'd never realized it before.

"So you think she's the one who paid Sam to off you?" Lou wanted to know.

He blinked at her. Even in the semi-darkness, her skin looked impossibly clear, her cheeks smooth as cream. "Who?"

She was looking at him like he was slow. "Meryl Streep. You know. 'Cause she's mad she was left out."

"You know," he said, his mouth feeling dry all of a sudden. "Somehow I doubt it."

She just smiled and broke off another piece of peanut brittle. Jack had never met a woman who carried peanut brittle around in her purse. Listerine Pocket Paks, maybe. Vicky had always had echinacea. But actresses, who were perpetually on diets, didn't tend to carry high-calorie candy in their handbags. The foil, he was able to see, had some writing on it. It said, *Thank you for supporting the Sherman Oaks Central High School band.*

Sherman Oaks. That must be where she lived. Hardly the section of southern California in which you'd expect to find an Academy Award–winning screenwriter living. The hills, maybe. Or the canyon. But not Sherman Oaks, which wasn't a bad part of LA. It just wasn't . . . well, it wasn't very glamorous.

"How about you?" he heard himself asking. "I mean, now that Barry's . . . you know. You seeing anyone?"

She narrowed her eyes at him. "Yeah," she said. "Robert Redford. Hey, maybe we could double. You and Meryl and me and Bob."

He took a pull from the Cutty. "I was only asking," he

said. "I mean, you're a vital, attractive woman. There must be—"

She plucked the whiskey bottle from his hands. "Don't even try," she advised him, after taking a long swallow.

"What?" He shrugged. "I was only asking."

"Yeah, well." She reached up to wipe her mouth—cherry-red, and without, he knew, the help of lipstick, since he'd have noticed if she'd put any on—with the back of a smooth white hand. "Don't."

He whistled, low and long. Her voice, which was full of a note of warning, had said more than her words.

"Sorry," he said. "I didn't know. I mean, you and Barry—you were going out with him back when I was on 'STAT,' right? And that was—"

"Six years ago," she finished for him, handing the bottle back. "What part of *don't* didn't you understand?"

Maybe it was the Cutty. Maybe it was their near-death experience. Maybe it was the fact that the two of them were trapped in a nine-foot-by-nine-foot room, with a blizzard raging outside its walls, and only each other's body heat to keep them from freezing to death. Or maybe it was just those brown eyes, so filled with intelligence, wit . . . and pain.

In any case, he ignored her warning, and blundered on.

"Six years is a long time," he said. "I mean, you two were living together, right? In Sherman Oaks? What happened?"

She scissored an incredulous look in his direction.

"*What happened?*" she echoed, in a voice that cracked. "What do you *think* happened? Your girlfriend Greta, that's what happened. Too bad you didn't keep her on a shorter leash."

He raised his eyebrows. "Hey," he said. "I could say the same thing about you. I mean, your boy Barry isn't exactly blameless in this."

She took the bottle from him, took an enormous swig, and this time neither choked nor coughed. Her eyes did not even water.

Her enunciation, however, was not exactly clear.

"For your information," Lou said, pointing an accusing index finger at his chest, "Barry would have married me, if your shtupid Greta hadn't come along. I mean, he was getting ready to make a commitment."

He took the bottle of Cutty Sark from her. She had clearly drunk her limit.

"Honey," he said. "I got news for you. If, after six years, the guy still hadn't made a commitment, he wasn't gonna."

"Ten," she said.

"I beg your pardon?"

"Ten years," Lou said. "We were together for ten years. Until shtupid blond Greta Woolshton came along. We were gonna get married. We were gonna buy our dream house in Santa Barbara. We were gonna have kids. Were you and Greta gonna have kids?" She punched him in the shoulder—surprisingly hard, too, for a woman. "Huh? Were you?"

"No, we weren't," he said, moving the whiskey bottle carefully out of her reach. "Hey, you weren't kidding about not being able to handle hard liquor, were you?"

Lou did not appear to have heard him. She placed both hands on her chest, just above her high, round breasts, and said, emphatically, "I was going to *marry* him. You were just using Greta for sex. Therefore, *my* loss is greater than yours."

Thinking back to the day he'd first met Barry, on the "*STAT*" set, he said, "Believe me, Lou. You didn't lose a thing."

She dropped her hands back into her lap. "I did, though," she said, with a sniffle, looking suddenly tragic. "I lost my girlhood. I lost the best years of my life. I wasted them on a guy named *Barry*." She said the name again, in tones of utter disbelief. "*Barry.*"

Jack regarded her solemnly. "The best years of your life, huh? What are you, twenty-eight?"

"Nearly twenty-nine," Lou declared, her eyes wide at the horror of it all.

"Ancient," Jack said. "You're right. You better chuck it all in. You'll never love again."

The big brown eyes narrowed. "At least I *have* loved," she said. "*Tis better to have loved and lost than never—*"

"That," Jack said, quickly, "is one movie I have seen. I've even read the book. Listen, you better eat some more of those crackers, or something. You're crocked."

Again, she did not appear to hear him.

"*You*'ve never loved anyone," she said, accusingly. "Not like I loved Barry."

He blinked at her. "How would you know?"

"Oh, please," she said, waving a hand at him as if to say, *Go on*. "Melanie Dupre. I am so sure! What do you guys talk about, anyway? Her cuticles?"

This seemed to strike her as riotously funny. She clutched her stomach, she was laughing so hard. Jack regarded her unsmilingly. It didn't matter that she was right—conversation with Melanie was never brilliant. It was the fact that she seemed to think she was so morally superior to him because during the course of her ten-year, monogamous relationship with one man, he'd been with . . . well, a lot of women.

But hey, in the end, who was the loser, huh? Him, whose heart was still unabashedly, unapologetically whole? Or her, whose heart was broken?

Abruptly, Lou stopped laughing.

"Oh my God," she said, all trace of humor wiped from her face. "I killed a guy." She looked at him, naked panic in those big brown eyes. "Jack! I *killed* a guy today!"

Then she pitched forward, landing with her face between his jean-clad thighs.

Looking down with some surprise at her bright copper curls spread out across his lap, Jack reached over and shook her by the shoulder. "Lou?"

When she didn't respond, he shook harder. "Hello? Lou? Are you all right?"

A muffled groan came up from his crotch. It sounded like she'd said, "Barry Kimmel can kiss my ass." He sat her up, just to make sure she was still breathing, and she said it again. Yep. Barry Kimmel was clearly no longer one of Lou Calabrese's favorite people. Much like . . . well, Jack Townsend.

Not knowing what else to do, Jack stretched her out on the cot. It smelled musty, but he figured in the state Lou was in, she wouldn't notice. He put one of the moth-eaten blankets over her and reflected that, so long as they had one another's body heat to warm them, they might just be all right until morning.

At least as long as those snowmobilers didn't come back.

11

"**M**a'am," the flight attendant said. "I'm sorry. But you'll have to put your dog back in its carrier."

Eleanor Townsend looked dismayed.

"Oh, dear," she said, stroking Alessandro's silken ears. "But it's such a long flight. And really, he is such an angel. He won't bother anyone, I promise you."

The flight attendant frowned prettily. "I'm sorry, ma'am. But we can't have animals running around loose during the flight. It's a safety issue, you understand."

"Oh, but he isn't running around loose," Eleanor said. "He'll just sit here on my lap, quiet as you please. He won't be a bit of trouble. I'm sure this nice gentleman doesn't mind. Do you, sir?"

The tall, white-haired gentleman seated beside her, looking distinctly uncomfortable, shook his head rapidly.

"Oh, no," he said to the flight attendant. "I don't mind at all. I love dogs. Well, bigger dogs than this one, actually. But this dog seems all right. He isn't bothering me. He's pretty well behaved."

Eleanor could have kissed him. Would have, if she

hadn't thought he'd have jumped right out of his skin. He was holding onto the grips of his arm rests as if he half expected the seat to eject at any moment.

"There," she said, giving the flight attendant her most dazzling smile, the one Jack had always called her now suffer smile. "You see? My dog isn't bothering this gentleman, and he's the one most likely to be disturbed. And it isn't as if there's anyone else in the cabin to be bothered by it." She looked meaningfully about first class, which was empty, save for her, the white-haired gentleman, and Alessandro. "Can't he just sit and look out the window for a little while?"

The flight attendant, charmed not so much by the Yorkie as by its owner, said, "Well . . . I really shouldn't. But . . . I guess. Just this once."

"Oh, thank you," Eleanor gushed. "You can't know what a comfort it is to me." The flight attendant went into the forward cabin to see to her passengers' suppers, and Eleanor said, to the gentleman beside her, "I can't thank you enough, sir, for being so understanding."

The white-haired gentleman gave her a perfunctory smile. Clearly, his mind was on other things, however.

"No problem, ma'am," he said. "Happy to oblige." Then he turned his face back towards the front of the plane, as if he, not the pilot, was flying it.

Eleanor, recognizing immediately a man who was used to being in control and disliked the feeling of not being so, even for a ten-hour flight, held her dog out towards him.

"Would you like to hold Alessandro for a little while?" she asked. At his look of bewilderment, she added, "I find that petting animals can be so soothing. It's actually been scientifically proven to lower the blood pressure. And if you don't mind my saying so, you seem nervous." When he hesitated, Eleanor pointed out, "He's just a little dog. And he's never bitten anyone in his life."

Looking as if he very much would have liked to decline, the white-haired gentleman nevertheless held out his hands. Eleanor placed Alessandro in them, and to her delight, the dog immediately began lapping the man's kindly, rather good-looking face.

"There," she said happily. "He likes you! I knew he would. Alessandro is actually quite particular, you know. It's quite an honor for him to accept you so quickly into the pack."

The white-haired gentleman smiled shyly. "Well," he said, between laps of Alessandro's pink tongue. "How nice. I didn't know they let people in first class have their dogs on their laps while they fly. They don't in coach, you know."

Delighted to have a conversation to keep her mind off her son, Eleanor said, interestedly, "Oh, you normally fly coach, do you?"

"Yes," the white-haired gentleman said. Alessandro, satisfied that he had licked his new friend's face enough, settled upon his chest and panted rapidly. "The only seats available on this flight were in first class. And I need to get to Anchorage as soon as possible."

"So do I," Eleanor said wonderingly. "My son was in a helicopter crash there."

The white-haired gentleman blinked at her. Alessandro, sensing the man's sudden tension, stopped panting and whined a little.

"So was my daughter," he said.

Eleanor reached out and grasped the man's wrist. "My goodness! Is your daughter a screenwriter?"

"Yes," the white-haired gentleman said. Then as if suddenly remembering something, he thrust his right hand at her, startling Alessandro. "Frank Calabrese. My daughter Lou's gone missing."

"Eleanor Townsend," Eleanor said, slipping her fingers into his. "My son Jack is missing as well. They say . . . they say he might be dead. That there's a blizzard in the area where the helicopter went down, and they can't get rescue planes there before morning."

Frank Calabrese's fingers were very warm and reassuring. It was no wonder Alessandro liked him.

"They told me the same thing," he said. "They're worried the survivors—if there were any survivors—will freeze to death in the night."

"Yes," Eleanor said. "That's what they said to me, too."

Neither of them said anything more for a while. There was nothing to say, really. They both declined the champagne the flight attendant offered them a few minutes later. And when the movie came on, neither accepted her offer of headphones. Instead, they sat exactly as they were, holding one another's hands, and staring through the window at the blackness of the night sky.

"No," Tim Lord said into his cell phone. It was simpler to use it than to figure out the intricacies of the phone service provided by the hotel. "I'm telling you, Andre, we've got enough footage of Jack that we can digitally superimpose shots over anything I don't have. Except that there won't be a need to, because I have everything we could possibly need."

"Daddy," said a small voice at the director's side.

"Listen, Andre," Tim said into the phone. "I'm telling you, I've got it. There's just that one last shot, of the mine exploding. And once we get rid of these crazy tree-huggers, we can—"

"Daddy." A dark-haired boy tugged on the tail of Tim's coat. "Daddy, what's wrong with Vicky?"

Tim brought the phone away from his face. "Vicky's resting, Elijah," he said. "Leave her alone. Go ask Nanny, if you want someone to read to you. Anyway, Andre—" He spoke into the phone again. "—I don't anticipate going a day over schedule. Once we get the mine shot, we're done. We can pack up and—"

"I don't want Nanny to read to me," Elijah cried, giving another tug to his father's coat tails. "I want Vicky! I knocked and knocked on the door to her room, and she wouldn't open it."

"Hold on a minute, Andre," Tim said. He lowered the cell phone, then stooped down to say to his son, "Elijah, listen. I told you before. Vicky isn't feeling well. She's in bed. She's sick."

"What's she got?" Elijah wanted to know. "Flu?"

"Well, she doesn't have anything," Tim replied. "She's just . . . she's sad."

"Why is she sad?"

"Because . . ." Tim sighed. Why him? Really. Why today? Tim put the phone back to his face and said, "Look, Andre. I'm going to have to call you back." Then he made a face. "Look, I know the studio's upset. Tell them they've got nothing to worry about, we've got everything we need. I gotta go." He pushed a button, then muttered, "Can't even wait until the body's cold." Then he looked down at his son.

"Look, Elijah," he said, taking the boy by the shoulders and sinking onto one knee in the deep pile of the hotel suite's white carpeting. "You remember Uncle Jack, don't you?"

"*I need a bigger gun*?" Elijah recited.

"Right. Uncle I-need-a-bigger-gun. See, there was a helicopter crash, and people are worried Uncle Jack might have—well, that Jack might have died in it. And Vicky's other friend, too. You remember Aunt Lou, right?"

"Sure," Elijah said. "From *Hindenburg*. A triumph of the human spirit."

"Right," Tim said. "Aunt Lou is missing, too."

Elijah blinked. "Is that why Vicky won't come out of her room?"

"Yes," Tim said. "You see, Vicky was very fond of Uncle Jack and Aunt Lou. So she's very worried and sad. And I need you to be a good boy and leave her alone for a while. And to tell the other kids, as well."

Elijah blinked once more. "Okay," he said.

His father's cell started to chime again. Looking tired, Tim Lord lifted the phone to his ear. "Lord," he said into it. Then, after listening a moment, he exploded, "No! Paul, you can't let her. No statements. We are issuing no statements at this time. I mean, my God, the blizzard hasn't even let up yet. Tell Melanie she is not to issue any comments, and no press conferences until morning, when we have more news. . . ."

Elijah drifted away from his father, back to the glass-topped dining room table, where his crayons and paper lay. Climbing into one of the high, silk-covered chairs, he took a clean sheet of paper, then carefully selected his crayons. Red for Aunt Lou's hair. Brown for her eyes. Black for Uncle Jack's hair . . . but there was some gray in there, as well, so Elijah carefully dotted it. Then he found some blue for Uncle Jack's eyes.

Satisfied with his creation, Elijah slipped from the chair and, carrying the drawing, padded across the hotel suite floor in his bare feet, while outside, snow came down in a steady white curtain, and in the center of the room, his father barked into his phone.

"No!" Tim Lord yelled. "No, Paul. All we need is an 'In Memory of,' right before the credits. Like they did for Vic Morrow in *Twilight*—well, why not? I think it would be tasteful. Why wouldn't it be tasteful?"

Elijah made his way to the door of the room his step-mother shared with his father. He reach up and tried the knob. Still locked. This, however, did not bother him. He leaned down and shoved his drawing beneath the door.

"There you go, Vicky," he called through the crack. "Now Uncle Jack and Aunt Lou can be with you always."

Then, satisfied at a job well done, Elijah went to join his brothers and sisters in the next room, where they were watching a Disney video and spraying one another with bottles of hotel shampoo.

Hinky.

That's what Sheriff Walt O'Malley felt about the crash scene. He had been at the site of a lot of aircraft accidents—mostly smaller, private planes, as they didn't get a lot of commercial jets this far north. But he had never seen anything as hinky as this one.

He couldn't say what it was, exactly, about this wreck that set his internal alarm bells ringing. It lay in a twisted heap, it was true, in the snow. It wasn't smoking anymore. Last night's blizzard had handily put out the fire that had charred and blackened the metal frame, disintegrating anything that wasn't made of steel.

Maybe that was part of what made him so suspicious. Because aside from the fire damage, the 44 wasn't that badly beat up.

Oh, the thing would never fly again, that was for sure. But it had landed in more or less one piece. Sure, the nose was flattened. He didn't doubt that the pilot had been injured in the crash.

But the passengers? There was no reason that Walt could see that they shouldn't have survived the crash.

So where the hell were they?

They'd found the remains of only one person. Charred beyond recognition, it would take the ME back in Anchorage to determine if the corpse had been male or female. On the whole, however, Walt suspected it was the pilot. The plaid jacket the fellow had been wearing was flame retardant, the same jacket worn by bush pilots throughout the region. Walt couldn't see a big star like Jack Townsend wearing a jacket like that. Townsend probably wore that what's-it-called, that stuff Walt's oldest daughter, Tina, was always going on about. Prada. Yeah. That's what movie stars wore.

Funny thing about the pilot, though. Sam Kowalski, the charter company had said his name was. Old Sam's body hadn't been found in the pilot's seat, where it ought to have been if he'd died in the crash. No, Kowalski had been in the rear seat.

Now, what would the pilot of the damned chopper be doing in the backseat?

"Walt."

Lippincott came over, looking red-faced. But then, Lippincott always looked red-faced. It was his first winter in the arctic, and he hadn't figured out yet that it was all right—manly, even—to use moisturizer. Hell, Walt had a complete collection of tiny bottles in his bathroom back home. The girls had had a blast at the mall, collecting samples for their dad, to see which brand he liked best. Mostly he preferred Oil of Olay. It didn't clog the pores, was what Lynn used to say.

Lippincott could have used some Olay. Or maybe some of that Burt's Bees stuff the girls put on their feet. The guy's face was a mess of cracked and peeling windburn.

"Something hinky, here, Chief," Lippincott said.

"I was just thinking the same thing myself," Walt said, slowly. It was past dawn, but the only way anyone could have told was by the faint lightening of the darkness in the eastern half of the sky. The snow had finally stopped, the storm having passed. It had dropped a good twelve inches in about a sixteen-hour period. Not a bad storm at all, by Alaskan measures. But still not one Walt would have liked to weather out in the open, the way it appeared two of the chopper crash victims had.

"Only one body," Lippincott said. "No sign of the other two. You think they would have wandered off? You know, 'cause they were dazed from the accident, or whatever?"

"Not both of 'em," Walt said. He squinted up at the thickly clouded sky. "More likely, when the snow got bad, they decided to look for shelter."

Lippincott's gaze swept the snow-covered mountain-side. "Geez," he breathed. "You mean they're out there somewhere? Wouldn't they—I mean, wouldn't they have frozen to death?"

"Probably so," Walt said thoughtfully.

Lippincott looked at the charred ruins of the chopper. "You'd think they'd have stayed close by," he said. "I mean, the chopper had to have been giving off plenty of heat. If they'd stuck by it, we'd've found 'em, soon enough. Why didn't they stick by it?"

"That," Walt said, his gaze scanning the snow-covered treetops around the crash site, "is what I'd like to know."

12

Lou opened one eye and immediately closed it again, having felt a stabbing pain through her head that indicated more sleep was necessary.

Except that she couldn't sleep any more. She couldn't sleep any more because something was wrong. Just what that something was, she couldn't exactly put her finger on—not without opening an eye again, and that she was reluctant to do, given the pain that had shot through her the first time.

Still. Something wasn't right. Something was, in fact, very, very wrong. She did not think, for some reason, that she was back in her own bed in her Sherman Oaks bungalow. For one thing, her room back home was painted in soothing blues and creams. She had seen neither of those colors when she'd cracked her eye open. Instead, she'd had a disconcerting glimpse of wood paneling. Wood paneling! Where was she, anyway? Her parents' basement?

And another thing. She was fairly certain she was not alone. And there'd been no one but her in her bedroom back in Sherman Oaks since Barry had moved out.

So whose arm was under her head?

Oh, yes. There was definitely an arm beneath her head. Which didn't make the least bit of sense, because Lou was not a promiscuous person. Since Barry had moved out, her Saturday nights had been spent working, or maybe dinner and a movie with Vicky, when she could get away from her stepchildren. Lou had never in her life had a one-night stand, or even allowed herself to be picked up in a bar. She was, simply, not that type of girl. For her, it was love or nothing.

So what was she doing in bed with a man who was definitely not Barry? Because Barry had never been a spooner. He had, in fact, always been vaguely annoyed when Lou strayed the slightest bit over to "his" side of the bed . . . except during sex, of course.

And then she realized that there wasn't just an arm beneath her head. There was an arm draped across her, as well. Not just across her, either. No, this arm was curled around her, like she was some kind of security blanket. Except that the hand at the end of the arm around her was cupped over one of her breasts. Oh, no, there was no mistaking it. Those fingers were splayed right across there, holding on as if for dear life.

And then memory came flooding back, and Lou realized where she was, what she was doing there, and who that hand belonged to.

She sat up with a scream.

Jack, who'd been curled against her on the narrow army cot, sat up, too, and looked around, wild-eyed.

"What?" he demanded gruffly. "What is it?"

Lou leaped from the cot, dragging the blankets with her, keeping them clutched to her chest.

"You!" she cried, pointing at him with one trembling finger while holding the blankets with the other hand. "I can't believe you!"

Still not fully awake, Jack ran a hand through his thick

dark hair. "What'd I do?" he wanted to know. "I didn't do anything."

"Yes, you did," Lou said, her cheeks beginning to flame. "You . . . you . . ."

But even as she was struggling to find the right words, she realized that, beneath the blankets, she was still fully clothed. Not a stitch out of place, in fact. Even her boots.

So she quickly shifted gears, and said, with much less rancor, but still some indignation, "You got me drunk!"

Jack regarded her groggily. But unfortunately not groggily enough. He was awake enough to observe, with undisguised amusement, "Hey. You're blushing."

"I am not," Lou said, grandly, though she knew the heat with which her cheeks were burning belied her. "I'm just . . . it's warm in here."

"It is not," Jack said. "It's like ten degrees in here. You're *blushing*."

Lou threw down the blankets and began to zip up her coat. Her hair fell over her face, mercifully covering her flaming cheeks. "I am not," she said, as she struggled with her zipper.

"Oh, yeah, you are," Jack said from the cot, where he lay, grinning maliciously. "You know, I think you must be the last woman in Hollywood who still blushes when she's embarrassed. And who can't handle hard liquor."

"For your information—" Lou jerked her head back to get a better look at him and instantly regretted the action as pain flooded her head. She could not help letting out a groan.

Jack was still grinning at her from the cot, his long, lean body looking perfectly relaxed. Somehow, even though he, like her, was still fully clothed, he managed to give off the impression of being naked. Lou didn't know how he did it, but there it was.

And he seemed supremely indifferent to what she thought of him, naked or clothed.

"You know, I thought girls like you had gone the way of Pop Rocks," he said.

Lou, furious with herself, bent down and picked up her purse, which she immediately began to rifle through.

"Yeah?" she said, into the depths of her bag. "Well, I've got news for you. We still exist, and guys like you make us mad as hell." Her fingers seized on the object she'd been looking for, and she gave a sigh of relief.

Jack, over on the cot, looked interested, and not in the least offended. "Guys like me? Really? What'd we do?"

Lou pried open the lid to the aspirin bottle and shook out three tablets. "As if you didn't know," she said darkly, then looked around the room for something to wash the pills down with. All she found was the bottle of Cutty, now only a third full. The mere sight of it caused the vise around her skull to tighten.

"You shouldn't take those on an empty stomach," Jack remarked from the cot. He'd twined his hands beneath his head and was watching her with as much fascination as if she were an exhibit at the zoo: The only female on the planet who'd ever woken up in Jack Townsend's arms and hadn't been happy about it. "Eat some of those crackers, or something."

"Thanks, Ma," Lou said and popped all three tablets into her mouth, swallowed, and retched a little at the bitter taste.

"Hey, as someone who's been there, I'm just giving you a word of advice." Jack might have been lounging poolside, he looked so relaxed. His brain wasn't cracking in two, clearly. "Or you could try a little hair of the dog."

Lou winced. "No way."

"Suit yourself." Now Jack stood, swinging up off the cot as easily as if he'd been exiting a limo, or sliding out from behind a table at Spago. He was so tall that the top of his head nearly brushed the ceiling of the ranger station. Lou wondered why she hadn't noticed this the night before.

Also why she had never seemed to notice how Jack filled a room. Really. It was uncanny. He seemed to consume the space, as if he owned it and everything around him.

"Well, the snow stopped, anyway," he said, as he glanced out one of the dirty-paned windows. "What do you say we try to make our way back to the helicopter? They'll have gotten people out looking for us by now."

Lou, who didn't fancy having a stomachache to go with her headache, had surreptitiously begun to nibble on some of the leftover crackers, as he'd suggested. It was amazing to her how good something like a simple saltine could taste, and how much better they were making her feel. Why, she thought to herself, in some amazement, the two of them had survived a night in the Alaskan wilderness. No one would have believed it, but it was true. They might actually make it out of this thing alive.

"Okay," Lou said. She picked up her computer bag and shouldered it, along with her purse. Whether it was the saltines or the aspirin, she was feeling better every minute. There was no reason to mention to Jack that he'd slept with one hand clamped over one of her breasts. No reason anybody in the world needed to know that but her. Things were going to be okay. Things were going to be fine.

At least, that's what she'd been thinking right up until they both heard the whine of a snowmobile engine outside.

Jack, who'd been just about to lift the trapdoor to the ladder leading to the ground, looked up sharply, meeting her gaze.

"You hear that?" he asked softly.

Lou nodded. The storm outside having ebbed, it was eerily quiet beyond the four walls of their shelter. The sound of the snowmobile engine seemed loud as thunder.

"Maybe," Lou ventured, "it's people out looking for us."

"I'm sure it is," Jack responded. "But are they the good guys, or more of old Sam's pals?"

Lou swallowed, not so much because of what Jack had said but because the sound of the snowmobile's engine, which had been growing louder and louder, suddenly ceased altogether.

Then Lou heard a sound more terrifying than anything she had ever heard in her life: the scrape of a boot on the rungs of the ladder leading to their shelter.

Jack wrapped his fingers around the handle to the trapdoor, then whispered to her, "The gun."

Lou nodded, and, her heart in her throat, drew the .38 out of her pocket. A single glance into the chamber, however, had her hissing, "There's only one bullet left!"

Jack, grim-faced, signaled for her to move behind him. "I'll take him," he whispered. "If it's one of them."

Lou did not like the sound of this at all. She didn't move from where she stood, directly in front of the trapdoor.

"He'll have a gun," she said, sotto voce.

"I don't care if he's got a flamethrower," Jack hissed. "Get the hell out of the way—"

But whoever was below the trapdoor was already pushing on it quietly, as if he didn't want to disturb whoever was inside. Lou doubted such caution was on account of fear of spiders. She held the revolver the way her dad had taught her, with both hands, the left cupping the right, and aimed for the center of the trapdoor, ignoring Jack, who looked mad enough to spit nails.

It was probably a Mountie, after all. Or whoever it was that came to rescue stranded people in this part of the world. But if it wasn't . . . if it wasn't. . . .

When the trapdoor had opened enough for Lou to see who was pushing it up, she saw at once that this was no Mountie. It was a man in a black ski mask and a camouflage ski parka, trimmed around the collar with what looked like coyote fur. He might almost have passed for a member of the National Guard if it hadn't been for the .44 magnum, drawn and ready, in his right hand.

The eyes Lou could see burning from the holes in the black wool were blue. Their gaze swept the interior of the ranger station, coming to a halt at her boots, then traveling upwards, until they widened at the sight of the .38.

Instead of yelling, "Police, drop the gun," or even, "I'm here to help you," the man in the ski mask fumbled with his own sidearm, trying to hold up the trapdoor and prepare to fire at the same time. . . .

He never had the chance. Jack, perhaps seeing from Lou's expression that their morning caller was foe, not friend, gave the trapdoor a vicious shove, cracking Ski Mask in the skull with the heavy wood panel and sending him plummeting back down to the ground below.

Impressed, Lou lowered the .38.

"Good one," she said to Jack.

"You know," he replied, "I think that's the first nice thing you've ever said to me." Then he yanked the trapdoor open again, peered down, and started climbing.

Lou climbed down after him, a little amazed at the change in the landscape all the snow the night before had effected. It had been snowy before, but now there was three feet of white covering everything, whereas before there'd only been two. When her feet finally touched ground, she sunk nearly mid-thigh into the snow.

Ski Mask lay a few feet away, one of his legs tilted at an ominous angle.

"Damn," Jack said, looking down at him.

Lou could see the breath coming from the unconscious man's nostrils frosting up in the frigid air.

"What's wrong?" she asked. "You didn't kill him. He's just out."

"Like a light," Jack said, grimly. "That's the problem. There were a couple things I wanted to ask him."

"I doubt he'd have talked," Lou said. "Unless you applied . . . pressure. And sorry, Jack, but you don't strike me as the pressure type."

"You'd be surprised," Jack said, enigmatically. Then he leaned down to extricate the .44 from the unconscious man's hand. "Here," he said, passing it to Lou. "Add this to your arsenal."

Lou took the pistol, checked the safety, then wordlessly dropped it into her pocket, along with the .38. She watched as Jack reached out and pulled the ski mask from their would-be assassin's face.

"Recognize him?" he asked her, his breath instantly freezing as it came out.

Lou looked down at the inoffensive-looking, middle-aged white man. Both of his cheeks were pink with the cold. "No," she said. "Should I?"

"I don't know," Jack said, with a shrug. "I don't recognize him either." Kneeling in the snow beside the unconscious man, he looked up at her and asked simply, "Why would a bunch of people I don't even know want me dead?"

Lou looked up sharply. "I don't know," she said. "But we better not waste time sitting around and thinking about it. Do you hear that?"

Jack tilted his head. Like her, he was hatless. The wind, gentle compared to the wind from the day before, but still just as cold, tugged at his dark hair.

"Snowmobiles," he said grimly. "Coming this way."

"They could be on our side," Lou said, but without much optimism.

"Until I see a shiny silver badge, I'm not trusting anybody." Jack wrapped a hand around Lou's upper arm. "Come on. At least this time we've got a ride."

She let him lead her over to the snowmobile Ski Mask had abandoned.

"You ever operate one of these things before?" she asked, skeptically.

"Sure," Jack said, swinging a leg over the seat. "We used to winter in Aspen when I was a kid."

"Oh," Lou said drolly. "You used to winter in Aspen. Of course. How stupid of me. And where did you summer? The vineyard?"

He started the engine, looking back at her over one broad shoulder. "The cape," he said. "You coming, or you want to stay here and make snide comments about my privileged upbringing?"

She eyed the wide black seat. There was room enough for two, but it would be a snug fit. Thankfully, there were handlebars along the back of the seat, so at least she'd have something besides Jack Townsend to hold onto. Jack Townsend, who a half-hour before had had his arms wrapped around her more firmly than she'd ever been held by anyone in her life.

Behind her, the sound of approaching snowmobiles was louder than ever. They were getting closer, whoever they were.

"Lou," Jack said impatiently. "Come on."

Well, what choice did she have? Get on the back of a snowmobile with Jack Townsend, or risk getting a bullet in the head.

She was probably, she mused, the only woman in America who'd hesitate over a decision like this.

But she didn't hesitate for long. That's because a bullet went winging past her, missing her shoulder by inches before plummeting into the snow a few yards away.

Like something propelled from a rocket launcher, Lou leaped onto the seat behind Jack, forgetting all about the handlebars on the back of the snowmobile. Instead, she twined her arms around the closest thing available—Jack—and screamed, "Go! Go!" at the top of her lungs.

Jack didn't seem to need any further urging. A second later, they were tearing down the mountainside, the wind ripping at their hair and cheeks, and bullets flying over their heads.

13

Thanks to Lou Calabrese's dislike for him, Jack had found himself in all sorts of situations while portraying the hapless Detective Pete Logan. There was the time in *Copkiller II* when he had been forced to wrestle a giant python in a mudpit in Belize. It had been a real python, too. A friendly one. His trainers called him Skippy.

Still, friendly or not, after several takes with Skippy, Jack had developed a profound dislike for snakes. He could not even see them on television anymore without hastily reaching for the remote control.

Then there'd been that time in *Copkiller III* when he had been forced to dive into freezing cold, choppy ocean water while having whaling harpoons launched at him. They hadn't been real whaling harpoons, of course. And the harpoons hadn't been what bothered him, really. It had been the temperature of the water, coupled with his state of undress—Pete had, as usual, managed to lose his pants—that Jack had found dismaying.

Lou had argued that the scene was necessary to his character's ultimate epiphany in the third act. The direc-

tor had believed her, of course. Jack had gamely leaped
into the water for take after take. The film had ended up
making a hundred mil its first week out.

Then had come *Copkiller IV. Copkiller IV*, where Logan
had to fling himself—stark naked, of course—into a
snowdrift. Otherwise, Lou insisted, the thematic arc made
no sense.

And Tim Lord believed her.

But not even Academy Award–winning screenwriter
Lou Calabrese, Jack was convinced, could have cooked up
something like the situation in which he currently found
himself, barreling down a mountainside on a Ski-Doo
with no idea where he was going, and bullets flying at his
head.

He did have one thing to be thankful for, however: At
least this time he had his clothes on.

His instinct, of course, had been to go up. Up was the
direction in which the wreck of the R-44 lay. They had
stumbled downhill in order to get away from that first
wave of pursuers.

It had been after eight by his watch when Lou had wakened him so roughly, though you wouldn't have known it
by the position of the sun in the sky, since all there had
been overhead was a sort of grayish haze. Surely by now
search and rescue teams would have located the wreckage,
and would be combing it in droves, looking for some hint
as to where Jack and Lou had disappeared to.

But evidently Ski Mask's cronies had realized this, since
they'd fanned out and, using some very convincing gun-
fire, had encouraged Jack to go down, towards who knows
what, instead of up, towards safety and potential rescue.

If he got out of this alive, was all Jack could think—as
he dodged trees and the occasional boulder, tears streaming down the sides of his face thanks to the cold, his ears
so numb with the chill that he thought they might fall

off—he was never doing another movie again. That was it. It was over. He was retiring. The cinematic career of Jack Townsend was at an end.

It had been a good career, overall, he thought. He'd enjoyed his stint as Dr. Rourke on *"STAT."* And the *Copkiller* series had given him both fiscal solvency and ample opportunity to exercise his skills as an actor. Lou might have written the scene in which his character had been strung up and beaten with bamboo poles out of some perverse attempt to humiliate him for the whole *I need a bigger gun* thing, but the scene had enabled Jack to show that he was capable of a wide range of human emotion, which had led to his landing roles in less well known but more critically acclaimed films.

And *Hamlet* had been funded entirely with *Copkiller* revenue. Jack had enough saved to start his own production company if he decided not to leave the business entirely. He could be like an American Kenneth Branagh, making movies of the lesser-known Shakespeare plays. Maybe even some Ibsen or Shaw. They'd be shown only in art houses in urban areas, but that was fine with him. It would give him more time to spend on the ranch. . . .

Yes, he'd had a fine career. He had certainly accomplished more than his father, exasperated by his only child's seeming inability to stick to any one thing, had ever expected.

Although Jack highly doubted his father would be very impressed if he could see him now, fleeing deadly assassins on the back of a Ski-Doo . . . a scene that was not part of some Lou Calabrese script but was actually a reality.

Zigzagging through the trees at a velocity that no one should travel over such terrain, it occurred to Jack that they could just as easily be killed careening into something as they could from any one of the bullets flying in their direction. Somehow, however, he'd have preferred to die that way—by crashing—than as the result of being shot. He didn't know who these assholes thought they were, or why they were shooting at him, but he wasn't going to give them the satisfaction of getting what they wanted. Not if he could help it.

He hoped Lou felt the same. She had her arms wrapped so tightly around his waist that he could barely breathe.

She wasn't, however, cowering back there like any other woman of his acquaintance would have been. Instead, she was shouting what he could only assume were driving instructions into his ear.

Fortunately the Ski-Doo's engine was so loud that he couldn't hear a word she was saying.

He could see her pointing, however. Every once in a while she risked letting go of him to point in a direction which she seemed to think he should take. How she could possibly have any idea where they were going, being as unfamiliar with Alaska as he was, he couldn't imagine. But clearly, Lou Calabrese was a woman who didn't like feeling as if she weren't in control at all times. The look on her face when she'd realized he'd joined her on that cot in the night had been priceless. Well, what had she expected, anyway? That he was going to sleep on the floor?

Besides, there'd been plenty of room for two. He didn't know what she'd been so bent out of shape about—

"Look out!"

He heard her this time, loud and clear. In spite of the fact that Ski Mask had evidently not kept his snowmobile in tip-top condition, as the engine was as loud as a jet's, he could still hear Lou.

What he could not do was see what it was that she was pointing at. At least until they'd hit it—a rocky outcropping, half-hidden beneath the deep snow—and gone sailing through the air.

"Oh my God," he heard Lou say, very distinctly—probably because her face was so close to his ear, "if you end up getting us killed, Townsend, you are going to be so—"

The Ski-Doo landed, with a jaw-snapping thump that he felt all up and down his spine. It was all Jack could do to maintain control of the vehicle as it skidded through a drift, kicking up plumes of snow eight feet into the air.

Still, he didn't miss it when Lou finished her sentence: "—sorry!"

He could hardly see now, his eyes were watering so badly from the cold. He knew he should have grabbed the snow goggles he'd seen hanging around Ski Mask's neck. But he hadn't wanted to touch Ski Mask, let alone any of his gear.

Still, he could make out the shapes of the trees as they barreled towards them. And there was Lou, who was sheltered from the wind by his body, shouting instructions at him at the top of her lungs: "Left!" Then, "Right!" Then, "Townsend, what are you doing? Left, left!"

He couldn't tell anymore if there were still bullets whizzing past them. On the whole, he thought not. It would be hard to operate a Ski-Doo at the velocity at which they were traveling, and fire a gun at the same time.

They were still in pursuit, however. He could see them out of the corners of his eyes, yellow and red blurs. The sight of them caused his blood to boil. Just what had he done to deserve this? He hadn't lied to Lou when he'd told her he didn't do drugs or gamble. Hell, his off-screen life was downright boring. He gave to the Make-a-Wish Foundation and Fresh Air Fund. He'd donated enough money to St. Jude's Children's Hospital that there was a wing named after him. He even rescued abused or abandoned horses and let them live out their days in equine luxury on his ranch.

So who the hell wanted him dead?

With his peripheral vision, he saw that two of the snowmobiles behind him—there were four in all—were gaining. Soon they'd be within a few feet of the Ski-Doo. Easy firing distance.

Ahead of him was a wide open area, strangely treeless. He didn't see why. Not right away, anyway. All he thought was that it was possible that, by pushing the snowmobile to the limit, then jerking it into a sudden turn and making for the woods to his left, he could lose his pursuers.

He would probably, however, also lose Lou, who was currently shouting something hoarsely in his ear. He had no idea what. Was she aware of the fact that, if the gunmen behind them did get close enough to fire, she'd take a bullet first? Her body would, in fact, shield him, for a while, from the rain of bullets.

He didn't think she was aware of it. All she was concentrating on was his steering, which, like most backseat drivers, she apparently found execrable.

He couldn't allow her to die. Lou Calabrese had, for years, been far from one of his favorite people.

But life without her would definitely lose a certain flavor. There weren't many women who categorically despised him. Certainly none, except for Lou, to whom he was attracted. Why he should be so drawn to her when she'd made her own, very different feelings for him so clear, he could not imagine. Maybe *because* she seemed to dislike him so much?

In any case, he couldn't let her die, either by flying off the back of the Ski-Doo because of an evasive maneuver he pulled, or because of any bullets that might be fired in his direction. It was, he saw, a no-win situation. Either she was going to die, or they both were.

And then he saw it. A gorge. That was why there were no trees ahead of him. Because they were careening towards a six-foot rip in the earth, at the bottom of which was probably a stream, picturesque in summertime, frozen solid now. There was no bridge, not this far in the wilderness. It was, without question, the end of the road.

He could turn, of course. Turn right into firing range. Or he could keep going straight. Either way, he realized now, was certain death.

He accelerated, heading straight for the gorge.

"Townsend!" Lou shrieked. She'd seen it now, what they were headed for. And she didn't like it very much.

"What are you doing? Are you insane? Turn! Turn!"

Jack kept his fingers gripped on the accelerator, and his gaze on the gorge.

"You ever see *Smokey and the Bandit*?" he called to her, over his shoulder.

"I thought," she screamed back, "you don't like *movies*—"

The word *movies* ended on a shriek so loud, he imagined it could have been heard all the way down in Anchorage. It certainly echoed through his head, the whole time they were sailing, suddenly weightless, through the air, over the snowbank that had formed to one side of the ravine, and across the chasm. He had a startling glimpse, as he looked down, of cascading rapids far, far below. The current would have to have been pretty strong not to have frozen over in this weather. He had time to wonder if, when they plummeted down into the water, they'd be dashed across the rocks, or simply be plucked up by that current and drowned. . . .

And then the front runners of the Ski-Doo were connecting with the bank on the opposite side of the gorge, while the back of it, its rotor still spinning, began to sink. . . .

"Jump!" Jack shouted, grasping Lou's arms, which were still wrapped around him, and hurling his body with all his might to the left.

She fell with him, and the two of them landed in the snow on the far side of the ravine, while the Ski-Doo, behind them, tottered, then dropped a hundred feet to the rapids below.

Across the gorge, their pursuers were not so lucky. Instead of accelerating, as Jack had, they threw on the brakes—one of them, on a red Arctic Cat, not soon enough. He went plunging headlong, snowmobile and all, into the chasm.

Jack didn't hang around to see what happened to the others. Scrambling to his feet, and pulling Lou up along with him, he yelled, "Run!" Then, keeping a grip on her arm, began tearing towards the trees.

He expected to feel the sting of bullets in his back at any time. He ran all out, the frigid arctic air piercing his lungs. Beside him, Lou kept up, the color in her cheeks high, her breath coming out in puffs of white. Jack tried to remember to zigzag—a target that wasn't moving in a straight line was harder to hit, one of the cops he'd had a ride along with all those years ago, when he'd been researching the character of Pete Logan, had informed him. He pulled Lou along with him. She came, unprotesting, the laptop around her shoulders banging heavily against her hip.

He didn't know how long they'd run before he realized no one was firing at them. He started slowing down, realizing that they were in woods deep enough that no snowmobile could follow . . . even if their hunters could figure out a way to cross that gorge.

Lou, however, her pupils so dilated that her eyes looked completely black, kept tugging on him.

"Come on," she said. "Jack, come on. They're still back there. Come on, Jack."

"No." Jack stopped and, leaning against a tree and panting heavily, looked back. "No, they're not, Lou. Look. They're still across the gorge. We lost them. For now."

Lou, her face white as the snow around them, except for the twin spots of red on her smooth cheeks, looked. Her breath, like his own, was coming out in ragged gasps.

"Oh my God," was all she could say. "Oh my God, Jack."

Her eyes, he noticed, were so large that they seemed to consume the rest of her face. Her breath wasn't coming out in gasps either, he now realized. She was sobbing. Tearlessly, but still sobbing. He'd never seen anyone look so terrified.

"It's okay," he said, reaching out to wrap an arm around her neck, and dragging her towards him. "Hey. It's okay."

For a minute, it was like she was someone else. The cocky, contemptuous Lou Calabrese he was so used to disappeared, replaced by this stranger with dewy eyes and trembling lips. Lou reached up to cling to his jacket, burying her face in his chest, suddenly as soft and vulnerable as a kitten. He felt her warm breath against his neck, felt her breasts, firm and round and vital, against his chest. Amazingly, a twinge of desire shot through him.

It was incredible. He could be stranded in the arctic, hundreds of miles from nowhere, with no clue as to whether or not he was going to survive the next hour, let alone the rest of the day, but his body still reacted to the touch of a pretty woman . . . even a woman like Lou Calabrese, who had tried, for so long, to make his life as unpleasant as she could. *Especially* a woman like Lou Calabrese, who could be prickly as a cactus when she wanted to, but who was also, he was now discovering, capable of being as tender as a lamb. . . .

It was just as he was wondering if he ought to make a move—it wouldn't really be taking advantage of her momentary weakness, he thought, to tilt her chin up and kiss those lips that for once were still, and so beckoningly red and moistly parted—that Lou suddenly tensed, stepped out of his embrace, and hauled back and slugged him, hard, in the upper arm.

"Ow!" he cried, not so much from the pain the blow had caused—which was not inconsiderable—but because it had caught him so off guard. "What is your problem?"

"What is my problem?" Lou cried hoarsely. Her pupils, he saw, had retracted to their normal size. She was no longer scared. Quite the opposite. She was mad as hell. "What is *my* problem? What is *your* problem? Who the hell did you think you were back there, anyway, Evel Knievel?"

Jack rubbed his arm where she'd punched it, indignant and more than a little ashamed that he had felt even a little attraction for her.

"I got us out of there, didn't I?" he demanded. "You might be surprised to hear this, but those were real bullets they were firing at us, not blanks, you know."

"Firing at us?" she echoed. "Firing at you, you mean. I'm not the one who—"

"Who what?" he interrupted, hotly.

"Who did whatever you did to get somebody mad enough to want to kill you," she finished.

Jack closed his eyes, praying for strength.

"For the last time," he said, as slowly and evenly as he could, "I didn't do anything to get anybody mad enough to kill me."

"Oh, yeah? Then who is that back there?" Lou asked. "The Myra, Alaska Gun Club? What is this, a Pauly Shore flick?"

Jack took a deep breath. "Look," he said. "I told you. I don't know why these guys are after me. All I can do is suggest that we get the hell out of here before they figure out a way to get across that gorge and come after us. Does that sound all right to you?"

She glared at him. "And just where," she asked acidly, "do you suggest we go? In case you haven't noticed, we're lost."

He looked around. They were standing in a wooded area, noiseless except for the sound of the wind moving between the dry, brittle branches overhead. He could see nothing in all four directions but snow, trees, and rock.

It was easy enough to choose a direction. He pointed downhill and said, "That way."

Lou looked unimpressed.

"That's the direction they want us to go," she said. "They were practically herding us that way."

"Precisely why we should keep heading that way," he said. "They'll be expecting us to go up, back towards Myra and the crash site. With any luck, that's where they're heading, looking for us. Only we'll outsmart'em. We'll head down, back towards Anchorage."

She didn't look pleased.

"I don't know, Townsend," she said, skeptically.

He gave her his most charming smile, the one that, the first time he'd used it on "*STAT*," had generated more fan mail than any other single episode.

"Trust me," he said.

She looked at him like he was out of his mind.

But when he started down the mountainside, trying to ignore the snow that crept up the legs of his jeans with each step, then trickled down into his boots, she followed him.

It wasn't much, he knew. But it was a start.

14

Flowers covered every flat surface of the hotel suite. Frank hadn't seen so many flowers—lilies, white roses, bunches of flowers he didn't even recognize—since Helen's memorial service, ten years earlier. The concierge—that was what the guy who'd met them in the lobby and brought them here, to Tim Lord's suite, had said his title was—said that so many floral arrangements were pouring in that they'd been forced to start putting them in the hotel conference and banquet rooms. The entire world, he'd said, was in mourning for Jack Townsend.

And Ms. Calabrese, too, of course, he'd added with a quick glance at Frank. Frank hadn't minded, though. Lou had explained to him long ago that on the Hollywood food chain, movie stars like Jack Townsend—and now, thanks to *Hindenburg,* that wimp Barry Kimmel—were filet mignon, while screenwriters, like Lou, were considered potatoes. Not even fries, either. Baked potatoes. Or sometimes even Rice-A-Roni.

The flowers in the hotel suite had a funereal look about

them. Or maybe it was just because it was so quiet in the elegant white room. Tim Lord supposedly had kids—a half-dozen of them, from various different marriages. But none of them seemed to be around now. The suite was as silent as a mortuary. The floral arrangements didn't help. One was even shaped like a wreath. Across the wreath was a white silk banner. On the banner, in gold letters, were the words, "With Our Deepest Sympathy."

Eleanor Townsend, who, instead of going to sit down on the white couch, as the man who'd met them in the hotel lobby had suggested, was looking at all the cards that had come with the flowers. Slender and elegant in her dark suit—now covered in pale gold hair, courtesy of Alessandro, who sat alertly in her arms—she bent to examine the card belonging to the wreath.

"From the movie studio," she said to him with some disgust. "You would think they'd wait until we actually knew for sure they were gone before extending their deepest sympathies."

Frank looked into the cup of coffee that sat, steaming, on the glass-topped table in front of him. He hadn't touched it yet, but it smelled like good coffee.

"Tough call," he said. "What else were they gonna put on it? *Good Luck?*"

Eleanor shook her head. "They oughtn't to have sent anything at all if they couldn't send something with an uplifting message."

Frank, as he had so often in the past twelve hours, found himself agreeing with Eleanor Townsend. It was amazing how frequently this seemed to be happening. It was ridiculous, because of course the two of them had absolutely nothing in common.

Look at that dog of hers, for instance. Frank had never been able to stand little yapping dogs. The Calabrese family had always had big dogs, German shepherds and labs. Frank had never had any patience for the more exotic breeds, like Yorkies and shih-tzus.

But even he had to admit there was something appealing about Alessandro. There was intelligence in those black beady eyes, and a sort of foxlike cunning in that furry little face.

And Alessandro wasn't the only thing Frank liked about Eleanor Townsend. No, that lady had a lot more going for her than just a smart and friendly dog.

Then the door to the hotel suite burst open, and Tim Lord—Frank recognized him from the Oscars. Lou had taken her good old dad to the ceremony. He'd gotten to meet Paul Newman. Helen would have loved it—came in, followed by another, much taller fellow in a suit and tie, and carrying a briefcase.

"Frank!" Tim Lord cried when he saw him, his eyes looking unnaturally bright. Unshed tears? Or too much blow? It was impossible to tell with these movie business types. "And Mrs. Townsend, what a pleasure to meet you at last. How I wish it could be under better circumstances—"

Tim Lord darted forward and grasped Eleanor's hand in his. The guy was, Frank noted, only an inch or so taller than she was, and Eleanor Townsend was not a large woman.

"I'm so sorry I wasn't there to meet you in the lobby," Lord was saying. "But the press . . . well, I'm sure you saw them. They're like vultures, they really are. Disgusting creatures. I've been trying to give them as wide a berth as possible since . . . well, since the tragedy."

Frank Calabrese didn't know much about Hollywood, it was true, beyond what his daughter had told him. And she, he was pretty sure, painted a prettier picture of it than she should have, so as not to worry dear old dad.

But Frank hadn't spent forty years on the force without learning a thing or two. And one thing he'd learned was to detect bullshit.

And when Tim Lord approached them, Frank Calabrese's bullshit detector swung into full alert.

"Not quite a tragedy yet, Mr. Lord," Eleanor said in that voice of hers, that voice that reminded Frank of those old movie actresses Helen had liked, that Kate Hepburn, and the other one, the one that had married a prince. "After all, no bodies have been recovered, have they?"

Tim Lord didn't say anything. Instead, he just looked troubled. The taller man in the suit, however, set his brief-case down on the coffee table and said, "No, they haven't. And Mr. Lord and I are praying, like the rest of the world, that both Mr. Townsend and Ms. Calabrese are alive and well. In the meantime, however, there are a few things we need to discuss—"

Up went the lid to the briefcase. Frank, gazing in disbelief at the guy in the suit, found himself curling a lip. A lawyer. Tim Lord had brought a lawyer along with him. Unbelievable. Their kids were out there somewhere, and all the studio could worry about was covering its ass. . . .

Then the door to the hotel suite swung open again. This time there was some sort of outburst from the other side, as if there'd been someone standing guard by the door—someone who did not want the person who was entering to do so.

But since the person striding towards them was a county sheriff in full uniform, Frank had a pretty good idea whoever it was trying to keep people out hadn't stood much of a chance.

"Um, excuse me," the lawyer said, looking alarmed. "May I help you?"

The sheriff was a tall guy, going gray beneath his fur-lined hat. He was followed by a much younger deputy, who had what looked like a painful case of windburn all over his face. The sheriff's gray-eyed gaze went from Tim Lord to the lawyer, then to Frank and Eleanor Townsend. It stayed on Eleanor Townsend. And a hand went up to hastily remove the fur-lined hat.

"Mrs. Townsend, ma'am?" the sheriff asked politely. Behind him, his deputy also removed his hat.

Eleanor, looking alarmed, seemed to squeeze Alessandro too tightly, if the sound that came out of the little dog was any indication.

"Yes," she said. "I'm Eleanor Townsend."

"And Mr. Calabrese?" The sheriff shifted his gaze towards Frank, who, despite what he felt sure was coming, had to hand it to the guy. He'd wanted to give them the news himself, rather than foisting off what was always an unpleasant duty to the departmental chaplain. Frank had to respect the guy for that.

"I'm Franklin Calabrese," he said, and was surprised that his voice did not sound like his own. It sounded like the voice of an old man, not the voice of Frank Calabrese. Sure, Frank might have been past his prime, but sixty-five wasn't really all that—

"Sheriff Walter O'Malley," the tall man said evenly. "I've just come from the crash site of the R-44 your daughter and your son, ma'am, were on yesterday morning. I thought I'd better be the one to inform you that it appears both Mr. Townsend and Ms. Calabrese survived the crash."

"*Survived?*"

A woman's voice rang out. But it wasn't Eleanor who'd spoken. The voice came from the opposite side of the room. Frank turned his head and saw a tiny woman, in a pair of gray silk pyjamas, her blond bob heavily mussed, standing in what appeared to be the doorway to an adjoining bedroom. On her impossibly pretty face was a look of complete and utter joy.

"Do you really mean it?" the woman asked, bounding forward on a pair of prettily pedicured bare feet, until she'd reached the sheriff's side, at which point she reached out and laid both hands upon his arm, hugging it to her. "They're alive?"

Walter O'Malley looked uncomfortable. He was evidently not a man used to having strange young women press their breasts up against his arm.

"Um," he said. "Well, ma'am, there was only one body in the wreckage, and that belonged to the pilot. We're combing the area, of course, looking for Mr. Townsend and Ms. Calabrese. It appears that they must have wandered away from the crash site, perhaps in search of shelter—"

"You've got to find them," Tim Lord said, firmly, coming up beside the young woman in the pyjamas, then putting his arm around her. "Don't let cost be an object, either. The studio is fully prepared to pay whatever it takes to get those two back here safely."

Walter O'Malley looked down at Tim Lord with some distaste on his face. So the sheriff, too, had a bullshit detector, Frank reflected.

"It's not cost that's interfering with the search," the sheriff said, successfully managing to extricate his arm from the blonde's grip. "Quite frankly, it's the weather. We've got planes in the air—the FAA is working on getting some more—but there's another storm front moving in. We can expect to get hit again with another blizzard tonight—"

"Oh, no." Eleanor Townsend, who had stepped away from the table with the floral arrangements on it, sank down onto the couch beside Frank as if her legs could no longer support her. She reached out blindly, as if for his hand. He closed his fingers around hers, as Alessandro anxiously lapped at her chin.

"If they managed to live through last night's storm," the sheriff said, "there's a good chance they'll live through this one, as well. It's expected to be only a little more severe—"

"Oh, God!" The blonde in the pajamas raised a hand to her face, as if she couldn't bear to hear more.

The sheriff glanced at her briefly, then turned his attention back to Frank.

"What Deputy Lippincott and I came here to find out," Sheriff O'Malley said, "was whether or not the two of you were aware of either your son, Mrs. Townsend, or your daughter, Mr. Calabrese, having any sort of wilderness survival skills."

Eleanor blinked at the sheriff blankly. "I beg your pardon. I don't know what you mean."

"Well, whether or not you'd think either of them would know what to do in a situation like this," Sheriff O'Malley said politely. "For instance, Mr. Townsend. Is he a hunter, at all? Maybe used to the outdoors?"

"He has a ranch," Eleanor said. "He keeps horses on it. But it's in Salinas. It doesn't snow in Salinas."

Sheriff O'Malley nodded. Frank could see he was disappointed.

"What about your daughter, Mr. Calabrese?" the sheriff asked. "Has she had any sort of experience at all in the arctic that you think might help her know what to do in a situation . . . well, like this one? I'm only asking, you see, because it might give us some clue as to where to start looking. There's a lot of space out there for our planes to cover, and if you think your daughter might know, for instance, how to find her way without a compass. . . ."

Frank carefully considered what the sheriff was saying. Lou, as far as he knew, had never been camping in her life.

She had never been a very outdoorsy girl. As a kid, she'd spent most of her time curled up with a book. Or in front of the television. It had been hard, in fact, to drag her from the screen, she loved it so much.

Helen hadn't helped discourage this sort of behavior, either. In fact, while Frank would never have accused her to her face, it was partly Helen's fault that Lou had had that little weight problem growing up. Instead of encouraging the girl to go outside and ride a bike, she had let Lou watch all the TV she wanted, because, as Helen used to say, "She loves it so. And who is it hurting? Her grades are good."

Lou's grades were always good, even in the days before they'd been able to afford a VCR, when Helen had routinely called Lou's school and informed them that she was sick in bed, when really, Helen had just wanted to make sure Lou didn't miss the channel eleven afternoon movie, if it was one she particularly thought their daughter would enjoy—generally anything starring Jimmy Stewart, or that actress with the skinny neck, Audrey something.

Thank God by the time Lou turned twelve Frank had finally been able to afford a VCR, or the girl might never have graduated from high school.

It was as he was thinking this that it hit Frank. No, Lou had never been a very outdoorsy girl. She disliked camping, and would hike only through the mall.

But she had seen every movie ever made. Of that, he was certain.

And so he said, "Movies," and looked expectantly at the sheriff.

Who seemed, unlike everyone else in the room, to understand him.

"She's seen a lot of survival movies?" O'Malley asked.

"Every damned one," Frank said. Then added, with a glance at Eleanor, "Sorry."

But Eleanor seemed untroubled by his slip. "Movies," she said, thoughtfully. "I wonder. . . ."

But Frank didn't. Wonder, that is. Because he knew. If there was a movie about surviving in the arctic, Lou had seen it. The only question, of course, was would that be enough?

15

"Jesus, Lou," Jack called over one of those impossibly broad shoulders—those shoulders that Lou would have liked to hurl darts at, if she'd happened to have any handy. "Come *on*."

Lou pushed a long, stray lock of red hair from her eyes and pried her foot from the drift into which it had sunk. Even though she had stopped a long time ago and tucked her pant legs into the tops of her knee-high boots, snow still seemed to get down them, trickling slowly to her frozen toes.

"*Come on, Lou*," she muttered to herself. "*Hurry up, Lou.* Easy for you to say. You try walking through four feet of snow in two-inch heels and see how fast you go."

She took a cautious step forward. In some places, a layer of ice had hardened over the top of the snow, and she could occasionally walk across it without sinking into the deep white powder.

Not this time, however. Down, down, down went her foot, until she could not see it anymore, or any of her leg, for that matter, from the knee down. Damned stupid snow. There was a reason she'd moved to California, and it hadn't just been because Barry had insisted they move there in order for him to pursue his acting career. No, she'd been happy to move there, because it meant she'd never again have to wade through knee-deep—

"Snow." She looked up, blinking, at the gray sky. No. It wasn't possible. It simply couldn't be.

But it was. It was snowing. Again. The sky was filled with flakes, falling fast, and not looking likely to stop any time soon. Damn. Damn! As if things weren't bad enough—

"Lou," Jack called from where he stood twenty feet away. "Pick it up. I'm telling you, we have to make that rise before nightfall."

"Why?" Lou demanded crankily. "What the hell do you think we're going to find behind that rise? A damned Sheraton?"

"It's just a goal," Jack explained, sounding like a man who was coming close to the end of his rope. Well, if so, he'd put himself there. Lou certainly didn't have anything to do with the fact that they were stranded in the Yukon with armed killers after them. "Haven't you ever been on a run before? You pick landmarks and you say to yourself, I'll keep going until I reach that tree. And then when you reach the tree, you pick another one, and that one becomes your goal."

"I don't run outside," Lou said flatly. "I run until the end of Judge Judy, and that's it."

Jack didn't look very impressed. "You can't build up any kind of stamina on a treadmill."

"I've got plenty of stamina," Lou said. "And you can't trick me into thinking there's going to be anything that great beyond that rise. Except more of the same. Snow. Trees. More snow. And then, guess what? Oh, maybe some more trees and snow."

"What would you like me to do, Lou?" Jack wanted to know. "Lie to you? Tell you there's an In and Out Burger over the next hill?"

"It might be nice," Lou said. "It might inspire more confidence in your leadership abilities. Certainly I haven't seen anything too impressive so far."

Even through the now thickly falling snow, she could see his look of disbelief.

"What do you mean?" he asked. "I kept us from being shot, didn't I?"

"Yeah," she said, with a snort of disgust. "But how do I know we're not walking out of the frying pan and into the fire? You don't even know what *direction* we're going. You know, Tony Hopkins, in *The Edge*, made a compass out of a paper clip and a leaf. I haven't seen any brilliant innovations like that from you."

"Yeah, well, I don't have a paper clip on me," Jack said, the look of disbelief disappearing. "And if you see any leaves, you let me know. Because all I see are pine needles. And snow. Sorry, but I didn't play MacGyver, remember? It was that other guy. You need to be intubated, though, I'm your man."

"Ha," Lou said. "As if I'd ever let *you* put something down my throat."

Then, realizing belatedly how that sounded, Lou added hastily, "I think this new snowfall is getting serious. We ought to think about finding a place to hole up until it blows over. I saw this episode of 'Little House on the Prairie' where they built an igloo. Maybe we should—"

But Jack wasn't about to let her off that easily.

"You're blushing again," he pointed out.

"I am not," Lou said stiffly, not meeting his gaze. "I'm just cold, that's all."

"Why, I wonder, would the idea of me putting something down your—"

"It's just windburn!" Lou shouted. Because of the falling snow, her voice didn't carry very far. He heard her, however.

"Sure it is, Lou," Jack said.

She was close enough to him now that she could plainly see him through the thickly falling white stuff. To her very great consternation, he was smiling.

"That wasn't what I meant," she said exasperatedly. "Okay? When I said that about putting something down my throat, I was talking about an intubation tube—"

But Jack didn't seem to hear her. Instead all he said was, "What kind of name is that, anyway? Lou? Isn't that a guy's name?"

"It's a nickname," Lou said, stopping to shake snow from her boot top. "It's not my real name."

"Really?" Jack sounded incredibly interested. Though why he should be so, when he'd never expressed the slightest interest in her before now, she could not imagine. Unless it was because she was the only female within a hundred miles. Not counting moose. Or elk. Or moosettes, or whatever female moose were called. "What's your real name?"

Lou muttered it as she took her next step, but the sound of the snow breaking beneath her weight swallowed the word.

"I beg your pardon?" Jack said.

Yanking her foot from the drift, she said, through gritted teeth, "Louise."

"Louise?" He hooted. "Louise Calabrese?"

"Oh, that's very mature, Townsend," Lou said tartly. "Make fun of my name. Go right ahead."

He sobered at once. "Sorry," he said. Still, the smile crept back across his face. She could see it, even with the snow. "What were your parents thinking?"

"They weren't, all right?" Lou snapped. "Louise was my

mother's mother's name. And besides, you don't pronounce it Cala*breeze* if you're Italian, it's Cala*braizai*, and so—"

"Whoa," Jack said, holding out both gloved hands. "Easy there, pardner. You act like you're the only one who ever got her name made fun of in school."

Lou said, with some bitterness, "Oh, right. Like the name Jack Townsend is so full of teasing potential."

"It can be," Jack pointed out. "I went to an all boys' school, remember. And guys aren't particularly inventive. All they did was add an *off* after the Jack. . . ."

Lou had to think about it for a second. Then she went, "Oh," and realized she was blushing harder than ever.

Fortunately this time Jack did not appear to notice. That's because at the same time she started blushing again, she put her foot down into another particularly deep drift of snow, sank in all the way to her mid-thigh, and nearly stumbled.

She would have landed right on her face if Jack hadn't reached out and caught her by the shoulder.

"All right," he growled, when he'd got her perpendicular to the earth once more. "That's it. The laptop's gotta go."

Lou looked at him like he was demented—no easy feat with snowflakes sticking to your lashes.

"Wh-what?" she said. "What are you talking about?"

"You've hauled this thing around long enough," Jack said, reaching for her computer bag. "It's no wonder you can't keep up, it weighs a ton. Come on." He tugged on it. "Say buh-bye to the laptop."

Lou laid both hands on the bag's shoulder strap and started backing away from him. "Are you crazy? This is a two-thousand-dollar computer. I'm not leaving it in the middle of the woods."

"So you'll buy a new one when we get back to civilization," Jack said, not releasing the bag, and following her, step for step. "You can't tell me you're hurting for cash, Lou, I read in *Variety* that you got seven figures for *Copkiller IV*. So hand it over. It's making you top heavy and slowing you down. It's gotta go."

"No way," Lou said, still moving backwards. "You don't understand. I have stuff on here. Stuff I don't want to lose, okay?"

Jack stopped moving. He just looked at her like she was nuts.

"You don't back your *stuff* up?"

"Of course I do," Lou said, taking another step backwards. Only he didn't move with her, so she stood there with the bag's straps stretched out between them. "There's just this one new thing I put on it the other night that I don't have on disk, all right? And I'm not going to lose it. It's very important to—"

"Lou." Jack, even with two days' growth of beard on his face—maybe especially with two days' growth of beard on his face—looked impossibly handsome. "We're talking survival here. Do you understand? The laptop's just making it harder for you to get through the snow. Leave it here. We'll come back for it—"

"Oh, right," Lou interrupted with a humorless laugh. "And how are we going to find it? Computer-sniffing dogs?"

"I mean it, Lou," he said, giving the bag a tug. "Let it go. It's not worth it. We could die out here. Some stupid screenplay tends to pale in comparison to death by hypothermia . . ."

"It's not a stupid screenplay," Lou said, yanking on the bag's handle. "All right? And it isn't too heavy for me. My boots are what's slowing me down, okay? Not the computer. Now let *go*—"

On the word *go*, Lou tugged with all her might—not

realizing until it was too late that Jack had got hold of the bag's zipper. In one neat motion, he'd unzipped the bag all the way around. Then it was just a matter of tearing the computer from its Velcroed safety harness, and, magically, he had the laptop, while all she was holding was the empty bag.

Stunned, Lou stammered, "D-don't you even *think* about it—"

But it was too late. He'd thrown it, as hard as he could, in the direction of the rise he'd kept going on about.

Then he brushed his gloved hands together, as if to say *That takes care of that.*

"There," he said. "Now get rid of that bag, and let's go. We should make a lot better time now. You won't have half so much trouble getting through the really deep stuff. . . ."

His voice trailed off, possibly because he'd gotten a good look at Lou's face. It had, she was sure, gone as white as the snow around them. She could not remember ever feeling quite so angry—except maybe the day that Barry had announced that he hadn't felt quite ready, after ten years, to commit.

She reacted now the way she'd reacted then. With white-hot, uncontrollable rage.

"*You!*" she shrieked, launching herself at Jack Townsend.

Jack looked startled. He took a quick step away from her—well, as quickly as the deep snow would allow, anyway. And then another.

"Now, Lou," he said. "Look. Be reasonable. That thing weighed a ton. It's of no use to us out here, and it's just holding you back. We've got to—"

But he didn't get out anything else, except for an *oof* as Lou sank her shoulder into his midsection, bringing him down to the snow as neatly as her brothers, who had

thought tackling an important part of any girl's educa-
tion, had taught her. Once she had him down, she swung
a leg over his waist and sat on him, then pinned his shoulders back with her hands, just like Nick had showed her.

"Are you out of your mind?" she shrieked down at him,
her face just inches from him. "That computer was the
only thing keeping me sane, do you understand? I'm
scared . . . and I'm hungry . . . and I'm freezing . . . and I
can't feel my toes . . . and I'm stuck in *Alaska*, in a *snowstorm*, with *you*! *And it's all your fault*! So you had better
go find that computer and it had better still be in one
piece, because if it isn't, *I'll shoot you myself*!"

Jack, regarding her from the snow with an expression
on his face that could only be called bemused, said, "You
know something? You're kind of cute when you're mad."

For a heartbeat or two, Lou just stared down at him,
not certain she'd heard him right. Then she made her first
mistake. She let go of his shoulders. She let go of his
shoulders so her hands would be free to wrap around his
stupid, egocentric, overprivileged neck—

It wasn't easy, however, to choke someone who was
laughing as hard as Jack Townsend happened to be. Especially since as soon as she got her fingers in the vicinity of
his neck, he grabbed hold of both her wrists and neatly
flipped her right off him, into the snow beside him.

And the next thing Lou knew, he was on top of her, exactly the way she'd been on top of him a few seconds before. Only instead of pinning her shoulders, he was
pinning her wrists, so that she could not, as she would
have liked to do, jab her thumbs in his eyeballs. Instead,
her entire field of vision was taken up with his big, stupid,
handsome, laughing face.

And there was nothing she could do about it.

"*Let me up*," she grunted. It was *really* uncomfortable,
lying like that. Snow was going down the collar of her coat,

under her sweater, and down her neck. She hoped plenty had spilled down his. "Did you hear me? Let me *up*."

"Now, I'd have to be pretty stupid to do that, wouldn't I?" Jack said, with a laugh. His teeth were even and white and one hundred percent his, every last one of them. Lou had found that out courtesy of her dentist back in LA, who also happened to have filled Jack's last cavity. "I mean, you said you were going to shoot me."

"Jack," Lou said, suddenly becoming conscious of the fact that his eyes, so pale blue they were almost gray, were rimmed in a darker shade that was almost black. "Look. Let me up and help me find the computer, and we'll call it even. For now."

The tanned skin around those incredibly blue eyes crinkled as he considered this offer.

"No," he said, after a few seconds. "Sorry. Not good enough. I mean, after all, you looked pretty homicidal there for a minute or two. I'm not convinced that if I turn my back on you, you're not going to drive an icicle through my skull—"

"Jack," Lou said. The heat from his body was actually making her feel, for the first time all day, warm. It was a pleasant feeling. Too pleasant. Alarmingly pleasant. It had been weeks—months, even—since she'd last felt a man's body this close to her . . . not counting what had happened this morning, that is. But she was pretty sure Jack hadn't been aware of what he'd been doing then.

He knew now. Oh, he certainly knew now.

"Snow is going down my back," Lou said. "Okay? So let me up."

"I don't know," Jack said, pursing his lips thoughtfully. Unfortunately, this action only caused Lou's gaze to be dragged towards his mouth. That laughing, insolent, sarcastic mouth. Which she did not want anywhere near hers. No, thank you. "Things have suddenly gotten kind of interesting. I can't help asking myself what Detective Pete Logan would do in a situation like this."

Lou, starting to feel a little breathless—though not because his body weight was making inhalation difficult, since it was only her hips he was straddling—said, in a warning voice, "Townsend. I'm serious. Let me up."

"If this were a *Copkiller* script," Jack went on, as if she hadn't spoken, "by none other than the Academy Award–winning Lou Calabrese, Pete Logan would undoubtedly find himself out here in the twenty-degree cold without any pants on. Now, why is that? Can you tell me, Lou?"

"I am giving the people what they want," Lou said, keeping her gaze on the sky, instead of his hypnotically blue eyes.

"Are you?" Jack asked. "Or are you just trying to punish me, script after script, for the *I need a bigger gun* thing?"

"Of course not," Lou said. "I happen to be a professional. I do not let my personal feelings get in the way of my work. I'm sorry to disappoint you, Townsend, but the reason Pete Logan keeps ending up in his birthday suit is because the American viewing public enjoys looking at your ass."

"The American viewing public," Jack said, one of those dark eyebrows rising, "or Lou Calabrese?"

"Don't flatter yourself." But even as she said it, she could feel her face turning crimson. Suddenly the snow on her neck did not feel half so cold as it had. In fact, it almost felt refreshing. "My God, Townsend. This may come as a shock to you, but contrary to what you apparently believe, there are some women who care more about what a guy's got in his head than in his pants."

"Oh, yeah?" Jack's face, she noticed, had gotten disturbingly close to hers. "Then why are you blushing again?"

"I'm not blushing," Lou said, blushing harder. "If my

face is red, it's because you are cutting off the circulation to my upper body."

"Oh, right," Jack said. "I mentioned that I think you're cute when you're mad, didn't I?"

"You said something along those lines," Lou said. "But—"

"Good," Jack said. "Then this shouldn't come as too much of a surprise."

And then that mouth—that laughing, infuriating, perfect mouth—came down over hers.

And Lou died and went to heaven.

16

She ought to have known, of course, that this is what it would be like. Kissing Jack Townsend. Or rather, being kissed by Jack Townsend. Because Lou was not the one doing the kissing. Oh, definitely not.

Except that it was sort of difficult, when one was being kissed as thoroughly and as expertly as Jack Townsend was kissing her, not to kiss back.

Which wasn't to say she liked being kissed by Jack Townsend. Well, in theory.

In practice, however . . . well, in practice was another matter entirely.

Because Jack Townsend kissed like he meant it. This was no polite peck, no Beverly Hills air kiss. This was full-on, open-mouthed oral exploration—tongue wrestling, as her brothers had called it whenever they'd caught her engaged in it with Barry.

But kissing Barry had never been like this. Barry had never, as Jack was doing, conducted such a leisurely investigation of the territory in and around her mouth. Barry had never made her feel, as Jack was somehow managing to, that kissing her was absolutely the only activity on his agenda that day, and that there was all the time in the world with which to accomplish it. Barry had never, with a mere kiss, made her feel as if her heart was going to explode within her chest from the sheer physical pleasure of it.

But that's exactly how Jack Townsend's kiss made her feel. She could feel him, his heat, his weight, his intensity, from her lips all the way down to the tips of her toes—which were, she noticed, in some dim recess of her brain, not so frozen after all, if they could curl in her boots the way they did at the first electric touch of his mouth to hers.

It was ridiculous, of course, that her body should react this way to his. She was no starstruck teenager, no sex-starved old maid. She was a sophisticated professional, a woman whose meteoric career—not to mention love life, until recently, anyway—was an inspiration to chubby red-headed girls everywhere. . . .

And a single kiss from America's sweetheart, Jack Townsend, had turned her into a puddle of quivering feminine Jell-O.

On ice.

This, Lou was able to think in a part of her mind that had not been reduced to a mere gelatinous mass of misfiring neurons by the searing intensity of his kiss, was completely impossible. She *hated* this man.

So how was it possible that he, merely by putting his mouth against hers, could make her feel this way . . . as if, for the first time in months, she was actually alive? Why did the weight of the length of his body on top of hers make her long to spread her legs—God help her—and wrap them around him? Why did the razor stubble on his face, scraping against her smooth—probably scarlet by now—cheeks, make her want to run her tongue all the way down his long, lean body?

It didn't make any sense. One second she'd been ready to belt him between the eyes. The next, he had her purring like a kitten.

It wasn't the magic of Hollywood, either. Oh, no. There were no visual effects involved. This was honest to God, old-fashioned chemistry.

Chemistry! Between her and Jack Townsend? Impossible!

Except that it wasn't. She knew it wasn't because of what was happening, she was very sorry to have to admit, between her legs.

Which was quite a lot, actually. Enough so that Lou, suddenly conscious of it—and of who was causing it: Jack Townsend. Jack Townsend, who'd broken the heart of her best friend. *Jack Townsend*, an *actor*. And she had forever sworn off actors—suddenly tensed and, ripping her wrists out from beneath his fingers, put her hands on his elbows and raised a knee until it rested against that famous ass.

Then, pulling on his elbows and pushing with her knee—a self-defense technique her father had taught her before she'd left for college, in case, he'd said, she happened to run into trouble at a frat house—she managed to send him flying over her head and crashing into the snow behind her.

The expletive that came out of Jack's mouth as he landed was one that would have earned him an NC-17 rating from any Hollywood censor.

Lou climbed to her feet and, brushing her hands together the way Jack had done, after he'd sent her computer airborne, said, in a voice that was surprisingly steady, considering the fact that her knees were still quivering from his kiss—not to mention what still seemed to be going on in the crotch of her panties—"If I don't find that computer in one piece, you'll wish those guys back there had shot you after all."

Then, striding through the snow—with difficulty, it had to be admitted, thanks to that traitorous dampness between her legs, though she was determined he would never, ever know about that—Lou headed towards the rise over which he'd heaved her laptop.

Lying in the snow, feeling as if his spine might be broken, Jack blinked up at the darkening sky and wondered what had just happened. Had he actually kissed Lou Calabrese? What had he been thinking? What could he possibly have hoped to accomplish?

Well, he knew what he'd accomplished, all right. He'd answered a question that had been bothering him for some time. . . .

Well, since the night before anyway.

And that question—which had occurred to him as she'd sat there on that cot, with all that glorious red hair slipping down her shoulders, and those dewy lips of hers seeming to beckon to him—had been *What would it be like to kiss Lou Calabrese?*

Well, he'd gotten his answer, all right:

Painful. That was what it was like to kiss Lou Calabrese.

But before the pain . . . ah, yes. Before the pain, there'd been pleasure. And a lot of it.

He couldn't imagine what had possessed him to actually act upon his desire. Of all the women in the world for him to find himself attracted to, he would have to have picked the one—certainly not the only one, but the only one he'd ever personally encountered—who hadn't the slightest interest in him that way. Or any way, he suspected. Lou Calabrese was as immune to his charms—and Jack knew he had a few—as the screenplays she penned seemed immune to flopping.

She hated him.

But maybe not quite completely. Because there'd been a moment there, when he'd been kissing her, that he could have sworn she'd been kissing back. He'd felt the tentative, almost experimental touch of her tongue to his. He'd felt her breasts, even through all their various layers of clothing, seem to swell against him, almost daring him, he'd felt, to touch them.

Oh, no. She'd liked being kissed by him. Maybe just for a minute or two. But she'd liked it.

Now if he could just get her to admit it. . . .

Not that he didn't have more pressing concerns at the moment. Granted, he was hungry and cold, and seemingly lost in America's largest state. It was snowing, and night was closing in, and if he kept on lying here, either the armed men who were after him or hypothermia would eventually get him.

Yet somehow, the most urgent of Jack's problems seemed to be the one that was pressing so insistently against the zipper of his fly.

Wasn't that always the way of it though? A guy could be starving in the middle of a blizzard, with assassins after him and a chance of survival that he'd be willing to place at about, oh, twenty percent, and all he was really concerned about was whether or not a girl liked him.

He ought to have known what kissing her would be like. It seemed like he'd known all along. It was like taking a live electric wire in his arms and wrapping his mouth around one end. That was how fully charged Lou Calabrese was, how filled with life and passion she was. If that's how she kissed a guy she didn't even like, he couldn't imagine what she'd be like if she actually had some iota of affection for him.

Barry Kimmel was a fool.

So, he realized, was he. Because she'd been right there, under his nose, for the past six years—*six years*—and what had he spent all that time doing? Arguing with her over line deliveries instead of attempting, as he ought to have been doing, to make her his. Vicky had never kissed him with half as much abandon as Lou had, and Vicky had professed to love him with all her soul! And Greta?

Holding Greta was like holding a dishrag, when he compared the experience to holding Lou.

It was amazing, he thought, as he slowly sat up, and discovered, to his surprise, that he'd apparently suffered no broken bones. But for the first time in a long time, he actually felt . . . well, alive. Hungry, yes. Cold, certainly. But alive. Thanks to Lou Calabrese. And not just because she'd proved to be so handy with a gun.

Limping a little—where had she learned a move like that? All the women he'd been with lately had had a distinct preference for Pilates over self-defense. Lou evidently wasn't the Pilates type—he followed her over the rise, noticing that the snow was starting to fall more thickly than ever. It would be dark soon. If they didn't get out of this wind and start a fire soon, they'd be polar bear bait.

Lou, he saw through the snow, was kneeling beside something at the bottom of the rise he'd tossed her computer over. She glanced over her shoulder at him as she heard the crunch of snow breaking beneath his weight.

"You're lucky," she informed him darkly as she dusted snow from her laptop. "It's still in one piece."

"Lou," he said, coming to a halt a few feet away from her. He had to raise his voice more than he liked to be heard above the roar of the wind, which had picked up, this side of the rise. "We have to talk."

He was not, by force of habit, a talker. That was one of the reasons, he'd often thought, that he spent so much time at his ranch. He wasn't called upon to say very much there—except of course when he made the mistake of bringing a female companion along. Women had this incessant need to discuss things, to talk about their feelings, rather than simply letting them happen. Jack had never been able to understand it.

But this was one of the few times Jack thought a conversation about feelings might just be necessary. Not that he was anywhere close to understanding his. Feelings, that is. Just that, well, something pretty powerful had happened back there, and he wasn't going to ignore it. He *couldn't*.

But Lou, apparently, could, since all she said was—being careful, he noted, not to meet his gaze—"There's nothing to talk about."

Jack, feeling the wind biting at his back, said, unable to keep the sarcasm from his voice, "Uh, I'm afraid I don't agree with you there, Lou. What just happened back there was—"

"What just happened back there was a big, colossal, stupid mistake," Lou said, crisply. She was looking up at him now, squinting against the wind. "Okay? It's over. There, you don't have to say it. I already did. Now, in the unlikely event that we ever get back to civilization and I plug this thing in and find out that I can't access any of my documents, I want you to know right now that I intend to hold you personally responsible for any loss of income such an occurrence might engender. You got it, Townsend?"

Jack, however, was barely listening. That's because while she'd been blathering away—the first woman he'd ever met who clearly did *not* enjoy talking about her feelings—he had spied something tucked against the trees a few hundred yards away. He couldn't be sure what it was, with the snow swirling all around him, and darkness falling so fast. But it appeared to be . . . it almost looked like . . .

"Townsend, are you listening to me?" Lou was zipping

her computer back into its padded case. "Look, we've got to get out of this wind. Maybe we should start gathering fallen branches for a lean-to, or something. Isn't that what they're called? That thing Tom Hanks built in *Cast Away*, you know, before he found the cave. At least it'll cut the wind. . . ."

Without taking his gaze from the thing in the trees, Jack reached down and took her by the arm. "I don't think we're going to need a lean-to," he said, pulling her up to her feet, then pointing. "Unless that turns out to be a mirage."

Lou looked in the direction he was pointing. Even with shadows under her eyes and snow in her hair, he noticed, she was breathtakingly beautiful. How he ever could have thought her a coldly calculating ice-bitch—which, he freely admitted, he'd once called her—he could no longer imagine.

Then she inhaled sharply.

"Oh, my God," she cried. "Is that a *house?*"

Jack dropped his arm. A sort of lethargy came over him. Was it wrong of him to feel that at last, they might be safe?

"So you see it, too," he said. "I wasn't sure whether or not I was imagining it. . . ."

"No, you're not imagining it. Come on."

Lou took his arm and began to drag him excitedly through the snow towards the wooden structure that seemed to have risen up, from the gloom, like a specter. It appeared to be, Jack realized, as they got closer, an A-frame, on the smallish side, but with large glass windows on either side of the front door affording those inside what was probably a spectacular view of the mountain-side behind them.

Considering the fact, however, that the snow was now blowing almost perpendicular to the ground, Jack couldn't imagine that most of the year, the owners of the house would be able to see much at all through those windows. He was unable to tell whether or not there was a road leading up to the house, or even any vehicles parked nearby it, and he was standing almost in front of it. It was all he could do just to keep his eyes open, they were being bombarded so heavily by surprisingly weighty snowflakes.

He could see, however, that the house had a distinctly deserted look to it. There were no lights on inside. And the snow that lay across the front porch was unbroken by footprints.

Not for long, however. Lou, letting go of him because he did not seem to be hurrying enough, bolted forward, her computer case banging against her hip. She pressed her face up against the first window she came to.

"Oh, Jack!" she wailed, cupping her gloved hands around her eyes as she peered inside the house. "Nobody's home! What are we going to do? Oh, my God, there's a kitchen, Jack. With a refrigerator. And is that . . . oh, my God. There's a bathroom. I see a shower curtain! A bathroom, Jack! A *bathroom*!"

Jack ambled up behind her, beginning to realize, now that enough time had passed since their embrace, that his toes, fingers, and ears were half-frozen. Still, he managed to wrap a hand around the doorknob and attempted to turn it. . . .

"What are you doing?" Lou stepped away from the window and stared at him. "Jack, what are you—we can't go in if no one's home. That's breaking and entering!"

The knob didn't budge. Locked. Undoubtedly, Jack thought, this was someone's summer getaway cottage. It would be abandoned, just like this, until spring, when the snow thawed and the roads once more became accessible.

He dropped his hand from the doorknob.

"If you think," he said, "that I am going to stand out

here and freeze when I could be inside there taking a long hot shower, you are going to need to think again. Stay here."

And he began to wade painfully through the snow towards the back of the house.

Lou called after him nervously, "Where are you going? What are you doing?"

But all he said was, "Stay there. I'll be back in a minute." Then he disappeared around the corner of the house.

That was the last she saw of him for nearly five whole minutes.

They were the longest five minutes of her life. The wind was so strong now that it seemed to slice right through her. Her ears, she decided, had to be frozen to her head. If she touched them, she feared they'd snap off. Why hadn't she thought to bring a hat? Sure, she'd have had to suffered the indignity of hat hair. But at least she wouldn't be losing eighty percent of her body heat through her head, like she was doing now.

And what was going on with her stomach? The saltines she'd downed for breakfast seemed like a distant dream. For once, she thought she'd be able to achieve that concave belly thing at the beach that other women seemed to be able to pull off so easily.

And what was with her eyes? They were watering so hard now, thanks to the wind that she could hardly see.

But she could still think. And what she thought wasn't about the fact that, if she stood out in the cold like this much longer, they were going to find her, like the Little Match Girl, frozen solid.

No, what she thought about was Jack Townsend. Jack Townsend, and the way he had kissed her, and made her feel, for the first time in a long time, like something desirable, something actually other than a walking word processor. She had seen an episode of "Star Trek" once in which Captain Kirk and his crew had come across a race of aliens so highly evolved that they no longer needed bodies. They were simply brains, floating around in a glass encasement.

That was how, since Barry had left, Lou had felt. As if she were a brain, unattached to a body.

And she hadn't minded very much, either. It was easier just to be a brain, to be unburdened by want and desire.

Astonishingly, it was Jack Townsend who had made her feel whole again, who had made her remember that there might actually be a purpose to her having a body other than needing one to house the brain that seemed to be in so much demand since it had spat out *Hindenburg*. He had, not to put too fine a point on it, made her body sing.

No wonder she'd freaked out the way she had. It was *Jack Townsend* who'd made her feel that way. Jack Townsend, who every woman in Hollywood—every woman in *America*, practically—was after. Lou had had enough of dating a celebrity. She was not about to make a habit of it.

But oh! How his kiss had made her feel!

Except that afterwards, he'd wanted to talk about it. As if analyzing just what in the hell had happened back there was going to make it fade from the recesses of her mind. Not very likely. She'd be thinking about that kiss on her deathbed, she was certain.

It was just like Jack to want to discuss it, however. He was always wanting to discuss his character's motivations. It made sense he'd want to talk to death his own, as well.

Well, she wasn't going to give him the satisfaction. Besides, that kiss was hers now. He couldn't take it away with reasoning and rational explanations. It had happened, and she was glad. Glad because it had proved she wasn't dead inside, as she'd been starting to suspect.

And glad because he'd gotten it out of the way. It wouldn't happen again. They'd tried it, it hadn't worked—she'd taken care of that with that back-flipping maneuver—and now they could go back to the way they'd been before: hating each other's guts with equanimity. It was done. It was *over*.

And then, to her surprise, a light came on inside the house. She didn't need to cup her hands over her eyes to see Jack through the plate glass window beside her, navigating the living room furniture. She stared, and was still staring when he unlocked the door and opened it to her.

"Oh, hi," he said with his best smile, the one he generally reserved for the press. "You're right on time. Won't you come in?"

Lou continued to stare. "B-but how? . . ." she stammered. "What . . . ?"

"Basement door wasn't locked," Jack explained, dropping the smile. "People generally don't lock the basement doors to their summer homes. I know we never did."

And then he was pulling her inside.

Lou just had time to think, *Oh, my God. I lied. It is so not over,* before he closed the door behind her.

17

It was a hunting cabin, not a summer house.

Lou was able to make this distinction almost at once by the number of weapons in the house—.30-.30s on the wall, along with numerous stuffed heads—and the plethora of frozen venison in the freezer. There was also a dearth of summer clothing in the single bedroom's closet. All she found were flannel shirts, long johns, jeans, and a stockpile of wool socks.

That fact, coupled with the apparent lack of a telephone, television, or radio—at least, their first frantic search had turned up none—caused Lou to deduce that she was the cabin's first female visitor. Its owner—whose name, they discovered, from a crumpled American Express bill they found in a drawer, was Donald R. Williams—was either single or married to a woman who was not fond enough of the great outdoors to accompany her husband on his hunting trips, as there was not so much as a nail file anywhere in the house.

From the looks of the fridge's contents—which had all expired a month earlier—Donald had not been to his cabin in weeks. Lou hoped he did not mind their appropriating it for the time being . . . though she could not say she cared very deeply what Donald thought. She was warm, and that's all that mattered. Warm and clean, thanks to the shower, which, after Jack had fiddled around in the basement, had proved to have a plentiful supply of hot water. Lou had not spent as long as she would have liked under that showerhead, conscious that she'd have to save *some* of the deliciously hot water, anyway, for Jack.

Still, the few precious moments she'd taken to wash and condition her hair—more proof it was a man-only habitat: the shampoo in the shower had been the kind with the built-in conditioner—were amongst the most glorious she could remember. . . .

Outside of that kiss Jack had given her, of course.

But she was determined not to think about that anymore. Emerging from the shower, delightfully scalded from her scalp to the soles of her feet, Lou put on one of the flannel shirts she'd stolen from the bedroom closet—nothing would induce her back into the clothes she'd had on for the past forty-eight hours straight—coupled with a pair of men's long johns, which, if they weren't exactly stylish, were at least warm and clean.

And since she was determined that whatever had happened out there between her and Jack had just been a fluke—and that if it had been anything more, needed to be discouraged immediately—she did not bother with makeup, but emerged from the bathroom in her borrowed clothes with a towel wrapped around her head.

"Hey," she said to Jack, who had just lit a fire in the living room's massive stone hearth. "Shower's yours."

"Thanks," he said, turning to look at her. . . .

. . . and dropping a lit match onto the wood floor.

"Jeez," Lou said, as he slapped out the resulting flame.

"It's bad enough that we broke into the guy's house. Do you have to burn it down, too?"

Jack's glance was sour. "Funny," he said. "Listen, I got two steaks defrosting in the microwave. If the timer goes off while I'm in the shower, and they seem like they're done, rub 'em with a little of that vegetable oil I found, then put 'em in that pan I've got sitting out, and start a flame under them. Got it?"

Lou blinked at him. She couldn't help it. He'd taken his coat off, and in the firelight, the lines of his body were perfectly evident beneath the cashmere of his sweater and form-fitting denim of his jeans.

Even unshowered, with two days' growth of beard on his chin, the guy looked good. What else could she say?

"You can cook?" was all she managed to get out, however, and even that sounded pitifully lame.

"Of course I can cook," Jack said, walking around the rattan couch towards the bathroom. "Can't you?"

"Um," Lou said, suddenly feeling as if the towel over her wet hair might have been overkill. "Sure. Sure, I can."

"Well, good," Jack said. "Throw those steaks on when they're ready."

Then he disappeared into the bathroom. Lou, though she was standing a good ten feet from the fire, felt as if she might expire from a sudden wave of heat that passed over her body. She reached up to unwind the towel from her hair, thinking her cold wet curls might soothe her suddenly feverish cheeks.

"Oh," Jack said, popping his head out from behind the bathroom door. "I found a bottle of wine in the basement. It's breathing on the counter. Pour out a couple glasses, will you? Unless," he added, with what she could only call mischievousness, "wine's gonna knock you out like that scotch did last night."

He closed the door on Lou's aggrieved expression, as she did not appreciate the reminder.

Alone in the living room, Lou draped the towel that had covered her hair over the back of one of the many chairs that were arranged around the big dining table just off the open kitchen. The cabin was basically made up of a single big room, what she supposed people were calling "great" rooms these days, though she highly doubted that's how the owner of this one referred to it. The furniture was comfortable and sturdy, but hardly the height of decorating chic. At least the kitchen was equipped with all the modern conveniences . . . with the exception of a phone.

Still, Lou was determined to make the best of her situation. At least she was warm and, for the moment anyway, safe. Outside, another blizzard was apparently upon them. She could hear the wind—she certainly hoped it was the wind, anyway—howling, and she could see the snow, reflected in the lamplight from the living room, coming down hard and fast against the black night sky.

But she was warm, and she was clean, and she was about to be fed—if it was true Jack could cook. What more could a girl ask?

Um, well. Some dignity might be good.

Lou was pretty much convinced that, after that display out there in the snow, she had none left. Dignity, that is. She had kissed that man with as much abandon as . . . well, a groupie. Really. No wonder he wanted to "talk." He probably wanted to remind her that they were both coming out of failed relationships, and that it probably wouldn't be "wise" to rush into anything right now. As if she'd ever even consider dating Jack "I'm not ready to settle down yet" Townsend. No way. Not more actors for her, thanks. If she ever got into another relationship again, it was going to be with someone who had a normal career. Like a cop. Or a CPA.

The microwave beeped. Lou opened the door and poked the steaks she found inside. They were no longer frozen. She pulled them out and rubbed them with olive oil, as Jack had instructed, then put them into the waiting skillet, and turned on the heat. As she watched the oil begin to sizzle, her mouth started to water. That was when she spied the wine bottle.

Barry was the one who'd made an effort to educate himself about wine. He'd tried to impress upon her the difference between a merlot and a montepulciano. Lou could never be bothered really to pay attention. She'd always had more important things to figure out, like how to bring her characters together in the third act without the dialogue sounding unconvincing. She wondered if Greta was a wine aficionado, and if that was something she and Barry had in common.

After an inspection of the refrigerator—mostly empty—and pantry—ditto—proved unsuccessful by way of providing something to eat until the steaks were done, Lou poured herself a glass of wine. Just one, she told herself, wouldn't hurt. Besides, she was able to handle beer and wine just fine. It was the hard stuff that did her in.

Taking her wine glass, she sat down on a counter stool to watch the steaks, thinking, as she did so, that if someone—Vicky, for instance—had told her that she might, one night, be making venison steak in someone's borrowed clothes, with wet hair and no makeup, while Jack Townsend was in the next room, showering, Lou would never have believed it. These kinds of things simply did not happen. Not to Lou. These kinds of things happened to other people, and Lou wrote about it. That is what Lou had done, for almost her entire life: recorded her observations about the lives—sometimes invented by herself—of others. She herself did not lead a life worth recording.

At least, not up until recently.

Suddenly, however, things had gotten very complicated in the life of Lou Calabrese.

The wine was rich and full-bodied. Lou knew enough about wine to know that. It felt delicious in her mouth, smooth on her tongue. She was warm already, from the shower and then the way Jack Townsend—what had he been thinking, anyway?—had looked at her right afterwards.

But now she was warmer than ever, with a few swallows of wine in her empty stomach.

Then the shower switched off, and a few seconds later, Jack came out of the bathroom, wearing nothing but a towel slung low across his hips.

And Lou could not help thinking that, even with as many times as she had seen him in even less clothes—and that was just about in every movie she'd ever written in which he had starred—it was still a good thing she'd swallowed just before he'd emerged, or she might have spat wine across the room, the sight of him set her heart slamming so hard against her rib cage.

"How are those steaks?" Jack asked.

"Fine," Lou replied, unable to meet his gaze.

"Great," he said. "I'll be out in a minute to finish them up."

Lou nodded, and mercifully, he went away . . . hopefully to put some clothes on in the bedroom. She was probably, she reflected, the only woman in America who, upon encountering a half-naked Jack Townsend, actually would have preferred to see him with some clothes on.

That was because she was probably the only woman in America to whom the idea of having her heart broken by Jack Townsend was not an appealing one.

Whether Jack had heard her unspoken plea, she didn't

know, but when he came from the bedroom a few minutes later, he was fully clothed . . . after a fashion. He too had formed an apparent aversion to his own clothes, and had donned, as she had, one of the hunter's flannel shirts. Only instead of selecting long johns as his choice for legwear, he had on a pair of the homeowner's jeans. Lou could not help noticing that both the shirt and the jeans were just a tad too snug.

"All right," Jack said, coming up to the stove and turning the steaks—the aroma of which were causing Lou to feel slightly lightheaded . . . unless, of course, that was due to the wine. Or possibly the man pouring it. "What else have we got? Man cannot survive on venison alone."

He pulled open the freezer, giving Lou a long and leisurely view of just how snugly the borrowed jeans conformed to the famous Townsend posterior.

"Eureka," he said, pulling an ice-encrusted object from the depths of the freezer. "Creamed spinach. Perfect. We couldn't ask for better at Peter Luger."

Then he was ripping the packaging off the frozen creamed spinach and shoving it into the microwave.

Lou, whose knowledge of the culinary arts extended to toast and the occasional egg sandwich, said, in a voice that sounded strangely unlike her own, it was so faint and polite, "I didn't know you could cook."

"Oh, sure," Jack said, turning the steaks over with a fork he'd dug out of a drawer. "I had to learn to fend for myself in the kitchen at an early age. I was a picky eater as a kid, and if I wouldn't eat what Cook was serving. . . ." He shrugged. "Well, house rules were, if you didn't like what Cook was serving, you cooked what you wanted for yourself. So, yeah, I learned to cook."

Cook, Lou thought. He said it so casually, as if everyone had had a Cook in their childhood.

But hey, so far he was more comfortable in the kitchen

than either Lou or Barry had ever been, and neither of them had grown up with servants in the house. In fact, if it hadn't been for takeout, she and Barry might well have starved to death before either of them ever picked up a pot to boil some pasta.

Then she realized that, beyond the fact that Jack had grown up rich, the heir to the Townsend Securities fortune, she knew virtually nothing else about him.

"Did you, um, have any brothers and sisters?" she asked, again in that weird voice that sounded so unlike her own.

"Nope," Jack said. He splashed some wine from the bottle into the remaining empty glass. "Just me and Mom and Dad."

"Oh," Lou said. Then, because she could think of nothing else—except how nice his butt continued to look in those jeans—she said, "That must have been lonely."

"That's what all you people who come from big families think," Jack said, with a grin. "But how could I miss what I'd never had? And I got along with my parents." The grin disappeared. "At least until I decided I wanted to be an actor."

Lou, relieved the grin was gone, because it had done something to her pulse she had not liked at all, figured this would be a topic on which they could dwell until bedtime, if it was going to keep him from smiling and messing up her resolve to have nothing to do with him . . . at least physically, anyway.

"Oh? Your parents didn't approve of you pursuing an acting career?"

"Well, my mom didn't mind," Jack said. "My father wanted me to take over the family business. Or, at the very least, go to law school." He took a sip from his wine. "When I disagreed, he pretty much cut me off. I don't think playing a janitor on an extremely short-lived sitcom was exactly what he had in mind for his only son."

Lou said, "Oh, but you've done lots of stuff since then. I mean, that was just when you were starting out, right? You've had incredible success since then. I mean, he must have been proud of the work you did on '*STAT*.'"

"Maybe," Jack said with a shrug. "But he never exactly had a chance to tell me. He died during the second season. He never even made it to the first *Copkiller*."

"Oh," Lou said. Amazingly, she really did feel badly for him. For Jack Townsend! "That must have been hard."

"No harder, I expect, than growing up the only girl in a houseful of boys." The grin was back. "They the ones who taught you that move you executed on me back there?"

She felt her cheeks growing hot at the reference, however oblique, to the kiss they'd shared. Fortunately, the timer dinged on the microwave, and Jack had to go see to the creamed spinach.

"No," she said, carefully. "That was my dad. He was worried about me, you know, when I went off to college. He wanted to make sure I could take care of myself."

"Yeah," Jack said, stirring the spinach. "Well, you can tell him from me that he succeeded. That must have been pretty intimidating for your boyfriends back in high school, huh? I mean, dating a girl with four big brothers and a dad who owned firearms."

Lou didn't know if it was the wine, the ease with which they were conversing—without rancor, for practically the first time all day, or the fact that she was finally, after a nightmare forty-eight hours, starting to relax. In any case, she found herself laughing at Jack's question, and saying, "Well, I don't know. There was only the one."

"Only the one what? Gun?"

"No," she said, with a giggle. A giggle! Lou, who never giggled, but practiced laughing throatily, like Linda Fiorentino, whenever she was stuck in traffic on the freeway! "Boyfriend."

Jack apparently burnt his hand on the creamed spinach. He waved it in the air as he asked, with some bewilderment, "What? *Barry*? Barry Kimmel was your only boyfriend? *Ever*?"

Belatedly, Lou realized what she'd just confessed. To a man who'd been linked romantically with as many women as Jack had—and that was just since he'd become famous—the grand total of Lou's past partners had to be an astonishing, even off-putting thing.

But what did she care if he was put off by it? She didn't want to have a relationship with him, anyway. Vicky had cured her of any tendency in that direction. And besides, Lou had sworn off actors, remember? Wasn't that what the towel on the head and the no makeup thing had been all about in the first place?

So she lifted her glass of wine, took a fortifying sip, and said, "Yep. Just Barry."

Jack stared at her in utter disbelief. The last time she'd seen him look this astonished was during the readthrough of *Copkiller IV*, when he'd gotten to the part where Detective Pete Logan's hand was forcibly broken by an Inuit crimelord.

"My God," he said. "Just one guy, your entire life? You're practically—" He broke off.

She narrowed her eyes at him suspiciously. "Practically what?" she asked.

"Nothing," he said and turned back to the stove. "Oh, hey, these look about done. Let me just grab a couple of plates and—"

"Practically what, Townsend?" she asked, her voice hardening.

"Well, you know," he said, with an embarrassed shrug. "A virgin."

18

"Oh!" Tim Lord's wife cried, clapping her hands together. "He *didn't!* That is just *too* funny. It sounds like just the kind of thing he would do. Doesn't it sound like the kind of thing Jack would do, Mel?"

Melanie Dupre—that, Eleanor thought, was another one of those stage names Jack's friends all seemed to be so fond of taking; the girl couldn't actually *be* French. No Frenchwoman of Eleanor's acquaintance would name her daughter *Melanie*—smiled, but only just. Unlike Vicky, Melanie did not seem particularly interested in hearing stories from Jack's childhood. Not that Eleanor blamed her, particularly. Jack had been a sweet child, of course. But it could not be entertaining for a young woman like Miss Dupre, who was so ravishingly beautiful, to sit around on a Saturday night in a hotel suite, listening to a mother's affectionate stories about her son, a man the girl hardly knew.

Or perhaps Melanie knew Jack better than she let on, since she said, politely hiding a yawn behind a pretty hand—though the girl's fingernails, Eleanor could not

help thinking, were really a bit too long for her taste—
"Oh, Jack told me that story a million times."

Mrs. Lord shot the younger girl a look that Eleanor
could only describe as venomous.

"Did he?" Vicky said acidly. "Well, he never told me."

Then, the angelic-looking Vicky—who, after she'd
learned that there was a chance Jack was still alive, had become positively animated, and had changed out of her
pyjamas and actually run a comb through her hair—
turned back towards Eleanor and said, her blue eyes wide
as a child's, "Tell me what Jack did next, Mrs. Townsend."

"Oh," Eleanor said. She glanced at Mr. Calabrese—or
Frank, as he'd urged her to call him. Eleanor did not, as a
rule, approve of nicknames, but Franklin seemed too for-
mal a name for this kindly man. Poor thing. He looked as
sleepy as she felt, almost nodding on the white couch.
Poor, sweet man. What a darling he had been since the
moment they had met, letting Alessandro sit on him like
that.

And how invaluable he'd proved in speaking with the
police! As a retired officer himself, he quite understood
the "lingo" and had explained all manner of things to her,
such as how the police go about conducting a search and
rescue mission like the one they'd currently embarked
upon to find Jack and Frank's little Lou. Eleanor had already developed quite a soft spot for the unfortunate Miss
Calabrese, who'd had the great misfortune to be called
Louise. If anyone should have demanded a stage name, it
ought to have been Frank Calabrese's poor daughter.
Louise Calabrese indeed!

Still, she was quite a pretty girl—Frank had shown her
a photo—and very successful, too, in her career, so
Eleanor supposed the poor thing's name hadn't hurt her
that badly. Still, that awful business with that di Blase
man, the one Frank called Barry, the one that horrid

Greta Woolston had left Jack for. Eleanor did not like to cast aspersions upon people she had never met, but she quite agreed with Frank's assessment that this Barry fellow was "smarmy."

Such delightful new words Frank had taught her! Really, but he was a delicious discovery. Eleanor slid a look at him from the corners of her eyes. Good looking, too, and quite a gentleman. Why, Eleanor could not remember the last time a door had been held open for her by anyone—excluding Richards, of course.

Much more gentlemanly than that horrible Tim Lord. Imagine, that man having directed the highest-grossing motion picture of all time—that one about the blimp that Frank's daughter had written. It was no wonder, really, that the little man was so full of himself. Still, it was unconscionable of him and his wife, keeping them like this. He must have known that she and Frank had spent the entire day in and out of interviews with the police, the Federal Aviation Association, the press. . . . Why, it had been enough to exhaust a much younger person, and here was Eleanor, getting on towards sixty-five . . . though wild horses would not have dragged the truth of this from her.

Still, it might have occurred to their host and hostess that the two of them were still on eastern time. It was past midnight back home! Even Alessandro was quite unconscious in his little wicker basket.

"Mrs. Townsend?" Vicky Lord was looking at her expectantly. Oh, dear. She must have asked a question. Eleanor was simply so tired. How could she remember . . . ?

Oh, yes. The story she'd been telling, the one about Jack.

"Well, Jack, being just a little boy, hadn't any real interest in art," she said, "and so he was running this little automobile he had—a toy one, you know—along the wall . . . of the Louvre! I had no idea until a guard came up to him and said, '*Petit monsieur*—' So polite, the guards at the Louvre, have you ever noticed? '*S'il te plait, ne conduis pas sur le mur.*' Please don't drive on the wall. Isn't that amusing?"

Tim Lord's wife laughed, but Miss Dupre did not. A beautiful but rather dense creature, Eleanor thought to herself. She was rather like Greta Woolston in that way.

This realization caused Eleanor to take another look at her son's costar. Good heavens, she thought to herself. Could this girl, and Jack—

No. It was preposterous. Surely Jack had learned his lesson by now. He could not possibly be involved with this girl. Not *another* actress. No. . . .

But then the girl said, glancing at Mrs. Lord through her eyelashes, "Yes, Jack told me about that, last time I was at the ranch. You've been to the ranch, haven't you, Vicky?"

Mrs. Lord had been taking a sip from her champagne glass. At the other girl's question, she choked a little. Tim Lord, who was sitting on a chair across from his wife, looked concerned. "Are you all right, sweetheart?" he asked, so courteously that Eleanor, had she not been convinced of the man's disingenuousness, might have thought better of him.

"Fine," Vicky said, coughing into her closed fist. "I'm fine. Sorry. Just went down the wrong tube, I guess. I'm so sorry."

Beside her, Frank Calabrese stirred, apparently wakened by the coughing. He looked around, his blue eyes wide, as if he were not sure where he was. Eleanor understood the feeling.

"What time is it?" he asked.

Tim Lord looked at his watch. "Only half past nine," he said. "Let me get you scotch, Mr. Calabrese. I have a twelve-year-old that'll knock your socks off—"

"No, thank you," Frank said, climbing to his feet. "It's late for me. Past midnight. And we've got another long day ahead of us tomorrow. Eleanor, are you all right? Or would you like me to escort you back to your room?"

Eleanor felt a rush of gratitude for the man.

"Oh, I *am* tired," she said. "You've all been so kind, but if you don't mind—"

"Not at all," Vicky Lord said, jumping to her feet as if suddenly anxious to see them go. Which was odd, since she'd been the one so insistent upon their coming up to the suite for drinks after their dinner—which had been lamentable; it was always a mistake for a restauranteur not to stick to simple American fare if his chef was not highly skilled in the culinary arts—in the hotel restaurant. "I'm sure you both must be exhausted. Let me walk you to the door."

She did, too, hovering about quite unnecessarily, Eleanor thought, while Frank retrieved Alessandro and his basket. Still, at least there was something likable about the young Mrs. Lord. Pity the same could not be said of Melanie Dupre. A sulkier girl Eleanor had not encountered in quite a while. If Jack was seeing her, it could only be because of her looks, which were of course extraordinary. But as Eleanor had been reminding him for some time, looks were not everything. Why couldn't he seem to find a *nice* girl, someone to settle down with on that ranch of his, and raise something more than just horses? Her grandchildren, for instance?

Well, that certainly wasn't going to happen any time soon. Not if Jack continued to consort with sulky starlets like that horrible Melanie Dupre.

"Let's hope there's good news in the morning," Vicky Lord said at the doorway, squeezing Eleanor's hand.

"Yes," Eleanor said. "Let's."

"Good night," Vicky said.

"Good night," Frank said.

Then Vicky closed the door to the suite, and Frank, who had Alessandro's basket in one arm and the dog in the other, said, "What's the matter with those people?"

It was all Eleanor could do not to burst out laughing. But really, they might overhear. Still, she had never heard her own thoughts voiced so exactly by another human being.

"I don't know," she said, pushing the down button beside the elevator. Tim Lord had taken the only penthouse suite. "It was a bit strange, wasn't it?"

"Strange?" Frank Calabrese shook his head. "Downright stupid, was what it was. I mean, our kids are missing, and they wanted to drink champagne. That may be how they do things in Hollywood, but I'll tell you, back on Long Island, somebody's kid goes missing, nobody's pouring champagne."

"I think," Eleanor said, as the elevator arrived, and Frank politely stepped aside so that she could board it first, "that's what they drink as a matter of course. The way we drink coffee."

"Well, I could've used a cup of java or two," Frank said, pushing the button for their floor. They'd been assigned rooms across the hall from one another. "Might've kept me awake while that Tim Lord was going on about that *Hamlet* business. Guess Jack hit big with that one, huh?"

"It was quite critically acclaimed, I suppose," Eleanor said. "But, oh, dear. It doesn't give me much confidence, Frank, that Jack and Lou are ever going to be found, if that's an example of the type of people out looking for them."

"Well, it's not," Frank said. The elevator door slid open to their floor. Frank held it for her as she stepped into the long, carpeted hallway. "The folks that are out looking for our kids aren't Hollywood types. They're the real thing.

Especially that sheriff. He looked as if finding a polar bear in a snowstorm wouldn't be too much for him. So don't you worry, Eleanor. They're going to be all right."

Eleanor wished she could believe him. But how could two people simply walk away from a helicopter crash, and vanish without so much as a trace into the woods? It didn't make sense. Yes, of course, the weather was hampering the search, all of this dreadful snow—she was so glad she'd sold the ski cabin in Aspen; really, she never wanted to see snow again.

But how long could they last, the pair of them, in this cold?

Not long. No one had told her so, but Eleanor had seen the look Frank and that sheriff who'd come down from Myra, the one who'd been to the crash site and driven all that way just to tell them Jack and Lou had not been found there, had exchanged when the subject had come up. They were protecting her from the truth, she was certain of it.

And the truth was that no one—no matter how many survival movies they might have seen—could last out of doors in the arctic for going on forty-eight hours.

Eleanor was not, of course, unaccustomed to loss. She'd lost both her parents long ago, and more recently, her husband. She had weathered all three losses, weathered them with the best humor she could, as well as a little grace . . . or so she hoped.

But how could anyone weather the loss of an only child? It couldn't be done. If Jack was gone . . . if Jack was gone. . . .

She might as well be dead, too.

Then Frank was putting Alessandro and his basket down. Only instead of asking her for her key, so that he could open her door for her and then politely bid her goodnight, he took her arm, and said, "Now what's this?" while peering down into her face.

Eleanor, who was quite certain she must look very sulky indeed—sulkier even than that nasty Melanie Dupre—tried to smile bravely.

"Nothing," she said. "It's nothing. Only I . . . I've got something in my eye."

"Now, Eleanor," Frank said, in his deep, kind voice. "We talked about this. You and I have a couple of real hotheads for kids. You really think a couple of hotheads like those two are going to let a little cold and snow get to them?"

Eleanor sniffled. She couldn't help it. Her handkerchief was in her purse, but she didn't feel like fishing it out just then. She was so tired. So terribly tired.

"You listen to me," Frank said. "My daughter's the stubbornest person I ever met, outside of her mother. If you think she's going to let a little something like a blizzard get in her way, well, you don't know her. And from what I hear about your Jack, well, hypothermia shouldn't bother him a bit. They are going to be fine, Eleanor. Just fine. They're probably holed up in a cave somewhere right now, snarling right back at the bear they kicked out of it."

Eleanor could not help laughing a little as she pictured this.

"Yes," she said. "That does sound like Jack."

"Am I right?" Frank said. "Or am I right? Now you get yourself to bed and grab some shut-eye. By morning, you can bet they'll have pinned down those kids' location, and the two of 'em'll be joining us for breakfast."

"Not, hopefully, at that unfortunate establishment downstairs," Eleanor said, dashing a tear from the corner of her eye.

"Are you kidding me?" Frank said. "I had to down half a bottle of Mylanta after that sirloin. I don't know how you can ruin a steak, but that place managed. We'll find a nice mom-and-pop operation downtown somewhere, and have some real food for breakfast. How does that strike you?"

"That strikes me just fine," Eleanor said. And then, impulsively, she stood on her toes, and pressed a quick kiss to Frank Calabrese's cheek. "Thank you," she whispered.

To her surprise, Frank turned a rather startling shade of pink. It took Eleanor a second or two to realize that he was not having a heart attack but blushing. It had been so long since she'd last seen anyone blush that she was completely unable to keep herself from blurting, "Why, Frank! You're blushing!" even though Eleanor thought personal remarks the height of rudeness.

After she said it, she flung a hand over her mouth and looked up at him guiltily. To her dismay, he only turned a deeper color of burgundy.

"I know," he said miserably. "It's a family curse. We all do it."

Eleanor brought her hand away from her mouth and said, taking his arm, and giving it a little squeeze, "Well, I think it's *delightful*."

Frank looked pleased, but a little disbelieving. "Really?"

"Absolutely," Eleanor said, firmly. "It's refreshing, actually. Sometimes it seems to me as if nobody gets embarrassed anymore . . . especially the people who have the most to be embarrassed about."

"I feel exactly the same way," Frank said, smiling broadly. "Isn't that funny?"

Eleanor felt a curious tug from within—almost the way it felt when Alessandro tugged on his leash because he wanted to conduct a closer inspection of something. Only this time, the tug wasn't on her arm, but—and she was quite certain of this—on her heart, instead.

This was startling, because Eleanor could not remember having felt such a sensation before, except possibly the first time she'd seen Gilbert, at Maude Gross-Dunleavy's cotillion, so many years ago. . . .

Good heavens. Was *that* what was happening here?

"Well," Frank said, his face having gone back to its normal, still somewhat ruddy shade. "Goodnight, Eleanor."

"Goodnight, Frank," Eleanor said, and she hurried Alessandro into their room and closed the door, before he could notice that it was her own face that had now gone up in flames.

19

Lou speared a piece of venison with her fork. The meat was delicious as was the creamed spinach but she was not about to let Jack Townsend have the satisfaction of knowing she thought so.

Although the fact that her plate was very nearly empty, as she'd devoured most of what was on it, might possibly give her away.

"Let me get this straight," she said, though the warm, full feeling in her stomach was making staying angry at Jack Townsend very difficult. "You think that because I've only been with—and I use *been with* in its biblical sense, of course—one person, that I am a virgin?"

He looked uncomfortable. But then, he'd been looking uncomfortable ever since the word virgin had first slipped from his lips.

"Look," he said. "Can we just drop it?"

"No," Lou said, "we cannot just drop it. I want to know what you meant by that. Because I am hardly a virgin, Townsend. I mean, I lived with a guy for six years. Six *years*."

And he still wouldn't freaking propose, she added . . . but not out loud, of course.

"Look, Lou," Jack said, laying down his fork. "I'm not making any judgments, or anything. It's just that . . . well, you have to admit. It's a little rare these days."

"What is?" She blinked at him where he sat across the table—the rough, uneven table that she had set with the mismatched cutlery from Donald's silverware drawer. It was the least she could do, she figured, since Jack had made the meal.

Now, however, it occurred to her that she oughtn't have bothered. Jack's opinion of her was obviously pretty well determined.

"Are you talking about *monogamy*?" she asked, a little incredulously.

"Well," he said, taking a sip of wine. "Yeah. I sort of thought it had died out with sock hops and milkshakes down at the local drugstore."

She continued to stare at him over the piece of venison she'd skewered.

"You do realize I'm the one with the guns, don't you?" she asked. "I could very easily just shoot you and leave your rotting corpse here for Donald to find."

"No judgments, I said." He picked up the wine bottle, and refilled her glass. "I don't know why you're being so defensive."

"You called me a *virgin*," Lou pointed out.

"Practically," Jack reminded her. "I said you're *practically* a virgin. How's your venison?"

"Don't try to change the subject," Lou said, although she herself was having difficulty staying on the topic at hand. How could she be expected to, when he was sitting so close, just a tabletop away, and looking better than . . . well, than she felt he had a right to. He had clearly applied one of Donald's Bic disposables to his lean, square jaw, since the razor stubble that had coated his face since yesterday morning was gone. His thick dark hair was still damp from his shower, and it stuck to the back of his neck in short, swirling curls. More dark curls—these of chest hair—peeked from the V at the opening of the flannel shirt he'd put on. Even though Lou had seen his naked chest a hundred times before—in wide-screen, even—somehow the fact that she could reach across the table and, with the undoing of a few buttons, have all that hard masculinity to herself was making her feel. . . .

. . . well, a little warm.

Maybe it was the long johns. Maybe it was the roaring fire in the hearth a few feet away. Maybe it was the rich and well-cooked food sitting at the bottom of her stomach.

Or maybe it was the fact that Jack Townsend was proving to be surprisingly unactorlike, for an actor. He hadn't uttered the word craft once, or made a single reference to his agent. What kind of actor was he, to be so lacking in self-absorption? Just the fact that he hadn't mentioned Stanislavsky in the entire time they'd been together was enough to make Lou suspicious.

"I'm not trying to change the subject," Jack said. "I am genuinely interested in your gastronomic experience here at Chez Donald."

She narrowed her eyes at him. "The food is delicious," she said. "As I am sure you are well aware."

He shrugged and picked up his wineglass. "Well, I never know. I think everything I cook is delicious. Others have been known to disagree. Interested in dessert at all?"

Lou forgot all about her annoyance with him. "Dessert?" she asked, her eyes wide. "What kind of dessert?"

"Donald's got some Breyers in the freezer, and I noticed a bottle of Hershey's in the fridge."

Lou leaned across the table and plucked up his empty

plate. "I'll do the dishes," she said. "You dish out the hot fudge."

Only he didn't. He just sat there looking at her as she moved around the table, stacking the dirty plates and throwing the used silverware on top.

"What?" she asked, when she finally noticed his stare. "Do I have spinach in my teeth?" She reached up to scrub them with a finger. "Where is it? Did I get it?"

"You don't have spinach in your teeth," Jack said, that fifteen-million-dollar grin of his at half-wattage—maybe a seven point fiver. "I'm just not used to dining with women who take such an eager interest in dessert."

Lou snorted and started into the kitchen with the stack of used plates.

"Color me shocked," she said as she started running the hot water to soak the plates in. "And I was so sure Greta Woolston carries peanut brittle around in her purse, just like me. Whatever, Townsend. Let's just say that for the most part, your recent taste in women leaves something to be desired."

"Oh," Jack said, leaning back in his chair and folding his hands behind his head—causing, Lou could not help but notice, his biceps to bunch up in an alarming manner beneath the flannel of his shirt, "and Barry Kimmel was such a fine choice for a life partner."

"At least," Lou said, squirting dishwashing liquid into the sink, "Barry's not a walking cadaver."

"Maybe not," Jack said. "But you can't tell me all that guy's kernels are popped. And you spent what, ten years with him? At least I only wasted a couple of months on Greta."

"Oh." Lou flattened a sudsy hand against her chest. Donald, of course, did not seem to own dishwashing gloves. "My God. You're right. You are *so* much the better person than I am." She dropped her hand and eyed him derisively. "For your information, Townsend, I was in love with Barry. I'm not proud to admit it. But at least I was trying to have a mature, adult relationship, instead of just amassing a collection of discarded fuck bunnies."

Something about this pronouncement seemed to cause Jack, who'd been leaning back in his chair, to tip it a little too far, until he nearly fell over. He righted himself at the last minute, but only because he leaped from the chair. When he turned around to face Lou afterwards, he wore an expression of puppy-dog hurt.

"Fuck bunnies?" he echoed.

Lou turned back to the dishes. "Oh, I'm sorry," she said. "Are you implying that you're attracted to Melanie Dupre for her intellect? What, the two of you sit around discussing Kant in her trailer? You know, somehow, I can't seem to picture that."

"You know something," Jack said, in a tone of wonder. "I don't know if it's on account of you having all those brothers, or your dad taking you to the shooting range instead of out for ice cream when you were a kid, or what. But you are a real ball-buster."

"Yeah?" Lou said, turning from the sink to face him. "Well, I'd rather be a ball-buster than a big good-looking wind-up toy who just walks around in front of a camera saying lines other people have written for him, and who spends all his time off camera being led around by his dick."

"Oh," Jack said, looming over her until her nose was level with that opening in his shirt, the one that revealed all that crisp dark chest hair. "So that's what you screenwriters think. That without you, there'd be no movies."

"Well," Lou said. "Wouldn't there?"

"You think I can't write my own lines?" Jack demanded. "I did a pretty good job with one, didn't I? I mean, I don't see anybody driving around with *It's always funny until somebody gets hurt* bumper stickers, do you?"

Lou inhaled sharply. She could feel herself getting red in the face, but she didn't care. She reached up and swiped furiously at her nose with the back of a hand.

"No, thanks to you," she spat. "Instead people are going around saying that idiotic *I need a bigger gun* line. You know, it's not the size of the gun that matters, it's the amount of fire power that the— *What do you think you're doing?*"

Because Jack had reached up suddenly, and was mopping at her nose with the bottom of his shirt.

"Hold still a minute," he said, since Lou was trying to squirm away from him. "You've got suds on your nose."

Lou, alarmed to find her back up against the sink, and her front up against Jack Townsend, was not happy when her face was suddenly seized by him between both his hands.

Even more alarming than his proximity and his grip was the fact that before Jack dropped the bottom of his shirt to grab her face, Lou had been awarded a long glimpse of his hard, flat stomach. Worse, the dark strip of hair that snaked down that stomach from the broader expanse of it on his chest disappeared down the front of the jeans he was wearing like an arrow pointing to a hidden treasure. The goody trail, Vicky had always called this phenomenon.

Jack's goody trail was something, of course, that Lou had seen before.

But never this close. Never not on a screen, and from several rows back . . .

Lou was apparently not the only one suddenly aware that the mood in the room had taken a sudden and dramatic shift. Jack, holding her face between both his large, darkly tanned hands, looked down at her with that same speculative expression he'd worn back when she'd tackled him in the snow . . . right before he'd kissed her.

Lou, feeling a spurt of something that wasn't quite fear but wasn't exactly excitement, either, was conscious only that her heart was slamming very hard against her ribs, and that her breath had grown a little short. In the nanosecond of time that they stood like that, with her back against the sink and Jack's hands holding her face, she was still able to reflect that this was precisely what she hadn't wanted to happen.

"Jack," she said, her voice sounding strangely unsteady, even to her own ears. "Don't even think about it. It will never work. I do *not* want to get involved with another self-absorbed actor."

"You think I want to get involved with a ball-busting know-it-all like you?" he asked pointedly.

And then, with that cleared up, he kissed her, hard, on the mouth.

Lou felt that kiss, just like the first one, slam down her spine like a roller-coaster. Suddenly she was flattened against him, could feel every button of that flannel shirt through hers, was singed by the hard muscles beneath it. His heat was pouring into her like steam from a mochachino grande, curling up from her toes, in their borrowed socks, all the way up her legs, making stops along the way at all the major erotic thoroughfares. It was all she could do to keep herself from wrapping her legs around his waist and yelling, *Take me*, like Marlene Dietrich in. . . .

Wait. Had it been Marlene Dietrich? Oh, God, who *cared*?

His hands went from her face to her shoulders. Suddenly, he was pushing her away, breaking the contact between them.

"Did you use Donald's toothbrush?" he asked her. At least she thought that's what he'd asked her. She was in too much of a daze really to understand him properly.

"Of course," she said. "Didn't you?"

Then he was pulling her back towards him, this time wrapping both arms around her and pushing her back against the sink, until she heard the water in it slosh. Not that she cared. Why should she? It was hard to care about anything when she was being kissed as deeply and as intrusively as Jack was kissing her. It was impossible to believe, in fact, that he disliked her as much as he claimed to when he was kissing her the way he was.

And it was hard to remember that he was her least favorite person in the world when his kisses were making her feel the way they were . . . like she was the most beautiful, exotic creature that had ever walked the face of the planet. Jack wanted her. He was making that perfectly clear. Jack wanted her, Lou Calabrese, even though she hadn't a splotch of makeup on her face and was wearing a pair of men's long johns. And yeah, maybe she was the only woman for miles and miles, but he wanted her, and she could feel that want, pressing hard and insistent through the front of his borrowed jeans.

There was no doubt about it: Jack Townsend was warm for her form.

And she was happy to say she felt the same. Who even cared if the guy was a womanizing commitment-phobe? Look at the way he was making her *feel*. Look at what his tongue was doing, conducting what appeared to be, to Lou, a very thorough and entirely necessary investigation of the inside of her mouth . . . while at the same time, his hands had launched an investigation of their own, right up the bottom of her borrowed shirt. There was one of them now, finding a bare breast, and expertly cupping and then palming it, causing Lou's spine, which had barely recovered from that first body-slamming kiss, to go weak. Suddenly, it seemed like her knees could no longer support her.

But that was okay, because Jack seemed to understand. Impatient with their difference in height, he was already slipping his free hand around one of her hips and boosting her up so that she was sitting on the edge of the sink, her legs spread apart and that part of him in which she was most interested pressing solidly against her pubic bone. He had her shirt pulled up—Jack Townsend was not a man to concern himself with buttons—and happily it seemed that now that she was sitting at counter level, her nipples were within reach of his very persistent, hard-working lips.

The first burning touch of that mouth to one of Lou's sensitive pink nipples nearly caused her to slip backwards into the sinkful of hot dishwater. Fortunately his other hand, the one not holding her shirt up, held her steady. Thank God, because the world seemed suddenly to have turned upside down. It had to have, for Lou to be doing what she was doing, which was reaching down and undoing the buttons of Jack Townsend's button-fly jeans. *Pop. Pop. Pop.*

And suddenly that part of him that she'd felt so reassuringly hard and hot against her was heavy in her hand, the only part of Jack Townsend's body that she'd never seen before, but of which she found she was able to approve most heartily, as it was everything a girl would expect from a star of the big screen, and oh so much, much more.

Jack's goody trail, it was comforting to know, did not lead to disappointment.

The minute her hand went to grip him, Jack, as if unaccustomed to such direct attention to that area—hardly likely, considering the assiduousness of the attentions of his past paramours—inhaled sharply and buried his face against Lou's throat. His hot breath scorched her neck. And the hand that had dipped beneath her shirt to fondle her breasts suddenly left them and dipped down, towards the sagging elastic waistband of the long johns she wore. . . .

And then Jack's fingers had slipped between her legs and found the hot, wet place there. Lou couldn't stifle a moan as his lips came down over hers again, his tongue as unrelenting as his fingers. All she had to do, she realized, was put what she held in her hand in the place where his hand was, and she'd be *practically* a virgin no longer. The thought was immensely tempting. In fact, it was with difficulty that she kept from throwing herself against that hot thick organ, throbbing its need in her hand—

But Jack seemed to have other ideas. He suddenly slipped both hands under her and lifted her from the sink, then started, with Lou held high against him, towards the bedroom door. Jack evidently had something against skewering women against the kitchen sink—that was the only reason Lou could think of for the sudden change in venue.

But she was more glad than she could say for his decisiveness when, a second later, he'd lowered her onto Donald's bed . . . and then lowered himself on top of her. Suddenly she could feel that goody trail against her own bare stomach . . . his goody trail, and so much else.

Then he was pulling at her clothes. Off came the flannel shirt. Goodbye went each of her socks. Last to go were the long johns, and those he peeled from her with care, watching intently as inch after inch of bare skin was revealed in the sliver of light that spilled into the bedroom from the fire in the next room.

"So you *are* a natural redhead," he observed hoarsely, running his fingers through the triangle between her thighs.

"You doubted it?" Lou asked huskily.

"Honey," he said, "I'll never doubt anything again, where you're concerned."

And then he was kissing her again, another one of those breath-stealing, toe-curling kisses that made her feel as if the sole reason he'd been put on this earth was for this, and this alone . . . to kiss her. As he kissed her, he ran his hands up and down the length of her nude body, doing things, touching things, Barry had never done or touched. Making love with Barry had been fun, but there'd been a certain perfunctoriness to it. They'd done it regularly, three times a week, and it had been satisfying.

But Barry had never pressed her up against a sink and kissed her as if his life had depended on it. Barry had never made the noise Jack had when she'd wrapped her hand around him, then buried his head in her neck. Barry had never made her feel as Jack was making her feel, as if there was just her and him in the entire world, and that the only thing that mattered at that very moment was the two of them.

And Barry had never, as Jack was suddenly doing, torn off his own clothes, as if he could not stand to have them on a second longer.

And there it was, in all its glory, the famous Townsend ass.

And it was, for the moment anyway, hers, to do with exactly as she pleased.

What she pleased to do with it at that moment was run her hands over its perfectly round smoothness. . . .

Then pull it very hard towards her.

Jack got the message and seemed to need no further urging. A second later, he had buried himself in her.

Home. That's all Lou could think. That after months—years even—of journeying, she had come home at last. Which was ridiculous, of course, because there was nothing remotely homey about Jack. Jack wasn't comfortable. Jack wasn't relaxing to be with. Except for the whole cooking thing, Jack didn't even strike her as very domestic.

But they fit. Oh, God, how well they fit together, as if his body had been created for the sole purpose of coupling with hers. Lou had never experienced anything like the sensation of fullness that swept over her when all that hardness entered her, embedded so deeply that she could have sworn she felt it all the way to her spine—that spine he kept managing to debilitate with his kisses. Lou could not remember ever feeling so complete, so less like a brain, and much like a woman. In fact, she was fairly certain that she had just died and gone to heaven.

Until he moved.

Just the barest fraction of an inch. But still, it sent sensations shooting through Lou's body that she had barely known existed. Suddenly she was on another roller-coaster, but this one a roller-coaster of need. She needed Jack to move like that again. She needed to move along with him. . . .

And to her everlasting joy, he did. And she, moving against him, realized that this was what sex was supposed to be like, not that dry, mechanical thing she'd been doing with Barry since that night after their senior prom in the back of his mother's Chevette. No, it was this, wet, hot roller-coaster love, the thing everyone had been talking about, the thing that she'd spent years writing about but never experienced herself, never understood. . . .

Until now. Now she understood. Now she knew, as she lay beneath Jack Townsend, her body molded to his, their lips and tongues entwined, what all the fuss was about.

The only question, really, was how in the hell had she done without it for so long?

And then something started happening. Something was building inside her, a pressure she recognized dimly as being like what she'd used to experience with Barry, but was a hundred times more intense. Surely she couldn't be orgasming already. It normally took her at least twenty minutes to climax, and that was only after a half-hour of messing around.

But something was definitely happening, welling up from some fiery place deep within her, then beginning to grow, like a flame on a match head.

Only instead of burning itself out, the way a match would, this flame kept growing and growing, until soon it was bigger than a candle flame, bigger even than a camp-fire, a housefire, burning out of control. No, it was a rag-ing forest fire, and it was consuming her, and making her do all manner of things she had never done in her life, such as sink her fingernails into Jack Townsend's fifteen-million-dollar ass and call his name in a ragged voice that sounded completely like her own, as what felt like a wall of cool blue water went crashing over her, putting out the flames and drowning her in sun-kissed waves of blessed wet. . . .

And then Lou opened her eyes and realized that for the first time in her life, she had orgasmed without fantasiz-ing that she was with someone else—such as that hot guy from the "Horatio Hornblower" series on A&E. No, she had come all on her own—well, with a little help from Jack—and in record time.

And Jack, she soon realized, if the heavy weight that was collapsed on top of her was any indication, had come, too, no doubt at some point during her own frenzied cli-max. The only sign that he was not in fact dead was his heartbeat, which she could feel thudding very fast against her breast.

"My God, Jack," she said, when she could finally sum-mon the energy to speak. "What *was* that?"

20

"Look," Jack said as he dug the spoon into the ice cream container. "It happens. I mean, when two people fight as much as you and I do—"

"—there's a lot of tension," Lou finished for him, doing some excavating with her own spoon. "Sure, I get that. But come on. I mean, I may be practically a virgin—"

"I told you I take that back." Jack frowned at her from across the bed. "And stop Bogarting the chocolate sauce."

"Bogarting's only for smoking," Lou said, passing him the squeeze bottle.

"Whatever," Jack said. "And that wasn't what I was going to say. Sure, we fight a lot. But *why* do we fight? See, that's the question you ought to be asking."

"I know why we fight," Lou said. "It's because you're a jackass."

"That," Jack said, squirting chocolate sauce directly into his mouth, then adding a spoonful of ice cream to it, "is not why we fight. We fight because you can't control your insatiable lust for me, and it makes you cranky."

"Do you talk with your mouth full to all your girlfriends?" Lou wanted to know. "Or am I just the lucky one?"

He swallowed, then rolled over until he was resting his head against one of her naked thighs. Lou, he'd discovered, from that first moment he had slipped a hand under that flannel shirt she'd been wearing, out in the kitchen, had skin the consistency of ski wax, as smooth and as firm and as buttery soft. He hadn't felt skin like hers since . . . well, he couldn't remember when. Possibly never.

He knew one thing, though. He hadn't gotten enough of it yet. Not by a long shot.

"What do you say we just stay here?" he asked, reaching up and fingering one of her long, auburn curls. "Forever. Or at least until the snow melts."

She had picked up the ice cream container and was scraping the bottom of it with her spoon. "We can't," she said. "We're out of butter pecan. Besides, there's no TV."

"We don't need TV," Jack said. "We have each other."

"Right," Lou said, with a laugh. "We'd kill each other in a day, maybe two, tops."

"No, we wouldn't," Jack said. "Did anybody ever tell you that your hair reminds them of a Key West sunset?"

"No," Lou said. "Did anybody ever tell you that when you come, you make a sound like a howler monkey?"

"See," Jack said. "This is why we work so well together. You are the only woman I have ever met who is absolutely immune to flattery. In the past forty-eight hours, I've come to realize that most of my past relationships have just been a series of meaningless, empty sexual encounters—"

"Speaking of which," Lou said, "if you've given me a disease, I fully intend to go to the press."

"Would you please," he said tiredly, "let me finish? I am trying to convey something to you that has a deeply personal meaning to me."

She held up one hand. "So long as what you're trying to

convey isn't chlamydia, I'm all ears. But next time, we are totally using a condom."

Jack took a deep breath. He had no idea why this was so difficult. Maybe because she kept making wisecracks. Maybe because he was emotionally and physically spent—though in a good way. Maybe it was because he was used to being the one pursued, not the one in pursuit.

Or maybe it was because, for the first time in his life, he actually found himself caring—caring more than he wanted to—about what a woman thought of him.

In any case, he was finding this far harder than he'd ever expected.

"Look," he said. "I know that in the past we've had our differences. But in the past forty-eight hours, I've really come to respect you, Lou. You're level-headed, brave, and good in a crisis. Not to mention totally hot in bed. I realize now that in sleeping with, um, some of the kind of women I've slept with in the past, I've been limiting my growth as a human being. There is something to be said, I now know, for intellect over physical beauty."

"If you think I'm going to give you a blow job now," she said, licking the spoon, "you're high."

"You know what I mean," Jack said. "Lou, you are the first woman I have ever been with who not only ate all of the food I prepared for her, but offered to do the dishes afterwards . . . let alone wasn't afraid to eat a little dessert."

"Obviously," Lou said, "you haven't led any of your other dates on a forty-eight hour tour of terror, the way you did me. Running from armed assassins tends to make a girl hungry."

"Lou," Jack said. "I'm serious. I think when we get back to civilization, maybe . . . we might want to consider . . . well, I was thinking we should move in together."

It was, he knew, a risk. He had never asked a woman

to move in with him before. They had always just sort of done it. One day he'd gone off to the studio, and that night, when he'd got home, all their stuff was in his closet.

And he didn't want Lou to get the wrong idea. He was not talking marriage. Only a fool would marry a woman he'd slept with a grand total of once. Well, okay, twice, if he counted fooling around in the shower afterwards.

But living together. That was different.

Except that he had a feeling Lou Calabrese was the kind of woman who wasn't going to just show up on his doorstep one morning with a suitcase and a box of CDs. No, Lou was definitely the type who would wait for an invitation.

So he was extending it, and now, before someone else could swoop in and get there first.

But if he'd expected gratitude for his kind offer, he was destined for disappointment.

She leaned over and patted him, very kindly, on the shoulder. "Thanks, buddy," she said. "But why don't we wait and see if we can get through the next twenty-four hours without anybody shooting at us before we make any big decisions about our future domestic arrangements."

He eyed her uneasily. He wasn't sure she understood what he'd just said.

"Lou," he said. "I'm not talking about the ranch in Salinas. I've got a place in the hills, you know. Seven bedrooms, with a pool that's got a vanishing horizon . . ."

Lou handed the empty ice cream container, both spoons, and the chocolate sauce to him. "That's great, Jack," she said. "But why don't we sleep on it? I imagine we're both pretty exhausted."

She slid from the bed, then padded, stark naked, from the bedroom into the bathroom. A few seconds later, he heard her employing Donald's toothbrush yet again.

That was another thing. How many women did he know who would use a stranger's toothbrush? None.

Jack wasn't sure what was happening to him. Why was he having this reaction to sex with Lou? Just because it had been the best sex he'd ever had was no reason to go overboard like this. If he didn't watch it, she was going to start thinking he was in love with her, or something. Which he wasn't. He definitely wasn't.

He just never wanted to be away from her again. That wasn't love, necessarily. It was just . . .

Interest. He was interested in her. She was like some new and exotic line of car. He'd test driven her, and liked what he'd found. Now he wanted to lease. Not own. *Lease.*

With an option to buy, maybe.

Lou turned out the bathroom night and came back into the bedroom. See, now this was the problem. How was he supposed to remain rational about all of this when she was going to do stuff like walk around stark naked?

Because of course it turned out that under that baggy wool sweater and slacks was a body that was curvy in all the right places, and slender in all the others. That fact, coupled with a pair of perfectly shaped, tip-tilted breasts, the ends of which were a tantalizing pink, and that damned distracting thatch of red hair—she kept, Jack had not been surprised to discover, what Tim Lord, who could be surprisingly lewd when there weren't any women around to overhear him, would have referred to as a "trim quim"—was what spelled his doom. Because how was he supposed to resist something that was wrapped in such delectable packaging?

Maybe, he thought hopefully, as Lou slid back into bed beside him, she snored. He could never live with a snorer. Snoring would put him right off.

Lou looked at him, one of those little elvish smiles she sometimes wore, curving her lips.

"Goodnight, Townsend," she said before reaching for the pullstring to the lamp by her side of the bed.

"Goodnight, Lou," he said.

The room was plunged into darkness. The fire in the other room had died long ago. Now the house was perfectly still . . . except for the wind that still raged all around it, making a howling noise that might, to someone with an imagination, almost have been the mournful cry of an arctic wolf.

He lay there, the empty ice cream container filled with used spoons and the chocolate sauce bottle not the only barrier, he felt, that was between them.

At least those, however, were easily removed. And as soon as he'd done so, Jack moved across the mattress until they were spooned together, her back to his front, one of his arms tucked around her, and a hand curled possessively around one of her breasts.

"Not this again," Lou said, not exactly pleasantly.

He looked down at her. "What are you talking about?"

"Nothing," she said. "Only that you are a creature of tenacious habit."

He didn't have the slightest idea what she was talking about. He did, however, know that whatever it was, it didn't matter. Not anymore.

"You might as well admit it, Calabrese," he said into the darkness of her hair, fanned across the pillow between their heads. "You're smitten with me."

Her chuckling was now the only sound he could hear, besides the wind. He had meant to stay awake, just in case Ski Mask and his buddies found them out. But he drifted off to the sound of that chuckling and the flowery scent of her hair. He didn't realize the fragrance was Donald's shampoo and conditioner in one. He thought it was the scent of Lou's soul. He fell asleep thinking that it was a miracle they'd found this cabin, but an even greater miracle that they'd found each other. He fell asleep fantasizing about all the time they'd spend together in the cabin, waiting to be rescued: the meals he'd cook; the games of cards—Donald seemed like the type who'd have cards somewhere—they'd play in front of the fire; the stories they'd tell each other.

And the love—especially the love—they'd make.

Except that when he woke up the next morning, she was gone.

This was not as it should be. When women spent the night with him, they tended to stay exactly where he wanted them to, which was in bed. They did not get up and go roaming around without him. Not unless they wanted to surprise him with breakfast.

But Lou hadn't gotten up to surprise him with breakfast. He realized this as soon as he stumbled, wearing only the sheet and one of the heavy comforters from the bed, into the living room. Lou wasn't in the kitchen, or the living room, either. The bathroom door was wide open, revealing another empty room.

And that wasn't the only thing that was wrong. It took a bleary-eyed Jack a few minutes to realize what else was bothering him. And that was the light. Yes, light was pouring in through the windows, and even through a skylight he hadn't realized was there the night before. Bright sunlight, the kind he'd caught only the barest glimpses of since his arrival to Alaska.

The sun was high in the cloudless blue sky—he could see that through the skylight. It made the snow all around the cabin gleam with almost blinding intensity.

And that's when he realized just where Lou had disappeared to. She was standing, wrapped in a comforter of her own, on the front porch, a cup of something that steamed in one hand, the other shading her eyes as she gazed out at the gleaming white snow.

He opened the front door and instantly sucked in his breath as the frigid cold hit him in the face.

"Lou, what are you doing?" he demanded. "It's freezing out there. Get back in bed."

She glanced at him. Her hair was tousled and wild from having gone to bed with it wet, and all she had on beneath the comforter was another one of Donald's shirts and the long johns she'd worn the night before. Her feet were tucked into a pair of enormous men's workboots, at least five sizes too large for her, and the cold had turned the tip of her nose pink, like a rabbit's.

And Jack was convinced that he had never seen a more beautiful woman in his life.

"Call me crazy," she said, pointing off into the distance. "But does that look like a road to you?"

21

"I can't believe I let you talk me into this," Jack said bitterly, his breath coming out in little white puffs like steam from a train engine.

"Look." Lou had worked up a nice healthy sweat, and she actually felt fairly comfortable as they chugged along. "I told you. If we don't run into civilization by dusk, we can turn around and head back."

"So a pack of wolves can attack us in the dark and dismember our corpses," Jack said. "Good plan. Do you have to go so fast? I never learned cross-country. I only know how to downhill."

Lou glanced over her shoulder at him. He looked, as always, impossibly handsome. Even the stocking cap and wool scarf he'd borrowed from Donald, which might have looked ridiculous on a lesser man, looked hot on him. Rolling her eyes in disgust—she knew exactly how stupid she looked in her own borrowed gear—Lou threw some shoulder into her ski poles.

"Didn't you ever own a Nordic Track?" she asked. She liked the *shoosh-shoosh-shoosh* of their skis against the crisp white snow. If it hadn't been for the fact that she was afraid armed men were going to come roaring up at any moment and blast holes through them both, she might almost have been enjoying herself.

And why not? She couldn't explain what had happened when she and Jack had made love, why their bodies had seemed so well-suited to one another, and how he had managed to send her into ecstasies of pleasure she'd never before known existed, let alone what had happened after—Jack's inexplicable invitation for her to move in with him, surely a result of far too many endorphins on the brain.

But she had to admit, even though she couldn't explain it, she had liked it. A lot.

"No, I never owned a Nordic Track," Jack growled. "Who do I look like to you, Suzanne Somers?"

She wrinkled her nose at him thoughtfully. "Maybe," she said. "But she does the Thighmaster, not Nordic Track. I don't think her butt is quite as nicely contoured as yours, though."

"You leave my butt," Jack said, "out of this."

Lou just laughed and shot ahead a few yards. It wasn't exactly easy going, and she'd had reservations about their traveling on the road she'd discovered . . . a fairly wide one, and one that, when it wasn't covered with three feet of snow, was probably pretty well traveled. The two of them, shooshing along that road, would be sitting ducks if Jack's friends with the guns happened to get hold of another helicopter.

So they were sticking to the side of the road, where they had the overhang of the branches from the pine trees on either side of the road to protect them from view. The ground wasn't nearly as level as it would have been if they'd been skiing down the center line, but at least they didn't have to worry about aerial assaults.

Jack had been against appropriating the skis, which they'd found in one of Donald's closets, along with two sets of ski boots that, though big on Lou and small on Jack, had fit both well enough for the short term. He hadn't even wanted to try the road, to see if it led to a town or perhaps a highway, where they might flag down a car or a trucker with a CB.

"Why can't we just stay here?" he'd wanted to know.

"Because people are probably worried about us," Lou had explained. "I'm sure everybody thinks we're dead. Who knows what kind of story Sam cooked up for them about what happened to us?"

"What makes you think Sam's told them anything at all?" Jack had wanted to know. "Who's to say he even survived that first night?"

"You told me you thought his little friends on the snowmobiles would have picked him up," Lou had said, her eyes suddenly wide with concern. "Don't you think they did?"

Jack had said "Sure," but Lou hadn't sensed that he'd cared either way. Well, Sam *had* been going to shoot them, so that was somewhat understandable. Still, Sam had been a father, after all. What was going to happen to his poor kids if he froze to death?

In typical star fashion, Jack seemed concerned only about those things that affected him directly. Although when it had come to figuring out how to reimburse Donald for his unknowing hospitality, Jack had swung to the other end of the spectrum, caring, Lou felt, far too much.

"Write him a check for a thousand," Jack had said.

Lou, who had pulled out her checkbook, since neither she nor Jack was carrying a lot of cash, paused with her pen poised on the amount line.

"A thousand dollars?" she'd echoed, her eyebrows raised very high. "Jack, all we did was eat a couple of his steaks and mess up his sheets a little. I was thinking three hundred would be more than enough."

"Spare me your midwestern frugality."

"I'm from Long Island," Lou had reminded him.

"We used his toothbrush," Jack had remonstrated with her. "And we're about to steal his skis."

"We'll send the skis back," Lou had said, "when we reach civilization."

"A thousand bucks," Jack had said. At her bewildered look, he had added, "I'm good for it, I swear."

Which only bewildered her more. Jack couldn't be less concerned about a human life, but he wanted to make sure a man he had never met was more than adequately compensated for any inconvenience Jack had caused him.

On the other hand, Donald had never tried to kill them. That in itself, Lou decided, was worth a grand. Certainly very few of his neighbors had been as accommodating.

Jack brought her out of these reflections by catching up to her now and, for a few heartbeats, anyway, falling into step—or shoosh—beside her, and asking, "This is all going into your next screenplay, isn't it?" he asked.

She looked at him. The sun, which had put in such a dazzling appearance earlier in the day, had quickly disappeared behind another bank of clouds. But these clouds, at least, were white, and did not look as if they intended, at any point, to drop buckets of snow on them.

Sun or no sun, however, Jack Townsend looked fine. Jack Townsend always looked fine. She found herself worrying about how she looked—she hadn't, after all, really bothered with makeup, except for some lip gloss. How in the hell was she supposed to compete with Jack's past loves, none of whom had even needed makeup to enhance the natural beauty they'd all been born with?

Then she shook herself. What was she thinking? She wasn't going to compete with any of Jack's past loves, because there was nothing going on between her and Jack. That boink fest the night before had been a fluke, a result of having been in one another's company far too long. That was all. She wasn't going to date another actor. She *wasn't*. She was going to find a nice veterinarian or school teacher or something.

And certainly she wasn't going to let herself fall for Jack Townsend. She knew how he operated only too well, thanks to Vicky. Sure, last night he was rambling about the two of them moving in together. But what about in another month, or maybe two, when he was throwing her out again? No, thanks. Lou Calabrese was not about to let Jack Townsend break *her* heart.

"For your information," Lou said, gripping her ski poles very tightly, "I am out of the screenwriting business."

Jack glanced at her sharply. "What?"

"You heard me," Lou said. "I'm not writing any more screenplays. *Copkiller IV* is my last."

"Really?" Jack, to her fury, didn't sound very convinced. In fact, his *Really?* sounded suspiciously polite. "Retiring before thirty, are you?"

"Not retiring," Lou said, ducking beneath a particularly low-hanging, snow-covered branch. "Just not writing for the screen anymore."

"I see." Jack ducked, too. "And just what are you going to write, then? Commercial jingles?"

"Ha-ha," Lou said sarcastically. "If you must know, I am thinking about writing a novel."

"A novel," Jack said.

Encouraged by the fact that he had not broken out into peals of uproarious laughter, Lou said, "Yes. A novel. In fact, I've already started it."

"I see," Jack said again. Then his glance fell upon the computer case she had slung across her shoulders. "Now I understand your determination to hang onto that thing."

Lou blushed. That's because when Jack had, earlier that day, offered to carry it for her, she had refused to let him, remembering all too clearly the way he'd mishandled it the last time he'd gotten his hands on it.

"Yes," was all she said now, however.

"And may I ask," Jack inquired, "what this novel is about?"

"Oh," Lou said, feeling the familiar warmth she always experienced when someone asked about her work. "Well, it's about a woman who is betrayed by her first love but finds redemption through . . ."

She broke off, mortified. Good Lord, she couldn't tell Jack the plot of her book! He might think it was about him! Which it most certainly wasn't. She'd come up with the plot for it well before she'd ever slept with Jack.

And besides, the character in her book was going to find love again in the arms of a *good* man. That was most certainly not Jack. Jack wasn't good. He was *far* from good. He was, in fact, a very, very bad man. A good man would never have been able to make Lou feel as she'd felt the night before in bed with him, as if the top of her skull was going to blow out, just like Mount St. Helen's. There wasn't a grain of good in Jack.

Or was there? Because he had, after all, made her that dinner. And hadn't he, both nights they'd spent together, exhibited a very atypically male propensity to cuddle?

In point of fact, she didn't really know anything bad about Jack. Except, of course, what he'd done to Vicky. And the fact that someone wanted him dead.

"Finds redemption through what?" Jack wanted to know.

"Oh," Lou said, knowing she was turning a fiery red and hoping he didn't notice. "Through her work with the poor."

Jack blinked at her. "You're kidding me, right?" he

asked. "A Lou Calabrese joint, and it doesn't have any explosions in it?"

She managed a smile. "Hard to believe, isn't it?" Then, in an effort to change the subject, she asked brightly, "How about you? What's the next Jack Townsend venture?"

He frowned. Even frowning, of course, he was still delectably handsome. It seemed perfectly incredible to her that just twelve hours ago, those impressively chiseled features had been buried between her—

"Direct," he said.

It was her turn to blink. "I beg your pardon?"

"I want to direct," he repeated. Then he groaned. "Oh, God. Everybody says that, I know. But I directed a film last year—I doubt you saw it, it wasn't very widely released. Anyway, it made me realize how much power directors have. I mean, I'm not saying you're right about that thing you mentioned last night—about me being a wind-up toy that just walks in front of the camera and says lines someone else has written—"

Lou winced. "Look, about that. I'm sorry. I didn't mean it."

"Yes, you did," he said without rancor. "But that's okay, because in a way, you're right. There's more to it, of course. I mean, than just saying the line. Or at least, there should be, if the person saying it knows what he's doing. Anyway, this directing thing. I really enjoyed it. And since I've, you know, worked at both ends of the camera now, I think I'd be a good director. A kind of actors' director. Not a megalomaniac fuck like Tim Lord."

Lou was so surprised to hear this that she nearly broke a ski on a rock she hadn't noticed sticking out of the snow. Jack, however, reached out in the nick of time and righted her.

"You all right?" he asked.

"Yeah," she said, laughing. "It's just . . . megalomaniac

fuck. Is that really how you guys think about him? Tim Lord? I mean, he won best director last year—"

"I know he did," Jack said. "He deserved it, considering what he had to work with. Not your script, which was, as you know, perfect. But he had Greta and Barry to deal with. That had to have been like directing two pieces of particle board—"

Lou was laughing so hard that she nearly tripped again, but Jack, who still had a hand on her arm, tightened his grip and kept her upright.

"Oh, God," she said, wiping tears from her eyes with the tip of her glove. "Particle board. And you're wrong, I did see it."

Jack still hadn't let go of her arm. "Saw what?"

"*Hamlet,*" Lou said. "The movie you directed. It was good."

His handsome face brightened. "Really? You thought so? I—"

But he never got a chance to finish. That's because, from just above the treetops, came a new sound, a *whomp-whomp-whomp* that seemed to reverberate not just from the air, but inside Lou's chest, as well.

"Shit," Jack said and pulled her hard into the nearby brush. Knocked off balance, Lou fell, but fortunately—for her, anyway; not so much for Jack—she landed across his midriff, causing him to let out an *oof* that quickly turned to an *ack* as the helicopter blades stirred piles of snow from the branches above them and sent it raining down on them in hard clumps.

"Maybe it isn't them," Lou shouted, to be heard over the sound of the chopper.

"You want to break cover and find out?" Jack shouted back.

Well, no. Not really. Lou didn't relish scrambling out from the underbrush only to be sprayed with machine-gun fire, or whatever. So she lay where she was in Jack's arms—not exactly an uncomfortable position—waiting to see if the helicopter would land, as there was plenty of room for a landing on the road, or move on.

Five of the longest heartbeats Lou could ever remember later, the helicopter moved on, heading in the direction they'd just come from. Through the branches above them, she caught a glimpse of it as it departed. It was a white eight-seater, with a big red cross painted on its underbelly.

"Did you see that?" Lou shouted, turning to pound Jack in the chest with a fist. "It was an air rescue chopper! They were looking for us!"

"Well, how was I to know?" Jack demanded, throwing up an arm to fend off her blows. "I wasn't exactly going to stick around to find out."

Muttering, Lou climbed to her feet and started looking for her skis. One of them had slid several yards down the road.

"We could be on our way back," she said, to no one in particular. "Right now, we could be on our way back to the hotel, and our own toothbrushes, and fresh underwear, and real coffee, not instant."

"Hey," Jack said, limping after her. One of his own skis had come off, as well. "We haven't had it so bad. I mean, you seemed to like the creamed spinach, if I'm not mistaken."

Lou, reaching her ski, which had slid all the way around a bend in the road, turned towards him, her hands going to her hips.

"Yeah, I liked the *creamed spinach*," she said. "But guess what? I could have had *creamed spinach* back in Anchorage, thanks very much."

"No, you couldn't," Jack said. "Because back in Anchorage, you weren't interested in having *creamed spinach* with me. It's only since you've gotten to know me out here that you've developed a taste for *creamed spinach*."

"Let's get this straight right now," Lou said, raising a gloved finger. "I have always liked *creamed spinach*. I just never gave it much of a chance—"

"—until you were stranded with it out here," Jack finished for her, impatiently. "See, that's exactly what I meant."

"Well, maybe," Lou said, "that's because *creamed spinach* was too busy screwing his brains out with girls named Greta, and Melanie, and Winona—"

It was Jack's turn to raise a finger. "Hey," he said. "I never laid a hand on Winona. She's not my type."

"Oh, why?" Lou wanted to know. "Because she can read?"

A look of annoyance temporarily creased Jack's features. He did not, however, look one iota less appealing.

"Come on, Lou," he said. "You know that's just. . . ."

She didn't interrupt him. His voice just trailed off. She couldn't figure out why, at first. Then she realized that he was staring very intently at something behind her. Thinking it was more of Sam's friends, she spun around, fast. . . .

And saw herself staring at a ramshackle building just off the side of the road, with a large neon sign out front that said, in blinking blue and red, Bud's Bar.

22

Bud himself wasn't tending bar when Jack cautiously pushed open the door and peered inside. Instead, a slightly haggard dishwater blonde was wiping down some glasses, a cigarette dangling from one corner of her mouth. She shot a glance at Jack as she felt the cold air he was letting in.

"We're closed," she snarled at him. "Come back in half an hour."

Jack could not quite believe what he was seeing. It was an honest-to-God bar, with a jukebox and pool table, an oversized TV in the back, neon Coors and Strohs signs in the windows, an aged blow-up figure of Spuds MacKenzie hanging from the ceiling, and a long, shining bar, against which twenty or so stools had been shoved.

It looked, to Jack, like heaven.

"Do you have a phone I could use?" Jack asked. "I'll only be a minute."

The blonde pointed wordlessly at a pay phone on the wall beside the jukebox.

"Make it quick," she said.

Jack held the door open wider, so that Lou, who was standing behind him, beating eagerly on his back with her fists, could come in. Her smile, as she surveyed the place, was like the sun.

"Bud's," she said appreciatively. "I *love* Bud's!"

"Bud ain't here," the woman behind the bar said. "And you can't stay. I told you. We ain't open yet."

"Oh," Lou said, leaning her skis in the doorway and hurrying towards the television, which was on. "TV. Look, Jack. TV."

Jack had put his own skis aside. "Yeah," he said, watching as Lou stripped off her gloves and ran her hands appreciatively over the sides of the television with all the affection of a jockey for a beloved horse. "Great." To the woman behind the bar, he said, as he slid onto one of the stools, "I know you're closed, miss. But listen. I could really use a beer."

He gave her his best smile, the one that had won him the part of Dr. Paul Rourke on *"STAT,"* over better-known, more experienced actors.

It hadn't, apparently, lost any of its effectiveness, since the blonde, staring at him like a jack rabbit stared at a rattler, not blinking, not even moving to flick the enormous ash from her cigarette, said, "Sure thing. And call me Martha."

"Thanks, Martha," Jack said, winking at her. "You're a peach."

Martha didn't blush. He didn't know any women who blushed anymore, with the exception of the one in the corner, going into ecstasies over the television. But Martha did remove the cigarette from her lips and, with a shy smile, tucked some of her lank hair behind her ears.

"It's satellite," Lou said, sliding onto the stool beside Jack's. "Seven hundred channels. Nine of them are HBO."

"That's great," Jack said. He took the beer Martha slid

in front of him and tipped the glass in her direction. "Cheers."

Martha smiled, then looked darkly in Lou's direction. "Get you anything?" she asked tonelessly.

"Oh," Lou said, dragging her gaze from the television. "Whatever he's having. Thanks."

Martha nodded and, the smile gone, began to fill a mug from one of the taps.

Lou had pulled her cell phone from her purse.

"Look at this," she was saying. "Seven hundred channels, but still no cellular service. This thing's completely dead. Maybe I should have charged it last night. But I doubt that would have made a difference. It should still have *some* juice. So—"

"Shhh," Jack said, holding up a hand and nodding in the direction of the TV.

Lou turned her head and found herself staring at her own image.

Or at least an image of her in a long, pink hoopskirt.

Lou let out a shriek. "Oh my God! What *is* that?"

Jack looked at Martha and asked politely, "Would you mind turning that up?"

Martha obliged, and a CNN news correspondent's deep, reassuring voice filled the bar.

"It's been almost seventy-two hours since the helicopter carrying action-adventure star Jack Townsend and Academy Award–winning screenwriter Lou Calabrese crashed in the vicinity of Mount McKinley." Lou's picture disappeared and was replaced by one of Jack in a tuxedo. He recognized it as a shot from last year's Golden Globes.

"Search and rescue crews are still combing the area in hopes of finding survivors," the reporter continued. "Neither Townsend's nor Calabrese's bodies were recovered from the crash site. Winter storms have hampered the search effort. A spokesman for the McKinley National

Forest says that the longer the couple remain missing, the less chance there is of their being found alive, as the conditions in the area are simply too harsh to support human life." Video footage of the terrain Jack and Lou had just spent nearly three days traipsing through was shown, along with a shot of helicopters exactly like the one they'd just hidden from.

"A spokesman for Tim Lord, director of the film Townsend was in Alaska to shoot, states that the thoughts and prayers of the entire Hollywood community are with the loved ones of the victims, whose safe return everyone is praying for."

The reporter shifted to a story about the continuing struggle for peace in the Middle East.

"Jeez!" Lou cried, with no small amount of indignation. "Did you see that photo of me? *That* was the best photo they could come up with?"

Jack said, "I thought it was kind of cute."

"I'm going to kill Vicky," Lou said, looking as if she meant it. "That picture's from her wedding to Tim, you know. I was one of the bridesmaids. God, I *begged* her not to go with hoopskirts."

Jack said, "You looked like Little Bo Peep."

Lou let out a frustrated exclamation, then headed for the pay phone. "My *driver's license* photo is better than *that* one," she said as she stomped away.

Jack, smiling, turned back to his beer. It was only then that he noticed that behind the bar, Martha was staring at him, wide-eyed.

"That was you, weren't it?" she said breathlessly. "On the TV?"

Jack sighed. Then he summoned up another smile.

"Yes, Martha," he said. "That was me, all right."

"You're Jack Townsend," Martha said. "From that show about the doctors. And those *Copkiller* movies."

"That's me," Jack said.

Slowly, Martha slid a napkin towards him.

"Can you sign this for me?" she wanted to know. " 'Cause otherwise, ain't no one going to believe me."

Jack took the pen she offered and scrawled his name on the napkin. Then, beneath it, he wrote, *It's always funny till someone gets hurt.* Then he handed it back to her.

Martha picked up the napkin and squinted down at it, her lips moving as she read what he'd written. Then she looked up.

"What's that mean?" she wanted to know.

"Well, it means—" Then Jack shrugged. "Here, just give it back." She did so, and he crossed out Lou's line, and wrote instead, *I need a bigger gun.*

When Martha read this, a smile broke over her face.

"Oh," she said. "Sure. I remember that." Then she looked at Lou, who was chattering animatedly into the phone. "She somebody famous, too?"

Jack nodded. "She wrote the movie *Hindenburg.*"

Martha's eyes widened. "Really? *Hindenburg*'s my favorite movie of all time. You know we got that song—you know, the one from the movie? 'My Love Burns for You Tonight'? We've got that on the jukebox. You want me to play it?"

"No," Jack said quickly. "No, actually, that's all right. I think we're just gonna, you know. Have a beer and use your phone and check out the scores on the TV, if that's all right."

"Oh, that's just fine," Martha said.

Across the room, Lou was having some trouble making herself understood. Her phone call had gone well enough so far. She had gotten through to the Anchorage Four Seasons, and asked for Tim Lord's room.

But when the phone was picked up by Vicky and Tim's housekeeper, and Lou said, "Lupe? Hi, it's Lou Calabrese.

Is Mrs. Lord there, please?" she was greeted by a high-pitched shriek followed by a cry of, "Nombre de Dios!"

Then there was a clatter, as if Lupe had dropped the phone.

"Hello?" Lou glanced at the bar. But Jack was no help. He was watching the television. "The *Jets* won?" he exclaimed to no one in particular, sounding indignant.

Lou heard a click, and then Tim Lord's voice sounded in her ear.

"Who is this?" he demanded. "If this is some kind of a joke, allow me to assure you that it is in the worst kind of taste. I want you to know I am having this call traced—"

"Tim," Lou said. "Calm down. It's me. Lou."

There was a stunned silence. Then Tim burst out, "Lou? Oh, my God! You're alive? You're alive!"

"Of course I'm alive," Lou said. "I'm calling you, aren't I?"

"Where are you?" Tim wanted to know. "Is Jack with you?"

"I don't know where I am," Lou said. "And—"

There was the sound of a slight struggle on the other end of the phone. Then Vicky's voice came over the line.

"Lou?" she cried. "Lou, is that really you?"

"Hi, Vicky," Lou said patiently. "Yes, it's me. Jack and I are all right. We're—"

"Oh, thank God!" Vicky broke down, sobbing in what Lou could only describe as a semi-hysterical manner.

Lou, not for the first time that morning, felt a twinge of guilt. She had, after all, just slept with her best friend's ex. But that was all Jack was: Vicky's *ex*. Vicky was happily married now. So what could Lou possibly have to feel guilty about? Nothing.

Accordingly, she growled into the phone, "Vicky, what were you thinking, giving that picture of me from your wedding to CNN? You know I freaking hate that picture.

And now the entire country has seen me in that dress—Vicky? Vicky?"

All she heard was sobbing. Lou sighed and looked heavenward. "Vicky. I'm sorry. I didn't mean it. I love that picture. I do. I even love the dress. Look, put Tim back on the phone, will you? Vicky? Vick?"

Then the sobbing grew fainter, and a new voice came over the line.

"Lou? Lou, honey, is that you?"

Lou found herself blinking down at the receiver. It took a few seconds for her brain to register what she was hearing. Even when it did, it still didn't make any sense.

"*Dad?*" Lou said incredulously.

"Yes, honey," her father said. "It's me. Are you all right? Where are you?"

"Oh," Lou said, because she could not believe she had called Tim Lord and somehow managed to reach her father. Which could only mean one thing, of course. That her father, notified of her disappearance, had come all the way out to Alaska to look for her.

It made sense, of course, for Frank Calabrese to have done so. He was that kind of man, the kind who liked to be in control. He'd probably wanted to supervise the search and rescue crews himself.

But still. Her *dad* had flown all the way to Alaska to look for her. Could there be anything sweeter—or more humiliating?

"Oh," Lou said, again, beginning to sniffle. "I'm just . . . well, right now, I'm in a bar, Dad."

"A bar?" Her father sounded stern. "Now you listen here, young lady. Did you know that a lot of people happen to be out looking for you? We've been scared silly! And you tell me you're in a *bar*?"

"Dad," Lou said. "It's kind of a long story."

She hung up a few minutes later, feeling completely

numb. Slowly, she made her way back to the bar and sat down.

Jack glanced away from the television. "Jets won," he said. "Can you believe that?"

Lou picked up the beer Martha had left for her and drained half of it while Jack watched her, a little astonishedly.

"Got some bad news?" he asked.

Lou put the beer down with a thump.

"I'll say," she said. "Guess who was in Tim Lord's suite when I called there just now."

Jack seemed to deliberate on this for a moment. Then he brightened. "Oh, I know," he said. "Robert Redford and Meryl Streep."

"No," Lou said, without even cracking a smile. "My *dad*."

Jack raised his eyebrows. "Really? What's he doing there?"

"Jack, everybody thought we were dead. Apparently there's a whole family contingent gathered there at the Four Seasons. My dad, your mom—"

"Excuse me?" Jack asked quickly. "My *what*?"

"Your mother," Lou said, reaching for her beer again. "Your mother, Eleanor Townsend. A very kind and elegant lady, my dad says."

Jack reached quickly for his own beer.

"Oh, Jesus," he said, when he'd lowered the glass again.

"My dad," Lou said faintly, "and your mom know each other. Not just know each other. Apparently, your mom's dog—"

"Alessandro," Jack said, closing his eyes tightly, as if by doing so he could drive a painful image from his mind.

"Yes. Apparently Alessandro really likes my dad—"

"Oh, God," Jack said, lowering his head until it rested against the bar. "Please stop."

"I wish I could. They had breakfast together this morning."

Jack jerked his head back up.

"They *what*?"

"You heard me," Lou said. To Martha, she called, "Excuse me, miss? Could we get a couple more beers over here?"

"Tell me," Jack said urgently, "that you did not say what you just said."

"My dad," Lou said, "had eggs over easy with Canadian bacon, even though his cardiologist, after his bypass, advised him to lay off the greasy stuff. Your mother's apparently a much lighter eater. All she had was whole wheat toast with half a grapefruit and hot water with—"

"—lemon and honey," Jack finished for her. "I know. I know. That's what she's had for breakfast every morning since I was born."

"Well," Lou said, "it certainly impressed my father. He likes sensible eaters."

Jack looked alarmed. Still, he tried to be reasonable about the whole thing. "Well, breakfast," he said. "So they had breakfast together. I mean, that doesn't mean . . . I mean, it's just breakfast."

Lou, realizing his meaning all at once, made a disgusted face. "Of *course* it's just breakfast," she said. "You think my dad and your mom would—"

"No," Jack said hastily.

"Of course not," Lou said. "Jeez. Get your mind out of the gutter."

"Still," Jack said, uncomfortably, "I mean, just the fact that they know each other—"

"I *know*," Lou said. "Stop talking about it. You're giving me the heebie-jeebies. They're sending some sheriff up to get us. Apparently he is familiar with Bud's. And listen. We are not saying anything"—she held up a warning finger—

"about us. What happened between us. Back at Donald's. To anyone. Especially our parents. Understand?"

"God, yes," Jack said, nodding vigorously. "Can you imagine the headlines? *Spurned lovers find comfort in arms of one another*."

"Headlines?" Lou snorted. "You've got a lot more to worry about than mere headlines, my friend. My dad still carries around his service pistol. He finds out how you took advantage of me in my moment of weakness, he'll pop you one."

As Jack choked on the mouthful of new beer he'd swallowed from the mug Martha had slid in front of him, Lou smiled at the bartender and said, as she refilled Lou's mug as well, "How much do I owe you?"

Martha shook her head. "Oh, nothing, nothing. The beers are on the house. I just wanted to say, Mr. Townsend here, he tells me you wrote the movie, that *Hindenburg*?"

Lou nodded. "Yes. Yes, I did."

"Well," Martha said. "I just wanted you to know. It's my favorite movie of all time. Really."

"Well, thank you," Lou said politely. "Thank you so much. And for the beers, too."

"And it really is true, you know," Martha said, conspiratorially.

"What is?" Lou looked confused. "You mean the story? Yes, it was based on a true incident."

"No," Martha said reverently. "I mean that it truly was a triumph of the human spirit."

23

"Let me see if I got this straight," Sheriff Walter O'Malley said, glancing in the rearview mirror so that he could watch their expressions as he spoke. "You say armed men on snowmobiles chased you through the woods."

"That's right," said the redhead, nodding vigorously. "Shooting at us."

"Shooting at you," Walt said. "And that you, in turn, shot at them. With a gun you'd taken from the pilot, Sam Kowalski, who also tried to shoot at you."

"He was supposed to kill me," the tall guy, Jack Townsend, said. Walt was finding it difficult to believe that this guy, and the guy he was used to seeing on the movie screen when he plunked down his nine fifty, were one and the same. The guy on the movie screen was so much . . . bigger. Though Walt supposed that, at six foot or so, in real life, Townsend was big, too. He just wasn't twenty feet tall, the way Walt was used to seeing him.

This, Walt thought, for the hundredth time at least, was one hinky case. Between that hot little number the director was married to, the one who kept grabbing his arm—

not that he minded, as it had been quite a while since his arm had last been grabbed by a female who was not one of his daughters, their mother having passed on almost five years earlier—and this story he and Lippincott were hearing as they transported the crash survivors from the town of Damon, population three hundred, to Anchorage.

Well, let's just say Walt was glad Lippincott was the one struggling to get it all down, not him.

"You say Mr. Kowalski was supposed to kill you, Mr. Townsend," Lippincott said now, from the front passenger seat, where he sat poised with an incident report form and a clipboard and pen. "May I ask how you knew this?"

"Because he freaking said so." Townsend, at least, Walt was somewhat relieved to note, had the same short temper as the character he played on the big screen. In some small way, this made the whole height thing easier to bear. "What do you think, we're making this up?"

In the rearview mirror, Walt saw the redhead put her hand on Townsend's arm. He may have been the one who played a cop on-screen, but she was the one who actually understood how cops worked. At least if her next statement was any indication.

"Mr. Kowalski informed us that someone had paid him to kill Jack," she said evenly. "He didn't say who this person was, but he did seem to feel that if he failed in his mission, he was going to be in big trouble."

Lippincott wrote this down but could not seem to restrain a comment as he did so.

"Well, good thing for him he got crispy-crittered in the crash, then," he said, mostly under his breath.

Still, Walt wasn't the only one who overheard. The Calabrese girl heard it, too, and leaned forward.

"I beg your pardon?" she asked.

Lippincott blushed, but the only person in the car who realized it was Walt. The guy's skin was too fried from windburn for anyone else to realize that deep shade of puce wasn't his normal coloring.

"Nothing, ma'am," Lippincott said hastily.

"Listen, can you go any faster?" Townsend did not apparently share Ms. Calabrese's interest in the deputy's remark. "We've got a bunch of people waiting for us back at the hotel, and we're kind of anxious to—"

"We'll be there soon," was Walt's laconic reply. He had the departmental Trailblazer going thirty, which was plenty fast enough for this snowy road. He could understand the guy's impatience, though. The accommodations, wherever the two of them had been staying, could not have been of the cushy variety a big movie star like Jack Townsend would be accustomed to. A ranger's station? Somebody's hunting cabin? Did they really expect him to believe this crap? But why, he wondered, for the thousandth time, would they make it up? Unless they were involved in whatever hinky stuff had been going on up at the crash site. . . .

"So you took Mr. Kowalski's gun," Walt said to the redhead, "and you shot at one of the snowmobilers—"

"What did he mean?" Lou wanted to know. She always went by Lou, never her real name, Walt had been informed by her father—the only person connected to this case so far, with the single exception of Eleanor Townsend, who didn't seem to be full of shit. Everyone else struck Walt as hinky as that helicopter crash . . . probably because everyone else involved was one of those Hollywood types.

"He said something about a crispy critter," Lou went on. "I'm not an idiot, you know. I know what that means. Who's a crispy critter?"

"Beg pardon, ma'am," Walt said, coming to his deputy's rescue. "What he meant to say was, perhaps it was fortunate for Mr. Kowalski that he perished in the helicopter crash, since that way he was not forced to admit failure to his employers."

There was silence in the Trailblazer for a few seconds. Then Townsend said, "Kowalski didn't die in the crash."

Lippincott, who'd lifted his pen to record this, stopped writing, and looked into the backseat.

"Could you repeat that, sir?" he said.

A glance in the rearview mirror proved that Jack Townsend looked angry.

"Kowalski didn't die in the crash," he said, again. "He was alive when I pulled him out of it. Unconscious, but alive."

"Pulled him out of it?" Walt slowed down. He wanted to make sure he had heard correctly. "The chopper?"

"Yeah," Townsend said. "He was banged up pretty bad, but he was definitely—"

"When we arrived at the scene of the crash site," Walt said carefully, "we found a body in the aircraft that has since been identified through dental records as belonging to one Samuel Kowalski."

The redhead sucked in her breath. "Oh my God," she said, seizing hold of Townsend's sleeve. "Oh my God, Jack. They killed him. They killed Sam."

Walt saw Townsend lift his arm and wrap it around Lou. When he spoke, he sounded tired, but firm. "The pilot was alive when we last saw him," Townsend said. "I'd dragged him a good ten yards from the wreckage. He was breathing fine. He wasn't burned. Not in any way."

Suddenly Walt, who hadn't quite known what to make about the pair's story of masked gunmen and flight through the arctic wilderness, sat up a little straighter.

"And you say you shot at one of these guys?" he asked Townsend. "One of the ones on the snowmobiles? And hit him?"

"I didn't," Townsend said. He met Walt's gaze in the

rearview mirror and nodded towards Lou's head, which was buried in the front of Townsend's sweater.

"We didn't find any signs," Walt said carefully, "of any bodies, except the pilot's."

Lou looked up, her eyes wet.

"That's impossible," she said. Her voice was ragged. "The guy slammed into a tree, and his snowmobile—not to mention its driver—blew into a thousand bits. And you're trying to tell me you didn't find any *signs* of that?"

Lippincott cleared his throat uncomfortably. An unmarried rookie, he wasn't used, as Walt was, to dealing with females.

"Uh," he said. "Maybe they cleaned up after themselves."

Walt coughed meaningfully, and Lippincott shut up.

"More likely," Walt said, "the snow covered up whatever was out there—"

It was Townsend who interrupted in an incredulous voice, "You don't believe us."

"Now," Walt said. Fortunately, he was beginning to see glimpses of the Anchorage city lights ahead of them. This ride wasn't going to last much longer.

This case, however. This case he had a feeling was going to last a long, long time. Just what he needed. Like it wasn't enough he had to deal with all those tree-huggers who'd come out of the woods on account of that damned movie. Now he supposedly had some kind of team of hired assassins to track down, if these two were telling the truth.

"Nobody said they don't believe you," Walt said, in what he hoped was a reasonable voice. Too bad, he was thinking, they couldn't call in the FBI. How he would have liked to hand this one over to the feds, let them deal with it. All he wanted to do was get home and take a bath. Maybe put some of that Aveeno the girls used in the water, to help with his dry skin. That's what he needed. A hot bath, some Aveeno, and maybe one of those fancy cigars Mitch had passed out when Shirl had her last baby. . . .

Walt saw Townsend nudge the girl. "Show them," he said.

And the redhead nodded and dug into the pockets of her parka. . . .

"Hey!" Walt cried, nearly losing control of the wheel, he was so surprised. Well, who wouldn't have been? It wasn't every day he got a pair of revolvers pointed at him. In fact, he'd gone twenty years on the force without ever having to draw his own weapon.

"Jesus H. Christ!" Lippincott yelled when he saw the guns. He dug frantically for his own sidearm, crying, "Now, ma'am, let's talk about this. Believe me, you don't want to shoot us—"

"Don't worry," Lou said drily. "The safeties are on. I'm just trying to show you that we're telling the truth. We took this .38 off the pilot—the man you say burned up in the crash—and the .44's from the guy who tried to attack us in the ranger's station. Go ahead and take them. Maybe you can trace the serial numbers and find out who they really belong to."

Walt managed, with difficulty, to get control of the wheel—and his rapidly beating heart. "Deputy Lippincott," he said. "Would you please relieve Ms. Calabrese of those firearms?"

Lippincott gingerly took each gun from Lou's hands, then placed them carefully in the Trailblazer's glove compartment.

"Now," Townsend wanted to know, "do you believe us?"

What could Walt say except, "Yes"?

But that wasn't exactly true, of course. And it certainly didn't mean that what they'd been saying made any more sense than before.

"And you say you have no idea," Walt asked Townsend, "why someone might want you dead?"

"None at all," Townsend replied. Then, with a sideways glance at Lou, he added, "I'm certainly no angel, but I've never—to my knowledge—done anything that'd make anybody mad enough to want to off me. Mess up my hotel suite, maybe, but not, you know, shoot me."

"Who messed up your hotel suite?" Walt wanted to know. "There may be a connection—"

"There isn't," Townsend said, flatly. "Believe me."

"You never know." Walt gripped the steering wheel more tightly now that he saw the silhouette of the Anchorage Four Seasons, one of the tallest buildings on its block, looming before them. "Mr. Townsend, I'm going to suggest that you have twenty-four-hour protection until you leave the state—"

"No way," Townsend interrupted.

"Mr. Townsend," Walt said in his most reasonable tone, the one he used when any of his daughters took it into her head to wear Lycra. "Several attempts on your life have been made—"

"Sure," Townsend replied. "Out there. Not here."

"Not yet," Lou Calabrese reminded him.

Townsend, Walt saw through the rearview mirror, glanced down at her. She was gazing up at him earnestly.

"Jack," she said. "Please listen to the sheriff. He knows what he's talking about. Whoever is behind all this, he could just as easily be in Anchorage as in Myra. And until we figure out who he is, you're a walking target—"

"Lou." Townsend had lowered his voice to an angry whisper, but Walt heard it easily enough anyway. "I don't want to have a cop following me everywhere I go."

"You'd prefer to have a bullet in your skull?" Lou wanted to know.

Townsend didn't say anything. Now they were swinging into the circular driveway to the Four Seasons. In the rearview mirror, Walt saw Lou Calabrese sit up a little straighter when she saw the crowds of protesters standing along West Third.

"Oh my God," she breathed. "They're still out there?"

"Yes, ma'am," Walt said cheerfully. "And they're still plenty mad about that mine shaft Mr. Lord's planning to blow up."

Some of the protesters shook their fists angrily at the Trailblazer, though they could have no idea that the passengers within it were in any way connected to the film. Many of them held signs with messages like "Save the Mine" and "Protect the Arctic Fox" and, most notably, "Take Your Toys Back to Tinseltown." A film crew from one of the entertainment news shows was interviewing a particularly hairy protester as they drove by, clearly getting the real scoop about the threatened mine from an actual mountain man.

"It could be one of them," Lou said from the backseat. "Any one of them."

Jack made a contemptuous noise, halfway between a laugh and a snort.

"Those weren't environmentalists out there on those snowmobiles, Lou," he said. "Believe me."

She glanced at him. And in that glance, even though he only saw its reflection in the rearview mirror, Walt saw fire.

"You're getting police protection," Lou said in a hard voice. "And that's the end of it."

And, to Walt's surprise, it was. Townsend didn't say another word about it.

Walt didn't blame him. If it was between a band of shooters and Lou Calabrese, he'd put his money on the redhead any day.

24

"**L**ou!" shrieked the reporter from "Extra." "What was it like to be stranded for three days in the woods with America's hottest hunk, Jack Townsend?"

"Lou!" screamed the *Us Weekly* journalist. "Did Jack Townsend confide his feelings to you about Greta Woolston's elopement with Bruno di Blase?"

"Lou!" A representative from Greenpeace waved a sign that said "Hollywood Doesn't Care." "How can you justify the slaughter of hundreds of innocent woodland creatures for the sake of a film that glorifies violence?"

"Ms. Calabrese," a teenage girl wailed, trying to thrust something in Lou's hand. "Can you get Jack Townsend my phone number? Please! I want to have his baby!"

"Okay, Dad," Lou said, as her father pulled her from the throng of reporters into the safety of the hotel elevator. "That is the last time we are going out to eat, understand? From now on, it's room service only."

Frank Calabrese pounded the button to their floor and said, "Honey, you don't understand. I ate that hotel food last night, and let me tell you, I was up swilling Mylanta until—"

"Fine," Lou said as the elevator doors slid shut, mercifully cutting off all the shouting from the lobby. "We'll order pizza. Whatever. I just can't go through that lobby again. I can't take it, on top of everything else."

"Now, honey," her father said. "I told you. Jack is going to be fine. Sheriff O'Malley's arranged for round-the-clock protection for him, courtesy of the Anchorage PD. If anybody is trying to kill Jack, those boys in blue won't—"

"If?" Lou could hardly believe her ears. "Oh, great. You don't believe us, either?"

"I didn't say that." Frank watched the numbers above the doors light up as they rode. "Of course I believe you. We all do. I'm just saying, you shouldn't worry about him so much. He's a grown man, and besides, he's got Anchorage's finest looking out for him."

Lou didn't say anything about her lack of faith in Anchorage's finest. She knew they were doing their best. Besides, there was no point in starting an argument with her father at this point. After all, they'd managed to share a nice, cordial meal at Shandy's Shrimp Shack—a guy in hotel security had told her father it was the best place to eat in the city. Frank had wanted to have a quiet meal with her after all the hoopla surrounding her and Jack's homecoming. Exiting Sheriff O'Malley's Trailblazer, Lou and Jack had walked unsuspectingly into a party Vicky Lord had arranged, with "welcome home" balloons and a buffet spread and every single person remotely associated with the film in attendance.

Including Lou's father, and Jack's mother.

All Lou had wanted to do was slip into her own room, take a shower, and go to bed. But she hadn't been able to. Oh, she'd managed to squeeze in the shower before dinner. But there'd been no nap. Instead, she'd worried.

First about Jack. Someone had tried, several times, to kill him, and they still had no clue who it might have been, or if he'd try to do it again. Sure, Sheriff O'Malley had the .44, and would try to trace its owner. And maybe he'd succeed.

But what if he didn't? And what if despite the extra security the hotel had arranged, and the police escort Jack was to have everywhere he went, something happened—something like what had happened to poor Sam?

"Lou?"

She glanced up from her shoes to see her father peering down at her.

"You all right, honey?" he wanted to know.

She shook herself. "Yes," she said quickly. "I'm fine. I'm sorry. I was just . . . I was just thinking. . . ."

. . . about America's hottest hunk. Oh, God! How pathetic was she? This was what came from falling in love with actors. Why hadn't she taken her own advice? Was she a masochist? This was the other thing she was worried about: Jack's invitation to come live with him . . .

. . . and the fact that she was so sorely tempted to accept it.

Then the elevator doors slid open, and Lou's face went up flames. Because standing there on the eighth floor—her floor, not Jack's, because Jack had moved up to the tenth floor after Melanie had trashed his suite on the eighth—was none other than America's hottest hunk himself . . . and his mother.

"Why, Frank," Eleanor Townsend said, in tones, if Lou was not mistaken, of delight. "And Lou. How lovely to see you. We just stopped by your room, Lou, to see if you and your father would be interested in coming to dinner with us, but you weren't there. But here you are! How wonderful to catch you."

"We just ate," Lou said quickly, hoping neither Jack nor

his mother would notice the blush that was turning her entire head, she was sure, beet red.

Her father was more gracious.

"What a shame," he said, in a voice Lou had only heard him use once before—and that had been up in the Lords' suite, when she and Jack had first arrived. Her father had introduced her to Jack's mother in that same too-hearty tone . . . a tone that had caused Lou and Jack to exchange nervous glances, especially since it seemed to induce in Eleanor Townsend a high-pitched giggle that was clearly unfamiliar to her son.

"That buffet up in the Lords' suite earlier this evening was nice and all," Frank went on jovially, "but a man can't survive on crudités alone, can he, Jack?"

"No, he can't," Jack said with a smile. "That's too bad. It would have been so nice if you could have joined us—"

"Oh, yes," Eleanor said eagerly. "Even if only for a cup of coffee—"

"We'd love to," Frank said, losing his grip on the elevator door, which he'd been holding open for Jack's mother. "Wouldn't we, Lou?"

But Lou had noticed something. And that was that Jack and his mother were standing alone in the eighth-floor hallway—all alone. Suddenly, she forgot she was blushing and didn't want to draw attention to herself.

"Where's the police officer?" Lou demanded, turning an accusing gaze on Jack. "The one who's supposed to be keeping an eye on you?"

Jack grinned at her, those electric blue eyes of his full of something Lou couldn't quite put a name to—had never been able to put a name to.

"I gave Officer Juarez the night off," he said.

"Jack." Lou felt as if her head might explode. She really did. "The whole point of having police protection is that they've got to be around at all times. You can't give them the night off. What if somebody tries to attack you here in the hotel?"

"We're just going downstairs to the hotel restaurant," Jack said.

"What, there's a no-shooting policy in the hotel restaurant? No shoes, no shirt, no silencer, no service?"

Jack gave his mother and Lou's father a salty smile. It was only then that Lou noticed that the two of them were staring at her. Well, at her and Jack.

"Why don't you two," Jack said, "go on ahead. I'm not really all that hungry."

Eleanor looked startled. "Oh, but Frank already ate—" she fluttered.

"Always room for more," Frank said, jovially. "Haven't had dessert yet, either."

Lou could not believe what she was hearing. Her father was offering to dine with Jack's mother in a place he'd complained had given him heartburn. And he was going to risk going back through that throng of reporters in the lobby to do it! What was happening here? Was this just parental bonding between two people whose children had been through an ordeal together? Or was it—God forbid—something more?

"See you later, you two," Frank said, as he guided— hustled might have been the more accurate word— Eleanor into the elevator. "Jack, listen to Lou. She knows what she's talking about. And don't wait up!"

The elevator doors closed on Eleanor Townsend's giggle. Giggle! The woman had *giggled!*

As soon as they were gone, Lou turned around and smacked Jack in the shoulder as hard as she could.

"Ow!" he said, though he looked amused. "What was *that* for?"

"Encouraging my dad," Lou snapped. "Can't you see he's got a crush on your mom?"

"Him?" Jack rubbed the spot she'd punched. "All my mother can talk about is *Frank this* and *Frank that*. Do you know your dad makes his own spaghetti sauce? Well, I do. I even know what's in it. The Calabrese family spaghetti sauce recipe. And I know it. I swear I've spent most of the past hour wishing I still had one of those guns you handed over so I could put a bullet through my head."

Lou, furious, paced the hallway. "Great," she said. "Just great, Jack. Like we don't have enough problems. Somebody's trying to kill you, and now our parents have crushes on each other." She froze in her tracks, and threw him a look of horror. "My God, Jack. What are we going to do if they start dating?"

"Well," Jack said thoughtfully. "I admit it might be hard to explain to the kids. I mean, why their mom and dad's parents are married. Maybe if we moved to Appalachia they wouldn't get made fun of as much in school—"

"Can't you, just for once, be serious?" Lou wanted to know.

"I think," Jack said with a perfectly straight face, "that you're overreacting. And not just about the whole rent-a-cop thing, either. Lou, no one is going to take a hit at me here at the hotel. Too many witnesses, okay?"

Lou opened her mouth to argue, but Jack held up a hand.

"And so your dad and my mom like each other," he went on. "So what? Let them have their fun. I personally can think of a few things—" He stepped towards her and wrapped both hands around her waist. "—I'd rather be doing right now than worrying about what our parents are up to. How about you?"

She pulled away from him—or attempted to, anyway. He had a pretty good hold on her, and didn't seem too willing to release her. And she, it had to be admitted, felt something inside of her wilt a little as she breathed in the scent of freshly showered Jack . . . damn him.

"Jack," she said, trying to hold herself as stiffly as possible as he bent his head and placed his lips alongside her neck. "I told you. This will never work."

"You never told me any such thing," Jack said, keeping his mouth where it was . . . and causing, as she was certain he was no doubt aware, all manner of havoc where her pulse was concerned. "You said last night that you needed to sleep on it. Well, now you've slept on it. And if it's all the same to you, I'd like to take up where we left off before we were so rudely interrupted by cross-country ski trips and barmaids named Martha. . . ."

"Jack," Lou said weakly. Still, she was determined to stick to her earlier resolve. "You know perfectly well this is a bad idea."

"I think this a great idea," Jack said against her throat. "And I have an even better one. Let's order up a bottle of champagne, put the 'do not disturb' sign on the door, and take a nice, long, bubble bath together."

"Jack," Lou said as his lips slid towards her jawbone. Her heartbeat was skittering like a pebble over the surface of a glass-smooth lake. Still, she refused to give in to carnal longing. That's what had happened with Barry. And look where that had got her. "Forget it. I am not getting involved with any more actors."

"Good thing I'm quitting the business, then," he said, his lips on her earlobe. "Hey, I've got an idea. Let's get a dog. A golden retriever. We can name it Dakota and when 'Entertainment Tonight' comes to interview us about our blissfully happy relationship we can stroll down the beach and throw Frisbees to Dakota, just like John Tesh and Connie Selleca. . . ."

"Jack," Lou said, her eyelids, completely against her will, closing. "We are not getting a dog together."

"Just one dog," Jack whispered, his fingers slowly un-tucking her blouse from the waistband of the slacks she'd changed into before leaving for dinner with her father. "To start out with. To go with our beach house."

"We are not getting a beach house together," Lou said, even as she felt his mouth sliding towards hers. "I told you. I am never dating an actor ag—"

Her protest, however, was smothered against Jack's lips. She felt herself melt in his arms. A part of her cursed her own weakness.

But another, much larger part of her reveled in the feel of Jack's long, hard body against hers . . . the fiery brand of his tongue as it met hers . . . the tantalizing feel of his fingers as they traveled up under her blouse, until first one, and then another of his thumbs dipped, with infinite gentleness, beneath the lacy cups of her bra. . . .

She moaned, softly, against his mouth. She couldn't help it. She could feel that now familiar hardness in the front of the charcoal wool trousers he'd put on for dinner, pressing urgently against her.

"What do you say?" Jack tore his lips from hers long enough to ask. As they'd kissed, he'd backed her slowly up against the hallway wall. Now he had her pinned there, with both his hands under her blouse, cupped over her swollen, straining breasts, while his need, rigid and im-perative, throbbed against her belly. "A little Dom Perignon and Mr. Bubble to forget your troubles?"

It would have been so easy to say yes. So easy to let her-self go limp in his arms, let him do whatever it was he wanted, what she knew he could do so well.

And she would have said yes. To her everlasting shame, she would have said yes, screamed it, even. . . .

. . . if right at that moment the elevator doors hadn't slid open to reveal none other than Melanie Dupre, carry-ing a bottle of champagne and two glasses, and wearing only a negligee, a pair of feathered mules, and a determined expression.

The determined expression vanished, however, when she noticed them. Suddenly, Melanie started screaming, loudly enough, Lou was convinced, to wake the dead all the way over in Canada . . . perhaps even all the way down to Mexico.

"You liar!" she shrieked, pointing at Jack with one talonous nail. "You damned liar! You told me there wasn't anyone else. You told me you just wanted to try being single for a while. And the whole time—the whole time— you were messing around with *her*?"

The look of horror on Melanie's face as she said the word *her* was all Lou needed to catapult her out of the haze into which she'd sunk at the first touch of Jack's lips to her skin. Tensing, she shoved him away from her, causing several of the buttons on her blouse to go flying off. She didn't care. All she could think was, *Must get away from here, and fast.*

Jack was holding up both hands to protect himself, as if Melanie were a slowly approaching cobra or fragrance-sample sprayer in a department store.

"Mel," he said, in a voice Lou supposed he was trying to keep low and soothing. "Listen to me. The other night, when I said I wanted to try being single for a while, I meant it. I really did. But then, as you know, I went through a near-death experience. And that can really make you reorganize your priorities, you know? And that's when I realized that maybe I haven't quite given monogamy a fair shake—"

"You," Melanie shrieked, "want to be monogamous with *her*? With *her* and not *me*?"

Glass exploded against the wall behind Jack's head as Melanie heaved one of the champagne flutes she'd been carrying.

Fortunately by that time Lou had managed to dig the card key to her room out of her purse. She wasn't sure it was fair, exactly, to leave Jack alone with this raving lunatic. On the other hand, *she* wasn't the one who'd been stupid enough to have an affair with Melanie Dupre—or give Officer Juarez the night off.

A second eruption of glass decided her on the matter. She was getting out of the line of fire—especially since Melanie seemed to be blaming Lou for Jack's decision to break up with her. Inserting her card key into her door lock, she waited breathlessly for the electronic light to turn green, while Melanie shrieked, "Do you have any idea how humiliating it's going to be when it gets out that you've left me for a *screenwriter*? I mean, my God, she doesn't even have a SAG card!"

The light turned green. Lou pushed on the door with all her might. It swung open, and she hurried inside, then slammed the door shut behind her and threw the deadbolt into place, just in case.

She was just turning to reach for the phone to dial security when she realized she was not alone in the room. No, there was a man sitting on her bed. A man in a cashmere sweater, suede jacket, and jeans. A man who looked disturbingly familiar. A man who turned out to be. . . .

"Hi, Lou," Bruno di Blase, aka Barry Kimmel, said to her.

25

Lou stared at him in complete bewilderment. What was Barry doing here, in Anchorage? Barry, who had, just a few nights ago, eloped with Greta Woolston, and was supposed to be on his honeymoon with her?

"Uh," Barry said. "Lou. Your, um, shirt is kind of—"

Lou looked down and realized that her blouse, where the buttons had popped open, was hanging wide open. Her white bra was out there for anyone to see.

"Barry," she said, spinning around and reaching for the terrycloth hotel robe she'd left on a chair after she'd showered. "What are you doing here?"

"Oh," Barry said, blinking a little. "I slipped some guy at the desk a fifty to give me one of those card keys. You know. To your room."

"No," Lou said, as she put on the voluminous robe, then tied its sash securely around her waist. "I don't mean here in my room. I mean here in Anchorage."

Barry's face, always so smoothly handsome, looked almost impossibly so when he was incredulous about something, which he evidently was just then.

"Lou!" he said, standing up. "How can you even ask that? I thought you were dead. Of *course* I came!"

It took Lou a minute to digest this. "Barry," she said slowly. "I don't know how to break this to you, but we broke up. Remember?"

"And because of that, I'm not allowed to worry about you?" he asked. "I mean, Lou, you were out there—" He gestured towards the large picture glass window that, when it wasn't dark out, had a view of the Alaskan mountain range. "—stranded in the frozen tundra—"

"Woods," Lou corrected him.

He regarded her with his sleepy brown eyes. Barry had always moved through life looking perpetually drowsy, as if he were just waiting for the right woman to come along and wake him up. Lou, obviously, had not been that woman. But it didn't look as if it was Greta, either, since Barry still seemed fairly droopy-eyed.

"Whatever," Barry said. "I mean, come on, Lou. Of course I had to come. I know we had our differences towards the end there, but whatever else happens, you'll always be my best girl."

"Really." Lou glanced at his left hand. It was noticeably bereft of the glint of gold. She said, "Barry, aren't you supposed to be on your honeymoon right now?"

Barry looked offended. He'd had a way of doing that, of looking pained whenever she'd pointed out his transgressions, as if her mention of them was somehow worse than his having committed them.

"Do you really think I could enjoy myself," he asked, "knowing that you were in moral danger?"

Lou coughed. "I think you mean mortal." Though, under the circumstances, his version fit as well.

"Whatever," Barry said. "As soon as I heard, I took the first flight I could find out here."

"Really?" Lou said. "Well, wasn't that nice of you." This

was weird. More than weird. Unreal, was what it was. She
and Barry had not parted on friendly terms. So what was
he doing here, really? "And Greta? Did she come, too?"
Lou glanced at the door to the bathroom. "She isn't hiding in the shower, is she? I told you before, Barry, no
three-ways."

Barry's darkly handsome face clouded over. He looked,
once again, resentful of her for having brought up such an
indelicate subject.

"Lou," he said. "Please. Don't cheapen the moment. Of
course Greta isn't in your shower. She didn't come with
me." He did not elaborate on this, but his tone was brooding enough to set off a few warning bells in Lou's head:
Uh-oh. Trouble in paradise.

"Lou," Barry said, with what she called his melting
look, the one that he'd given Greta in *Hindenburg*, just before the two of them had swung down to safety from the
doomed airship—a look *Cosmo* had suggested could turn
a glacier into tap water. "I am more glad than I can say
that it turns out you're all right."

More alarm bells sounded in Lou's head. As if Barry's
mere presence wasn't enough to arouse her suspicions,
the almost unprecedented fact that he had actually parted
with a fifty in order to establish this contact, Barry being
one of the most tightfisted people she had ever met,
coupled with the fact that he claimed he was glad to see
her, pretty much convinced her that either he was trying
out a new personality—something Barry did with a fair
amount of regularity—or had suffered a debilitating head
injury.

"Barry," Lou said, cautiously. "Did something heavy
fall on you recently?"

Barry knit his perfectly waxed brows. "What?"

"Never mind," Lou said. Barry, it was strangely good to
see, was still Barry. He, like the rest of Hollywood, would

never change. There was something reassuring about this. "Look, Barry, it's nice of you to cut your honeymoon short to come and see me like this, but I've really had a long day, and if it's all the same to you, I'd like to hit the sack."

Barry put on his crestfallen expression.

"Lou," he said. "I was really hoping . . . I mean, I really need to talk to you. I know you're busy, and everything, but . . . well . . . we never talk anymore."

Lou sank onto the bed. "Barry," she said, "that's because you left me for another woman. Remember?"

"See, that's just it." Barry looked behind him, found a chair, and pulled it towards the end of the bed where Lou sat. "I mean, just because I'm with someone else now, that doesn't mean I've stopped caring for you, Lou."

"Really," she said without inflection. Inwardly, of course, her mind was racing. What, she wondered, was going on here? People said bad things happened in threes, but this was getting ridiculous. First Barry dumps her for Greta Woolston, then she gets shot at by strangers in the Alaskan wilderness, then Barry decides he wants her back? Too weird. Unless. . . .

Unless they were all connected. It couldn't be . . . it wasn't possible that Barry was behind the attacks on Jack. Why would Barry want Jack dead? To take over the role of Pete Logan? It was true that since *Hindenburg*, Barry had been having trouble finding scripts that he felt suited his new superstar image. But to resort to murder to get his hands on the perfect role? That just wasn't like Barry. It would have required way too much effort . . . not to mention money.

No. Her writer's imagination was overreacting again. She needed to calm down. She needed to get a grip. She needed to . . .

. . . get Barry Kimmel's hand off her knee. Because that's where he'd put it, suddenly.

"Of course I still care, Lou," Barry said. "We were together, what, ten years? You think I can just turn my affections on and off, like a faucet? No. It doesn't work that way. I will always care for you, Lou. *Always.*"

He had on his sincere face. He'd worn this expression in the scene in *Hindenburg* where Greta's character had questioned him about his intentions. He'd also, Lou remembered, worn it frequently in front of highway patrol officers, whenever he got pulled over on the freeway for speeding.

"Barry," Lou said in a hard voice, not falling for his sincere face any more than she'd fallen for his melting look. "What do you want?"

Sincere face disappeared to be replaced by an expression Lou liked to call *who me?*

"Want?" Barry echoed. "Lou, I already told you that. I wanted to make sure you were okay. That's all." He shook his head, looking bewildered. "I don't understand where all of this hostility is coming from."

"Gosh, Barry," Lou said. "I don't know. Maybe it's because for ten years, you told me you weren't ready to commit, that you needed to get to know yourself before you could fully get to know another. And then I find out from '*Access* Freaking *Hollywood*' that you and Greta Woolston got hitched in a quickie ceremony in the Elvis Chapel—"

"It wasn't," Barry said, offended again, "the Elvis Chapel. It was the Hindenburg Room at the Trump Casino, and—"

"Whatever, Barry," Lou said. "I don't want to fight. I just—"

"Neither do I," Barry said earnestly. "Because in spite of our past differences, Lou, you're still one of my favorite people of all time. You don't know how much I wished you could have been at the wedding. You were the only thing missing, really."

"Uh," Lou said, reluctant to point out the obvious, but fearing he really didn't get it. "Because you dumped me to marry someone else, Barry. Remember?"

Barry made a face. But even with his features squinched up with distaste, Barry Kimmel—Bruno di Blase to the rest of the world—was one of the handsomest men alive.

One of them. The other one, as Lou could hear only too well, was still getting his fifteen-million-dollar ass kicked by a size two model/actress in the hallway outside.

"So it didn't work romantically between us," Barry said, in the exact same tone he might have said *I prefer pepperoni on my pizza.* "You're still like a sister to me. Which is another reason why I had to come to Alaska personally to see you, Lou."

Barry cleared his throat, and Lou realized, with a sinking heart, that he was getting ready to make a speech. His last speech—the one about her having grown so hard and cynical that he hardly recognized her anymore as the sweet girl with whom he'd moved out west—was still ringing in her ears, and that had been delivered weeks ago. She wondered what she could possibly have done to deserve further punishment.

"I had an idea," Barry said grandly, as if announcing something highly unusual. Which, considering that it was Barry, was actually true: he was not a man prone to many ideas.

"An idea," Lou said.

"Yes," Barry said. "I had it on the plane on the way to the Cayman Islands. That's where we're honeymooning, Greta and I. You know what the Cayman Islands are made up of, don't you, Lou?"

Lou knit her brow. "Offshore banking accounts?"

"No," Barry said, with a laugh that revealed all of his even, capped white teeth. "Volcanoes, Lou! The Ring of

Fire. And that's when it hit me. An idea for a project that would make *Hindenburg* look like *Airport '77*. And the minute I thought of it, I told myself I have to tell this to Lou. Because she's the only person I know who could pull it off."

Lou smiled at him weakly, afraid she knew what was coming. "Really."

"Really," Barry said. He held out both his tanned, manicured hands—hands that had, for ten years, roamed over just about every part of Lou's body at one point or another, but had never once managed to make her feel the way Jack had made her feel in one night. "Are you ready?"

Lou thought longingly of crawling between the cool white sheets she was sitting on and going to sleep. "Ready," she said.

Barry made a little movie-screen shape out of his hands. "Pompeii," he said, dramatically.

"Pompeii," Lou repeated tonelessly.

"Right!" Barry leaped up from his chair and spread his arms open wide. "There's never been a movie about the destruction of Pompeii. Picture it, Lou. A cultured, sophisticated people—artisans, really—unknowingly living on the mouth of a volcano. They are going about their normal, artisan business when all of a sudden—POW!— the mountain explodes, sending molten lava through the cobblestoned streets of their town, destroying everything in its path. Will our two young lovers—you've got to have two young lovers, see. Two young lovers whose parents disapprove of their relationship—be able to escape the magma and volcanic ash in time? Talk about a triumph of the human spirit."

Barry lowered his arms and stood, grinning down at her. "Well?" he said. "What do you think? I see me as the part of the young lover. A young Roman general, or something. And the girl could be, you know, from a long line of pan-flute players, and her parents don't want her to marry a soldier, because they want her to carry on the pan-flute business, or some crap like that. And the general, see, he can be the only person who knows the volcano's gonna blow, because the same thing happened on his native island. He's like an ancient volcanologist. So he's trying to warn everyone, only they won't listen, on account of being all obsessed with the pan-flutes—"

"Gosh, Barry," Lou interrupted. She hadn't wanted to interrupt, but Barry did not seem close to winding down, and she wanted to get him out of her room before midnight, if at all possible. "That is such a great idea."

Barry grinned down at her. "See. I knew you'd like it. That's why as soon as I thought of it, I was like, I have to talk to Lou. Only, you know, you were lost in the tundra."

"Woods," Lou said, standing up. "And I think that's just a great idea for a movie, Barry. And you know what's best about it? The way you tell it. So compelling. In fact, you tell it so well, I think you should be the one to write the screenplay, not me."

She had taken his arm and begun to walk him towards the door. Now, however, Barry jerked his arm from her reach.

"But, Lou," he said. "I'm not a writer. That's why I came to you. You can have it, Lou. You can have full story by, screenplay by credits, whatever, I don't care, so long as I get to star. See, Lou, the scripts I've been getting since *Hindenburg* . . . well, they're all really bad. I mean Jim Carrey, Robin Williams bad. I need you to write something for me. Another star vehicle. . . ."

Lou smiled up at him. She didn't want to do it. It really was like shooting fish in a barrel.

But the thing was, he'd completely asked for it.

"But Barry," she said, with her eyes very wide. "Remember when you told me I'd grown so hard and cynical you barely recognized me as the same girl you'd moved out to California with?"

He eyed her uneasily. "Yes. . . ."

"Well, I realized then, Barry, that you were right. I *have* grown too hard and cynical. So I've decided to quit the film writing business."

Barry stared down at her, so astonished that he didn't even remember to put an expression on his face.

"Quit the film writing business?" he echoed.

"Yes," Lou said, taking his arm again and steering him towards the door. "You see what an enormous influence you've had over me, Barry? And I just can't thank you enough for it."

"B-but you can't," Barry stammered. "You can't just quit. I mean, what are you going to do instead?"

"Well," Lou said. "I'm working on a novel."

Barry looked hopeful. "Really? Do you think it would translate to the screen? Because you know I bet the studio could adapt it, and if you mentioned my name for the lead character—"

Lou laughed. She couldn't help it.

"Well," she said. "I don't know about the lead character. But there's definitely a part in it for you, Barry."

He brightened. "Really?"

"Uh-huh," Lou said. "You can play the ex-boyfriend who uses the heroine and then dumps her when someone prettier comes along."

The smile left his face. "Hey. Hey, now! That's not called for."

"Isn't it, Barry?" Lou asked. They'd reached the door now. All she had to do was pull back the deadbolt, open it, and shove him through.

But she still had one thing left to say.

"*Hasta la vista*, Barry."

Then, just as she'd planned, she lifted the deadbolt,

opened the door, and got ready to shove Barry through it.

Except that she couldn't. Because a very haggard-looking Jack Townsend was standing there, holding a bottle of Dom Perignon in one hand, and in the other, a bright pink box of Mr. Bubble.

26

"I can't believe you did that," Jack said, a little while later. "Left me alone to deal with the Attack of the Five-Foot Fuck Bunny."

"Hey," Lou said, from the bathroom, where she was brushing her teeth. "She was your fuck bunny, not mine."

"Oh, right," Jack said. "Like I didn't rescue you from your own fuck bunny attack just now."

"For your information," Lou said, "Barry was not a fuck bunny. He and I once shared a deep and abiding love for one another."

Jack, stretched out on her bed, the bottle of Dom resting against his flat abs, said, "Once more, in English, please."

Lou spat the toothpaste from her mouth, rinsed, then, wiping her face on a hand towel, stomped out of the bathroom to say, "I was in love with Barry. For years and years."

Jack winced. "That is not something I would go around repeating," he said. "It doesn't cast you in the most positive light, you know."

"Oh, and your having sex with Melanie Dupre makes you what?" Lou demanded. "Ghandi?"

Jack observed her from the bed where he lay. "What have you got on under that robe?" he wanted to know.

Lou felt, to her fury, her cheeks start to heat up. "Nothing," she said. "And not for the reason you think. I happened to be showering when you reappeared. I didn't expect to see you again tonight. I thought you were going to escort Barry back to his room, then retire to yours like a good little actor. You're supposed to be at the set at nine tomorrow morning, if I read the call sheet correctly."

Jack rolled onto his side, and, propping his head up on one hand, said, "Hey, a guy can't be too careful where a woman like you is concerned. I turn around to deal with an irate ex, and next thing I know, you're in here with a guy I thought was not only long gone out of your life, but who was supposed to have been safely wed to another. You're damned right I came back. I wasn't sure who I'd find in here next. I thought I saw Matt Lauer wandering around down in the lobby, looking for a scoop. Seemed a good bet he'd show up on the old eighth floor eventually. Everybody else seems to."

"You," Lou said, "are a sick, sick man."

"I know." He patted the mattress suggestively. "Come and sit down over here. I think I need to have a look under that robe."

Lou, who'd picked up a bottle of moisturizer, sat down on the opposite side of the bed from him and began industriously to rub the cream into her newly shaved legs. She did this in order to keep her gaze from roving too hungrily over his long, lean body, laid out so enticingly across her bed. She was not going to fall into temptation again. Not this time.

"I think I recall, Jack," she said, "my saying just a short

time ago that this little flirtation you and I seem to be having is never going to work."

"Well, not if you won't take that robe off, it won't."

"I'm serious, Jack," she said.

"So am I."

"Jack." Lou sighed. "What happened out there—you know, while we were, um, lost. That was just a fluke. All right? That wasn't me. I don't do things like . . . well, what we did in Donald's cabin. Okay? I'm not that type of girl."

"Could have fooled me," Jack said, with a suggestive laugh.

"I know." Lou felt herself starting to blush as she remembered all the things she'd done to merit that laugh. *Be strong,* she told herself. *Remember what happened with Barry. Jack could break your heart ten thousand times worse.* She shook her head. "Look, I'm sorry if I misled you. But this—whatever this is—it's got to stop. It's got to stop now, tonight."

Jack's dark eyebrows rose. "Wait a minute." He looked—and sounded—incredulous. "Are you *breaking up* with me?"

She couldn't blame him for being shocked. She was probably the first woman who'd ever turned down a chance at being Mrs. Jack Townsend for a month, or however long his romantic liaisons tended to last.

And she was, she told herself, probably one of the few women to walk away from him with her heart still intact.

Or at least she would be, if she broke things off with him now, tonight, this very minute. . . .

"Listen," Lou said. "In order for me to break up with you, we'd have to have been in some kind of relationship. Which we never were."

"We weren't?" Jack looked even more incredulous. "You could have fooled me."

Lou gave a nervous laugh. She didn't know what else to

do. She certainly had never expected him to fight her on this. She'd thought he'd be relieved. Weren't all serial daters like Jack just dying for an excuse to dump their current flames, so they could move on to the next one? He ought to be on his knees before her in abject gratitude.

Instead, he looked troubled.

"Who's going to break the news to Dakota?" he wanted to know.

She stared at him. "What are you talking about?"

"Well, just that you can't break up with me now," Jack said. "We haven't even figured out who's going to get custody of Dakota. And have you considered the impact this is going to have on his fragile little psyche? He may be in therapy for years over this."

He was joking. It had taken Lou a little while to realize it, but of course it turned out he was joking. His resistance had been token after all. He didn't care. He didn't care in the least.

She told herself that this was a good thing—that now she'd be able to extricate herself with ease.

Except a part of her was hurt. A part of her—the same part of her that believed in the happy endings she penned, that really did think love could triumph over all—was wounded to the quick that he could joke over something that, however briefly, had meant more to her than . . . well, than she'd been able to admit to herself.

But it was better this way. So much better. Now they could go back to squabbling over his nude scenes and the *I need a bigger gun* line. Things would go back to the way they were. Things would go back to normal.

Everything, she knew, except for her. Lou Calabrese, she knew, would never, ever be the same.

And that's why it was good she was getting out now, before the damage was irreparable, and he ruined her for any other man.

She tried to match his flippant tone, so he wouldn't know she cared. "I thought Dakota," she said, drily, "was a golden retriever."

"Changed my mind," Jack said. "The dog's name is Ranger. Our firstborn is Dakota."

Lou sighed. He was only teasing, she knew. That's what Jack did. Teased.

But this kind of teasing hurt. He didn't know, of course, how in high school, when she'd been planning out her and Barry's life together, she'd been sure they'd be married with their first child by her thirtieth birthday. Sure, she still had a year or so to meet that deadline.

But it still wasn't a subject she could joke about.

"You shouldn't have come back here, Jack," she said seriously.

"I had to," Jack said. "I left my Mr. Bubble here."

"I mean it, Jack," she said.

"Hey." He looked genuinely irritated. "I thought we had a date. Remember? In the hallway? Before we were so rudely interrupted. I was getting definite date vibes back there. Then I come back in here, and all of a sudden, you're breaking up with me. I don't get it. What changed? Was it Officer Juarez? Look, I swear tomorrow I'll hand-cuff myself to him. Tim won't like that for the shot he's planning on filming, but he'll just have to edit the guy out later—"

"It's not that," Lou said. "Though I wish you'd take the fact that someone wants you dead a little more seriously."

"What is it, then?" Jack demanded. "Is it Melanie? Haven't I said how sorry I am about that? But honest to God, Lou, I never made her any promises, and when I found out how attached she was getting, I tried to break it off—that's how my hotel room got trashed. I had no idea what a headcase she was—"

Lou, who knew perfectly well that Melanie Dupre had,

in fact, been a headcase long before she'd ever gotten involved with Jack, couldn't help feeling a little sympathetic towards her. God knew Jack Townsend was a man worth lighting a love seat for. Look at him lying there on her bed. He looked completely delectable, like a newly unwrapped candy bar.

Too bad she'd sworn off chocolate.

"I can't do this, Jack," she said, no humor in her voice at all. "I really can't."

Blinking, he sat up straight. "This is all starting to sound very ominous," he said. "What can't you do, exactly?"

"This," Lou said, lifting a hand and then letting it drop back into her lap. "You. I can't do the casual sex thing, Jack. I've never been able to see the point of it. And I especially can't do it with a guy who's pretty much the king of casual sex. I just don't have it in me. I think I had better just pull the plug on this thing before it goes any further."

"Oh," Jack said, and to her surprise, the teasing tone was gone from his voice. Now he sounded . . . well, wounded.

But that was impossible. Because he was Jack Townsend. Jack Townsend never got wounded. He only did the wounding.

"That's all I was to you, then?" he asked. "A casual fling?"

If she hadn't seen the expression on his face, she might have thought he was joking. But for once there wasn't a hint of humor in those ice-blue eyes.

"Well, Jack," she said, giving a nervous laugh in an attempt to break some of the tension in the room. "I mean, come on. You can't tell me you ever meant for this to go any further than that. A casual flirtation. Right? I mean . . . did you?"

She tried not to look eager. The chances of Jack Townsend, notorious ladies man, ever settling down were exactly nil. He'd even told *Playboy,* in an interview, that he thought marriage was an antiquated institution, and that he didn't think humans were meant to be monogamous.

So when he said, "I guess we'll never know now, will we?" then gave her a brief, cold smile, she couldn't help staring at him. This was not the Jack that she'd come, over the past few days, to know. Here suddenly there was nothing flippant, nothing playful, nothing even remotely casual.

But how was that possible? Wasn't she just another in a string of leading ladies with whom he'd been involved? Oh, sure, this time he'd picked one who worked behind, rather than in front of, the camera. But that was the only difference, really. Wasn't it?

Or didn't he talk about Dakota with all his girlfriends? Had he talked about Dakota with Vicky?

Lou took a deep, trembling breath. When she released it, she said, "Jack, I told you before, I can't get into another relationship with an actor."

"Good thing *Copkiller IV*'s my last acting gig, then," he said.

She shook her head. "I'm serious."

"So am I."

He looked it, too. She had never seen his gaze so somber.

"No." Her voice shook. She tried to get it under control. Now was not the time to crumble. "I mean it, Jack. I just can't let myself get hurt that way again, not right now. There'll be . . . there'll be nothing left of me."

There was silence. One heartbeat. Two.

Then Jack got up off the bed.

Lou assumed he was leaving. She hung her head, feeling the prick of tears beneath her eyelids.

But this, she told herself, was for the better. She had

told him the truth. She could not afford to be hurt again . . . especially not by someone like Jack, who, unlike Barry, was so quick, so eminently capable of causing real, lasting pain. The disappointment she'd felt over what had happened with Barry had, after all, been tinged with relief, since she'd managed to escape her relationship with him with only her pride, not so much her heart, broken.

With Jack, she knew, it would be different. Her love for Barry had been like a habit she'd clung to since adolescence. What she felt—was beginning to feel, anyway—for Jack was something far deeper . . . and so much more dangerous. If she did not extricate herself now, she knew, she'd only fall deeper. And with Jack, it wouldn't just be her pride that would suffer. Oh, no.

But to her surprise, Jack did not leave. Instead, he came around the bed, until he was standing in front of her. She looked up at him, wondering what he could possibly want. She had made herself, she was sure, perfectly clear.

But she should have known. She should have known when he bent down and tugged the bottle of moisturizer from her hand. She should have known when, after setting the moisturizer down on the nightstand, he knelt in front of her, his knees sinking into the deep pile of her hotel room's carpet. She should have known when he placed both his hands on her bare knees, still pink from her shower, and gently, but firmly, spread them apart. . . .

. . . then buried his face against the damp curls between her thighs.

"Jack!" she cried, her fingers flying to his head, each grasping fistfuls of his thick dark hair. "What are you— Jack, stop it. You can't—"

But he could. And he did. His mouth pressed against her as tightly as a hand. His hot, competent tongue laved her. His arms, moving beneath the robe, circled her hips and brought her more firmly against him, his fingers singeing the soft flesh of her less-than-fifteen-million-dollar ass.

And she could do nothing but tighten her grip on his hair and moan, her back and neck arching with each expert caress of his tongue. . . .

Was it any wonder she fell back against the bed, all of her arguments against their doing exactly this completely forgotten? Was it any wonder that her fingers left his hair to travel along the ropelike sinews of his forearms, until she came to the hands now gripping her thighs, keeping her anchored to the bed since his lips and tongue were causing her hips to roll with each new stroke? Was it any wonder that she sank her fingertips into the backs of those hands, urging them higher, until they'd parted the robe and found her aching breasts?

It was wrong. She knew it was wrong. He was using weapons against her for which she had no defense system in place. He was bad for her, bad for womankind in general. He would hurt her, in the end, the way he'd hurt so many others. And then she'd be the fuck bunny standing in a negligee in a hotel hallway, throwing champagne flutes.

She knew all this. She knew it perfectly well.

So why did what he was doing feel so very, very right?

And then his mouth slid out from between her thighs, to burn a course over her belly and up her rib cage, with stops at either breast, teasing each of her pink nipples, while one hand slipped between her legs, where his mouth had been, his fingertips as thrillingly callused and hard as his tongue had been teasing and soft.

When his face finally came level to hers, he looked down at her, his blue eyes dark with desire, his mouth wearing a crooked smile.

"You know what your problem is, Calabrese?" he said. "You think too much. Sometimes you have to stop thinking, and just *be*."

On the word *be* he replaced the fingers that had been inside her with something much thicker. She didn't even have time to wonder how he'd managed to get his pants undone without her noticing. The only thing she knew was, that part of him which she'd felt pressing against her with such urgency in the hallway had found its way inside her at last, filling what had begun to feel like an aching emptiness. His weight—not to mention his erection— pinioned her to the bed, and she liked it. Look how much she liked it, if the way she was moving against him was any indication. She was lifting her hips to meet him, thrust for thrust, while his lips sought her neck and his hands, oh, his hands slipped behind her shoulders and pulled her up, so that each time he drove himself into her, he went even more deeply home.

It was madness. It was heaven. It was going to have to stop. Really, she could not go on like this, like some kind of writhing, gasping slave to desire. . . .

But oh, how good he felt. Here at last was something that was stronger than the voice inside her head telling her none of this was going to get her anywhere good. Here at last was something that drowned out all the voices, all the words of advice she'd heard over the years, all the warnings about bad boys and men who just wanted one thing. . . . He could *have* it, as far as Lou was concerned, so long as he kept making her feel like this.

And then she was there, trembling on the edge of a dark chasm, so deep she couldn't see the bottom. At any minute, she was going to fall. All she needed was one last, final push—

He pushed her.

And then she was falling, falling down and down. And now she could see the bottom of the chasm rushing up at her, so fast she barely had time to register that it was filled with water until she'd plunged into it. Cool, silver drops kissed her bare skin all over . . . then, hardly giving her a chance to recover, did it again.

Oh, yes, Lou reflected, as she lay in a damp heap a few minutes later, feeling Jack's heart drumming hard against hers. Bad boys *were* more fun.

"Now," Jack said conversationally, lifting his head from one of her bare breasts. "What was that you were saying about why it is we can't be together?"

![clapperboard icon] **27**

Eight stories below the bed in which Jack and Lou lay, emotionally and physically spent, Frank Calabrese picked up a microphone and crooned into it.

"My love burns for you tonight," he sang, in a surprisingly pleasant tenor voice. *"Nothing ever felt this right."*

Eleanor Townsend, one of the only other customers, besides Frank, in the Anchorage Four Seasons Hotel bar, applauded merrily. She had never heard of karaoke before, and found it most surprising that a hotel the caliber of the Four Seasons offered it. But then, this *was* Alaska.

Besides, she found that she most heartily approved of karaoke. It was quite a lot of fun. In fact it was too bad, she thought, that Jack had been too tired to join them for dinner. He would have enjoyed it very much, especially the elk burger—really quite delicious, and so low in fat!—which she had had, along with a beer, at Frank's suggestion. The two did seem to go quite well together. Rather like Frank and karaoke.

"And when my heart fire's burning," Frank sang, *"you know it's for you I'm yearning."*

Eleanor had, unfortunately, been taking a sip of beer as Frank sang that line. Now, having snorted at the absurdity of the lyrics—really, that such a song could have won an award of any kind, let alone an Academy Award, was perfectly ludicrous—she felt some of the beer go up her nose. Good Lord! Laughing so hard that liquid came out her nose! This hadn't happened to her since she'd been a little girl at her parents' camp in the Adirondacks.

Mortified, Eleanor pressed a napkin to her nose. Fortunately neither Frank nor the bartender seemed to notice.

"*When the world goes up in flame,*" Frank sang, coming in for the big finish, "*and nothing stays the same, I will whisper your name . . .*"

Frank finished the chorus with a flourish. Then he bowed to her applause, laid down the microphone, and came back to their table.

"Now you do one," he said.

Eleanor set aside her napkin and said, "Oh, Frank, no. I can't sing!"

"Who cares?" Frank asked. "Here, here's the songbook. You must know one of these. Here. How about this one. 'You Light Up My Life.' You must know that one. Everyone knows that one."

"Oh, Frank," Eleanor said, laughing again—but this time avoiding taking a sip of her beer as she did so. "You don't know what you're asking. I really can't carry a tune."

"This one." Frank held up the song book. "You must know this one. 'You're So Vain.' Sing 'You're So Vain.' "

"Frank, no!" Eleanor could not quite remember when she had had so much fun. Certainly not since Gilbert had died. Gilbert, for all his staid ways, had been quite amusing, when he'd wanted to be. Life had gotten dull since he'd passed away, though Eleanor had tried to keep herself busy with her volunteer work.

Still, volunteer work could only be so interesting. This,

however—eating elk burgers and singing karaoke with a retired policeman from New York City—was imminently more exciting. Who would have thought that, in traveling to Alaska to look for her lost son, she would find a man who made her feel like a teenager again? Certainly not Eleanor.

"You have to sing something," Frank insisted. "I did it, so you have to, too."

"Oh, very well," Eleanor said, with a mockly exasperated sigh. "But I will pick my song, thank you very much."

Seizing the songbook, she began to flip through the pages, gazing at all the titles listed there. So many songs, and almost all of them about one thing—love. Well, and what better topic for a song than something that produced in otherwise sensible people such a feeling of giddy silliness, rather like. . . .

Well, rather like what Eleanor was feeling right now.

Effervescent as bubbles in a glass of champagne was how Eleanor felt. Which was perfectly ridiculous, because it was nearly midnight Alaskan time, which meant it was close to three in the morning back in New York. When was the last time she'd stayed up until three in the morning? She couldn't even remember. It was quite impossible that she should be in love with a retired police officer, and father of five, whom she'd only met three days earlier.

And yet Alessandro had liked him from the start. And Alessandro was never wrong about people.

Gripping the songbook, feeling as bright and as gay as she had at fifteen, Eleanor stood up.

"I'll do it," she announced. "I'll sing."

Frank burst into applause while the bartender very kindly took down the song number, then punched it into the computer.

Then Eleanor, holding the microphone very tightly, turned to face her audience of one—the bartender being too deeply engrossed in a game of solitaire to pay her the slightest bit of attention—and launched into a rendition of a song she had never heard before, let alone knew how to sing.

It was, however, the first song she'd laid eyes on after realizing she was in love with Frank Calabrese, and for that reason, in Eleanor's heart, there would always be a special place for "Kung Fu Fighting."

Twelve floors up from the Four Seasons Hotel bar, Vicky Lord couldn't sleep.

She ought, she knew, to have been enjoying her first good night's sleep since the disappearance of Jack and Lou. They were, after all, safe now. When she'd first heard what had happened—that their helicopter had gone down, and that they were feared dead—it was as if a part of her had died, too. Really, that's how she'd felt. She'd been unable to get up out of bed for almost thirty-six hours. . . .

But then she'd heard there was a chance they'd survived. A good chance. Her elation had known no bounds. She'd even given Lupe a hundred-dollar-a-week raise.

And now they were back. They were back, and they were safe, and for that, she was more glad than she could say. She had arranged the little welcome back party in the penthouse suite, buying out the hotel's supply of Dom Perignon and cocktail shrimp for the occasion. The party had gone quite nicely. Both Jack and Lou had seemed appreciative of the gesture.

It was what had occurred during that party—and then later, on the eleven o'clock news—that had Vicky so wide awake that even the sleeping pills her doctor had prescribed shortly before her wedding, when she'd been so jittery, weren't doing the trick. No, she was awake, and likely to remain so as long as her mind kept replaying the horrible, startling news Jack had told her.

And that was that he'd been shot at.

Not only shot at, but chased—*chased*—through the forest, by men wielding guns. Their own pilot, the one who'd died in the crash, apparently hadn't died in the crash at all. That much had been confirmed in a late-breaking news story on one of the local channels.

"In an intriguing twist involving the fatal crash of the helicopter that was carrying action-adventure star Jack Townsend and one other passenger to the set of *Copkiller IV*, currently being shot outside of Myra, Alaska," the Channel Eleven news reporter had said, "the Anchorage medical examiner's office reports that the pilot of that aircraft, Samuel Kowalski, did not, as was formerly assumed, die in the crash. Instead, it appears that Kowalski was killed by a bullet that entered his skull sometime before his remains were charred in the wreckage of the downed R-44 he piloted for a private firm hired by the film studio. The Myra sheriff's department refuses to comment on this latest development in this bizarre case. Townsend was stranded for nearly seventy-two hours in the Alaskan wilderness with the screenwriter who penned the block-buster film *Hindenburg*. Mr. Townsend's publicist reports that the former star of television's hit medical drama '*STAT*' and current star of the successful *Copkiller* films is resting after his ordeal, and is expected to continue working on his current film according to schedule. In other news—"

But Vicky didn't hear what the other news might be. All of her attention had been riveted by one word, and one word only. And that word was *bullet*. Bullet. A bullet had entered the skull of Samuel Kowalski. He had not, as had been previously reported, died in the accident that had brought down the helicopter. The story Jack and Lou had told, at her little party, of basically being stalked by armed men for what turned out to have been dozens of miles, was true. It was absolutely true, and it could only mean one thing.

And it was that thing which was keeping Vicky up, seated on the couch in the suite's living room with the television remote in her hand, flicking from channel to channel, but not seeing any of them.

Someone was trying to kill Jack. Not Lou. No, Lou was safe. It was only because she'd been with Jack that her life had ever been in any danger in the first place. It was Jack who'd been the target, Jack who was still in danger.

She had to warn him. She knew she had to warn him.

And yet there'd never been a chance. He had stayed at the party for such a brief time before his mother had whisked him away, wanting—and the sentiment was understandable—some quality time alone with the son she had thought she'd lost.

And when, after the party, Vicky had called his room, there had been no answer. She had tried calling again on the hour, every hour, since, but Jack never picked up. . . .

She had to tell him. She had to. Before it was too late—

"Vicky?"

The voice, coming from the darkest part of the living room, startled her so badly that she nearly fell off the couch. But it was only her husband, after all, calling out to her sleepily from their room.

"Vicky." Tim Lord, in gray silk pyjamas and a black dressing gown, came shuffling out of the shadows and towards the couch. Tim didn't much care how he looked while he was working—in fact, he seemed to prefer jeans and his ubiquitous cowboy boots. But he also dressed splendidly for bed. That was because, as he'd once confided to Vicky, his mother, who'd raised Tim single-handedly after his father had left for parts unknown, had been able to afford food and school clothes for her only child, but very little else.

"What are you doing up so late?" Tim wanted to know. "Are you not feeling well?"

Vicky hit the power switch on the remote. She didn't want him to see, in its blue glow, how pale she was without her makeup.

"No," she said. "No, I'm fine."

"Well," Tim said. "Then come to bed, will you? You know I can't sleep without you. And I have a big day ahead of me tomorrow. We're shooting the mine scene. It's the last shot, you know. The last shot before we call it a wrap and head back."

Vicky obediently left the couch and let her husband steer her back to the room they shared.

It was a testament to her acting skills that he never knew, never even suspected, what she had discovered. He had no clue. No clue at all. Anymore than he knew that she lay awake beside him for the entire night . . .

. . . right up until everyone in the entire hotel—those who weren't awake already—was jolted by the explosion that ripped through Jack Townsend's room, two floors below theirs.

28

Jack Townsend wasn't in his new room on the tenth floor when it went up in a ball of smoke and flame. He was still in Lou Calabrese's room on the eighth floor. To be exact, he was in Lou Calabrese's room on the eighth floor. To be exact, he was in Lou Calabrese.

But he wasn't having as much fun—at least then—as he might have expected. That was because Lou, against his express wishes, had answered her phone when it had begun to ring at the ungodly hour of six forty-five in the morning.

Never mind that just minutes before it rang, Jack, who had wakened to find himself pleasantly plastered against Lou, her back to his front, both his arms around her, had discovered that he was suffering from an erection about the size, if he wasn't mistaken, of a SCUD missile.

While this was not a wholly unusual situation, it was the first time it had happened with Lou.

And, happy occasion, she appeared to be stirring as well. Jack—who knew only too well that Lou wasn't exactly a morning person, if her behavior that time in the ranger's station had been any indication—gave her time to wake up, nuzzling only her shoulder, and that gently.

Lou opened her eyes and said, in a voice rough with sleep, "You know what? You were wrong. You do *not* need a bigger gun."

"Ah," Jack said, against her shoulder. "Ever the romantic."

"You," she said, "are insatiable."

"Most women would be appreciative of that fact," he pointed out.

Lou rolled over with a sigh, and, flat on her back, said, "Okay. Do me."

Jack did so. Happily they were both still naked from the night before, so there was no fuss about clothing. Instead, Jack was able to fling back the sheet and set to work at once, pressing his lips to one of her pink nipples, which until he kissed it had lain sweetly dormant. At his touch, however, it sprang to life, burgeoning under his gaze to full, rosy stiffness.

Gliding a hand down her smooth, flat belly, he found the tangle of russet curls that he'd given so thorough an examination the night before. But this time, instead of his tongue, he slipped a finger there and found that she was as ready as he was for love, the way they made it.

A second later, he pulled her, squealing, on top of him, with the suggestion that she do some of the work for a change. . . .

A task she set about fulfilling with breathtaking aptitude. She had just pulled him deep inside her—so hot, so wet, so deliciously tight—when the phone rang.

He didn't think for a minute she'd actually answer it. Not with him inside her, so close—though she apparently did not know it—to exploding within her. Fortunately Lou was no laggard in the climax department. She came lustily and often and never once without him. She had to have been close, too.

And yet he saw her hand reach for the phone. . . .

"It's so early," she explained. "It's got to be important. It could be the police. Or my dad."

Lou's father was not a topic Jack wished to discuss just at that particular moment.

Then she lifted the receiver and said, "Hello?"

Only it wasn't the police or her father. It was Lou's agent, Beverly Tennant, calling from New York City, where it was almost ten o'clock.

Except, apparently, Lou's agent was as important to her as the police and her father, since Lou immediately got into a long-winded conversation with the woman about Tim Lord, and how Lou had to break it to Tim today that he could not, in good conscience, blow up a large chunk of the Alaskan wilderness; that this was a critical mistake on his part that was going to result in terrible press for the film and besides had all the tree-huggers in the country up in arms over the goddamn arctic foxes; that only Lou could do it, because he'd listened to her last time, on the set of *Hindenburg*, when he'd wanted to blow up a historic Hungarian train depot, merely because he'd happened to have the explosives on hand, and had thought the resulting flames would look good on camera.

At least this was what Jack garnered was the crux of the conversation. He could only hear one end of it, but he had a very personal stake in it, as he could feel Lou's growly voice all the way down her body, through the very intimate physical connection they were currently sharing.

"Get off the phone," Jack said eventually, when the conversation descended into what appeared to be a long-winded description, on Beverly Tennant's part, of some Italian floor tiles.

Lou made a face at him and hastened to put her hand over the mouthpiece of the receiver. Only apparently the gesture was too late, because Jack heard a woman's voice demanding, "Is someone there with you? My God, Lou, who is it?" And then something about having seen a documentary on the Learning Channel about Alaskan crab fishermen and their impressive forearms and had Lou managed to reel one in.

Jack made a move to grab the phone, intending to tell Beverly Tennant a thing or two about crabs, but Lou snatched the receiver away at the last minute, saying into it hastily, "Sorry, gotta go," before hanging up.

At which point Jack thought it safer to keep her out of reach of the phone, and flipped her onto her back, all without breaking their own connection. . . .

"I have to catch Tim," Lou murmured—but weakly, Jack noticed—"before he leaves for the set—"

"You have plenty of time for that," Jack said, lowering his lips to her neck. "He can't do anything until I get there, and I am not getting there—" he sank even more deeply into her—"until I'm good and ready."

What transpired after this was, in Jack's opinion, anyway, the very definition of good sex. It was extraordinary how well they seemed to fit together, how much each of their bodies appeared to have been made to complement the other's. He had never, not in his whole life, had a sexual experience that could in any way compare to what he and Lou shared—in heat and passion, anyway. Maybe it was because for the first time in his life, he had found a partner he was not only attracted to but actually liked, and even, to a certain extent, admired.

Plus she had a mouth on her. God, how he loved that mouth.

The problem, however, was that that mouth was starting to demand things of him, things he wasn't sure he could deliver. Why couldn't Lou be happy with the fact that he'd asked her to move in with him? Why did she have to want more? Didn't she know that more would come naturally, if she just let it?

No. No, she didn't. Because she'd been burned before. She needed to hear the words.

But those words were the ones Jack had the most trouble saying . . . because, of course, he'd never said them before. How did you ask a woman to be with you for the rest of her life? How did you say that you loved her and wanted to marry her and have kids and golden retrievers with her without sounding like a total bohunk? Jack didn't know. He could have said the words if they'd been printed on a script, but he would have felt contempt for the character he was playing, the one who was saying them.

Now, however. Now he understood those hackneyed phrases and the sentiments behind them. He just couldn't figure out how to utter them without sounding like as big a fool as the characters he so often played.

So he tried to show her, instead. Show her how he felt, instead of telling her. He made love to her, tenderly, he hoped, though there were a few moments towards the end there where there was nothing tender going on at all, where raw need gripped him and he slipped over the edge into fierce possessive want.

But one of the reasons he loved Lou—and how strange it felt to use that word, love, even inside his head—was that her need seemed as all-consuming as his own. In bed, all that hard-edged toughness she'd cultivated so carefully in order to compete in what was, for the most part, still a man's world, fell away to reveal a quintessential woman, someone who had bath beads and wasn't in the least afraid to use them, dammit. Someone who had peanut brittle in her purse. Someone who came unapologetically but so femininely that Jack sometimes forestalled his own pleasure just for the sheer joy of watching hers.

He did so that morning, holding back his own release so that he could revel in Lou's. Only when the last shuddery spasm had left her body did he allow himself to take his own pleasure . . . but when he did, it was rich and full and left him spent, like a wrung-out sponge.

Was that what he should say? That they had to be together forever, because she was the only woman he'd ever known who made him feel like a wrung-out sponge after sex? Somehow he did not think this would be received in its appropriately complimentary light. Why was it that for the first time in his life when it actually mattered what he said, he couldn't think of the right way to put anything? Lou couldn't be right. He was a lot more than just a robot who spewed out whatever was written in front of him.

But he would have appreciated a speech writer just then, someone, anyone, who could have told him the right thing to say, the thing that would keep her exactly where she was—well, all right, maybe not *exactly*—for the rest of their lives.

What was wrong with him? Millions of men did it every day. Proposed, that is. Surely he could do it, too, and without outside help. Yes, the moving in together suggestion hadn't worked out, but Lou had tried living with a guy already, and look what it had gotten her. Maybe what she needed to hear—was waiting to hear—was something with a little more permanency, a little more commitment on his part. He could do that. He *wanted* to do that, for the first time in his life. All he had to do was say the words.

"Lou," he said. There. That was good. He'd gotten that part out.

She opened her dark eyes and looked at him, her red hair spread across the pillow behind her like a halo. A copper halo.

"Yes?"

He took a deep breath. He could do this. He could totally do this. Hadn't he won a People's Choice Award for Favorite Actor in a Television Drama? Wasn't he one of *Los Angeles* magazine's most eligible bachelors? He was sexy. He was cool. She would say yes. All he had to do was say the words. Three of them. That was all. Three words, four or less letters each.

"I—" he started to say.

And that was when the hotel was rocked by an explosion that nearly flipped them both from the bed.

"Oh my God!" Lou cried, from the tangle of sheets and limbs in which they lay. "Jack. What *was* that? An earthquake?"

Jack, not too happy about having been interrupted, said, "Earthquakes don't make that much noise. Probably it was just a sonic boom. Listen, Lou—"

But it was too late. Lou was already shoving him off her. Wrapping a sheet around her nude body, she rushed to the window.

"Jack, look at that smoke," she exclaimed. "What do you think— My God, it's coming from a couple of stories above us, I think. What could have happened?"

Jack, over the initial shock of the explosion, wrapped himself in the bedspread, and sat dejectedly on the end of the bed, contemplating his failure.

"It's probably Melanie," he said. "Spontaneously combusting over this morning's script changes."

Lou was craning her neck to see out the plate glass window.

"No, Jack," she said. "I think it might be a little more serious than that. There are flames coming out the windows. Maybe we should, I don't know. Get dressed. Evacuate. Or something."

Jack brightened at this suggestion. Breakfast. Yes, that

was it. They could go down to breakfast, and he could propose over grapefruit and toast. Not very romantic, it was true, but he imagined coffee would fortify him. He stood up and, still holding the bedspread around his waist, began looking for his pants.

"That's a good idea," he said. "You want to shower first, or should I? Or should we both hit the shower at once—"

Voices became audible from the hallway just outside Lou's door. Lou, struggling into the terrycloth robe, knit her brow.

"Does that sound like my dad?" she wanted to know.

The next thing Jack knew, Lou was throwing back the deadbolt on her hotel room door, and looking out at the chaos beyond.

And it *was* chaos. Hordes of people were in the hallway, nearly all of them in some way connected to the filming of *Copkiller IV*, and most of them in various states of undress. Jack recognized Paul Thompkins, one of the assistant directors. Paul was wearing a pair of boxer shorts and a Knicks T-shirt, and was talking very rapidly into a cell phone.

"I don't know what it was," he was saying. "But just make sure you get the damned shot lists. If those go up in smoke, we're up shit creek without a goddamned paddle—"

In the center of the fray was Lou Calabrese's dad, calling for order.

"All right, everybody," Frank was saying. "Let's calm down. It's probably nothing. Probably just a transformer on the roof, or something. But why don't we do the fire department a favor and start heading for the stairs. No, not the elevator, now, the stairs. Come on now, orderly fashion please—"

Lou, her robe clutched tightly in front, shot past Jack.

"Dad," she said, rushing up to him. "Dad, are you all right? What's going on?"

"Oh, good morning, honey." Frank smiled at her. He was in a blue-and-green plaid bathrobe over blue pyjamas. His white hair stood up in comical tufts from the top of his head. He did not seem at all surprised to see his daughter in nothing but a hotel robe. "Nice wake-up call, huh?"

"Dad, what was that?" Lou looked up and down the hallway. "It sounded like an explosion. And this smoke seems pretty bad."

"Yeah," Frank said, waving people from the far end of the hallway through the doors marked "exit." "You'd think the—"

Suddenly an eardrum-piercing alarm kicked in, accompanied by bright, flashing lights that appeared to have been built into the sprinkler system in the ceiling, apparently intended to guide people towards the emergency exits in a smoke-darkened hallway.

"Ah," Frank said, in a satisfied tone. "There we go. I was wondering when that was going to go off."

It was nearly impossible to hear anything over the fire alarm. Still, Jack was certain for a moment that he heard his mother's voice.

And sure enough, she appeared through the filmy gray smoke, wearing a pink satin dressing gown and matching turban, clutching Alessandro in one hand and her jewel case in the other.

"Frank," she called. She sounded as near to hysterical as Jack had ever seen her. "Oh, Frank!"

Then Jack saw something extremely disturbing. Before he himself even had a chance to move, Jack saw Lou's father actually reach out and put a comforting arm around Eleanor Townsend's shoulders.

Then he said to her, his lips in her turban, practically, "It's all right, sweetheart. Just a little fire."

Sweetheart? *Sweetheart?*

But Eleanor did not apparently hear him. Surely if she had, she'd have objected to being called any man's sweetheart. Instead, she clutched one of Frank's lapels, Alessandro smushed between them, and wailed, "Oh, Frank! It's just awful! I tried to go to Jack's room just now, you know, to see if he was all right, and it turned out that's where it happened. The explosion! Jack's room is gone! There's nothing but black smoke and fire and—"

Lou, who'd been watching this little scene unfold with a troubled expression on her face, stepped forward and said, "Mrs. Townsend. Mrs. Townsend, don't cry. Jack's right here, he's fine. He was with me."

And Jack, wearing only the spread from Lou's bed, was forced to wave at them, lamely, from the doorway to her room.

"Hi, Mom," he said.

29

Breakfast was not going well.

This was probably due to the fact that a large chunk of the hotel's tenth floor was suddenly missing.

Still, one would have thought a simple thing like an explosion in a guest suite would not affect the waitstaff ten floors below.

"This," Tim Lord said, looking around the booth in which they sat impatiently, "is too much. Where's the waiter? I have to get out to the set. I've got a plane to catch."

Lou, seated across the table from the director, said, "Tim. Listen. The plane'll wait. I know this is a bad time, but we've got to talk about this blowing up the mine shaft thing. I mean, don't you think there've been enough fireballs for one day? Can't we just leave the mine the way it is?"

Tim continued to look around the nearly empty restaurant. Most of the guests had opted to breakfast elsewhere, even though the Anchorage Fire Department had ruled the building safe to reenter only an hour after the initial evacuation.

Still, Tim Lord was not a man who was going to let his schedule be disrupted by anything as piddling as an incendiary device being set off in his leading man's hotel suite. He had a film to shoot, after all.

"For God's sake, Lou," he said now, as he glared at the back of a waiter who was busy gossiping with a busboy, presumably over the tenth-floor fireball. "We're already running three days behind schedule because of that little chopper incident you and Jack went through. And now you're asking me to change the very fabric of the story I'm trying to tell—which, by the way, you wrote? You've got to have inhaled too much smoke this morning."

Lou glanced at Vicky, who was sitting next to her husband, looking, as always, angelic this morning in a cream-colored cashmere coatdress. Lou tried to make a semi-comical face at her, since Vicky looked unusually tense. But Mrs. Tim Lord wouldn't meet Lou's gaze, keeping her eyes on the cup of tea on the table in front of her.

"Tim." Lou tried again. "Arctic foxes. Cute, fuzzy little doglike creatures. They have dens in that mine shaft. You blow up the mine shaft, you leave a lot of cute puppies homeless. Is that the kind of message you want to convey to America? That Tim Lord doesn't care about puppies?"

"Kits," Vicky piped up.

Both Lou and Tim looked at her. "What was that, honey?" Tim Lord asked.

"Baby foxes are called kits," Vicky said, sounding a little faint now that she had so much attention being directed at her. "I think. Not puppies. I'm pretty sure."

"Kits, then," Lou said. She frowned at Tim in her most schoolmarmish manner. "Is that what you want, Tim? To be a kit-killer?"

The waiter, finally having noticed Tim's frantic waving, came over, looking pale and excited and younger than what Lou supposed were his nineteen or twenty years of age.

"Sir?" he asked, his voice wobbling.

"Yes," Tim said. "I would like the check please. And could you hurry? I have a plane to catch."

"Oh," the waiter said, looking taken aback. "There's no charge, sir. Because of . . . well, you know." He lowered his voice and whispered conspiratorially. "This morning's disturbance."

Tim gave the boy a brittle smile. "Fine," he said. "Thank you." To Lou and Vicky, he said, "Ladies. As always, it has been a pleasure. But I have a car waiting to take me out to the airport, where I have a plane waiting, to take me out to my film set, where I have a crew waiting, and costing me approximately two hundred thousand dollars an hour. This has been, Lou, the most expensive free breakfast I have ever consumed in my life. Now, if you'll excuse me—"

Tim started to slide from the booth.

"But, Tim," Lou said, realizing she was losing a battle she didn't feel she'd ever been completely equipped to fight in the first place. "There's no reason to blow up the mine. Really, I mean, narratively. It isn't even—"

"Lou." Tim had stood up, and now he reached for his coat, hanging on a peg at the end of the booth. "You know I respect you as a writer. But the American viewing public expects two things out of every *Copkiller* movie, as you well know. A shot of Jack Townsend's naked ass, and a great big mother of an explosion." He pulled on his *Hindenburg* crew baseball hat, which happened to be one of the most sought-after pieces of film-related memorabilia on eBay. "And I don't intend to disappoint them."

Then he turned and walked out of the restaurant.

Lou, not certain she actually believed what she'd just

heard with her own two ears, looked at Vicky and said, "Well. That went well. Don't you think so?"

There was certainly nothing in that statement meant to engender tears from its addressee. But that's exactly what happened. Vicky, who'd looked less than her usually radiant self—but Lou had put that down to the rude wake-up call they'd all gotten—began to cry.

Lou blinked astonishedly at her friend. It was true that, thanks to Jack, she'd been sort of . . . well, self-absorbed over the past twenty-four hours. But surely if she'd done or said something to upset Vicky this much, she'd have remembered it.

"My God, Vick," Lou said, leaving her own side of the booth and coming to slide into the place Tim Lord had just vacated, the one beside his wife. "What's wrong? Are you all right? Oh, God, it's all this talk about fireballs, isn't it? I am so sorry. I know how scared you must have been this morning. I mean, you all were just a couple floors up—"

"It—" Vicky, Lou couldn't help noticing, even cried beautifully. When Lou cried, her nose turned red, as did her eyes and most of the rest of her. Not so with Vicky. Her eyes welled, but that only made them look bluer than ever. And not a single portion of her face even pinked up. "I—it's not that," she stammered.

Lou leaned over their empty plates. Tim had eaten heartily, bacon, eggs, as well as pancakes, while Lou had settled, not very happily, for an egg white omelet, fearing for the size of her hips after all that butter pecan ice cream she'd consumed at Donald's house. Vicky hadn't had a thing, except for herbal tea. Lou pulled a wad of paper napkins from the dispenser.

"Here," she said, thrusting them at Vicky. "My God, Vick, don't cry. Everything's going to be all right. Maybe what I'll do is, I'll get some pictures of baby foxes from those protestors outside, and I'll fly up to Myra and show them—"

"Oh, God!" Vicky looked heavenward, while tears slid like pearls down her smooth white cheeks. "It's not the movie, all right? It's not the fucking movie! It's *Jack!*"

Lou stared at her old friend, feeling as if her heart had suddenly slowed down to a beat per minute. "Jack? But . . . but Jack's all right. He wasn't in his suite when it blew. And the Anchorage PD sent an officer right over the minute they heard. He's completely protected—"

"N-no," Vicky sobbed. "Not *that!*"

Lou felt her blood run cold. Great. Just great. Vicky knew.

It was bad enough Lou's own father—not to mention Mrs. Townsend and God, how Lou blushed to think of it—knew that she and Jack had spent the night together. Now apparently Vicky knew, as well. Word certainly sped fast through a film family.

"Oh, God, Vicky," Lou said. She felt terrible. Worse than terrible. She was the worst friend that had ever lived. Imagine, her having slept with the man who'd broken her best friend's heart.

But in her own defense, Vicky herself had moved on, had even remarried!

Maybe that wasn't even why she was crying, Lou thought, hopefully. Maybe she was crying because she was concerned for Lou's feelings, knowing that she wasn't exactly the casual sex type. Jack, Vicky was probably thinking, was going to rake Lou over the coals, emotionally.

Well, Lou had thought long and hard about all of this the night before while Jack, apparently exhausted from his labors on her behalf, had slept soundly. Lou had decided that she was going to risk it. Actor or not, Jack was fun to be with. Lou had spent her whole life being cautious, sticking with Barry even after she'd realized he was, not to put too fine a point on it, an idiot. She was not going to make that mistake again. She was going to take a risk, and for once in her life, live like one of her characters, take a chance on happiness, gamble on joy.

And if Jack ended up breaking her heart, well, at least she'd put her heart out there to be broken in the first place.

And until he did it—broke her heart, that is—what a fabulous, wild ride it was going to be.

"Listen, Vicky," Lou said, reaching over to take her friend's hand. "I am so, so sorry. But you said you were over him. You said you'd moved on."

Vicky only sobbed harder. Lou hardly knew what she said next. All she knew was that she desperately wanted to make Vicky understand why she'd done what she had.

"I know you're worried about me," she heard herself blather. "But honestly, I'm going to be all right. I mean, I know Jack has a reputation and all of that. I know he's never stayed with a woman longer than a couple of months. But I'm a big girl, and I have a lot of life yet to live and I want to make the most of it. I have spent almost all of my adult life behind a computer screen. Seriously. I write all the time about people who do these extraordinary things, but what have I ever done? *Nothing*! I'm tired of always doing the safe thing. I'm tired of protecting my heart. Dammit, Vicky. I'm going to live. Do you hear me? *I want to live!*"

It was Vicky's turn to blink at her. Possibly it was because of Lou's impassioned speech. Or possibly it was because, while delivering that speech, Lou had risen from her seat and pounded on the table for emphasis, causing a syrupy fork to fall to the floor and several of the waitstaff to stare in their direction.

In any case, Vicky, blinking up at her, went, in a dull voice, "What are you *talking* about, Lou?"

"Well," Lou replied feeling sheepish, and sinking back into her seat. "Jack Townsend, of course."

"That's what *I'm* talking about," Vicky said, a poignant throb in her voice. "Jack. And how my husband is trying to kill him."

Lou, her throat suddenly desert dry, could only stare at Vicky for a moment. It was like she was seeing a person she had never seen before. Suddenly the vain, shallow, indomitable Vicky, whom Lou had grown to love and appreciate, in spite of her very human failings, looked like a stranger . . . a beautiful, cold stranger, who had never told Lou she had ketchup in her hair, or referred to her stepchildren as the Stepford children . . .

"*What?*" was all Lou could come up with to say.

"It was Tim," Vicky sobbed into the wad of napkins Lou had handed her. "Tim was the one who paid the helicopter pilot to kill Jack. You weren't supposed to have been on it. If you'd checked your messages, like I did, you wouldn't have been."

Lou stared at her friend. "Vicky. What are you talking about?"

"Oh, God, Lou, don't you see?" Vicky blinked tearfully. "Tim hired those men who chased you, you and Jack. I wasn't sure—I couldn't be positive . . . but that bomb went off, the one that destroyed Jack's room this morning, and I knew . . . I just knew Tim had done it!"

Lou was not ordinarily so slow on the uptake, but this she simply could not understand. It was as if Vicky had started telling her some story about being kidnapped by aliens. Or about the Kabala. Vicky had been active in the Kabala for some time, and during that four-week period, Lou had had to avoid her, because she had not understood a word that had come out of her friend's mouth.

Now was no different, really, except that the words *truth* and *light* had been replaced by *kill* and *bomb*.

"Vicky," Lou said slowly. "Why would Tim want to kill Jack? Tim and Jack are friends, they've always gotten along great—"

"Sure," Vicky said, with a miserable sniffle. "Sure, they did. Until Tim and I—well, Tim and I, we've been having some problems, and so I suggested . . . I suggested maybe we should go see my therapist—the past-lives specialist one. I thought, you know, it would help bring us closer together. And in one of our sessions, Dr. Manke suggested we talk, you know, not just about our past lives, but about our past romantic relationships, as well. And I brought up Jack, and Tim, well, Tim didn't know—"

"You never told him?" Lou stared at Vicky in utter disbelief. "You never told Tim that you and Jack were once . . ."

"No," Vicky said, with a tiny shrug. "I didn't. Okay? So sue me."

"Vicky," Lou said, with a growing feeling of dread. "Vicky, you didn't—"

"Dr. Manke encouraged us to be honest with each other," Vicky said, with a spark of indignation. "And so I told Tim, you know, that Jack was really the one who got away."

Lou felt something not unlike a trickle of cold ice water slide down her back. She could not quite believe what she was hearing. Vicky still loved Jack? Still loved him, but had married someone else anyway? Not just someone else, but Tim Lord, one of the most powerful directors in Hollywood?

No. This was simply not happening. Not to her. Not the morning she'd decided to embark on her new career as someone who doesn't just observe life, but actually lives it.

And as if that weren't enough, Lou was apparently supposed to believe that Tim resented Jack so much over his wife's continuing ardor that he wanted to *kill* him? Impossible.

And yet . . . why else would Tim ever agreed to direct *Copkiller IV*? Everyone had been shocked when that had been the first picture he'd chosen to take on after winning the Academy Award for best direction for *Hindenburg*. Why on earth, most everyone in Hollywood had wondered, Lou included, would Tim choose, as his next project, a sequel—and number four, at that?

Some had said it was because he'd wanted an easy project while he refueled creatively for his next big endeavor. Some whispered that Tim wanted the money so that he could fund an indie arthouse project of his own, the way Jack had.

But now . . . now Lou wondered if either of those was, in fact, the reason. Was it because by accepting the *Copkiller* gig, Tim had a chance to work closely with Jack Townsend? Would have access to Jack's schedule? Would be able to set up something that would, if it had come off the way it had been supposed to, have looked like an accident? If Sam had been successful in killing Jack, and then had flown back to whatever rendezvous point he was supposed to, what would everyone have thought? Well, that Jack, and the copter, had gone down. It wouldn't even have been so strange for them not to find the wreckage . . . not with thousands of square miles of forest to comb.

The cold trickle in the middle of Lou's back began to feel more like a stream.

And now that it hadn't worked—that Jack was still alive—Tim was by no means out of luck. God, no. Oh, maybe he'd run out of patience with the hired guns he'd procured. But he still had a film set full of explosives.

"Vicky," Lou said, feeling goose flesh rise on her arms. "You didn't. Really. Tell me all this is some kind of bizarre acting exercise, and that you didn't."

"Of course I did." Vicky was definitely looking indignant now. Tearful, but still indignant. "I mean, Tim is my husband. If I can't be honest with my husband, who can I be honest with? A marriage built on lies isn't a marriage at all, it's a—"

Lou brought her hand down, hard, on the tabletop. *"You told Tim Lord you were still in love with Jack Townsend?"*

"Well," Vicky said, looking a little taken aback by Lou's vehemence. "Yes. Why shouldn't I have? I mean, Tim's been married twice before. It's not like I'm the only woman he's ever loved."

"But you're the only woman he's in love with *now*," Lou cried.

"Well, of course," Vicky said. "But I can't help it if a part of me will always be in love with Jack. He does that to women. Jack does, I mean. He gets under their skin. He's like a bad habit you can't break. I want to, believe me. But sometimes I just can't get him out of my head—"

"And you said all this—" Lou's voice was hard. She couldn't help it. If Vicky expected sympathy, she had definitely come to the wrong person this time. "—to Tim. You told him you can't get Jack Townsend out of your head."

"Well," Vicky said, beginning to look less indignant, and more fearful again—but this time, she seemed fearful of Lou. "Of course I did. Dr. Manke says if I ever want to break through to my true identity as a human being, I've got to be emotionally honest not only with myself, but those closest to me, as well—"

Lou lunged across the table. But not for Vicky's neck, like she wanted to. Instead, she seized hold of her purse.

"Great, Vicky," she said, sliding from the booth. "That's just great. I hope you feel really good about yourself. Because if you're right, and Tim is the one behind all this, two people are dead because of your emotional honesty, and Jack—" It was at this point that a cold, hard fear gripped Lou by the throat. "—who is at the set, which, if I'm not mistaken, your husband is on his way to, may be next—"

"I'm sorry," Vicky wailed. "Oh, God, Lou, I'm sorry! I'm so— Wait. What are you doing?"

"Vicky," Lou said, locking a hand over the smaller woman's wrist and dragging her bodily from the booth. "You're coming with me. You and I are going to have a little talk with that nice sheriff who was here yesterday."

"Oh, God!" Vicky cried. "Oh, Lou! No! If Tim finds out I know—if he finds out I told . . . he'll kill me!"

Lou smiled, though there was no humor in her expression. "Good," was all she said.

30

"You're wanted on the set, Mr. Townsend," called the voice through the door to Jack's trailer.

Jack looked up from the notepad he was scribbling on. He had decided that, since he did not seem to be able to tell Lou how he felt about her, he might as well try writing it.

Describing how he felt in writing to a writer, however, was even more difficult, he finally decided, than actually saying it. He had already gone through eight drafts—they lay in crumpled balls all around the floor of his trailer—and it wasn't even ten in the morning yet. The call to the set came as something of a relief. At least now he had something to do, something to keep his mind occupied.

As he stepped out into the frigid air and once white snow now turned to dirty clumps of gray he supposed he ought to have been worrying about his mortality, not his love life. Despite what the fire marshall had said—that the tentative cause for the explosion in his suite, pending a more thorough investigation, had been faulty wiring— Jack suspected the only faulty wiring involved had been in the mind of whoever it was that was trying to kill him.

A different man, having gone through what Jack had gone through in the past few days, might not have felt so resentful about the fresh-faced young police officer who, seeing Jack emerge from his trailer, climbed from his warm squad car and fell into step behind him. A different man might have noticed nothing wrong with this picture at all.

But Jack didn't like it.

Oh, Officer Mitchell was friendly enough. He smiled as he trudged along behind Jack, across the frozen set towards the mouth of the mine shaft, where the last scene to be shot was set. It was just that this thing, with the people trying to kill him, was getting kind of annoying. Supposing Jack had actually been in his room at the time that blast had gone off? More importantly, what if Lou had been there with him? He could not go about starting a new life with someone he actually cared for only to have her get blown to smithereens before his very eyes. He was, he decided, going to have to do something about all this. And soon.

In the meantime, however, he had a film to shoot. As he and Officer Mitchell approached Tim Lord, who sat perched in his director's chair giving Paul Thompkins, his AD, last-minute instructions, Jack couldn't help feeling a certain satisfaction that this was the last time he was ever going to have to stand in front of a camera. There was something liberating about the knowledge.

"Ah, Jack," Tim said, passing a clipboard to Paul, then leaning back in his chair. "You ready?"

"Ready as I'll ever be," Jack said.

"Great." Tim cast a single glance in Officer Mitchell's direction, smiled a little, then turned his attention to the set before them. It was the mouth of the mine shaft, some sixty feet away, which the special effects crew, seated at a table a few yards from where Jack stood, had rigged to explode. The snow in front of the shaft had been carefully swept so that there was no sign it was anything but virgin powder. Several rehearsals of the scene, with demo explosives, had shown the pyrotechnic guys exactly where to set the detonators. The mine was ready to blow.

All Tim wanted now, he explained to Jack, were a few shots of Detective Pete Logan running from the mouth of the mine and then diving into a snowbank—within which they'd hidden a foam mattress to support Jack's landing. They'd digitally insert the footage of the explosion behind Jack later.

"So what I'm going to need for you to do," Tim said, as film and camera crew milled around, their breath hanging frozen in the twelve-degree air, their faces fixed with a look that indicated they'd rather be just about anywhere in the world than where they currently were, "is just go into the mine, then when I yell action, come running out and make the dive, just like we rehearsed earlier in the week. Remember?"

"I remember," Jack said, his eyes narrowing at the mouth of the mine. It was dark in there. Warmer than it was outside. But still dark. Jack hadn't liked it.

"So it's the same thing as we rehearsed," Tim said. "Only this time, of course, we'll be shooting. Run and dive."

"Run and dive," Jack repeated.

"Right," Tim said. "And remember, a giant explosion will be going off behind you. Not really, of course," he added, with a glance at Officer Mitchell, who was staring dumbfounded at all the activity around them, never having been, as he'd informed Jack earlier, on a real Hollywood movie set before. "But we'll be putting it in later. So Jack. Look scared."

"Right. Scared," Jack said. He remembered the rehearsal,

when he had run from inside the mine shaft and jumped into the snowdrift. He had done it five or six times. They'd have shot the scene then if the light hadn't faded.

"Right," Tim said. "But not too scared. Because Pete Logan doesn't get too scared."

"No," Jack said. "No, he doesn't, does he?" Then he narrowed his eyes at the director. "So you're really going to do it," he said. "Blow up the mine."

Tim raised his megaphone and called over to one of the set dressers, "That snow over there on the right doesn't look fresh enough. Hit it, will you?" And the tech complied by blasting the clumps of semi-gray snow with a special white paint that simulated the virgin whiteness of fresh snowfall.

To Jack, Tim said, "Yes, of course I'm really going to do it. With the amount of money the studio forked over to the fish and wildlife department in order for us to shoot here, the Alaskan government ought to be letting me blow up the frigging capital. I highly doubt they're going to miss one crappy little mine."

Jack sucked on his lower lip. He wore no hat—costume wouldn't let him. Detective Pete Logan would never wear a hat. He could feel his ears beginning to feel numb already.

"And the arctic foxes?" Jack wanted to know.

"Fuck the foxes," Tim said.

This, as Jack knew only too well, was how Tim Lord talked when there were no women present. Everything was frigging this and fuck that. Some actors found Tim's earthiness refreshing after the pretentiousness of certain other directors. And Jack himself certainly did not mind foul language.

But he did mind that Lou had met with Tim—he knew she had, Lord himself had used their breakfast meeting as an excuse for why he'd arrived late to the set—and that

Tim was obviously disregarding everything she had said. Lou was, as Jack knew only too well, a persuasive and passionate orator. How her plea for the arctic foxes could fail to change Tim's mind, Jack couldn't imagine.

But clearly it had failed, and Tim intended to go through with his plan of blowing up the old abandoned mine shaft in which these foxes supposedly lived—though Jack had been in there several times and seen no sign of any wildlife whatsoever; on the other hand, the hustle and bustle of the movie set might have sent them scurrying away.

Which wasn't right. Blowing up their habitat. Not because Jack had any particular love for arctic foxes. He could, in fact, have cared less about them.

And he was certainly no tree-hugger. He loved red meat just as much as the next man.

But Lou cared. Lou had gone to the trouble of coming all the way out to Alaska to talk Tim Lord out of doing this. And the guy was blowing her off as if she were. . . .

Well, nothing.

It was for this reason that Jack said, "No."

Tim, who was peering through a lens, didn't even glance in Jack's direction. "No what?" he asked. "Don't worry, the mattress is all set up. I know it was off a couple inches earlier in the week, but we've moved it. It should be all right now."

"No," Jack said, folding his arms across his chest—not so much as a gesture of defiance, but because he was starting to feel frozen. "No, I'm not going to do it."

Now Tim did glance towards him. He glanced towards him with a laugh and said, "Funny, Townsend. Now come on. This is good light, I don't want to lose it."

"Maybe," Jack said, "I didn't make myself clear. I said no. I'm not going to do it."

All movement, all noise on the set suddenly stopped. Fifty people, from guys perched in the crane overhead, to the sound guys in the snow below, swivelled around to stare at the pretty much unheard of spectacle of Tim Lord being challenged by an actor. Even Melanie Dupre, who was standing in her place—her character, Rebecca Wells, was supposed to scream as Detective Logan dove for cover—looked stunned . . . and she was trying to pretend she did not know Jack.

Tim was, of course, used to tantrums. He was used to actresses like Melanie, who'd once locked herself in her trailer and refused to do a scene until she was brought a particular brand of bottled water.

But this—this quiet opposition—was something new. Tim stared up at Jack as if he had done something rude, like questioned the genius of Spielberg.

"What did you say?" Tim asked, his voice carrying across the snow as loudly as if it had been a shout, though really he had not spoken more loudly than a whisper.

"I said—" Jack was bored with the whole thing already. Disgusted, really. How Vicky could have married this clown, Jack could not imagine. "—I'm not going to do it. I can't have any part in destroying this beautiful—"

Even as he said it, he was wondering if he'd gone too far. The abandoned mine shaft was anything but beautiful. If anything, it was a blight on the landscape and quite probably a hazard to the locals, as certainly the children of Myra could not help but be tempted to explore this dangerous remnant of a time past.

Nevertheless, he went on.

"—piece of American history."

There, it was out. After he'd said it, he felt better. The beautiful part had been a bit much, maybe, but the rest of it had been all right.

Not to Tim Lord, however. At least, not if his expression was any indication. He looked mad enough to spit nails. Or at the very least, ram his Porsche into the back of someone's minivan.

"Townsend," he said. "Just because you've had a little taste of how it feels to direct doesn't mean you are in any sort of position to take over my job. Sure, the *Times* might've loved your Danish prince, but I know what your gross was, and it was nothing to write home about. And what we're doing out here today? Yeah, it ain't Shakespeare. So don't even think you're gonna go crunchy granola on me today. You get your ass into that mine shaft, and you stay there until I yell action. Got it?"

Jack said, "You want to shoot me anywhere near that mine shaft, you agree not to blow it up. You got that?"

Tim set his jaw. He wore a beard, a short gray number that was really more of a goatee, because he had something of a receding chin. Still, when he set his jaw, he looked formidable . . . sort of like an aging Robin Hood.

"Always have to do things your way, right, Townsend?" Tim shook his head. "Never think about anybody else's feelings, do you?"

"Excuse me," Jack said. "I'm considering the foxes' feelings right now."

"Right," Tim said, with a humorless laugh.

Then he said the one word Jack had never expected to hear from Tim Lord in his life.

"Fine."

Jack raised his eyebrows. He could not quite believe what he'd heard.

"Pardon me?" Jack said.

"You heard me." Tim might have said it once, but wild horses wouldn't drag it out of him again, that much was clear. "Now get into that mine."

Jack, a little astonished that his scheme had worked, said, "I really mean it, Tim. You blow up that mine, and I'll take it personally. *Real* personally."

Tim looked tired. "Jack. Just get in there, all right?"

And with that, it was over. This, Jack realized, was really it. This was the last scene of this film—possibly any film—he was going to have to shoot. After this, he'd be done with it. For good.

Turning around, he faced the dark mouth to the mine shaft. He saluted Officer Mitchell, who grinned back at him encouragingly. Then Jack began the long trek through the combed, spray-painted snow, to the top of the slope where the opening to the shaft sat, deeply embedded into the side of Mount McKinley.

Then, with one long look back at Tim Lord and all the other people gathered below, he stepped into the mine.

Below him, he heard Tim Lord say through his megaphone, "Okay, everyone, this is the real deal. Places. Places, everyone. Jack? You all right in there?"

Jack stepped towards the mouth of the shaft and waved, then disappeared back into its gloomy depths.

"Excellent," he heard Tim Lord say through his megaphone. "And . . . Action!"

31

"**C**an't this thing go any faster?" Lou, bouncing along in the front seat of the sheriff's four-by-four, crammed in between the sheriff and Deputy Lippincott, wanted to know.

"It can," Walt O'Malley said as he carefully navigated a hairpin turn in the road. "But I'm not going to risk plunging over the side into that ravine. That won't help your friend, and it certainly won't help us any, either."

"It's just," Lou said, feeling as if, not for the first time in the past hour, she were addressing a roomful of toddlers, "that a man might *die* if we don't hurry."

"I got all that," Sheriff O'Malley said. "I actually got that the first time you told me."

"Well, then could you please hurry it *up*—"

On the word *up* the four-by-four went over a deep rut in the road that caused the passengers in the backseat—Vicky Lord and, though Lou had not been happy about their tagging along, Jack's mother and her father—to become airborne for a second or two. When they landed again, Mrs. Townsend's dog, whom she'd apparently squeezed too hard, let out a squeak.

"Oh, my poor baby," Eleanor Townsend said, lowering her face into the dog's neck. "It's all right. It's going to be all right."

Lou wasn't certain if the woman was trying to reassure herself or the dog. Whereas Lou's father's intentions were clear: he was busy trying to reassure everyone.

"Now, don't get yourself in a tizzy, Lou," he said—had been saying that since they'd boarded the private plane Eleanor had chartered for the express purpose of getting out to Myra as fast as possible. "Jack's a grown man. He can take care of himself."

"With bombs going off right and left, and people with guns lurking around?" Lou threw her father an aggravated look over her shoulder. "I don't think so, Dad."

"I just don't understand," Eleanor said, for what had to have been the hundredth time, "what this Tim Lord has against Jack."

Some details Lou had thought pragmatic to leave out of the story she'd hastily told her father and Jack's mother when she and Vicky had run into them as they were exiting the hotel restaurant. It had been enough that they knew the gist—that Tim Lord wanted Jack dead, and that Jack had gone to the set—a set out of reach of their cell phones—where Tim Lord was expected to cause a very large explosion later in the day. They would know the truth soon enough, Lou supposed. The whole world would know.

"Don't you see?" Lou had asked her father when he'd expressed doubt about the efficiency of blowing up a mine shaft while Jack Townsend was in it. "Everyone will think it was an accident. People die during film stunts all the time, Dad. No one would ever suspect there was anything behind it."

Frank Calabrese had been dubious, but he'd been alarmed enough by his daughter's vehemence that he'd insisted upon coming along to Myra in a frantic effort to keep Tim Lord from making yet another attempt on Jack's life. It had to be admitted that, upon arriving at the Myra sheriff's department, Lou's father had grown a good deal less skeptical. That's because as Lou had hastily laid out the evidence in her case, the sheriff had not looked at all surprised. Instead, he'd flicked an inquiring glance at his deputy and asked, "You like him for our money man?"

Apparently, the guns Lou had handed over had been successfully traced to two Myra locals—"Deadbeats," the sheriff had described them—who happened to be missing. Their buddies, when brought in for questioning, had said, after pressure had been exerted on them, that they had been paid five thousand dollars each by an individual they would not identify to kill action-adventure star Jack Townsend, who, they'd been informed, had wandered away from a plane crash somewhere in McKinley Park.

"Five thousand dollars?" Lou had been disgusted. That's all Jack's life had been worth?

"Well," the sheriff had said. "Five thousand each. And we suspect there were seven or eight of them involved, not counting old Sam Kowalski. We haven't finished rounding them all up, but we expect to have 'em by the end of the week. Except for that one you killed, that is."

All of this talk, however, had only prevented them from getting out to the set as soon as Lou would have liked. While the sheriff didn't dispute the fact that someone had paid the men he was currently holding for questioning to kill Jack Townsend, no one seemed to believe that someone was Tim Lord, the Academy Award–winning director. How could the director of such a heartwarming film as *Hindenburg* be a killer—or at least have paid others to kill for him?

Lou had had to make Vicky explain it to them, something that Vicky, looking whipped and defeated, had done in a toneless and not entirely convincing manner. Certainly Eleanor Townsend, who had heard the whole thing, wasn't convinced.

"But that's ridiculous," she'd cried. "Why should Mr. Lord want to kill Jack, just because his wife says she's still in love with him? Lots of wives are married to one man while in love with another, and their husbands don't go around trying to kill anyone!"

Yes, but this was Hollywood, where Tim Lord was pretty much king, it would never have done for the queen's heart to belong to someone else. That was the thing about directors. They wanted control. And if they didn't have it, well, that was when things got messy.

Sheriff O'Malley had not been at all excited about transporting the four of them to the movie set. He'd have preferred, he'd explained to Frank Calabrese, as if speaking one cop to another might help, to bring the suspect in for questioning himself.

But Lou wasn't about to be left behind in the sheriff's stuffy office while Jack was in imminent danger of being blown to bits. . . .

And neither, she'd soon discovered, were any of her other companions, who piled into the back of O'Malley's four-by-four right along with her, and like her, refused to budge from it.

But she supposed the sheriff was happy she'd come along when, arriving at the set, they were met by a PA in a shearling coat and a headset. She tapped on the driver's side window of the four-by-four and said, "Sorry. Closed set. You'll have to turn back."

Sheriff O'Malley was just lifting out his badge and preparing to present it to the PA when Lou leaned over him and shrieked at the young woman, "Get out of the way before we run you down!"

The PA hastily backed out of the way, and Lou laid her foot down over the sheriff's. . . .

A gesture he did not appreciate, though it did propel the four-by-four several hundred feet at a considerably faster rate than they had traveled thus far.

"Miss Calabrese," Walt O'Malley turned to say to her when he had recovered control of the vehicle. "I am quite capable of doing my job. I really don't need—"

But Lou had already bailed from the car, having climbed over a deeply embarrassed Deputy Lippincott in her effort to get out.

And then she was running.

Lou was not dressed for the arctic, as she had hardly expected, when she'd met with Tim Lord for breakfast that morning, to be back on Mount McKinley an hour later.

But that's exactly where she was, in a skirt and Jimmy Choo heels, no less, running through the dirty gray snow that carpeted the ground between the trailers, icy wind stabbing at her lungs, and all the exposed parts of her skin feeling as if they were on fire. But she hardly noticed her own discomfort. All of her attention was on the crowd of people in front of her, looking expectantly up towards an old, abandoned mine shaft. One set of tracks led to the dark mouth of the mine. Lou could see no one standing in it, but she heard Tim Lord's voice clearly enough, yelling one word through a megaphone. One word that seemed to freeze the blood running through Lou's veins.

"Action!"

Lou let out a shriek that, had there been any loose snow on the mountainside above them, would have brought it all raining down upon their heads. As it was, every person on the set, from the key grip to the caterer, turned to stare at her. . . .

. . . including Tim Lord, whose pointed, foxy face was livid with rage.

"Cut," he called in disgust when he saw who it was who'd dared disrupt his shot. Then he lowered the megaphone and said, "Lou. I should have known. Don't you think you're going a little far with this save-the-animals crap? I don't think the studio's going to appreciate it when they hear—hey, where do you think you're going? You can't—Stop her! Somebody stop her!"

But it was too late. Lou had already staggered past the director's chair, and was laboring up the mountainside in her heels, screaming at the top of her lungs, "Jack, get out! It's a trap! Tim Lord is trying to kill you!"

Behind her, she could hear her father shouting. Not just her father, either, but Tim Lord and, for some reason, Melanie Dupre. Chaos had broken out on the set. The sheriff could be heard, calling for order. Alessandro barked shrilly.

But all of Lou's concentration was centered on getting up the hill to the mine, and getting Jack safely out of it before Tim Lord flicked the switch that would, Lou had no doubt, send the whole thing exploding—just like Barry's vision of Pompeii.

Except that when she finally reached the mouth of the mine and stumbled inside of it, thinking, only briefly, "It's too cold for spiders . . . way too cold for spiders," there was no Jack to be found. The opening was empty. Just a few old crates. But no Jack. Jack was nowhere to be seen.

"Jack?" she called hoarsely into the mine. "Jack, are you in there? It's me, Lou."

But when she heard him respond, it wasn't from inside the mine. It wasn't from inside the mine at all. His voice, calling her name, seemed to come from somewhere outside, and from far away.

And he was saying the strangest thing, too. Lou couldn't be certain, because it was hard to hear anything above the screams from the people down below, but she thought Jack was shouting, "Stay where you are!"

"Jack?" A beatific smile broke over her face. He was alive. He was still alive. She hadn't been too late. "Jack? Where are you?"

Lou turned around and headed out of the mouth of the mine, to see if she could find where Jack's voice was coming from.

And as she was stepping from the mine and back out into the snow, her foot caught on something—a wire. It tangled around her ankle and put a run in her hose.

"God dammit," she said, attempting to kick her foot free from the wire....

And that's when she heard Jack call, "No!" and she knew, instantly, what she'd just done.

She threw her arms up over head and waited for Mount McKinley to come down on top of her.

32

Except it didn't. Not then.

Instead, Jack Townsend came down on top of her, all two hundred pounds of him, hitting her with enough force to knock the wind straight out of her. Then they were falling onto the hard snow . . .

. . . just as a red-and-yellow fireball exploded behind them, sending down a hailstorm of rock and wood, and pouring a wave of thick black smoke over them.

The explosion was deafening, the heat intense. For several minutes Lou could see nothing but darkness. She wasn't even sure whether or not she was dead or alive. She could see nothing, hear nothing, feel nothing . . . nothing but cold, a cold that was seeping through the front of her blouse and skirt, causing her skin to feel numb.

Then, as the darkness cleared, she became aware of another sensation. Something heavy on top of her. It wasn't because of the smoke that she couldn't breathe. It was because of this enormous weight. . . .

And then the weight was being lifted, and she became dimly aware of voices. She could not tell what was being said to her, but as she blinked the grit and dirt from her eyes, and was finally able to see again—the bright blue sky above her had never looked so beautiful—she saw that faces, familiar faces, were gazing down at her and saying things . . . things she couldn't hear because her ears were still ringing from the explosion.

And then, slowly, the things people were saying began to make sense. She even began to recognize the people who were talking to her. There was her dad, looking panicky. She had never seen her dad look panicky before, except the night her mom had died. And there was Eleanor Townsend. She was crying. And there was Sheriff O'Malley, yelling at someone on the ground.

But not at her. Sheriff O'Malley was looking down, and he was yelling, but the person he was yelling at was not Lou, because Lou was no longer on the ground. Even now, her dad and Paul Thompkins, the assistant director, were trying to pull her to her feet. She tried to stand, but one foot wouldn't support her weight. She sagged in their arms.

And that's when she saw Jack.

He was lying on his back in the snow. There was black soot all over his face. His suede jacket was covered with it as well. He was not moving. His eyes were closed. Sheriff O'Malley was kneeling beside him, shouting. Dimly, Lou was able to hear what he was saying.

"Jack," the sheriff said. "Jack, wake up. Come on, Jack."

And then Lou was crawling through the snow toward Jack's prone body, tears streaming down her face.

"Jack," she whispered. Or maybe she screamed it. She didn't know. "Jack?" She reached him and put out a hand to touch his face. It was cold. So cold. "Jack?"

He still did not stir. She looked at his chest. It rose and fell, but slowly—so slowly. He was dying. She knew it. He was leaving her, leaving her alone, when they had only just found one another.

And then Tim Lord—Tim Lord, that bastard, that scheming, lying jerk off—was there, leaning over Jack and crying, in a desperate voice, "Jack! Jack, it's me, Tim. Jack, come on, you can't do this, buddy. You can't die. You can't."

That was when one of Jack's arms, which had been lying limply in the snow at his side, suddenly lifted. Lou watched, hardly daring to breathe as the arm rose into the air, until the hand attached to it grasped the thing that was nearest to it—the front of Tim Lord's leather jacket.

And then Jack's eyes opened—pools of blue in the middle of all that black soot—and his mouth opened, too, and he croaked, "I have no intention of dying, you self-righteous *prick*."

On the word *prick*, Jack hauled back his other arm and sent a fist plunging into Tim Lord's face.

Lou—along with just about everybody else who'd gathered around Jack's prone body—sprang back, fearful of being caught by a stray knuckle. Tim Lord put up a valiant struggle, getting a blow in now and then, but all the spinning classes in the world can't prepare a man for an assault by a livid action adventure star who's trained for months in preparation for his role.

Everyone stood paralyzed as Jack sent first one fist, and then another, into the director's head, mid-section, and sides. It was, Lou reflected in some small part of her brain that seemed detached from the scene before her, like watching a prizefight in which one of the contenders had simply given up from the sound of the very first bell. Lou hadn't any doubt that if her father hadn't stepped forward and put an end to the fight by wrapping his arms around

Jack's shoulders and pulling him away from Tim, they'd have had one dead Academy Award–winning director on their hands.

As it was, Tim broke down and, falling to the snow—now flecked not only with pieces of Mount McKinley that had come raining down on them after the blast but also with the director's own blood—exclaimed, hysterically, "Why won't you die? You're supposed to be dead! You were supposed to have died four days ago. What is wrong with you? *Why won't you die?*"

Jack, after shrugging off her father's arms, replied, "Because I've got too much to live for." Then he turned tiredly to Lou and asked, "Are you all right?"

Though she was still kneeling in it, Lou hardly felt the snow and ice beneath her. That's because the glow in Jack's eyes warmed her through.

"I'm fine," she said, unable to tear her gaze from his soot-covered, beautiful face. "But how did you—how did you know? Where did you come from?"

Jack shrugged beneath the blaze-blackened shoulders of his suede jacket.

"I figured he was up to something," he said, with a contemptuous nod in Tim's direction. "It was so damned important to him that I went into the mine. And the more I thought about it, the more I realized . . . well, who else would have had reason to pull Vicky off the flight that first day? Then something he said to me . . . something about how I never worry about anybody else's feelings. . . ."

His gaze strayed away from Lou's. Following it, she saw that he was looking at Vicky, who was staring owlishly at her husband, almost as if she had never seen him before

Jack's face, beneath the soot, looked pale. "Well, anyway," he went on. "I figured then that it was Tim. I saw the trip wire as I went into the mine . . . but I was looking for it. Then I just ducked out of a side shaft—this whole part of the mountain is riddled with them. I wanted to see if he'd actually come up himself and look for me when I didn't come down. If he stepped over the wire—" Jack shrugged. "—I'd know it was him. That he'd been trying to kill me, I mean."

Then Jack reached out and laid one finger, the knuckles of which were split open, on her cheek. "The last thing I expected was to see you come barreling up there. What were you *thinking?*"

Lou didn't realize until Jack took his hand away from her face and there was a clean spot on his fingertip that she was crying. She reached up, mortified, to wipe the tears away with the backs of her hands, and said, "Vicky told me this morning. I got out here as fast as I could. I tried calling—"

"No relay stations," Jack said, ruefully.

"Exactly." Lou's eyes were filled with love and tears. "I thought I was too late. . . . and when I opened my eyes and saw you lying there, I thought . . . I thought you were dead."

Now he brought both hands down to cup her face. "No way am I going to die," he assured her, "when things are just starting to get good."

Lou smiled up at him, and he smiled back, his teeth startling white against the black streaks across his face. Her gaze was so riveted on his that she only dimly noticed Deputy Lippincott snapping handcuffs over Tim Lord's wrists, then hauling him to his feet. She barely saw her father slip an arm around Eleanor Townsend, who was weeping joyfully into Alessandro's golden fur. Melanie Dupre's stomping off with a disgusted snort and a "That's it. I *quit!*" barely registered. And though she noticed that

Vicky Lord was sobbing fitfully into Sheriff O'Malley's shirt front, it didn't really seem to matter—any more than the fact that the sheriff had lifted one of his hands and was awkwardly patting Vicky on the head with it. All of her attention was focused on Jack, and his smile, and those blue, blue eyes.

"Want to get out of here?" he asked.

"More than you know," she said. "Except . . ." She looked down guiltily. "There appears to be something wrong with my foot."

"Not a problem," he said and leaned down.

And, before she knew what was happening, Jack had swept her legs out from under her, cradling her easily in his arms.

Then, like Richard Gere in *An Officer and a Gentleman*, he carried her away. The only difference, really, was that Jack Townsend was much taller than Richard Gere. . . .

. . . and he hadn't said he loved her.

33

Lou's ankle was broken in two places, x-rays revealed. She would be forced to wear a plaster cast for six weeks, then graduate to a foam brace for four. She would need to stay off her foot entirely for eight weeks.

How was it, she asked herself as she sat in the examination room she'd been wheeled into at Anchorage General Hospital, that heroines of movies—the ones who'd selflessly risked their lives in order to save others—always escaped with maybe a scrape or two, but real-life heroines, like Lou, ended up with spiral fractures to their tibia and had to get ugly casts put on their leg, and then had to hobble around like Sigourney Weaver in *Working Girl*, who was not exactly a sympathetic character?

Of course, Lou's lack of resemblance to a movie heroine did not end at her injury. No, she also hadn't got the guy. Heroines always got the guy at the end.

But not, apparently, Lou.

Oh, Jack had carried her down to Sheriff O'Malley's four-by-four. He had stayed with her during the ride to the landing strip, and had even held her hand all during the flight back to Anchorage. He'd come with her into the emergency room, where he'd been immediately mobbed by patients waiting in triage, who'd wanted to know if he was Dr. Paul Rourke, and if so, could he please just take a look at their rash. . . .

That had been the last Lou had seen of Jack Townsend before she'd been whisked off into the ER, where visitors were not allowed.

Now she was in her very own exam room, waiting for the doctor to return to do her cast. As long as she didn't move, her ankle didn't hurt. She lay on the examination table, staring out the window at the bleak view of the hospital parking lot. It had started snowing again, but she could still see Mount McKinley, rising gray and white and majestic behind a Kmart across the road. It seemed a million years ago that she had been lost on that mountain with Jack Townsend. In a way, she wished they were both back there, in Donald's house. At least there, they'd been safe from scenes like the one at the film shoot a little while ago.

Who would have thought that Tim Lord, award-winning director and all-around megalomaniac, would ever have become so consumed with jealousy that he'd orchestrate such an elaborate scheme to get rid of his wife's ex-boyfriend? Not Lou. She had thought Vicky and Tim's marriage a perfectly happy one.

Which just went to show what she knew.

She was lying there, musing over her apparent lack of insight, when there was a knock on the door to her room. Thinking with a suddenly rapid pulse that Jack had come back at last—but knowing deep down that he wasn't the type to knock—she called out, "Come in."

She was more surprised than she could say when the door opened to reveal Vicky Lord standing there, looking pale and thin and used up, like a tissue.

"Lou," she said faintly.

Lou stared at her best friend. She couldn't help it. She had never seen her looking so . . . old.

"Vicky," she said. "Are you all right?"

"That's what I came here to find out about you," Vicky said. Then suddenly, her face—still pretty, in spite of the pain and sorrow etched there—crumpled, and Vicky launched herself at Lou, throwing her arms around her and jostling her broken foot very badly.

"Oh, Lou, Lou," Vicky sobbed. "I'm so sorry! Will you ever forgive me?"

"For what?" Lou wanted to know. It was sort of hard to talk, as waves of pain were shooting all up and down her leg. But she managed. "Vicky, you didn't do anything. It's not your fault."

"It is," Vicky cried, her tears wetting Lou's hair. "If I had just kept my mouth shut . . . if I had just thought before I said anything. I never should have told Tim about Jack. I don't even know anymore if it was really true. That I still love him. I mean today, when I saw him hitting Tim like that, I was . . . well, I was more worried about Tim than I was about Jack. Which means I must care more for Tim than for Jack, doesn't it?"

"Well," Lou said a little drily. "I should hope so. Tim's your husband."

"Not for long," Vicky said, releasing Lou and stepping back with a sigh. "They've arrested him. I don't think even Johnnie Cochran's going to be able to get him off for this one. And I . . . well, I can't be married to a convict. I mean, I might as well move right back to the trailer park I crawled out of to get here, if that's going to be the case."

Lou winced. "Oh, Vick. I'm so sorry."

"It'll be all right." Vicky must have been feeling better, since she reached up and finger-combed her hair. "Besides, I sort of . . . well, do you think that sheriff guy is kind of sexy?"

Now Lou was convinced she'd heard everything. "Vicky!"

"Well, I can't help it," Vicky said, with a shrug. "He's got that big . . . gun. Anyway, I just wanted to see if you were all right. And say I'm sorry. Now I'd better go."

"Vick—" Lou held out a hand to keep her friend from going. "Look, there's something . . . there's something I've got to tell you. About me and . . . me and Jack."

Vicky blinked back at her from the doorway. "Oh," she said. "You mean about the two of you spending last night together?"

It was Lou's turn to blink. "How did you—how did you know?"

Vicky rolled her lovely blue eyes. "Lou, everyone in the entire hotel knows. I wouldn't be surprised if it turned up in *Us* magazine next week."

Lou bit her lip. "Do you . . . do you mind?"

"Mind?" Vicky shook her head. "Lou, you're a big girl, like you said back at the hotel. You can take care of yourself. Just—" Here Vicky's voice caught, just a little. "—just do me a favor, and don't get your heart broken, okay?"

And without another word, Vicky left the examination room—left it before Lou could call after her, "Too late."

But Lou wasn't left alone long enough to process what she'd just heard before the door opened again. Expecting to see the doctor, who'd been gone a pretty long time for someone who'd only gone to hunt up some plaster, she was surprised to see her father lay a finger to his lips. Then he and Eleanor Townsend came creeping into the room, looking conspiratorial.

"They said no visitors except for fifty minutes after the hour," Frank said when he'd closed the door behind them. "But we snuck past the guard while that Melanie Dupre was distracting him. Apparently she got a piece of Mount McKinley in her eye, or something, when the mine blew."

"Oh," Lou said, looking from her father to Jack's mother bewilderedly. They looked, she had to admit, as giddy as a couple of kids. "Well. Nice to see you."

"We brought you something," Eleanor said, and she fished from the depths of her Gucci bag a large box of chocolates and handed it to Lou. "Your father says you like candy."

Lou looked down at the chocolates. They were the good, expensive kind. She noted with approval that several of them were filled with peanut brittly goodness.

"Wow," she said. "Thanks."

"It's just a small token, really," Eleanor said, looking embarrassed. "I mean, you risked your own life to try to save my son's. Several times, from what I understand. I really don't know what I can ever do to repay you. But I'd like to start by inviting you to come visit me on the cape. I have a house there, you know, and I would be so pleased if you—and maybe your brothers—would come out this summer and stay with me awhile."

"I'm going, too," Frank chimed in. It was only then that Lou noticed he and Eleanor were holding hands.

Lou felt a stab of something. It couldn't have been jealousy. Jealous of her *father* finding happiness, after having lived so many years alone? No way. Not jealousy. Not over that.

But why was it so simple for her father and Jack's mother? They liked each other, they held hands. There was no second-guessing the other's motives, and worrying that next week, one of them might leave the other for Cameron Diaz.

No. Lou had to get a grip. She had to learn to live like a heroine. She had to trust her instincts, take a risk. . . .

It was as she was thinking this that she noticed a large

bulge coming out of Eleanor Townsend's handbag. A second later, the bulge disappeared.

"Um, Mrs. Townsend," Lou said. "I don't quite know how to tell you this, but your bag is moving."

Eleanor looked down with a laugh. "Oh, that's just Alessandro. They don't allow dogs in this hospital, can you believe it? I must say, I prefer the European attitude for dogs than the American one. Alessandro is really quite cleaner than some of the children I've seen running around here."

Lou gave her a wan smile. Then Frank leaned forward and, patting her on the arm, said in a low voice, "Kiddo. You done good out there. I couldn't have been prouder. I only wish your mom could've still been around to see it."

Tears sprang to Lou's eyes. Oh, great, she thought. Now I'm crying. Real heroine-like behavior.

"Thanks, Dad," she said in a muffled voice, dabbing at her face with her sleeve.

"Oh, look what you've done, Frank," Eleanor said, looking concerned. "Dear, are you all right? Have they given you any pain medication? You know, I know the Alaskan surgeon general. Do you want me to give him a call? It isn't right they just stick you in here without even a Tylenol—"

"No," Lou said, smiling at them through her tears. "I'm all right. I . . . You wouldn't happen to have seen Jack anywhere around, have you?"

Eleanor and Frank exchanged glances. "Um," Eleanor said. "Why, no, dear."

It was so transparent a lie, Lou did not even bother acknowledging it. So they'd seen Jack, but didn't want to tell her where they'd seen him, or what he'd been doing. Which could only mean, of course, that whatever it was, they didn't think Lou would approve.

Well, what had she expected? After all, he had already

pursued and won Lou. The challenge was over. The blush was off the rose. The guy was on to greener pastures.

God! Why was she such a paranoid *freak?*

"Oh, dear," Eleanor said, glancing down at her bag, which was bulging again. "Alessandro's getting over-heated. We'd better go, Frank."

"Okay," Lou's father said. Then, giving her a pat on the cheek, he said, "We'll be waiting outside when they discharge you, honey. We'll make sure you get back to the hotel safe."

Sure. Because Jack wasn't around anymore to do it.

But Lou managed a smile and wave, and they left, convinced she was all right.

And she was. Or she would be. After all, she was one tough cookie. She'd survived seventy-two hours on Mount McKinley. She'd survived a mine blast. She'd survived Bruno di Blase. She could survive Jack Townsend. No problem.

It was sort of ironic that, as Lou was thinking this, Bruno di Blase himself pushed open the door to her exam room and came in, holding a bouquet of pink carnations he'd obviously bought at the hospital gift shop.

"Knock, knock," he said, smiling so that all his capped white teeth showed. "How's my little detective doing? You know, it's all over the news, what you did."

Lou just stared at him. Really, she was thinking. Really, it's not enough that she had broken her ankle in two places, survived a murder attempt, and endured the apparent abandonment of the man she'd thought quite possibly might be Mr. Right. Now she had to be visited by her ex-boyfriend, on top of everything else?

"These are for you," Barry said, lifting the lid from the water pitcher the nurse had left for Lou to drink from, and standing the flowers in it. "I know roses are your favorite, but the hospital gift shop doesn't have roses. So. How does it feel?"

Lou looked down at her torn panty hose and grossly swollen ankle. "How do you think it feels, Barry?" she demanded. "It hurts like hell."

"Oh, not that," Barry said, looking unaccountably nervous. "I mean about . . . well, you know. Stopping a cold-blooded murderer in his tracks."

Lou said, drily, "Not as great as you might think."

"Well, you should be feeling on top of the world," Barry said while walking over to the exam table she was lying on, and sitting down on it without asking her if it was all right, of course. "You can bet you're going to have producers crawling all over you, wanting to develop a deal. People are calling it the story of the year. Of course, you knew it was going to have to happen sometime. Jack Townsend never has been able to keep it in his pants. It was just a matter of time until he made someone mad enough to kill him."

"Barry." Lou had been polite to her other visitors because . . . well, because she liked them. She suffered no such weakness for Barry. "What do you want?"

He looked startled. "Want? I want to make sure you're all right, of course. I mean, Lou, we're still friends, aren't we? I mean, ten years. You can't just throw ten years down the drain."

"Why not?" Lou demanded. "You did."

"Well." Barry looked down at his hands. She could see it coming before it even went up over his face: his contrite expression. Good God, she thought to herself. Barry is going to apologize.

"Lou," he said. "I don't know quite how to say this. But the fact is . . . well, I may have been a bit hasty when I moved out. I was confused. I hadn't really thought things through. Things with Greta . . . well, to be frank, things with Greta have not been all that great."

Lou said, "Barry. You've been married to her for four days. How bad can things have gotten?"

"Well," Barry said, with his trademark quick, charming smile. "I'm here with you, and I'm supposed to be on my honeymoon. If that's any indication."

Lou blinked at him. That's when she realized it was gone. Her animosity towards him, that is. It was gone, and it had been replaced by a feeling of tolerance . . . like what she felt for her brothers, only not quite as fond.

"You haven't given Greta enough of a chance, Barry," she said.

"I have, though." Barry got up quickly, jostling Lou's foot. She barely heard him through the haze of pain she was in as he exclaimed, "I don't know what I was thinking, leaving you for her. She's nothing like you, Lou. All she thinks about is herself. Everything is always Greta, Greta, Greta. She never thinks about me. You, Lou. You used to think about me. You wrote *Hindenburg* for me. That has got to have been the greatest gift any man has ever received from a woman. And like a fool, I took that gift, but I made the most unforgivable mistake a man could make. I threw the giver away. Lou." Barry swept up one of her hands. "Can you ever forgive me for my stupidity?"

"Yeah," Lou said, still cross-eyed with pain. "Whatever. Do you think you could maybe find a nurse, or something? My foot really—"

"Do you mean it?" Barry exclaimed, crushing her hand to his chest. "Oh, Lou, if you would take me back, this would truly be the greatest moment of my life. You could get to work on the Pompeii screenplay, and everything will be like it was—"

"Wait a minute," Lou said confusedly. "What are you—?"

"I knew you'd forgive me," Barry cried. Then he leaned down as if to kiss her—

Lou, with a reflex she never even knew she had, reached out, grabbed the water pitcher filled with carnations, and dumped it over his head.

At that very moment, the door to her examination room opened, and Jack Townsend, his arms filled with what had to have been at least four dozen pink roses, came into the room.

"Hello," he said, his blue-eyed gaze going from Lou, lying on the exam table and still clutching the water pitcher, to Barry, looking very surprised, with carnations and water all over him. "Am I interrupting something?"

"No," Lou said, at the same time Barry barked, "Yes!"

Jack sauntered over to the steel table in the corner that held glass jars of gauze and tongue depressors and set the flowers down.

"Sorry I was gone for so long," he said to Lou. "You know how hard it is to find decent roses in this town?"

Lou, looking from the pile of flowers to the man who'd brought them, felt her eyes begin to brim with tears. Oh, great. She was crying again.

"They're beautiful," she said. "Thank you."

"Well," Jack said with a shrug. "They're your favorite, right?" He looked at Barry, who was still plucking sodden carnations from his shirt front.

"Uh, Barry," he said. "Do you think you could give Lou and me a couple minutes alone?"

Only then did Barry seem to register the meaning behind Jack's presence, the roses, and the happy flush on Lou's face. He himself turned an unattractive shade of red as he blurted, "Oh, great. That's just great, Lou. You're taking up with him? Are you insane? He's broken the heart of every woman in Hollywood. I mean, just ask Greta."

Lou did not even have to reply. Jack did so for her.

"You," Jack said, lifting a hand and pointing at Barry, the wounds on his knuckles from where he'd hit Tim Lord still raw and undressed. "Get out."

Barry took a quick step backwards. Then, with a hasty glance at Lou, he said, "Fine. Fine, I'm leaving. But Lou, you're making a big mistake."

Then, with one last frightened glance in Jack's direction, Barry hightailed it from the room.

When the door closed behind him, Jack looked down at Lou and said, "He's right."

She picked up his hand and studied the cuts on his knuckles. "You should have someone look at these," she said.

"I mean it," Jack said, pulling a nearby examination stool towards Lou's bed and perching on it. "I haven't exactly ever been . . . well, in a long-term relationship before."

Lou looked up at his face. Someone had tried to clean it up—maybe Jack himself—but there was still a layer of soot around his hairline that didn't look as if it would ever come out.

"They aren't necessarily all they're cracked up to be. Long-term relationships, I mean," she said. "Believe me."

"But I don't think that would be true for us," he said, simply and sincerely. "It's different with you, Lou. I never . . . I mean, with Vicky, and Greta, and Melanie . . . I didn't love any of them. But you . . . It's different with you."

She stared at him, forgetting her ankle, forgetting his hand, forgetting even to breathe, forgetting everything except the fact that suddenly, the happy ending she'd once thought would never be hers seemed to be almost within reach.

"Because I love you," he went on, his gaze on her face. "So about this moving in together thing. I know you've tried it before and it didn't work out. So I was thinking, maybe we should try it a different way. I was thinking we should get married first. Because neither of us have tried that before, and I don't know, I'm thinking that it might work out better—"

Lou had to blink back another wave of tears. It was not the proposal that she'd have written for him.

But the fact that he had come up with it all on his own and that it had clearly come from the heart was good enough for her.

She said, in a choked voice, "Okay. That sounds good. But just one thing."

A look of anxiety replaced the wave of radiant joy that had been on his face a second before.

"What?" he asked cautiously.

"No more movies," Lou said.

"You got that right," he said and bent down to kiss her so deeply, so passionately, that when the head nurse entered the examination room a minute later, they did not even hear her approach, much less her embarrassed departure.

That kiss, though Jack and Lou never knew it, was the talk of the nursing staff for weeks.

34

Academy Award-winning director Tim Lord was found guilty of conspiracy to commit murder. He is currently serving ten to twenty in an Alaskan federal prison. His final film, *Copkiller IV*, was released one month after his trial and was one of the highest grossing movies ever released, despite the fact that environmentalists worldwide boycotted it.

Seven natives of Myra, Alaska, were likewise convicted in criminal court on charges of manslaughter, attempted murder, illegal weapons possession, and menacing. The children of Samuel Kowalski successfully sued them, as well as Tim Lord, in civil court for the murder of their father, and won a settlement sizable enough for them to pay off the mortgage on their family home, and to pay for beauty and technical college for them all.

Vicky Lord quietly divorced her husband and has since disappeared from Hollywood and the film business. Her wedding to Sheriff Walter O'Malley was a private affair, attended only by Deputy Lippincott and Walter O'Malley's four daughters, all of whom were very grateful to Vicky for taking their widowed father off their hands.

Elijah Lord and his brothers and sisters elected not to return to their respective mothers after their father's conviction, but to continue residing in Tim Lord's house under the parental supervision of the only stable influence they had ever known, their housekeeper, Lupe.

Donald R. Williams, owner of the hunting cabin in which Jack Townsend and Lou Calabrese sought safety from the cold, was quite astonished to find their check upon his return to his cabin in the spring. Nevertheless, he cashed it and used the money to put a down payment on an all-terrain vehicle he'd had his eye on for some time.

Bruno di Blase and Greta Woolston divorced six weeks after their elopement, citing irreconcilable differences. Greta is currently in Australia filming a movie based on the life of Eva Braun. Bruno di Blase has yet to find a studio willing to option his first screenplay, entitled *Pompeii!*

Frank Calabrese returned to Long Island after his Alaskan adventure, where his sons greeted him with a six-foot-long "big" sandwich and a brand-new power mower. Frank enjoyed the sandwich very much, but he told them he wasn't going to have much use for the lawnmower. He was, he explained, moving to Manhattan.

Eleanor Townsend did not particularly care what any of her friends had to say about the fact that a retired New York City police sergeant was moving in with her, though she did worry what her butler and son would think. Richards, however, only expressed his hope that Mrs.

Townsend would find joy, while Jack merely suggested that the pair might be happier if they married one another. Neither Eleanor nor Frank are ready to rush into anything that permanent, however.

Jack Townsend, true to his word, gave up his film career, as well as his ranch in Salinas and home in the Hollywood Hills, opting instead for a farmhouse in Vermont, where he moved with his wife shortly after their quiet wedding in the bride's hometown. Jack restored an old movie theater and reopened it under the name of the Dakota Playhouse, which has become quite well known for its annual Shakespeare festival, all productions of which are directed by former action-adventure star Jack Townsend, who's been found, to the surprise of theater critics everywhere, to have a real genius for stage direction.

Lou Calabrese Townsend sold her bungalow in Sherman Oaks and relocated with her husband and his horses to New England, where she quit writing screenplays. Soon after the birth of their first daughter, Sara, Lou's first novel was published. The novel, *She Went All the Way*, describes a woman's realization that, to find happiness, she had to risk her heart in order to gain what she treasured most.

Though the book has enjoyed considerable popular success, the author refuses to relinquish the screen rights to the story.

Six Tips to Planning the Perfect Wedding...

WITH A LITTLE HELP FROM AVON ROMANCE

Everyone knows that a great love story ends with "happily ever after"... and that means a perfect wedding. But before you get to the Big Day, you have to iron out the details ... picking out a dress, getting the right flowers.

Oh, and there's that little matter of finding the groom.

Now, take a sneak peek as these Avon Romance Superleader heroines ... as created by these talented authors—Cathy Maxwell, Victoria Alexander, Susan Andersen, Jennifer Greene, Judith Ivory and Meggin Cabot—go about finding that husband-to-be.

*When Anthony Aldercy, the Earl of Burnell, has the bad manners
to fall in love with someone other than his fiancée, he does everything in his power to change his own mind! But pert, pretty
Deborah Percival unexpectedly captures his heart in*

The Lady Is Tempted

BY NEW YORK TIMES BESTSELLING AUTHOR

CATHY MAXWELL

July Avon Romance Superleader

He turned—and for a second, Deborah couldn't think, let
alone speak.

Here was a Corinthian. Even in Ilam, they'd heard of
these dashing men about Town. Every young man in the Val-
ley with a pretense to fashion aped their casual dress. But the
gentleman standing in Miss Chalmers's sitting room was the
real thing.

His coat was of the finest stuff, and the cut fit his form to
perfection . . . as did the doeskin riding breeches. His boots

were so well polished that they reflected the flames in the fire, and the nonchalantly careless knot in his tie could only have been achieved by a man who knew what he was doing.

More incredibly, his shoulders beneath the fine marine blue cloth of his jacket appeared broader and stronger than Kevin the cooper's. And his thighs were more muscular than David's, Dame Alodia's groom's. Horseman's thighs. The kind of thighs with the strength and grace from years of riding.

He was also better-looking than both Kevin and David combined.

He wasn't handsome in a classic way. But no one—no *woman*—would not notice him. Dark lashes framed eyes so blue they appeared to be almost black. Slashing brows gave his face character, as did the long, lean line of his jaw. His lips were thin but not unattractive, no, not unattractive at all.

Then, he smiled.

A humming started in her ears. Her heart pounded against her chest . . . and she felt an *unseen* pull toward him, a *connection* the likes of which she'd never experienced before from another human being.

And he sensed the same thing.

She *knew*—without words—that he was as struck by her as she was by him. The signs were there in the arrested interest in his eyes, the sly crookedness of his smile.

Miss Chalmers was speaking, making introductions, but the sound of her voice seemed a long distance away. ". . . Mrs. Percival, a widow from Ilam. This is our other guest, a great favorite of mine, Lor—"

The gentleman interrupted her, "Aldercy. Tony Aldercy."

*Women never said no to Lord Matthew Weston, but he never
met one he'd wanted to say, "I do" ... until he impetuously
married a beautiful woman named Tatiana. So imagine
his shock when he discovered his marriage bed empty,
his bride gone ... and his wife was of royal blood!*

Her Highness, My Wife

BY VICTORIA ALEXANDER

August Avon Romance Superleader

"If you are to be my wife, you are to be my wife in the
fullest sense of the word."

"But surely you cannot expect me to—" Tatiana caught herself and stared. "What do you mean *fullest sense of the word*?"

"I mean my wife has to live on my income." Matthew's
grin widened. "It's extremely modest."

"I see." She bit her bottom lip absently. There were benefits
to being in close quarters with him. He certainly could not ignore her presence in a—she shuddered to herself—cottage.

"And I have only one horse and he is better suited to pull—"

"A carriage?" she said hopefully.

"It's really a wagon." He shook his head in a regretful manner she didn't believe for a moment. "In truth, more of a cart."

"To go along with the shack, no doubt." She would put up with his living conditions, castle or cottage scarcely mattered as long as she was with him.

"And there will be no servants," he warned.

"Of course not, given your modest income," she said brightly. "Is that it then? Your conditions?"

"Not entirely." He studied the apple in his hand absently.

"Really? Whatever is left? You do not mean—" She widened her eyes in stunned disbelief. "You cannot possibly believe—" She wrung her hands together and paced to the right. "Surely, you do not expect that I—" She swiveled and paced to the left. "That you—that we—" She stopped and turned toward him. "That you think I would— Oh Matthew, how could you?" She let out a wrenching sob, buried her face in her hands, and wept in the manner of any virtuous woman presented with such an edict.

"Good Lord! Your Highness. Tatiana." Concern sounded in his voice and she heard him step closer. "I didn't mean—"

"You most certainly did." She dropped her hands and glared at him. "*This* is exactly what you wanted. Was there a moment of regret over your beastly behavior?"

"There is now." He glared down at her but held his ground.

"Ha. I doubt that. Your intentions with this and every other of your ridiculous conditions was to shock me and, furthermore, to put me in my place. These stipulations of yours, especially the last one." She shook her head. "Did you really believe for a moment I would fall to pieces at the idea of sharing your bed? I am not a blushing virgin. I have been married."

"To me." His eyes narrowed dangerously. "Or have I missed another marriage or two?"

"Not yet," she snapped. "But the day is still young."

TIP #3:
THE PROOF IS IN THE KISS!
IF THAT FIRST KISS
IS AT THE ALTAR,
YOU REALLY ARE IN TROUBLE...

*Tristan MacLaughlin is sent to protect vulnerable dancer
Amanda Charles from the crazed man who is stalking her.
At first Amanda thinks MacLaughlin is overbearing—
and overwhelming—but she soon discovers
the unleashed passion in his arms.*

Shadow Dance

THE CLASSIC ROMANTIC NOVEL

BY **SUSAN ANDERSEN**

September Avon Romance Superleader

Tristan yanked her forward and kissed her. And, if before
that instant Amanda had thought he stood aloofly by and
observed life from the sidelines, she discovered then that she
was mistaken. For there was nothing detached about his hungry mouth moving over hers, nothing aloof about the powerful grip of his arms on her back as they pressed her forward

into the heat of his body, or in his blunt fingers, tangled in her hair, grasping her skull. There was nothing detached at all, and his intensity laid to waste her powers of reasoning.

He had pulled her to him so quickly, she had hardly had time to react. Automatically, she raised her hands to push him away. But, for just an instant, she was caught up in the contrast of how things as they appeared to be and as they actually were could be so devastatingly different.

For instance, MacLaughlin's mouth appeared hard and stern, but, Lord help her . . . it was soft. Strong. Hot. But not hard—not hard at all. The only remotely harsh element of his kiss was the heavy morning beard of his unshaven jaw, abrading the tender skin of her face.

Having hesitated for even that brief an instant, she forgot exactly to which it was she had been going to object. Being manhandled again, maybe? Um. Something like that. She didn't remember and she didn't care. Any objection she might have raised was swamped beneath a wave of sensation.

Tristan's mouth kept opening over Amanda's. Restlessly, he slanted his lips over the fullness of hers. When she didn't open to him immediately, he raised his head, stared into her eyes for a moment, and then came at her from another direction, using the hand in her hair to tilt her face to accommodate him. He widened his mouth around her lips and then slowly dragged it closed, tugging at her lips.

She didn't even think twice. Amanda's lips simply parted beneath his, and Tristan made a wordless sound of satisfaction deep in his throat.

His tongue was slow and thorough. It slid along her bottom lip and explored the serrated edges of her teeth. Releasing his grip on her head, Tristan pulled her closer into the heat of his body, moving his pelvis against her with suggestive need. His tongue rubbed along hers. Nerves Amanda hadn't even known she possessed flamed to acute, throbbing life. Her tongue surged up to challenge his and she arched against him, sliding her arms up to wrap tightly around the strong column of his neck, plunging her fingers into his crisp hair. She was aware of every muscle in his body as he pressed against her.

Murmuring soft sounds of excitement, she raised up on tiptoe, lifting her left leg with an agility borne of years of dancing, to hook the back of her knee behind his hard buttock.

Tristan groaned and kissed her harder, aroused nearly to a frenzy. Meaning only to lean her against a support, but misjudging the distance from where they stood, he slammed her up against the wall of the apartment and rocked against her with slow, mindless insistence. One large hand slid slowly up the leg locked around his hip, stroking from knee to thigh, pulling her closer into him before it eased beneath the high-cut leg of her leotard to grip her firm, tights-covered bottom with wide splayed fingers. "Oh, lass," he breathed into her mouth, and then, unable to bear even that slight separation, he kissed her harder, his mouth hungry and a little rough against hers.

Amanda tightened her grip around his neck and kissed him back, following his lead exactly.

He was frustrated by the tights and the one-piece leotard she wore. She looked smashing in it, but it protected her flesh from invasion like a high-security alarm system.

Susan Sinclair is strong, capable, and can deal with anything—
after all, everyone tells her so a million times a day!
Surely she can handle a man like Jon Laker . . . even if
she melts into a puddle every time he comes around.
After all, she "got over" Jon a long time ago—didn't she?

The Woman Most Likely To . . .

BY JENNIFER GREENE

October Avon Romance Superleader

When Jon realized his heart was beating like an overheated jackhammer, he stopped dead, determined to head back home and forget this nonsense. If Susan was in the area, then she was staying at her mother's. He could call her. And if she'd wanted him for something critically important, she could have—and would have—said something on the spot. It was stupid to think that he had to track her down this second . . .

He was halfway to the marina, when he spotted her. Her hands were in her pockets, her hair kicking up in the breeze; she was ambling near the docks, toward the beach, heading for nothing specific, as far as he could see.

He charged forward until he was within calling distance. "Suze!" An out-of-breath stitch knifed his side. His shop keys were still dangling from his hand. "Susan!"

She turned the moment she recognized his voice. From that angle, the sun slapped her sharply in the eyes, where he was in shadow, so he could clearly see how she braced, how she instinctively stilled. "Honestly, Jon, you didn't have to run after me."

"I figured I did. It's not like you go to the trouble of tracking me down more than once in a decade. What's wrong?"

"Nothing."

He wasn't opposed to wasting time on nonsense. But not now, and not with her. "You didn't show up at my place to discuss the weather."

"There's definitely something we need to talk about together. But it's not an easy subject to spring into. I can't just . . ."

"Okay. So. Let's sit somewhere."

"Not *your* place."

God forbid she should trust him after twenty-two years. As if he'd jump her if he caught her alone . . . well hell, come to think of it, he had. But only a few times. And only when she'd wanted to be jumped. And that hadn't happened in a blue moon because they'd both spun out of control the instant someone turned the heat up—and then they'd both been madder and edgier than fighting cats afterward.

Even the best sex in the universe wasn't worth that.

It came close, though.

*Stuart Aysgarth might be the Viscount of Mount Villiars—
and he might consider himself extremely important—
but that doesn't mean he is above the law . . . and
Emma Darlington Hotchkiss is determined he honor
his debt to her. And nothing—not even seduction—
will change her mind!*

Untie My Heart

BY JUDITH IVORY

November Avon Romance Superleader

There was nothing innocent in how his finger continued over the curve of her jawbone to her neck, taking the hem of her dress down her tendon all the way to her collarbone. His eyes followed his finger to the hollow of her throat, where at last he hesitated, paused, then—thank goodness—stopped. She shivered involuntary, tried to speak, but ended up only wetting her lips, dry-mouthed.

The path his finger had traveled left a tiny, traceable impression down her neck to her clavicle, a trail so warm and particular it seemed traced by the sun through a magnifying glass.

"You," he said finally, then paused in that soft, slow way he had that was mildly terrifying now under the circumstance, "are a very hard woman to frighten, do you know that?"

She blinked up at him. "I can assure you, you're doing a good job. You can stop, if that was the goal."

He laughed. A rare sound, genuine, deep, though she definitely didn't like his sense of humor, now that she heard it. For a second more—with him leaning on both arms, his shoulders bunching, pulling at his shirt where they held his weight—he hovered over her, surveying her in that very disarming way again. Then he stood up completely.

Good God, was he tall. From her angle, his head seemed to all but touch the ceiling.

He stared about them, perplexed for a moment, as if he'd lost track of what he was doing, then seemed to remember. And he backed up.

To take a gander at his handiwork, it seemed. Over her knee she watched him withdraw two feet to the window sill and sit his buttocks onto it, his back flattening the lace curtains. There, he crossed his arms over his chest, tilted his head, and viewed her incapacitation from this new angle.

He then said, "Do you know, I think I could do anything to you, absolutely anything, and there would be nothing you could do about it."

"What a cheerful piece of speculation," she said, a little annoyed.

"Save complain. Which you do very well."

She shut her mouth, advising herself to take John's advice and be humble. Or at least quiet.

Mount Villiars laughed again, entertained by his own iniquitous turns of mind. "And whatever I did, afterward, I could hand you over to the sheriff, and, even complaining, he'd just haul you away." The sarcastic jackanapes shook his head as if in earnest sympathy. "Such is our legal system and the power behind the title of viscount. I love being a viscount. Have I mentioned that? Despite all the trouble that arrived with my particular title, I find it's worth fighting for. By the way," he added, "I like those knickers."

TIP #6:
IF THE NEWSPAPERS ARE TALKING ABOUT THE "SURPRISE WEDDING OF THE YEAR," MAKE SURE IT'S YOURS!

Lou Calabrese never dreamed she would be left behind when her boyfriend ran off with a bimbo! And when she is accidentally stranded with that same bimbo's sexy, stubborn Hollywood hunk of an "ex" she learns that sometimes the surprise wedding of the year turns out to be your own!

She Went All the Way

BY MEGGIN CABOT

December Avon Romance Superleader

"Sorry," he said. "I don't really watch movies all that much." For a moment, Lou forgot she was the victim of an attempted murder and a helicopter crash, and gaped at Jack—Jack, the movie star—as if he'd just done something completely out of keeping with his manly image, such as order a champagne cocktail or burst into a rendition of "I Feel Pretty."

"You're an *actor*," she cried, "and you're telling me you don't really watch movies all that much?"

"Hazard of the trade," Jack said lightly. "The magic of Hollywood doesn't hold much allure when you know all the secrets."

Lou shook her head. Oh, yes. They were definitely in Bizarro World now. No doubt about it.

"Maybe," Jack ventured, as if he hoped to change the subject, "we should build a fire."

"A fire?" If he'd suggested they strip naked and do the hula, Lou could not have been more surprised. "A *fire?* What do you think *that* is?" She pointed at the burning hulk of metal a dozen yards away. "What, you're worried when they start looking for us they won't be able to spot us? Townsend, I don't think they're going to have any problem."

"Actually," he said, in the politely distant tone he reserved, as Lou knew only too well, for incompetent waiters and crazy screenwriters, "I was thinking a fire might warm us up. You're shivering."

She was, of course. Shivering. But she'd hoped he wouldn't notice. Showing weakness in front of Jack Townsend was not exactly something she wanted to do. It was bad enough she'd been unconscious in front of him. The last thing she wanted was for him to think she was afraid . . . or worse, uneasy about their current situation—that she was stuck in the middle of nowhere with one of America's hottest Hollywood idols. She had had more than enough with Hollywood idols. Hadn't she lived with one for eight years? Yeah, and look how *that* had turned out.

She was certainly not going to make that mistake again. Not that she was about to do anything as foolish as fall in love with Jack Townsend. Perish the thought! So what if he seemed to be concerned about her physical comfort, and had saved her life, and oh, yes, looked better in a pair of jeans than any man Lou had ever seen in her life? *Are we having fun yet?* Right there was reason enough not to give him the time of day, let alone her sorely abused heart. Besides, hadn't he had the very bad taste to, until recently, date Greta Woolston? There had to be something wrong with a man who couldn't see through that vapid headcase, as she knew only too well.

It was as she was thinking these deep thoughts that she noticed Jack had stood up and wandered a short distance away. He was picking up sticks that had fallen to the ground, branches that, too heavily laden with snow, had fallen to the earth.

"What . . ." She started as he leaned down and hefted a particularly large branch. The back of his leather jacket came up over his butt, and she was awarded a denim-clad view of the famous Jack Townsend butt, the one women all over America gladly shelled out ten bucks to see on the big screen.

And here she was with that butt all to herself.

In the middle of Alaska.